Acclaim for Abigail Wilson

"*The Vanishing at Loxby Manor* cleverly combines Regency romance with Gothic intrigue, and the result is a suspenseful, thoroughly entertaining read. Charming and lovely."

—Tasha Alexander, *New York Times* bestselling author of *In the Shadow of Vesuvius*

"Abigail Wilson's latest Gothic romance hits the notes readers have come to expect from her talented pen: romance, shadows and intrigue, and a brilliantly executed atmosphere. But it is the deep characterization, the sense of longing for the past and a love lost and reforged—not to mention the deeply humane flaws and fallibilities of its dimensional characters—that solidify *The Vanishing at Loxby Manor* as a must-read Regency. I will never tire of Wilson's intelligent voice, expert pacing, and heart-stopping romance. She is a master at her craft and a rare stand-out in a popular genre."

—Rachel McMillan, author of *The London Restoration*

"Weaving a shadow of mystery among the gilded countryside of Regency England, Wilson's tale of love lost, buried shame, and secret societies is a delicious blend of romance and intrigue. Flawed characters grace each page with a vulnerability and deep desire to be known for their true selves, which is a beauty unto itself. Splash in gorgeous historical Regency details, and murder brewing around every stone and readers will be burning through the pages until the riveting end."

—J'nell Ciesielski, author of *The Socialite*, on *The Vanishing at Loxby Manor*

"Like each of Wilson's novels, *The Vanishing at Loxby Manor* drew me in from the start and didn't let go. From the heartfelt characters to the twists that kept me guessing, I relished each turn of the page. Wilson is a master at historical mystery, and I cannot wait for her next story."

—Lindsay Harrel, author of *The Joy of Falling*

"In *The Vanishing at Loxby Manor* Abigail Wilson has created a gothic romance that is filled with great characters and a mystery that unfolds chapter by chapter. A perfect blend of mystery, family relationships, lost years, and star-crossed love. There is also an integral thread of letting go of past tragedy and moving into the future. This book is perfect for readers who love Regency fiction in gothic settings. Be warned, you won't be able to walk away from these characters."

—Cara Putman, award-winning author of *Flight Risk*

"This latest from Wilson (*Midnight on the River Grey*) has all the elements of a classic Regency romance, but the mystery adds another layer, enriching the plot . . . Recommended for fans of Tasha Alexander and Lauren Willig."

—*Library Journal* on *Masquerade at Middlecrest Abbey*

"This is a very well written Regency romance wrapped in a historical mystery involving murder, government agents, French spies, poison and kidnapping. The descriptions of house, grounds, furnishings and costume all immerse the reader in this 19th-century world. Well-drawn characters add a distinctive flavour to the action, and there are several mysteries to untangle . . . A very enjoyable read and recommended."

—Historical Novel Society

"This novel is so packed full of mystery, intrigue, and romantic tension that you will be turning pages until the wee hours while your heart hurts from the emotional tension."

—Austenprose.com

"Wilson (*Midnight on the River Grey*) weaves a splendid tale of murder and deception in this fun, suspenseful Regency . . . The main couple are well matched in spunk and intellect, and Wilson strikes a nice balance between intrigue and gentle romance. This delightful story is sure to entertain."

—*Publishers Weekly* on *Masquerade at Middlecrest Abbey*

"From the very first page, I was enraptured! Ms. Wilson delivers a timeless story made even better by a hero who epitomizes generosity of love like no other I've read before. *Masquerade at Middlecrest Abbey* has intrigue, mystery, and suspense beautifully enhanced by the vulnerability revealed through memorable characters, making this story impossible to put down. A must-read recommendation, this story is exactly what makes me love reading!"

—NATALIE WALTERS, AUTHOR OF THE HARBORED SECRETS SERIES

"Murder is far from no one's thoughts in this delicious new romantic mystery from Abigail C. Wilson. With scandal dodging every turn of the page, mystery hiding behind the visage of each character, and a romance brewing with an English rake of the worst—and best—sorts, readers will find nothing lacking! I was entranced, mesmerized, addlepated, and not a little bit bewildered as I wandered the halls of Middlecrest Abbey. While it was easily cemented before, it is now forever set in stone that I am a loyal fan of all things Abigail C. Wilson."

—JAIME JO WRIGHT, AUTHOR OF *ECHOES AMONG THE STONES* AND THE CHRISTY AWARD–WINNING NOVEL, *THE HOUSE ON FOSTER HILL*, ON *MASQUERADE AT MIDDLECREST ABBEY*

"Suspicion shades the affluent grounds of Middlecrest Abbey in this riveting novel by Abigail Wilson. The artful balance of mystery and romance cleverly blends with the Gothic tones of Regency England. With exquisite prose and a layered plot, *Masquerade at Middlecrest Abbey* is a compelling story not to be missed."

—RACHEL SCOTT MCDANIEL, AWARD-WINNING AUTHOR OF *ABOVE THE FOLD*

"With a wonderfully suspicious cast of characters, intriguing clues, and a lush backdrop that readers can easily get lost in, *Midnight on the River Grey* is a captivating novel."

—HISTORICAL NOVELS SOCIETY

"Abigail Wilson's debut novel is a story rich in detail with a riveting mystery . . . With enough jaw-dropping plot twists to give readers whiplash, it would be a severe oversight to pass this story up."

—*HOPE BY THE BOOK*, BOOKMARKED REVIEW, ON *IN THE SHADOW OF CROFT TOWERS*

"Readers who enjoy sweet romances, Gothic settings, innocent heroines, and mysterious heroes should enjoy this read."

—*Historical Novels Review* on *In the Shadow of Croft Towers*

"Abigail Wilson's *In the Shadow of Croft Towers* is the kind of novel I love to recommend. Well written, thoroughly engrossing, and perfectly inspiring. I honestly couldn't flip the pages fast enough."

—Shelley Shepard Gray, *New York Times* and *USA TODAY* bestselling author

"Mysterious and wonderfully atmospheric, Abigail Wilson's debut novel is full of danger, intrigue, and secrets. Highly recommended!"

—Sarah Ladd, award-winning author of *The Weaver's Daughter*

"What a deliciously satisfying debut from Abigail Wilson! *In the Shadow of Croft Towers* is everything I love in a novel: a classic Gothic feel from very well-written first person storytelling, a Regency setting, a mysterious hero . . . and secrets abounding! *In the Shadow of Croft Towers* is now counted as one of my very favorite books, and I can't wait for more from this new author!"

—Dawn Crandall, award-winning author of The Everstone Chronicles series

"Mysterious . . . Melodic . . . Thrilling and original . . . Abigail Wilson has crafted a debut that shines. Artfully weaving shades of Gothic romance in a portrait of Regency England, Wilson brings a fresh voice—and a bit of danger!—to the mist and hollows of a traditional English moor. With a main character both engaging and energetic, and a quick-out-of-the-gate plot that keeps you guessing, one thing is certain—if Jane Austen ever met Jane Eyre, it would be at Croft Towers!"

—Kristy Cambron, author of *Castle on the Rise* and the bestselling debut, *The Butterfly and the Violin*, on *In the Shadow of Croft Towers*

"Part mystery and part romance, Abigail Wilson's debut is an atmospheric period novel that will keep readers guessing to the very end."

—Amanda Flower, *USA TODAY* bestselling author of *Death and Daisies*

The
Vanishing
at
Loxby Manor

Also by Abigail Wilson

Masquerade at Middlecrest Abbey

Midnight on the River Grey

In the Shadow of Croft Towers

VANISHING
at
LOXBY MANOR

ABIGAIL WILSON

The Vanishing at Loxby Manor

Published in Nashville, Tennessee, by Thomas Nelson. Thomas Nelson is a registered trademark of HarperCollins Christian Publishing, Inc.

Thomas Nelson titles may be purchased in bulk for educational, business, fundraising, or sales promotional use. For information, please email SpecialMarkets@ThomasNelson.com.

ISBN 978-0-7852-3295-7 (trade paper)
ISBN 978-0-7852-3312-1 (epub)
ISBN 978-0-7852-3315-2 (downloadable audio)

Library of Congress Cataloging-in-Publication Data

CIP data is available upon request.

Printed in the United States of America

21 22 23 24 25 LSC 10 9 8 7 6 5 4 3 2 1

For my daughter, Audrey
The girl with an endless zest for life, a wicked humor, and a deep compassion for others.
I thank God every day He allowed me to be your mother as well as your friend.

PROLOGUE

1811
Kent, England
Village of East Whitloe

"Foolish. Impetuous. Risky. You needn't hold back now, Piers. I know precisely what's ticking in that mind of yours."

I forced my shoulders back against the bark of the oak tree where I'd spent the last few interminable hours shivering. Even the slightest movement of my hurt ankle caused knives to twist beneath my skin.

Piers Cavanagh merely shook his head as he looked over my injury. "I simply cannot deduce how the devil this happened. First off, it's nigh five in the morning. Second, I was under the distinct impression you were to return home this afternoon." He rolled his eyes heavenward. "Believe me, I've been counting down the hours till I would see you again, and I'm certain it was to be later today."

I threw my hands up, regretting the action at once as I winced. "I haven't the foggiest idea how the date of my arrival became confused. I was always to return on the seventeenth of March. Do you know, no one was sent to the coaching house last night to bring my maid and me home to Flitworth Manor. What a pickle we were in."

Having finished pawing at my ankle, Piers moved his hand to my resting fingers, his gaze following suit. "Yet here you sit with all the signs of a battered ankle. Thank goodness the bruising isn't worse."

"I admit my decision to borrow a few hacks and set out on the journey ourselves turned out to be a poor one. I was thrown . . . the little beast."

His eyes shot to mine. "Do you mean to tell me you left the coaching house on your own with no escort but your maid?"

"Don't scold me. I daresay I've paid enough for my foolishness. I was just so anxious to see you again." I tipped my head back. "'Pon my word, the last thing I wanted to do was to waste one solitary hour apart from you when I'm to be dragged out of the country tomorrow morning. Oh, Piers. I still cannot believe my family's move is actually happening . . . and so suddenly at that. My parents were quite devious to send me away to my cousin's house while they worked out all the details. I can't even begin to tell you how many miles Ceylon is from here."

Piers sighed. "A little over five thousand. I checked."

My heart squeezed, but I lifted my chin. Secret romance or not, surely no distance, however great, would squelch what Piers and I had discovered only a few months before. I toyed with the edge of my lip.

At least we would have letters. Really, all I had to do was wait for his proper proposal, and I would be whisked back to Britain and into Piers Cavanagh's waiting arms. If only his mother hadn't already decided on Honora Gervey for a daughter-in-law, this whole ridiculousness could have been avoided. Engagements entered into by parents at the infants' cribs rarely came to fruition, particularly when the parties involved had little interest in each other.

He squeezed my hand, a wry smile inching across his face. "And you're absolutely right. We haven't any time to lose." He rearranged his position on the ground, then leaned in close, pausing only at the last second to flick his eyes to the road. "Where exactly is your maid again?"

"I sent her for help hours ago."

He ran his finger down my hairline and around my ear, his deep blue eyes as alive as I'd seen them a week ago. "How I've missed you, Charity Halliwell."

Careful of my ankle, he closed the gap between us, pressing his lips to mine.

I melted forward, numb to the aching world beyond his kiss. There was no one in Britain like Piers Cavanagh, and he'd given his heart to me and me alone.

Suddenly he pulled away, fumbling for his pocket watch; his cheeks still slightly pink. "It's getting late."

A gust of wind rumpled his brown locks and made over his face. Disquiet filling his eyes, he turned to the road like he'd seen a ghost. "Do you think you can ride?"

"I don't know."

He ran a hand down his chin, a gasp of frustration on his breath. "It will be slow going either way. You've picked the deuce of a morning to have an accident."

I rubbed a chill from my arm. "You won't leave me to get help, will you? I've been alone in the dark for so long now. I'm certain I can manage with your assistance. In fact"—I moved to stand—"I know I can."

He hung his head, a curious tension filling the air between us. "All night, huh? You had to have been out here all night. What were you thinking, Charity?"

"I told you. How could I have known the horse would be so careless?" Nerves prickled down my back. What did it matter now? He was here. I was safe.

Another wayward glance down the road was followed by a difficult lapse into silence. I'd always been able to read Piers like an open book, but this odd intensity was nothing short of alarming. Had something happened in the week I'd been away?

He pushed into a squatting position. "Let's get you the rest of the way onto your good foot." One hand on my arm and another at my back, he tugged me effortlessly to a standing position. I would have been lying if I said the movement didn't send my leg throbbing, but I hardly noticed as I was lost in Piers's strange behavior, my mind afire to figure out what was wrong.

He placed his arm beneath mine, bracing me against his side, his other hand securing his horse's reins. "One hop at a time, and I suppose we'll get to Loxby Manor eventually."

I looked up into his troubled eyes. "What is it?"

He responded simply by pulling me close. "My estate is the closest by far. Don't worry, we'll fetch the doctor from there. I would never dream of leaving you." Then almost to himself, "Everything will work out." He pressed his lips together. "I have faith that it will."

He gave me a wan smile, but I'll never forget the look in his eyes, like he knew something I did not, like he'd lost something he knew he might never get back.

CHAPTER 1

Five years later, 1816

I knew something was terribly wrong the moment I stepped foot back inside Loxby Manor—the pervasive restlessness of the servants, the strained silence of the front room.

I'd spent much of my childhood visiting its inhabitants, but my pace turned tentative as I peered in each open doorway of the ancient house, searching for the telltale presence of a coffin, for I could have sworn I'd stumbled upon the start of a funeral.

The Cavanagh's elderly butler, Mr. Baker, whom I remembered all too well, emerged from the shadows of a distant hall. The candelabra in his hand lit a familiar, but rather disturbed face.

"Ah, Miss Halliwell . . . There you are. If you would be so good as to follow me to your room." He hid the remains of a grimace as he motioned to the grand staircase. "The family is regrettably engaged at present, and since you are likely tired from your extensive journey, they've arranged for you to rest for the evening in your bedchamber undisturbed."

For a moment I stood as if nailed to the parquet floor, digesting his words without fully understanding them. Where was Seline or Mrs. Cavanagh? Or even Avery?

I glanced wildly about the dim hall as a shiver tickled my shoulders. Could it be true? Not a single member of the family could be bothered to welcome me back to Kent? Of course Piers Cavanagh was from home. I'd made certain of that before ever considering a long visit in the first place.

Mr. Baker waited for me halfway up the stairs, his voice dipping to one of impatience. "This way, if you please."

With little choice, I hurried up the carpeted steps behind him, my gloved fingers sliding along the curved banister. Yet on the landing I hesitated at the balustrade, my unwitting gaze hunting the small alcove on the ground floor that was only visible from where I now stood.

Five long years had crept achingly by since I departed East Whitloe and my friends at Loxby Manor, but in that breathless moment I wondered if my heart had ever really left. I could almost see my sixteen-year-old self rushing into that alcove, far too eager for my own good, accepting Piers's outstretched hands with such reckless abandonment. How full of hopes and dreams I'd been then . . . Needless to say, that was before Ceylon. I turned back to the lonely corridor and the butler's retreating form. Everything was different now.

Mr. Baker deposited me in a small out-of-the-way room with pale green papers and golden drapes before deserting me with the promise of a supper tray. I crossed the room only to slump down upon a bow window seat near the fireplace and toss my bonnet at my side. How different my arrival had been from the one I'd anticipated. Perhaps Mrs. Cavanagh was not as pleased to host me as her letter had indicated.

The clatter of footsteps sent me roaring to my feet. My bedchamber door burst inward and a young lady spilled into the room. "Charity!"

Her delicate fingers lay across her chest, and she paused to appraise me before guiding the door shut.

My eyes widened. "Seline? Can it be you?" Her name wafted into a whisper as I took in the beauty before me. Was this the same girl I'd traipsed through the woods with, having escaped my governess time and time again, to pick berries and climb trees? Her hair had darkened to a pleasing gold, and her face balanced the perfect combination of innocence and allure. No wonder Avery had mentioned in his letters that she'd been declared the toast of the season. Seline Cavanagh had grown into nothing short of an artful goddess.

And she was here in my room . . . after I'd specifically been told otherwise.

She extended her arms, urging me to meet her at the center of the rug where she took my hands into hers. Those astute green eyes did a bit of talking of their own, measuring my worth. "What ladies we have become."

She produced a half-hearted laugh as she pulled me into an embrace, then drew away. "I'm so glad you have arrived at last. 'Faith but Mama has no sense at all. She thought it best I stay away so you could relax this evening, considering . . . Well"—an exasperated sigh—"let's just say, I could not wait to hear all the news of Ceylon."

My brows pulled in. Mrs. Cavanagh had told Seline to stay away . . . *from me*?

"I cannot believe you've traveled so far and have seen so much of the world when I've never even left Britain." She pursed her lips. "I'm quite jealous, you know. Tell me all about your travels. What is it like there?"

Although I'd prepared myself for questions about my time in Ceylon, my heart still quivered at her words and my muscles clenched. Would I ever lose the horrible impulse to flee?

I swallowed hard against the lump in my throat. This would not be the last time I was asked.

The truth was, Ceylon was nothing short of beautiful, the people kind, the tea plantations and estates a grand affair, but it took all my willpower to keep the tears at bay, to look past the *incident*, as my mother liked to call it. There was much more to my time in Ceylon than that terrible day.

I took a deep breath. "Ceylon is a different world from Britain. It is a beautiful island with rolling hills and a sweeping shoreline. Did you know they have elephants there?"

"No, I didn't." She checked. "Did you touch one?"

"Of course. They're quite friendly."

Seline blinked, her mouth puckered just so. "Mama would faint if she even saw an animal of that size. In fact, I'd advise you not to mention that part to her . . . among other things, like my being in your room. Your, well, let me just say, the timing of your arrival has proven to be a bit awkward."

"Awkward? Whatever do you mean?"

She gave an indifferent shrug, her hair glinting in the firelight. "Nothing all that dreadful. Certainly not worth the histrionics Mama has enacted this last hour or more. She's got the entire house in an uproar. Surely you remember how dramatic she can be." Seline shot me a coy glance. "Ridiculous, since the whole thing was nothing but a silly accident."

I inched down onto a nearby chair, lost as to what could possibly be amiss at Loxby that had turned the entire household upside down. Granted, at least now I wouldn't have to talk about Ceylon.

I fumbled with my fingers in my lap. When my mother proposed the idea to spend a year with the Cavanagh's while she and Papa visited my brother in Boston, I'd latched on to the notion at once. It was a golden opportunity—the perfect distraction from my difficult memories, time away to start anew. Yet the tone of Seline's voice and her uncertain countenance sparked an all too familiar wave of repressed nerves. Had I made the wrong decision after all?

Seline seemed to follow my thoughts as she knelt by my chair, patting my hand as if I was a child. "Do not fret. Everything shall be made right within the week."

I stared up. "Tell me what has happened."

A spark of mischief lit her eyes. "I suppose you must know the whole. Living in this house, you'll learn of it soon enough, only I beg your discretion as it is rather personal in nature."

Personal indeed. As a child Seline had steered headfirst into any trouble that came her way, and I was always right there with her, joining in, keeping her secrets.

There was the time she'd dared Lord Kendal to touch her ankle and laughed so prettily when he'd done so. And the day she tempted Hugh Daunt to take her fishing all alone for the afternoon. She never did reveal to me what they'd done on that riverbank, but Hugh couldn't take his eyes off her after that.

Thankfully her elder brothers had always shielded her. But now? I produced a weak nod. "Oh, Seline. Years ago we promised to look out for one another, and I have every intention of continuing to do so."

Her shoulders relaxed as that dainty smile she affected so well returned to her lips. "You were always so wonderfully trustworthy, and I can see you haven't changed a bit." She squeezed my hand. "Perhaps it is a good thing you came to Loxby at such a dreadful time. I daresay you can help protect me from Mama."

I angled my chin. "Only if you tell me what you've got yourself into this time."

"I'm afraid it is a bit of a bramble." She fought back a laugh. "Well, you know how men get?"

I sighed, for I did know just how men got around *her*. Even at fifteen she'd been enticing. How she'd made it to twenty without an engagement I couldn't guess.

She turned her attention to the arm of the chair, tracing the pattern with her finger. "It all started when Mr. Lacy, our head groom, took on a new stable hand—his nephew." She snuck a peek beneath her lashes. "His name is Miles, and you know how I love to ride early every morning."

I seemed to remember her sleeping until midday, but now was not the time to quibble.

"So you see, it wasn't exactly my fault. I couldn't help but interact with him alone day after day. It was only natural . . . I mean, I was simply humoring the man. Neither of us were the least serious. He knows full well I will settle for nothing short of a title. I told him so from the beginning."

"A title, hmm?" I wondered why Lord Kendal had not yet come up to scratch. The two had been inseparable since childhood.

She huffed, her hands suddenly animated. "Wouldn't you know, this morning, one of the dratted servants slunk into the stables and found Miles and me . . . well . . . you know, kissing."

I sat up straight. "Oh, Seline."

"Then the wretch dared to tell Papa. And now Mama thinks it likely the rumor will circulate the neighborhood."

Seline had been labeled the village flirt years ago, but kissing a stable hand—it was the outside of enough. No wonder the house had been a veritable mausoleum when I arrived. Mrs. Cavanagh was right. This was much more serious than Seline's usual nonsensical whims. Her very respectability was at stake. "What do you plan to do?"

"Well, deny it of course. Miles has been paid to leave the estate and keep his mouth shut. He is lucky Papa is willing to do that."

A line squirmed across her brow. "You needn't look at me like that. You always were such a curst innocent. I vow I never could say or do anything without ruffling your feathers." She leaned forward, the hint of a laugh on her breath. "There is more to discover than books, my dear, but I daresay you wouldn't have the least idea what I'm even talking about."

My jaw tightened. Why was it that people always assumed those who are quiet or shy know nothing of the world? How shocked Seline would be if she learned what actually happened in Ceylon, but I had no intention of sharing that day with anyone besides my mother. Not now, not ever.

I touched my forehead. "Won't there be a scandal?"

"Not if I can squelch it or head it off. I do have a plan."

A plan, hmm? I waited for her to say more, but she rose and made her way to the fireplace and poked the logs.

She angled her shoulders to steal a glance back at me. "What about you? Any special gentlemen you met at a ball? If you even had those in Ceylon."

I cringed as the memories of the dreaded house parties I'd been forced to attend on those blustery summer nights came to mind. Goodness, how I'd hated them.

"If you remember, I have great difficulty hearing and understanding people in crowded spaces. It's an affliction I've suffered since birth. Everyone's voices jumble together, particularly with the instrumentalists present, until the sounds form nothing but a mess of words and notes. Trust me, when a gentleman did take pity on me and asked for a dance, I hadn't the least idea what he'd said during the set to make conversation. I must have come across as dull as ditchwater, for I was rarely asked for a second dance. After all, nodding and smiling can only get you so far."

There was a beat of silence, and then she said dryly, "You poor dear. I do recall you struggling with something of the sort. At any rate, I remember how Avery used to tease you mercilessly when you misunderstood what was said, though you can't entirely blame him as you quite often did."

"Neither of your brothers had much patience with me."

"Well, the good news is Avery is in as much hot water as me at present. He was rusticated from university just last week. In fact, Piers was so angry he dashed off a letter informing us he means to arrive tomorrow. Can you believe it? With any luck my little indiscretion with Miles should slip quite nicely under the rug, particularly if I have a certain announcement to make."

My heart dropped. "Piers will be here tomorrow? I thought he hadn't returned home in five years."

How I wished my voice hadn't cracked, for Seline rounded on me, her eyes flashing. "Don't tell me you're still harboring that ridiculous calf-love you always had for my brother."

"Certainly not." Not after he'd ended our secret relationship in one cryptic letter, the first and only one I received from him. "I was just surprised to hear he was coming home is all."

She crossed her arms. "It was a shock to all of us, believe me. He's been hiding for so long at Grandmama's old cottage outside Liverpool, we thought he'd never return. At least I hoped he wouldn't."

"Why did he go to Liverpool?"

I'd spoken too quickly. Seline darted another knowing glance. "Why, the scandal of course. He can't face the shame of his public disgrace."

I stifled a gasp. Seline and Avery had written me a handful of letters over the years, and none mentioned one word about a scandal. Thoughts raced through my mind—cheating at cards, an illicit affair, a brawl—but nothing made any sense, not about Piers. He could never stoop to anything of the sort. Of course he had easily walked away from our relationship. Had I ever really known him?

I drew my arms in close. "What do you mean . . . a scandal?"

She glared at me as if testing the motivation for my question. "I suppose you wouldn't know, isolated as you were. It happened right around the time you left for Ceylon." She flicked her fingers in the air. "You remember when Lord Kendal and I got rather silly that one day, and I allowed him to touch my ankle?"

I dipped my chin. "How could I forget?"

"Well, Lord Kendal had the gauche to boast about our silliness at White's, and Piers caught wind of it. He got so angry he called Kendal out on the spot, only my illustrious brother never bothered to show up for the duel. Kendal declared him a coward that very day, and rightly so. Piers wouldn't even give a reason for his absence. I was never so embarrassed in my life."

The room blurred. Piers a coward? Why on earth wouldn't he show up for a duel he'd arranged? I lightly shook my head as a strong chin and a pair of resolute blue eyes came to mind. Surely there was some sort of mistake.

Seline went on, ignorant of the shock coursing through my body. "Piers received the cut direct first in London then everywhere else. He is completely beyond the pale at this point, and I decided years ago to have nothing to do with him. I'm certain Piers's disgrace is at the heart of why Lord Kendal never offered for me. My brother's absolute cowardice has left a blight on this entire family. Mama can hardly bear to be in the same room with him.

Her hopes are all with Avery now. If only Papa will change his will before the end and leave Loxby to Avery, this family might come about."

I looked up at the mention of her father. My mother had warned me about Mr. Cavanagh's accident. "How is your papa?"

She expelled a weighted sigh. "Not well at all. He spends most of his time in bed." She gave me a sideways glance. "His vision never did return."

"I'm so sorry to hear." Mr. Cavanagh had always been such a kind, thoughtful man. I could hardly imagine him confined to his bed, blinded by a kick from a horse.

Seline paced the rug as if she anticipated the ceiling to fall, her attention on each wall she faced as she turned. "And what about your parents?"

"They are well, extremely proud of the work my brother is doing in Boston. Arthur is a chemist. His work has even been lauded by the government."

"Oh." She paused by the window. "Is there a reason why they didn't take you with them to America?"

"Mama thought I might do better here." I studied the creases on my palm.

"Or perhaps she thought I might find you a husband and take you off their hands."

My shoulders slumped. "Something like that."

"You know, I think it a glorious idea. We have so many eligible gentlemen in the area." She clapped her hands. "Oh yes. Tony Shaw or Hugh Daunt shall do nicely for you. They've never been all that picky when it comes to looks. And you do have a little dowry."

I knew Seline hadn't meant to insult me, but her words stung. Of course she was right. I could hardly be called pretty. Plain, more like. Mousy brown hair, dull brown eyes, freckles. I was decidedly forgettable. The closest I'd received to a compliment was when old Colonel Baynes had referred to me as a taking little thing. Granted, he wasn't wearing his spectacles at the time.

The sound of a scuffle drew my attention to the corner of the room where I caught a flash of white. "What was that?"

Seline followed me to the far side of the bed where I leaned down to peek beneath the bedside table. There in the shadows hid a snowy white cat. Carefully I reached underneath the table and was rewarded with a touch of soft, velvet fur. The cat hesitated at first, but soon enough she allowed me to scoop her into my arms.

I turned to Seline, cradling the animal. "What a darling."

Seline waved her arms in the air as I approached. "Get that curst thing away from me. I cannot tolerate animals. Mama banished the beast from the house, but she keeps finding her way back inside, if for no other reason than to terrorize me."

The cat nestled her head against my shoulder, a low purr vibrating against my chest.

Seline seemed to shiver as she backed away. "Hugh should have known I would hate it when he gifted her to me last year." Her voice lightened. "You remember Hugh, don't you? He lives on an estate just to the south."

Certainly I remembered Hugh. She'd mentioned him as a possible suitor for me just moments ago—one of the less picky ones. He'd also been a staple at our pretend garden parties. It seemed he hadn't lost the affection he'd acquired the day he and Seline spent at the river. "Is he still a good friend of yours?"

"A silly one, but a friend nonetheless."

There was an edge to her voice that had seemed to grow over the course of the conversation. She wandered to the window again, this time thrusting back the drapes. She fell motionless for a split second, and then her mouth fell open.

"Oh my goodness. He must have returned sooner than I thought."

She was breathless as she spun back against the wall. "What shall I do? He'll hear about Miles and everything I've planned will be lost." She narrowed her eyes. "Unless . . ."

I laid the cat on the bed. "Unless what? He who?"

She pressed her hands to her cheeks, her gaze darting around the room. "It might work. It just might work." She stalked over and grasped my shoulders. "Stay here, and you must tell no one you've seen me this evening. Do you understand?"

I glanced at the darkened window. "Why? What do you mean to do at this hour? Who are you talking about returning home?"

"I cannot say at present, but I believe it will prove just the thing." She snapped her fingers. "Quickly, have you a black cloak in your wardrobe?"

"A cloak? Never tell me you mean to leave the house."

"All right, I won't tell you." She scampered to the looking glass, her fingers wild in her hair as she tugged and pulled each errant strand back into place.

I stood helplessly in the center of the rug, holding my hands out in front of me. "Seline?"

She glanced over her shoulder, a sly smile across her face. "So do you have the cloak or not?"

"I do in my trunk, but I cannot let you leave the house, not like this."

"Don't be such a prude. It's not like I haven't gone out at night alone before. I know full well what I'm doing." She laughed. "Besides, I haven't much of a reputation left to protect." Then her face changed, and she crossed her arms. "Listen, I do not dare risk a return to my room, and the back stairs are so wonderfully close to yours. Either you give me the cloak or I'll fish it from your trunk myself. I'm running out of time."

She knelt on the floor and swung open the trunk's lid. Caught up in a misguided desire to help my friend, I found myself kneeling beside her, pawing through my things. I was forced to remove several garments before locating the long black cloak I hadn't used in years.

She grasped it from my hand. "Charity, you are the dearest dear. I shall never forget your kindness. I promise to find you the perfect husband soon enough. You'll see." She touched my cheek, pushed to her feet, then slung the cloak over her shoulders, flipping the hood over her golden hair. She fumbled with the collar. "What's this?"

"Oh, that's my brooch."

"It's pretty." She fastened it beneath her chin.

"Please be careful with it. It was my grandmother's. She had one of my grandfather's favorite collar jewels fashioned into it."

"You needn't worry. I'll take good care of it." She flashed me a smile. "If everything goes according to plan, my whole life changes tonight. Mama will be so pleased. She'll regret the day she ever called me an ungrateful wretch." She seemed almost weightless as she bounded to the door.

"Please." My stomach clenched, and all at once I couldn't let her leave. I grabbed her arm. "I don't care how many times you've gone out alone. A lady should never do so, particularly at night. You could be assaulted or worse."

"Don't be absurd, not in East Whitloe. You've been reading too many novels."

An ache swelled in the back of my throat. If only it was just the novels. I went on, miserably aware of the pain seeping into my words. "Please, you don't understand."

She wriggled out of my grasp, a coy bend to her shrug. "Besides, I won't even be alone."

I stood breathless as she hesitated at the door for one final statement. "Wish me luck. I won't be long."

I didn't even have a chance to reply before the door closed and the room fell empty around me, the casement clock ticking away an uncomfortable silence. I stood like that for several seconds, trying to make sense of why Seline had darted from my room, before returning to the open drapes.

What had Seline seen through the darkness that set her off? I pressed my forehead against the cool glass, scanning the moonlit garden and the west lawn beyond.

Twinkling on the horizon, at the jagged tip of a nearby hill, something did catch my eye. A light, wavering in the evening breeze like a solitary ember fanned to life one breath at a time.

Hardly anything was left of the curved stone cloisters of Kinwich Abbey, but I recognized the glowing remains straightaway—a lonely remnant of another time, another place. The people who lived around the village of East Whitloe believed the ruins of the old abbey still housed the ghostly spirit of a monk who once lived there. As girls, Seline and I had been too scared to venture anywhere near the rubble.

I shook my head. Seline and I were girls no longer. My hand inched over my lips as I stared into the abyss. Whoever placed that light within the cloisters had drawn Seline racing from the house to meet them.

CHAPTER 2

I ate the supper on my tray by the bow window as I listened to the ebb and flow of the wind, my gaze glued to the light flickering amid the ruins of Kinwich Abbey. Who exactly had Seline scrambled from the house to meet, and what on earth did she have planned?

I tucked my feet beneath my nightgown and tipped my head against the window's hard wooden frame. June's daytime warmth had vanished with the sun and ushered in the cool, layered depths of nightfall in the countryside. Nearby tree branches whipped back and forth in the moonlight while the growing gusts charged against Loxby's ancient stones.

The wind had always fascinated me. I suppose it was the pure relentlessness of it. Heaven's invisible hand sweeping over the world. Sometimes it was as light as a feathered touch, a soft whisper on my skin, and other times a fevered fury that left nothing untouched. My father once explained that the wind was a promise of things to come. He said all we needed to do was listen to its call.

Another strong gust pounded the wall and my heart lurched. It was not an evening to be out and about. Why had I ever let Seline leave?

As I sat quivering on the window seat, still exhausted from the events of the day, the hours stretched on endlessly. The remains of my supper grew cold on the tray. Yet I could not abandon my post, not when Seline was out there somewhere in the gloom. I glanced at the clock for the hundredth time. Eleven thirty. Where on earth could she be? Whatever she had planned, she hadn't indicated it would take all that long.

A great deal of time had passed since she escaped my room, yet the strange beacon on the hill remained fixed in place. The impulse to leave the house and initiate a search wavered in and out of my mind, charging my nerves for flight. But it had been so long since I'd ventured into Loxby's expansive woods, and I'd promised myself in Ceylon that I'd never be so foolish about my surroundings again. Besides, I had little chance of finding my way in the darkness. I pressed the palm of my hand to my forehead. Why had I ever agreed to her ridiculousness?

The *pit-pat* of rain tickled the window, and I sat up just in time to see the light on the hill jolt and weave.

I pushed the drapes aside and pressed in close. The dithering glow seemed to vacillate then split in two, the smaller light bobbing its way toward Loxby, while the larger simply disappeared into the opposing hillside.

I kept my focus on the small glow as it crawled toward the house, dipping in and out of the trees, up and over the gradual curve of the land. I was forced to wait several minutes until a dimly lit figure scampered across the rose garden and I was rewarded by the outline of a black cloak.

I released a trapped breath. The onset of the drizzle must have sent Seline scurrying back to the house. Thank goodness. I sat for a moment, then took a few relieved steps onto the rug.

A door slammed somewhere in the distance, and Loxby's old walls seemed to groan in response. Muffled footsteps resonated through the twisting corridors of the ground floor, and then an unexpected silence took hold.

I stood for some time in the center of my room completely still, straining to hear the least movement beyond my door. But the quiet was deafening. Slowly, the hair began to rise on my arms.

Seline would have to venture back this way. The side stairs were the fastest and easiest way to the family wing. I inched to my bedchamber door and cracked it open, peering into the blackened hall. Surely it would only be a moment before my dear friend crested the stairs and I could calm my frantic heart.

"Seline," I whispered into the gloom.

Nothing.

I tied my dressing gown a bit tighter about my waist and tiptoed to the edge of the steps. "Seline."

Again, nothing but my heartbeat throbbing against my ears.

Where was she? I stared down the curved stairwell then fleetingly at my bedchamber door. It was possible she had taken an alternate way to her room. Perhaps she did not wish to discuss anything further with me tonight. I knit my brow—that is, if it was indeed Seline who had entered the house. My chest tightened.

I would never sleep if I didn't find out for certain.

Seline had occupied the same bedchamber at Loxby for all the years I knew her. Perhaps a quick peek in her room would ease my mind, and then I could make my way back to bed. The silvery haze of moonlight would be ample to guide my slippered steps. I secured the ribbons on my robe and turned down the main corridor.

Little had changed at the manor house in the years I'd been away—the same floor-length paintings hung in the hall, the sparse furniture with a flair for the Orient, the familiar white wainscoting that appeared gray in the dim light—every inch conjured a memory from my past.

It didn't even occur to me that I might need to be cautious until I heard a cough a few paces from the door to Seline's room.

Not any cough, mind you—a deep, manly cough. My gaze snapped to my robe. Heaven help me if I'd stumbled onto Baker or one of the servants. I was scarcely presentable. And worse, it could just as easily be one of the other inhabitants of Loxby Manor.

I grimaced at the thought. Now was a particularly awkward time for a reunion. I plunged behind the velvet drapes at the L in the hall seconds before the moving shadow clambered into view around the far corner.

From the fold of the curtains I was able to catch a glimpse of the candlelit figure as he took shape in the long corridor. Broad shoulders, medium build, dark hair, lanky gait.

Avery.

My shoulders relaxed, and I pressed my palm to my heart. I'd forgotten Seline said he'd been rusticated from school. Relieved, I nearly vacated my hiding spot, but I realized all too quickly I was in no condition to meet an old friend. Tomorrow would be better.

I held as still as possible as Avery, thankfully unaware of my presence, simply lumbered down the far hall and disappeared from sight. I allowed several more seconds to pass to be certain he had indeed retired to his room.

That's when I heard it. Another set of heavy footsteps, pounding toward me from around the corner of the dark corridor.

Someone else was up and about without a candle, and it wasn't Seline. I leaned against the window casement and closed my eyes. The pant of heavy breathing seemed to echo down the quiet hall. My skin crawled.

Tap, whoosh. Tap, whoosh.

The nature of the person's tread was strangely uneven, almost as if the individual dragged something behind him. The prickling fingers of fear scurried across my chest, tightening every muscle one by one as my memories of Ceylon threatened.

Tap, whoosh. Tap, whoosh.

Whoever it was, he was achingly close. *Run!* My feet itched to escape, but I gripped the edge of the wainscoting, willing myself to stay in place. It was probably just a servant—the butler or a maid—and they were simply doing their job.

I tried to breathe like my mother had taught me to whenever I imagined things differently from what they actually were. "*Everyone is not out to assault you. I promise it will get easier, Charity*," she'd remind me time and again. And she was right . . . about part of it. Time had dulled the pain my attacker left in his wake, but the wound would never fully heal, not when it was filled so deeply with grief.

It took several minutes for the sounds to drift away and my muscles to slacken and my pulse to slow, even longer for me to allow the silence of the hall to calm me.

Carefully I tugged open the drapes to find an empty corridor beyond the thick fabric. A quick look both directions, and I was relieved to see I was indeed alone. I rushed straight into Seline's bedchamber, sealing the door behind me without a sound.

Much of the yellow room lay as it always had. Heavy mahogany furniture dotting the various walls and a lovely poster bed with gauzy white curtains. I crept forward before resting for a soothing moment on the edge of Seline's crème coverlet.

She was nowhere to be found.

I looked around in confusion. She had said nothing about staying out the entirety of the night, nor did I believe she would ever do such a thing, not after all she'd revealed about her situation with Miles. I raked the ribbons on my nightgown through my fingers.

Though Seline told me Mrs. Cavanagh had been angry with her earlier in the evening, her mother would certainly want to know that her only daughter was not in her bed, particularly at this hour. I'd promised Seline my silence, but her continued absence was not something to take lightly. The strange footsteps I'd heard pounded over and over again in my head. She could very well be in trouble.

Recollections flashed through my mind as I debated my next move. If only someone had come looking for me that night in Ceylon, so much would have been different. The thought drove me to my feet. Mrs. Cavanagh must be told and straightaway.

I dashed from Seline's room and down the corridor to the long family wing without a moment's hesitation. It wasn't until I stood before Mrs. Cavanagh's door, my hand poised to knock, that a fresh wave of nerves sparked to life. I'd not seen Seline's mother in five years, and she had always been terribly proper. What would she think of me, pounding on her door in the middle of the night, forcing her from her bed? Would she brand me as an aid in Seline's flight from the house?

I swallowed hard and knocked.

The door thrust inward far more quickly than I had anticipated. Mrs. Cavanagh's hand flew to her chest. "Why, Miss Halliwell! What are you about at such an hour?" Her handkerchief trembled as she dabbed her face.

From the looks of her rumpled evening gown, she'd not been to bed. What mother could sleep after learning of a scandal that involved her own daughter? She'd had such high hopes for Seline. Even in our youth she paraded her about, a living trophy of wealth and privilege.

I rubbed my arms. What I was about to tell her would only make her evening worse.

"I'm sorry to disturb you, Mrs. Cavanagh, but I'm terribly worried. I've come about Seline."

"Seline!" Her eyes flashed, and she shoved the door open wide. "What now, child?" A moment's hesitation, then she yanked me into her bedchamber. She cast a weary glance over the hall before slamming the door shut.

I was directed into her private sitting room with a half-hearted gesture of hospitality, which she quickly betrayed with the emergence of a scowl.

The large apartment was a lavish affair, full of deep purples and sumptuous pinks. I couldn't help but take in the complexities of the room as I spoke. "Again, I am sorry to disturb you at such an advanced hour, but it is urgent."

Mrs. Cavanagh cast a shrewd peek at her clock. "I must say, I'm surprised to find you still awake after such a long journey. I vow you young people shall never cease to amaze me."

"Seline came to see me earlier this evening."

"She did, did she?"

"We talked for a bit, and then quite suddenly she told me she meant to leave the house. I tried to stop her, but . . ."

Mrs. Cavanagh's eyes narrowed as a flush lit her cheeks. "What do you mean . . . left the house? At night, my gel? Are you mad?"

"I assure you, I am quite lucid. When Seline came to my room, she was terribly distraught about what happened earlier today." My throat felt suddenly dry. "I-I'm at a loss as to where she intended to go, only there was this light we saw out my window and she decided—"

"You mean to tell me she left the house alone?" She fanned her face with her hand. "Oh, dear me, I'm feeling faint." She glanced around madly before collapsing into a chair. "Avery must be sent for at once."

She twisted her hands together as if washing them in the air. "You don't think she went to see *him*, do you? No, no, she would not do such a thing to me, not after everything." She tugged on her ear as if it might soothe her nerves as she rocked back and forth in her chair. "Avery's the only one who can possibly keep this wretched scandal at bay. I only hope he's returned from town."

I lifted my voice. "He has."

Her focus snapped to me, and I realized a bit too late how such an admission must sound. I stumbled over my next words. "I only know because I saw him just moments ago in the hall, walking to his room, I assume."

She cast a rather daring look at my nightgown, and I added quickly, "Good heavens, I didn't allow him to see me like this. I made certain of that."

She jerked the bell pull, her hand quivering in the firelight. "Well, at any rate, he must be sent for at once." Her fingers lingered on the embroidered rope for a moment as she stared into the shadows of the room. She gave it a quick tug, then slowly she turned to face me, her green eyes narrow, her jaw set. "I suppose Seline told you all."

It was difficult to find my voice, trapped as I was in her piercing gaze. "She told me about Miles Lacy if that is what you mean."

Mrs. Cavanagh crunched forward, dipping her chin into her chest. "And I can only hope you realize how important discretion is at such a moment."

"Certainly." I tucked a strand of hair behind my ear as I knelt beside her. "Seline has always been one of my dearest friends. I would never say anything to hurt her or anyone else in this family."

She lowered her eyelids. "That is good to hear." She curled her icy fingers around my hand. "Tell me, did Seline say anything that might help us ascertain where she meant to go this evening? I can only assume it was to see that horrid stable boy."

"As I said before, we saw a strange light in the valley through my bedchamber window. It must have meant something to her."

"I see. Another liaison perhaps."

A knock sounded at the door and Mrs. Cavanagh nearly jumped out of her skin. Her voice erupted from between her narrow lips. "Come."

An elderly woman in a dark blue dress sidled through the open door. "Yes, ma'am. You rang?"

"Harriet." Mrs. Cavanagh's voice turned distant. "Summon Avery to my sitting area at once."

The dark color of the maid's clothes sparked a memory. "Oh!" I squeezed Mrs. Cavanagh's hand. "There was something else."

Mrs. Cavanagh's arm shot up, silencing me with a flick of her wrist until the maid had left and the door was sealed. Then she gave me a hard smile. "My dear Miss Halliwell. You do understand what I mean about discretion, don't you? The last thing this family needs is for my lady's maid to catch wind that Seline has left the house."

I covered my mouth. "I didn't think."

"No, you didn't." She pursed her lips. "Well, go on. What were you about to tell me?"

"I don't know what it means, but Seline was determined to borrow my black cloak before she left."

Mrs. Cavanagh stared at me for a moment, then twitched a nervous laugh. "Well, of course she would need a cloak. There's a decided nip in the air tonight." Then she stood. "If that is all the information you have for me at present, I shall leave you for my sitting room. Avery shall be waiting for me, and I daresay you must be missing your bed."

Her voice softened a bit as she took my arm. "And don't worry your pretty head, my dear. You've done all you can do tonight. Avery and I will see that everything is hushed up and Seline is returned to her room as quickly as possible. We will all speak again in the morning." A sharp nod. "Good evening, Miss Halliwell."

I paused for a moment, considering whether I should tell her about the second set of footsteps, but they were so very odd, I might very well have imagined them. Goodness knows I had done so before.

Mrs. Cavanagh swung open her bedchamber door and waited as I passed through it, confusion heavy on my heart. However, I halted one step into the hall as Mrs. Cavanagh's maid flew around the far corner, a note gripped in her hand.

Her face was pale, her arm stiff as she strangled out, "Mrs. Cavanagh! Mrs. Cavanagh!"

Mrs. Cavanagh thrust the door wide and the rush of wind ruffled the paper in the maid's hand. "What is it?"

The maid shook her head like a baby bird, thrusting out the note in one fell swoop. "I passed by Seline's room and found her door open. This note was on her bed."

Mrs. Cavanagh snatched the letter from her maid's hand and angled it into the light. Her countenance shifted as she pored over every last word, her face transitioning from the harried look she'd worn since I knocked on her door to a pale grimace. She lowered the note, her whole body shaking in response.

I moved to support her arm, my own fear and curiosity extinguishing any qualms I had in addressing her. "What does it say? Where is she?"

The note fell to the carpet. "Seline's set off for Gretna Green with Miles Lacy. And we are all ruined."

CHAPTER 3

After a fitful night of sleep and the uncomfortable silence of an empty breakfast room, I realized my only hope for information regarding Seline's unfortunate situation would be to return once again to Mrs. Cavanagh's bedchamber.

The precipitous appearance of the letter the previous night wrought more questions in my mind than answers. First off, why hadn't I seen the note when I entered her room just a few minutes before? It was dark, yes, but was it really possible to miss such a vital item? And when exactly had Seline left the note? Nothing about the events of the evening made any sense.

An offhand comment from a maid in the hallway informed me that Avery had set off quite early in search of her, and it would probably be some time before he returned. Mrs. Cavanagh remained my only recourse in the house with whom I might mull over the inconsistencies that plagued my thoughts. If only she wasn't so easily affected.

The family wing looked oddly cheery in the daylight, the ghosts of the previous night's escapades tucked neatly beneath a warm, yellow glow. Even though I knew in my heart that as a mother Mrs. Cavanagh would wish to hear my suspicions, I couldn't help but fear the flurry of her nerves.

The shouts of a heated argument rent the cloying stillness of the hallway and arrested my steps. What at first I thought emanated from Mrs. Cavanagh's bedchamber, I realized only too quickly came from the room next door.

Seized by the shrill pitch of Mrs. Cavanagh's voice, I sank against a wooden pillar, numb as to which way to turn. Of late I tended to shy away from conflict, so it was strange of me to stand there and eavesdrop . . . but I did so like a curst statue.

As I feared, Mrs. Cavanagh's shock from the previous night had turned into hysteria by the light of day. I could almost see her hands fluttering before her as she spoke.

"Please, don't take a pet about Mr. Lacy. I only meant to—"

"How I continue to handle our curst situation is entirely up to me. Don't ever forget that." The second voice was that of an older man, an angry one. Considering the proximity to Mrs. Cavanagh's room, I could only deduce it was her husband. "It seems Mr. Lacy could not stop his nephew's abhorrent behavior any more than you seem able to manage our own daughter's."

A dramatic sniffle. "I've not been remiss in any way. Acquit me of that at least. I've been the best mother anyone could be to our daughter. And for you to question my judgment when I've done everything you've asked of me—everything. Who do you think handles Loxby in your stead?"

He gave a pointed sigh. "We both know Piers runs the entirety of the estate from Liverpool. All *you* have been left to worry about is how to spend my money."

There was a hint of the victim in Mrs. Cavanagh's voice. "I'm well aware that you've no choice but to lie there day after day, planning your next criticism of me, but—"

"Enough." The word boomed through the wall.

My eyes widened and my cheeks felt hot. What was I thinking

listening in on a private conversation? But her next words kept me firmly in my spot.

"Now I have that Halliwell girl to deal with. You would force me to let her come here."

My hand retreated to my mouth as my eyes slipped closed. I had been right in my assumptions. Regardless of my mother's enthusiasm, my visit was wholly unwanted.

Mr. Cavanagh's shrewd tone broke the amassing silence of the hall. "Miss Halliwell shall likely be a comfort for you as we wait for word on Seline's whereabouts."

Mrs. Cavanagh's voice shook, but she managed to carry on well enough, "Yes . . . well . . . I . . . That is neither here nor there. What I am most anxious about is Avery. You know how easily he can be entrapped. Thankfully the little mouse is as drab as she ever was. I do not believe his head could be turned where Miss Halliwell is concerned. And it's a good thing, too, for I have high hopes for him. As should you."

Another sigh. "Your memory seems to be selective at best. As I told you before, I have no intention of discussing my will with you again. Let it alone." A long pause. "Have Piers come to my room as soon as he arrives."

A huff. "I wasn't aware you knew he was coming."

Mr. Cavanagh coughed out an irritated laugh. "Interesting that you did not tell me so yourself. We promised to be forthright with one another, did we not? Thankfully I have Baker to apprise me of what goes on in this house. I may be weak and blind, but I am not on my deathbed yet, lest you forget."

"You needn't act like I withheld the information on purpose. We've been at sixes and sevens throughout Loxby since Seline's shocking disgrace. As you well know."

I heard footsteps approaching my position beyond the door, and I sprang into a brisk walk, my feet flying numbly down the carpeted hall, my mind awash with what I'd overheard.

Avery. High hopes that didn't include me. The utter notion!

I took a careless look behind me. Goodness, I had no intention of approaching Mrs. Cavanagh now. Not when she thought I came to Loxby to—my chest tightened—make a match with her younger son.

I gripped the banister hard as I hurried down the steps, my heart a wrangled mess. Avery Cavanagh was never anything more to me than a good friend, and there had always been Piers . . . How could she think I'd come here to set my cap at Avery?

My head hurt. 'Faith, but I'd come to Loxby to escape the thought of men entirely, and here was one waiting to engage me, only this time his mother wanted her children to have nothing to do with a drab little mouse like me.

Perhaps voyaging to America would have been the better option after all.

No. I knew full well conversation about marriage would have been front and center if I'd gone with my parents. Oh yes, I'd felt the undercurrent of hope when Mama had mentioned cousin Samuel would be meeting them in Boston. He had always been the family joke when it came to me. If I never found a suitable husband, I could certainly have him. Well, I didn't want cousin Samuel or anyone else. Not anymore. Why couldn't anyone understand that?

Mrs. Cavanagh could rest easy. Not only were Piers and Avery marked off any list of mine but I'd torn up the whole dratted thing and torched it to ashes in Ceylon. I had plans of my own, none of which involved a husband.

At some point during the upcoming year, I would find a governess position—one as far away from Loxby as I could get.

Unfortunately I'd made the decision to come to East Whitloe, and I had little choice but to stay at the manor house and await Mrs. Cavanagh's pleasure for the time being. I owed the family that much. Besides, I couldn't leave now, not after Seline had disappeared so suddenly, not if I could help her in some way.

I moved past Mr. Baker in the long corridor to the drawing room. There was a moment's hesitation in his step until he halted midway down the hall as if he meant to delay me. But then he gave his head a light shake and hurried on his way.

I plowed through those double mahogany doors as if I owned the world, only to stop short one measly step inside the room.

I immediately realized I was not alone—and my entire world flipped upside down.

Piers Cavanagh didn't turn from where he stood at the fireplace, but I knew he'd heard the click of the door, for his fingers clenched into a ball and his arm plunged from the mantel to his side.

The air in the room felt thin.

He'd grown taller over the years, his shoulders broad, his dress so terribly refined. Had I ever seen him wear a black jacket quite like that one? All of a sudden I didn't know where to rest my hands. In front of me or at my sides?

Goodness, the room was warm.

I stepped forward, my brow pulled tight, my chest heavy. Oh dear. What had he done to his hair? The curls I remembered so well had been cut short, leaving behind a tangle of thick locks dusted with a bit more brown and a little less red.

My heart rode painfully on a storm of nerves, and I could do little but mouth his name as I waited for him to turn and acknowledge me. Seline said he planned to return today, but had I ever really believed I would see him again?

Carefully he stepped back and glanced over his shoulder, the utter shock of finding me at Loxby all too evident in his blue eyes. "Miss Halliwell?"

It was hard to see anything but the young, carefree boy I'd spent the whole of my youth admiring. One letter had changed everything between us. I knew nothing of the gentleman across the room. "Good morning, Mr. Cavanagh."

There was a slight silence before he affected a smile. "What on earth are you doing here?"

"I suppose your mother didn't tell you."

Piers had always been a master at quizzical glances, and he took a moment to examine me. "No, she didn't."

I detected a curious note of wistfulness in his voice, and it drew my gaze painfully to his face. "I came for an extended visit while my parents are across the Atlantic. I'm to stay at Loxby for the next year." I swallowed hard, fear of what he might say swelling in my throat.

"A whole year? That's"—he looked away for a moment as if to hunt the right word, then turned back to me—"auspicious." He extended his hands as he crossed the rug toward me, but his eyes betrayed a rigid undercurrent that only grew with each second. "Tell me, is your family well?"

"Quite well." I forced myself to take his hands, only to drop them a second later at the sound of footsteps in the hall.

Piers's plastered smile vanished, and he stepped shrewdly away. It seemed neither of us was in the mood for playacting.

Mrs. Cavanagh breached the door and bustled past me on a whiff of lavender perfume, her eyes ticking like a clock between Piers and me before settling sharply on him.

Her voice, however, sounded defeated. "So you've come home at last."

She trudged to the sofa and settled down, staring for a moment before fluttering her eyes closed and extending her cheek.

I could read the insecurity in Piers's stark expression as he stooped to place a kiss. "Good morning, Mother."

She took a loud, quivering breath, then turned to me. "I suppose Miss Halliwell has been airing all our dirty laundry."

I could have sunk into the floor after what I'd overheard her say earlier in the family wing.

"Certainly not." Mortified, I made my way to the far end of the sofa and took a seat. "I came into the drawing room but a second before you did." I couldn't help casting a sideways glance at Piers. "I had no idea your son had already arrived."

Piers gave a shrug and wandered to the window. "If you are referring to Avery's situation, Mother, I've already heard all the blasted details. I scrambled off a note informing him I would consider writing his teacher a letter if he promised to start afresh. No more larks."

Mrs. Cavanagh snorted. "Start fresh indeed. Avery's the only one I count on at Loxby these days—certainly not Seline. Heaven help me if the two of you don't mean to drag this family through the mud at every turn." She pressed a handkerchief to her nose, and a slight wail accompanied her words. "I shall never be able to return to London at this rate."

Piers ignored her outburst and propped his shoulder against the wall. "What has Seline done now?"

"What hasn't she done?" Another sniffle. "You remember Mr. Lacy?"

He gave her a hard smile. "Who do you think I correspond with weekly on the running of the estate with Father indisposed?"

She waved her handkerchief in the air. "I really wouldn't know."

He crossed the room and took a seat in the opposing chair. "What about Mr. Lacy?"

She stiffened and tipped her nose in the air. "He has a nephew, that's what."

I listened as Mrs. Cavanagh recounted Seline's indiscretions, from her kiss to her desperate nighttime flight from the house, but it wasn't until she mentioned the letter Seline left behind in her room that I gave voice to the questions that had been brewing in my mind. "Mrs. Cavanagh?"

She jerked her head up. "Yes, dear? I nearly forgot you were there." She patted my leg. "Miss Halliwell was the last to speak with Seline before she left. Have you anything to add?"

Now was my chance. "I have been doing a great deal of thinking over the night, and I cannot help but ask, are you completely certain Seline wrote that note? You see, when she fled my room, the last thing she said to me was that she wouldn't be out long. I fully expected her to return straightaway."

Piers leaned forward, curiosity bending his brow. "What are you getting at? Do you think Seline's flight some sort of ploy?"

I tethered my lip between my teeth. "I don't know exactly. I mean, it is indeed possible that Seline changed her mind. Yet when she left my room, she made it perfectly clear that she had no intention of departing the estate." Of course Seline did say she had a plan. But to elope, and with Miles Lacy? Certainly not.

Mrs. Cavanagh's fingers came to life, wiggling in the air. "Then where else can she be?"

All eyes shot to me.

"Who could say, but taking flight for Gretna Green in the middle of the night? That doesn't sound anything like her, not unless it included a gentleman with a title."

Piers rubbed his chin, his eyes steady on me. "Miss Halliwell does have a point, Mother. Seline is impulsive and foolish, but why on earth wouldn't she wait to flee until morning?" He lifted his eyebrows. "I would like to take a look at this note."

I nodded quickly as it was just what I'd been hoping to do all night. The letter had to reveal something.

Mrs. Cavanagh's lady's maid was sent at once to fetch the letter from Mrs. Cavanagh's bedchamber, and the three of us were forced to wait patiently for her return—Piers with his stern brow and troubled gaze, Mrs. Cavanagh full of strained quivers, and me, taunted not only by my acute fear for my dear friend but by the added presence of her brother. Why did he have to come home at such a time?

The clock ticked away the seconds achingly slow until the maid rushed back through the door, the note thrust out in front of her. Mrs. Cavanagh accepted the letter as if it were a dead animal and unfolded it before us. We all stared at the crisp white paper, but Piers was the first to take the note into his hands and scan carefully over Seline's scrolled words. "It does appear to be her handwriting."

Mrs. Cavanagh scoffed, "Well of course it's her handwriting."

He passed it to me.

My dearest Mama,

Miles and I are off for Gretna Green this very hour.

Seline

Awfully short at such a moment. I narrowed my eyes. "Do you think she might have written it under some sort of duress? See how the ink blurs here."

Mrs. Cavanagh grasped the letter, smashing it closed. "Well,

I daresay she was under duress. The poor dear must have thought she was out of options. People can do all sorts of things when they are desperate."

"But to make such a rash decision before—"

"My dear Miss Halliwell, I can certainly understand your wish to find meaning in such a haphazard trip to Scotland, but this letter proves Seline took off with little regard for her family, particularly her mama."

Mrs. Cavanagh pressed her handkerchief to her nose. "I only hope Avery may find her in time, or we shall be forced to welcome the new Mrs. Lacy back to the house in a few weeks. I do hope she enjoys living out her days in one of the small cottages on the estate. I fear that is all her father will do for her now." She stumbled to her feet and made her way to the door before pausing to rest her hand against the doorframe. "I do apologize, but my nerves are far too raw to continue on in this way. I need to lie down. You must excuse me."

Caught up in the drama of her departure, I watched her sweep from the room before I turned back to face Piers. My fingers gripped the armrest of their own accord. He was studying me with that look of his that seemed to know and question everything. Yet at the same time he couldn't keep still, swinging his boot across his opposing leg then back to the floor.

A curious mix of emotions snuck over me as I watched his awkward dance—the delicious hint of exhilaration I'd felt the last time I'd seen him, accompanied by the inescapable veil of abandonment that swathed every last memory of our time together. I glanced up. Was Piers as affected by my unexpected presence at Loxby as I was by his?

He rested his elbows on his knees and his chin in his hands. "I suppose we've little recourse but to wait for word from Avery. Odds are my mother's right, and Seline did just as she wrote in that note."

I nodded in agreement, ushering in the wretched weight of silence once again.

I took a deep breath. Regardless of how things had ended between Piers and me, there was no reason to be uncivil, not anymore. Besides, my parents had trained me better than that, and he would be gone from Loxby soon enough.

"Piers." My voice faltered. "It is good to see you again."

I wasn't prepared for the look he gave me. Part hope, part dread, and his response, terribly slow. "I cannot guess what you must think of me."

I didn't move as the years melted away. Time would never dull my need for some kind of closure.

He kept his voice emotionless, yet he had difficulty meeting my eyes. "I never should have insinuated anything regarding our future before you left. It turned out to be a turbulent time for me." The muscles twitched in his jaw. "Of course I do realize excuses are futile. I've not the ability to rewind time."

And . . .

His letter about his responsibilities hadn't been enough explanation at the time for ending our relationship. This was even worse.

He ran his hand down his pantaloons, his focus vacant on the corner of the room. "You've probably heard, but I live a very different life now, one of isolation. Believe me when I tell you, I never would have come home if I'd known you were here."

My eyes widened.

He pushed to his feet and started for the door before stopping cold at the edge of the carpet, his voice hollow like a ghost from the darkest corners of Ceylon. "We'll have no choice but to be in each other's company over the next few days, and there is a part of me that is glad I got this chance to see you again, but I feel certain at some point you'll understand me when I tell you, the past must remain in the past."

CHAPTER 4

It wasn't until late the next day that I got my first sight of Avery Cavanagh. Seated at the escritoire in the crook of the bow window in the drawing room, I'd painfully managed only half a letter to my mother when I saw him galloping up the long, central drive.

At first I thought he meant to ride on to the stables, but with a billowing puff of dust, he jerked his horse to a halt and motioned to a servant. He swung his pristine riding boot over the horse and slid to the ground in one swift movement.

I stood to get a better view through the window, and I was not disappointed.

Everyone at Loxby had grown in the years I'd been away, but Avery had certainly changed the most. In place of the chestnut-headed, wide-eyed boy I knew as my childhood friend, a definitive gentleman waltzed up the front steps. Gone were the lanky clumsiness of youth and the red spots on his cheeks. In many ways he resembled Piers now, but—I narrowed my eyes—in others, he was quite different.

He caught sight of me through the window as he approached, and I gave an enthusiastic wave. The easy smile I remembered so well flashed onto his face, and he hurried toward the door. Avery had always been a mix of impulsive excitement and good humor, the perfect foil to Piers's brooding intensity. And as I stood there waiting for Avery to join me inside, I realized just how much I had missed him.

He passed his hat and riding crop into a servant's waiting hands, then burst through the open drawing room door. "Charity."

Dirt coated his superfine jacket and beige pantaloons, and we couldn't help but laugh as he accepted my outstretched hands. "You're a sight for sore eyes. Had a devilish few days, I'm afraid. When did you arrive?"

I stepped back a pace, reminded of the black cloud hanging over Loxby. "Shortly before Seline went missing. Please tell me you've heard something of her on your journey."

He rubbed the back of his neck. "I wish I had better news. Rode to every inn within a day's ride of East Whitloe. There's no word of the happy couple. All I can figure is that they gave assumed names or paid off someone on the road. They'd have to change horses somewhere."

I frowned, and Avery dipped his shoulder. "Seline has always been a step ahead of everyone else, but there is still a sliver of hope. Do you remember our uncle Charles?"

"Not at all."

He paused. "Well, that's neither here nor there." Then he gave a little laugh. "What I mean to say is the curst blunderbuss has decided to journey on to Gretna Green alone in hopes of intercepting the lovebirds along the way. I daresay he shall have a difficult time catching them. Miles Lacy knows his way around horses too well. He would not be so addlepated as to have no plan. Granted, I would not put such a half-baked scheme past Seline, but Miles . . . I told Uncle Charles that from the start. We'll never come upon them, at least not until this little liaison is right and tight and preferably legal."

My gaze clouded. Avery spoke as if he believed Seline and Miles Lacy had a longstanding plan to run away. That would mean she lied to me in my bedchamber the night she disappeared, which made no sense at all. We'd always trusted one another. It didn't feel quite right.

On impulse I touched his arm. "Then you completely agree with the assertion that she left in the middle of the night—to marry a stable hand?"

"That is what her note said, didn't it?" He ran his finger along his chin, his eyes focusing in on the far wall. "I will admit it doesn't sound all that much like Seline, but . . ."

He meandered to the sideboard and poured himself a drink before turning back to face me. "Cor, but it's good to have you back. It'll almost be like old times around here with Piers in residence, and you"—he raised his eyebrows—"you look well. Dash it all, but you do! Piers is already here, right? Do you think, uh, I mean, has he said anything about me yet?"

"Said anything about *you*?" We were both a bit startled by Piers's deep voice at the door. "I daresay we have bigger problems today than you."

Avery crossed the room and embraced his brother, patting him on the back. "Ordinarily, I'd be relieved to hear you say so, old man, but not this time."

Piers motioned for me to have a seat, and I eased onto the edge of the scrolled end sofa behind me. Of course my hasty selection only ushered in a bit of awkward footwork as Piers was forced to angle between Avery and me before slumping into an opposing chair. We both knew there would be no question of him joining me on the sofa. Not after his declaration yesterday.

Avery, clearly amused, watched us with a keen eye before crossing his arms. "'Fraid I need to freshen up before joining the two of you . . . in whatever that was. Mother would have my head if one fleck of this dirt got on her precious furniture."

Piers cast him a sideways glance. "Quite right."

Avery picked up his drink. "Tell me, how is Mother today? She was in a frenzy when I left."

Piers took a measured breath. "Not well. As to be expected, I suppose. She rarely leaves her room." He glanced up at Avery, his voice a bit tight. "I hope you've come across some news that might pacify her."

Avery pressed his lips together. "'Fraid not. I was just telling Charity there's not a trace of which way they went."

I couldn't help but catch the uncomfortable shift Piers made in his seat at the mention of my Christian name. Why shouldn't Avery and I use such familiarity? Heavens, we'd always spoken so as children.

"Baker told me you saw Seline the night she left." At first I thought Piers was speaking to me, but his attention was on Avery, who took a quick drink before answering. "Yeah, well, the boys and I were in the meadow. Seline came flouncing down there and, uh, had a few words with Kendal."

Piers's mouth fell open. "Lord Kendal was there? I didn't realize the two of you cried friends."

Avery tugged at his jacket sleeve. "Don't get in a pucker, Piers. Besides, he's not as awful as you remember him. After all, it was you who caused the rift. If only you'd have showed your face at that blasted duel, he never would have labeled you a coward."

Piers simply stared at the fireplace, wholly unconcerned with the eyes of the room. "What time did you last see Seline?"

Avery swirled the last of his drink in his glass. "I don't know exactly. I'm not her keeper. All I know is it was quite late."

Piers's attention remained fixed on the fire, but his voice was a bit more complicated, gruff even. "What did she say to Lord Kendal?"

"Curse it if I know. She pulled him off to the side. Whatever it was, it wasn't pleasant. There was a great deal of"—he imitated his sister's movements—"flailing arms and whatnot."

"An argument?" I couldn't hide the surprise in my voice. "You don't think she told Lord Kendal what happened with Miles Lacy?"

Avery shrugged. "I certainly hope not. She'd be a fool if she did, for I saw his announcement in the *Post* earlier that very day, along with the rest of Britain. Lord Kendal is engaged to Miss Honora Gervey. Can't get out of it now."

The room fell motionless around us, except for my eyes, which inched their way painfully toward Piers.

He seemed a bit stunned for a second, his face freezing in place, but he managed to straighten his shoulders and say rather passably, "It is a relief to know that Miss Gervey will be happy and taken care of. You know very well there was never anything official between us, and I have always hoped the best for her."

Avery gave a breathy laugh. "Still a bit ironic how she ended up with Kendal though."

I saw Piers's hand clench and release, and my heart twisted. What exactly had transpired after I left for Ceylon? Piers had always indicated to me he'd never been in love with Honora. A match between them was a fantasy of his mother and hers.

I leaned forward. "Kendal's engagement could certainly be a motive for Seline's sudden flight."

The boys looked to me, and I said quickly, "I know for certain Seline still harbored a tender for Lord Kendal. She was worried about how the scandal with Miles Lacy might affect her chances."

"The little nitwit." Avery returned his empty glass to the

sideboard. "Who knows? But does it really matter now? What's done is done." His arms fell loose at his sides. "Maybe Uncle Charles will come up with them after all. Either way, I ought to get out of these clothes and go check on Mother." A shrewd glance at Piers. "She never handles these things all that well, and she's bound to have heard I'm home."

Piers rose. "I need to dress for supper as well."

Moving quickly, I held out my hand to delay him just long enough for Avery to depart the room.

His eyes looked strained as he glared back at me. "What is it?"

I matched the severity of his countenance. "Clearly your mother and Avery believe Seline is on her way to Gretna Green, but do you, Mr. Cavanagh—the scholar, the scientist—honestly think that as well?"

His gaze drifted to the window. "I'm not certain what to believe."

"Piers."

His focus snapped back to me at the mention of his Christian name. I was already tired of keeping things formal between us.

I went on quickly, "I'm only asking you to weigh the evidence. When Seline came to my room that night, she told me she had a plan, but I am quite certain it did not involve the likes of Miles Lacy. She fled the house to see Lord Kendal, not for any elopement. Avery said so himself. You see, we saw a light on the hill at Kinwich Abbey. She must have known Kendal was the person who lit it. She said something to that effect, then left at once."

"What about the note she left?"

I stroked the armrest. "I'm not certain, but I didn't see a note when I entered her room that night before it was discovered. Maybe she wrote it, maybe she didn't. But I cannot help worrying she is in some sort of terrible trouble. I waited for her to return to my bedchamber for hours. I knew she was coming back, and now she's vanished. Wouldn't she at least have told me? She used to tell me everything."

He grasped the far side of a slat-back chair with both hands. "You've been gone . . . People change . . ." He lowered his head. "Yet I must confess, I, too, noticed inconsistencies in regard to the letter."

"Then why didn't you—"

He held up his hand. "I kept silent at the time in hopes of sparing my mother. She doesn't handle anxiety well. Goodness knows I've given her my own share of trouble. I don't want her knowing there could be more to this business than a simple elopement to Gretna Green. Not yet at least. And I certainly don't want my father catching wind of it. The shock could very well kill him. He has taken a turn for the worst over the last few days. Mother and I decided this morning that it's best to keep as much as we can about this business from my father."

"But you believe me and will look into it?"

"Once I hear back from Uncle Charles, yes. He may yet come upon them on the road."

"That could take weeks."

He opened his hands. "What other choice do we have? Seline has been reckless before. She never should have . . ."

My ears buzzed, drowning out his words. The disapproval written on his face was obvious enough. What woman would go out alone at night? Whatever happened to Seline was inevitably her fault. She deserved it.

Tears welled in my eyes as memories flashed through my mind.

I deserved what happened to me in Ceylon as well.

I know Piers never would have disparaged Seline if he'd had the slightest idea of how his words would affect me later that night. In the small hours, when the darkness ruled the recesses of my bedchamber and scaled the walls of my mind, I could no more stop the barrage of memories than I could cease breathing.

Back I fell into the past, to the year I moved to Ceylon, to the last cool night of the summer. The sounds of the ballroom still echoed in my ears. I'd become restless with the crowds and never even stopped to question my moonlit stroll alone in the tea fields. I'd not had cause to do so before, and I craved the beauty of silence and the simplicity of nature at rest. I had been missing home, missing Piers. A gentle breeze tugged me into the rolling hills bursting with the lush green tea plants.

My attacker must have been watching me when I left the house, because he timed his arrival perfectly. Thick rows of tea plants stretched out in concentric circles around me. As I crested a slight hill, I paused to admire the breathtaking view, unaware the estate had disappeared into the darkness behind me.

The man had a lazy air about his movements. He was a commoner, yes, but British and handsome. He said he was working as a groom for one of our government officials. I had no reason to distrust him, yet a wave of disquiet washed over me the minute he arrived with his sharp gaze and easy smile. He was so very friendly, and I'd always loved learning about people from every walk of life.

The house slipped farther and farther beyond the hill.

And my world was never the same. Though he was interrupted by the call of a farmworker before the whole of my dignity was taken, he still escaped with a great deal of my innocence and all my hopes for any sort of future. Besides my mother, I told no one. And neither did he.

CHAPTER 5

Mrs. Cavanagh gathered her scattered wits long enough to join us for supper the next evening. Avery was in rare form, seeing to all her needs. It was "Yes, Mother," and "Can I send a servant to get that for you, Mother?" throughout the meal. However, when we retired to the drawing room and the men to their port, her attention snapped to me.

Resting comfortably on the scrolled end sofa, she instructed me to place a blanket across her lap.

"Yes, dear, that is much better. With my nerves as they are, I wouldn't wish to catch a chill."

After ensuring the fireplace screen was just so, I took a hesitant seat at her side, conscious for the first time of an uncomfortable tension between us. I straightened my skirt. "How long do you believe it will be before we hear word from Mr. Charles Cavanagh?"

She expelled a huff. "Gretna Green is a full five-day ride from here. I cannot imagine we shall hear anything within the week." She toyed with the edge of her lace cap. "In the meantime"—a well-placed pause—"there is something I should like to discuss with you."

"Oh?" My mind scrambled for what she could possibly be alluding to. Piers had warned me to keep my concerns about Seline to myself, so I affixed a light smile.

She popped open a tortoiseshell fan and spoke from behind it. "Did your mother tell you that Mr. Cavanagh has not been well these past few years?" She tapped the side of her head with the corner of the fan. "He suffers greatly, and it has only worsened over the last few days."

I narrowed my eyes. Mr. Cavanagh had certainly seemed lucid when I overheard their argument, but I nodded. One never did know a person, not really. Besides, it was quite unlikely I would encounter Mr. Cavanagh often during my stay.

Ignorant of my confusion, Mrs. Cavanagh went on, fanning herself as she spoke. "Avery and I have decided it would be best not to tell him too much about Seline's elopement. He knows she's left, but I don't wish to give him further concern."

I seemed to remember Piers being the one to make the decision regarding his father, but I said nothing to that end. "Don't worry. I won't say a word."

She pressed her lips together. "Thank you, dear, but I would even take it a bit further."

My smile fell.

"I want you to avoid him in the house if at all possible. He's assisted from his room from time to time when he is able, and I'm quite cautious with his care." She touched my hand. "You must understand, Mr. Cavanagh tends to get confused at times. He's always been a bit volatile, but after the accident . . . well . . . When he learned of Seline's disgrace with the stable boy, for example, he refused food the entire day. The doctor warned us not to get him excited, and after everything that has happened, I think it prudent for you to stay away as best you can."

I darted one last glance at the door. Since he was so often from home, I'd rarely spoken to Mr. Cavanagh in all my time growing up in East Whitloe. He certainly wouldn't expect me to visit him now. "I'll be sure to steer clear."

She clasped her hands together, the sharp clap striking my nerves. "Thank you, my dear. You relieve my mind."

I answered with a listless smile as Piers and Avery wandered into the drawing room. By their expressions, I couldn't help but wonder if my presence at Loxby had been a significant topic of conversation. Goodness, Piers wouldn't even look my direction.

Avery walked straight to his mother. She answered his quizzical glance with a pert nod, his responding smile a curious one.

He turned his focus to me. "Would the two of you care for a game of Whist?" A glance at his mama. "We finally have four players. What do you say?" He looked over his shoulder at Piers. "At least I assume we do." He leaned in close to me. "Piers has been in a foul mood all evening. I shan't be surprised if he means to put us off."

Mrs. Cavanagh sat up in eagerness of the idea, brightening in turn but then lowering her gaze. "My dear boy, you know just how to anticipate your mama's pleasure; however, I must confess, this day has been a difficult one. There is no way I could possibly concentrate on a game of cards, not until Seline is safe at home." She splayed her hand across her chest. "I'm afraid I expect little sleep this evening but shall be forced to retire to my room nonetheless. If you would but give me your arm."

Mrs. Cavanagh lifted a brave face to the room, but the strain was evident. The days of worry had left dark circles under her eyes, and her gait was unsteady as she walked. Her Turkish robe and sarsenet gown lacked her usual precision to detail. One sleeve was bunched up above her elbow and a ribbon remained untied at the hem. I wished somehow I could lessen the pain of the unknown.

Piers had been right to caution me where his mother was concerned. She appeared to be at the breaking point. What mother wouldn't?

I, on the other hand, had questions. I pushed to my feet. "Avery."

He looked back as he supported his mother's arm. Mrs. Cavanagh echoed his movement with her own startled glare.

Oh dear, how had I already forgotten what I'd overheard from outside Mr. Cavanagh's room? Such familiarity with Avery would hardly go unnoticed. I was playing into Mrs. Cavanagh's suppositions. I regulated my tone to seem a bit more nonchalant. "If you have a mind to return to the drawing room after you've seen to your mother, I'd like a word with you, and Piers of course. It will take but a moment."

Avery's eyebrows peaked, but he nodded.

I watched them leave and returned to my seat on the sofa to find Piers in the strange humor Avery had mentioned.

He was calm enough on the surface, but something simmered beneath his brooding silence. He took a long sip of his drink before addressing me. "Just a few days back in East Whitloe, and I see you've already managed to wrangle Avery under your thumb."

I stared at him, then frowned. Had his mother aired her concerns to him about me and Avery? "What nettles you tonight?"

He didn't answer, focusing his attention out a window and into the dark night. There was a crawling wind beyond the glass, which left the room almost edgy with anticipation, as if Piers and I were merely pawns on a chessboard waiting for the next play to determine our fate.

"If you think my asking Avery for a quick chat is wrangling, I daresay you've been isolated outside of Liverpool for longer than I thought."

He waited a moment before scowling back at me, a bend to his brow, but then he opened his hands as if chastised. "As you say."

He sounded both aloof and cross, and I considered retiring for the night when his tone softened. "Forgive me. I don't do waiting well."

"Neither do I, as you well know, which is why I asked Avery to return. I have a few questions for him about Seline."

I must have sounded unsure of myself, for the look on Piers's face transformed. He was a young man again, my first love, my only love. I swallowed hard.

Willfully forgetting the feelings that had been a part of me for so long—the uncontrollable attraction that still churned beneath the surface of my scars—would take practice. However, Piers and I were different people now. I could not forget that.

I looked up, straight into Piers's sharp gaze. He, too, felt the distance between us—the impenetrable chasm neither of us meant to cross.

But what if a bridge was possible—one of friendship and mutual admiration? Granted, I'd have to be extremely careful how I handled myself. If only I could find my way back to the carefree young lady I had once been, we might find a way to civility. After all, I could use his help to solve the mystery of what happened to Seline.

"Piers?"

"Yes," he answered quickly and with complete control, which felt like a slap to the face after I'd been forced to work hard to control my own emotions.

"Do you think it possible we might cry friends?" My heart thundered in my ears as I waited for him to ponder his response.

Then a slight smile emerged, and he breathed out a laugh. "I suppose you've grown tired of my incessant ruminating. Goodness knows I have."

"I wouldn't call it incessant." I sat up and extended my gloved hand. "Friends, then?"

He hesitated a moment, then grasped it. "Friends." He settled back against his chair. "You know, I'm relieved really. Avery has already scolded me for behaving like a flat this evening. I told him I was only concerned about that temper of yours."

My brow shot up. "Of mine?"

He covered his mouth to hide a grin. "We used to call you Captain Halliwell for a reason."

"I thought that was because I always knew the answers."

"Or were rather good at dictating them, one way or another."

"You brute." I reached out to pop his arm as I'd done a thousand times in my youth, but I sobered all too quickly, memories flashing into my mind. Long strolls in the garden. The day he kissed me in the alcove. And then that letter. I would not be so foolish this time.

He, too, shifted his position in his chair before turning to the door, his expression changing. "Avery, what impeccable timing you have."

Avery strolled into the room and flopped into the large wingback chair across from us. "Would you expect anything less? Now what's all this about? I must tell you, I've got a devilish headache."

The two brothers looked to me.

"It's about the day Seline disappeared."

Avery flicked his fingers in the air. "What of it?"

"Would you mind explaining who else besides Lord Kendal was with you when Seline came upon you in the meadow?"

He glanced up at the crossbeams in the ceiling. "Just a couple of friends—Hugh Daunt and Tony Shaw. The four of us had something important to discuss."

"And you saw nothing of Miles Lacy that night?"

He shrugged. "No, why would I?"

"What did Seline say when she arrived?"

He tilted his head back against the chair. "Nothing all that remarkable. She said she'd come to speak with Kendal, and then he took her aside as she requested. Curst if I know what she was jabbering about."

"You didn't hear a word? Not a solitary one?"

"No. She just let in on Kendal for several minutes and then flounced off." Avery pinched the bridge of his nose. "Listen, as much as I'd love to stay and chat with you two lovebirds, this headache needs a dark, quiet room, and straightaway. I'll be happy to answer anything else you can dream up tomorrow morning, when I'm up to snuff."

Irritated by Avery's insinuation, I gave a pert nod.

He sprang to his feet. "G'night, Piers, Charity."

Piers and I waited until the sound of his footsteps disappeared, and the imaginary rope of curiosity drew us both forward. I lowered my voice, a curious spark of interest christening my words. "He's hiding something. Did you see how quickly he had to get out of here?"

Piers dipped his chin. "Like a scared rat."

CHAPTER 6

Avery was nowhere to be found the following morning, not in the house or about the estate. In fact, I didn't see either brother until Piers came upon me at the back gate of the rose garden in the afternoon.

He was a bit flushed when he appeared around the corner, and I wondered if he'd been running. A natural at evasion, he ignored my questioning look and motioned down the incline toward the River Sternway, tempering his voice. "Care for an afternoon stroll?"

I hesitated at first, then gave a vague nod, still a bit intrigued as to what brought him rushing this way. I could keep my emotions at bay. "Any word of where Avery got off to?"

He shook his head. "Baker says he left quite early. Apparently a letter came for him last night from Hugh Daunt."

"Hmm, so you don't think he's avoiding us?"

Piers ushered me onto the narrow gravel path with a flick of his wrist. "Not exactly, yet at the same time I wonder what was so urgent to take him from home at such a time. He could have easily found another way of putting us off."

The sun hung low in the sky, warming our backs while painting long shadows over the eastern slope. A slight breeze ran its wide fingers across the grass and tinted the air with the sweet scent of wisteria. I glanced over at Piers. Though I'd dreaded his presence at the house, it also seemed so natural that he should be here beside me, that we should be deciding between us what was best to be done about Seline.

"What do you think Hugh, Tony, and Lord Kendal were doing meeting Avery so late at the abbey? Seems a remarkably odd choice to me."

"Very odd, no doubt. Of course Avery has been friends with those first two since he was in leading strings, but Lord Kendal—that name was certainly a surprise."

A bird swooped low over the path, and I watched it glide for a moment on a stray gust of wind, the very embodiment of strength and peace.

"I've been doing a bit of thinking about the night Seline left. As I said before, there was a light out my window, which had to have been the very thing that set her off." I paused to catch his gaze. "From what she said before she left my room, she knew who would be at Kinwich Abbey, in effect, who had brought the light. I can only assume it was Lord Kendal she was after. She had just finished telling me she would only marry a gentleman with a title."

"My mother's words, but I see Seline adopted them as her own." He kicked a stone with the toe of his boot.

Piers paused at the woods' edge, placing his hand against a tree. "I am beginning to fear you're in the right of it though. After your questions in the drawing room, I decided to do a bit of questioning of my own. First thing this morning, I spoke with my man in the stables. Berkeley said he'd heard from Mr. Lacy that Miles was called to Mr. Cavanagh's room the morning of Seline's disappearance and was planning to leave early the next morning. He, too, thought the elopement extremely unlikely. He didn't know Miles well but said he was never one to take responsibility for anything. I wasn't able to speak with Mr. Lacy directly, as he accompanied Avery to town, but I intend to do so."

I was forced to focus on my steps as the path took a dip. "Then if Seline didn't go to Gretna Green with Miles Lacy, where on earth is she?"

He countered my question with a cunning look. "If Avery's description of what happened at the abbey is to be believed, only one person can possibly know for certain what happened to Seline once the group dispersed, and I doubt Lord Kendal would be keen on a visit from me." He shook his head. "Avery is the only one who can journey to Whitecaster Hall and demand answers from Kendal."

I rested for a moment in the steady rush of the river, dredging up some nerves before turning once again to Piers. "I may be out of line in asking, but what happened between you and Honora Gervey? When you wrote to me in Ceylon, I assumed the two of you would be married shortly. That is, until Seline's letter finally came and said otherwise."

He hesitated a moment, the awkward truth of a well-placed pause settling between us, and I got the strongest feeling he didn't mean to answer at all. But then he turned and leaned against the tree. "The arrangement between our parents ended rather quickly. She wouldn't have me, not after I disappointed Lord Kendal at the duel." He shrugged. "Would you?"

He'd certainly posed the question as some sort of joke, but warmth filled my cheeks nonetheless. "I'm hardly the person to answer such a question. I've done quite a bit of growing up over the past five years, and it may surprise you to learn I have no intention of marrying at all."

I thought I saw his eyes widen as he looked down. "Don't be ridiculous."

"I'm perfectly serious. I have my own plans—to pursue a governess position."

Without warning, he touched my arm, but I pulled away, feigning a distraction as I continued on the path.

My head throbbed, but I was glad I'd said it. Now we could stop all the self-conscious toying with each other and get on with the uncomplicated friendship I'd asked for. "I know my desire to be a governess sounds a bit premature in most people's minds, and it's not as if I don't have options. My parents would have me consider my cousin Samuel."

He coughed out a laugh. "Not Samuel. He wouldn't do at all. You can set your cap far higher than him." He studied me for a moment. "What about Tony Shaw? He's a nice enough fellow."

"I'm never short of matchmakers, am I? First my parents, then Seline, now you. What a pleasure you all are."

"I realize any attachment of yours is most certainly none of my business." His shoulders slumped. "Forgive me. Tony just came to mind when you were talking. Would you not consider him though?"

"I thank you, but no."

He sighed. "And then there's Hugh. Remember when he and Seline spent that day at the river? I was forced to say I'd been with them the entire time to save Seline's reputation."

"She did enjoy her little escapades."

He nodded, his breath tinted by a laugh. "We all enjoyed our little escapades, didn't we?"

My gaze rose to his. I knew he was referring to the moment we'd shared in the alcove in his house.

He took a deep breath, his eyes so terribly unnerving. "You've changed."

I don't know what I was expecting him to say, but it certainly wasn't that. The words cut straight to my heart because I knew them to be true. How many times had I been forced to endure that same sentiment? *"You look different, Charity." "Where is that beautiful smile of yours?" "You used to be more fun." "It's only a dance, Charity. Why must you act so awkward—take the man's hand!"*

My ears rang with all the people who knew better than I how I should feel and how I should act. Granted, most didn't know what had happened, but my mother did.

I realized belatedly I missed the start of what Piers had said.

". . . don't you think?"

I gave him a wan smile. "I'm sorry, Piers, I didn't hear you." I hated to blame my preoccupation on my hearing difficulties, but I had no intention of telling him what I'd been thinking.

His glance was a compassionate one as he tugged me to the side. Piers Cavanagh was the one person who never teased me about missing part of a conversation, yet for some reason, I couldn't meet his eyes.

"You know I never mind repeating." He pointed at the horizon. "I only said we should probably turn back, don't you think? The hour is advanced."

"Yes. It is getting rather late."

He offered me his arm. "And Avery knows full well when it's nearing dinnertime. Mark my words, he'll be home soon enough."

I gave a little laugh, more of a diversion than anything else. All I could think of was the soft texture of Piers's superfine jacket and the underlying warmth of his arm, the ease of friendship and the fear of the unknown. Was it possible? Could Piers and I move beyond our past? Could I forgive him for deserting me in Ceylon?

Piers caught sight of Avery seconds after we rounded the front of the house. "There's his horse. Perfect timing."

Avery had no choice but to meet us on the lawn. He acted almost amused, but his eyes told me otherwise. "You won't believe it, but Lord Kendal has returned to his country seat."

Piers crossed his arms. "Of course I believe it. He probably means to introduce his family to his fiancée."

Avery held up his first finger, the others clenched into a fist. "Quite right, but the curricle race is still on."

Piers shot a glance at me. "What curricle race?"

Avery angled his chin, his mouth practically falling open. "You haven't heard? I wondered why you didn't enter a bet. You best do so before it's too late. The race is scheduled for the close of the month."

"And who exactly would I be betting on?"

Avery leaned in. "Secret is Kendal's hiding some prime bit of horseflesh at Whitecaster Hall. I'd suggest going that way with any money you can swing. The odds are too good to pass up."

I stepped forward. "So the race is to be at Whitecaster? Might that provide the perfect opportunity to speak with Lord Kendal?"

Avery went motionless. "In regard to what?"

"If he knows anything further about Seline. You told us yesterday he was the last to speak with her."

His face relaxed. "Oh, I doubt he knows where she and Miles have run off to. Presently I need to change for dinner." His focus swung like a pendulum between Piers and me, and then a sly smile creased his lips. "What have the two of you been about today?"

Piers shoved his brother's arm. "A simple walk, nothing more.

Get on with you. We won't hold supper." He thrust the front door wide for Avery, but as soon as Avery passed, Piers extended his hand to stop me. "Allow me to apologize for Avery. You mustn't let him get under your skin. He likes to tease me is all. I assure you, I've no intention of burdening any lady with my disgrace, particularly you."

I couldn't help but touch my face as I took a step back. Was that what his letter was getting at? His responsibilities? "I, uh, never do take Avery seriously, at any rate."

"Good." He motioned me through the door, but I hesitated once inside.

"Piers?"

An idea had been growing all day, and Avery's artful evasion only solidified the notion. "If Avery continues to fob us off and Lord Kendal has left the area, should we not reach out to Tony Shaw and Hugh Daunt? It has been years since I've seen them, and it would give us the perfect excuse to broach more delicate topics. I seem to remember Tony had a rather loose tongue."

"You mean like a dinner party here at Loxby?"

"Something like that. We all cry friends, after all. Setting up an evening of entertainment would be a natural thing to do—a bit of a welcome party for me, perhaps."

"Except Seline is not in residence."

"No one is aware of that at present. We shall have to speak to your mother of course, but I think we should be able to come up with a plausible excuse for Seline's absence for one night. An unfortunate cold perhaps that keeps her abovestairs."

"And how do you propose to get our questions answered?"

I searched the ceiling for answers. "Carefully, I suppose."

"Extremely carefully, and there are a few things you are forgetting." He rubbed the back of his neck. "First off, I've never been one for parties. Surely you remember that I avoid them like the plague."

"Oh fustian. You danced with me at the Dowding's ball."

"Once."

I gave him a hard smile. "Then Avery can play host if you are too put out to do so."

He added quickly, "There's also that nasty little issue that I am decidedly *de trop*."

I knew Piers merely meant to weasel his way out of attending our little soiree, and I had no intention of letting him do so. He'd had five years outside of Liverpool to be alone. If I was willing to overcome my own reservations about a dinner party to help Seline, then he could do so as well.

"I don't think Mr. Shaw or Mr. Daunt will keep their obvious distaste for you from ruining an evening with me."

His mouth fell open, and then he laughed. "I suppose they wouldn't. Shall we set the date, Captain Halliwell?"

Footsteps sounded on the stairs, and we both turned to see Mrs. Cavanagh bustling down the steps. She grasped the banister, gasping for air. "Thank goodness I've found you at last."

I thought she meant Piers, so I was surprised when her gaze fell to me. She couldn't seem to speak without the aid of her hands. "Mr. Cavanagh is asking to see you."

"Me?"

"Don't act so shocked. He simply remembers your family and would like to send his best wishes to them through you." Her lips quivered as she pressed them together. "I'm afraid he won't be dissuaded. I promise you it will only be a quick chat, and I shall not leave your side. Now, come on, gel."

CHAPTER 7

Mrs. Cavanagh thrust open the door to her husband's bedchamber and flounced into the room on a rustling wave of muslin and lace.

Left alone in the hall with nothing but my teeming doubts, the first waves of nausea seeped into my body. Why had Mrs. Cavanagh been so adamant to keep me away and then turn around and force me to visit her husband? It didn't make any sense.

Mrs. Cavanagh trounced back to the door and motioned for me to enter with a sharp flick of the wrist.

I took a deep breath. I had few options really. As Mrs. Cavanagh's guest with nowhere else to go, I had no choice but to do as she bid. I pushed my shoulders back and trudged forward.

Almost at once the dull, grassy scent of age assaulted my senses. Mr. Cavanagh's private chamber seemed almost as if it stood frozen in time, an ornate reminder of his once grand position as head of the household. Neglect, however, had been allowed to creep in. Dust littered the pictures and nooks in the dressers as spiders were left to decorate the corners. I suppose Mrs. Cavanagh saw little need to address such issues with her husband blind, but the thought did not settle well.

I inched across the remains of a worn rug as a nurse with red-rimmed eyes shot me a cold stare. The bony woman did nothing but shuffle by me on her way from the room, leaving me to the bitter silence of the unknown.

An enormous gray fireplace flanked the whole of one wall and maintained the room in what I could only call oppressive heat. Mrs. Cavanagh did not address the figure in the great poster bed—not at first—as she shoved a chair near the head of the bed. She signaled with her chin for me to come closer, the solitary candle at the bedside highlighting a scowl on her face.

My mouth felt dry as I fought the questions rolling through my mind. What would Mr. Cavanagh look like now . . . after the accident? My feet grew heavy, then stopped as I clutched my skirt in my fingers. Was I afraid of him?

My muscles stiffened as I settled into the seat Mrs. Cavanagh had provided. The draped canopy kept Mr. Cavanagh's motionless body in shadows until Mrs. Cavanagh drew back the thin cloth and repositioned the candle.

Ever so slowly, I leaned forward and stifled a gasp. My body felt suddenly sluggish as I grappled to recognize the skeletal gentleman lying still before me.

His white hair was slicked back away from his forehead. His thick eyebrows curved at an angle above closed eyes. A jagged scar cut from one side of his cheek, across the orbit of his eyes, then plunged its red fingers into his wet hairline. I began to wonder if he might not be alive until his head lolled to the side.

Mrs. Cavanagh adjusted his bedsheets closer to his chin. "Miss Halliwell has come to see you, my dear, but she hasn't long before supper."

At the mention of my name, his eyes flicked open and a smile curved his lips. His movements were decidedly unsteady, jerky even, as he rotated his head, but his voice was strong. "Thank you for coming. It's been some time, has it not?"

His eyelids were thin now, his cloudy gray eyes so like an owl's in the muted firelight. He moved to say more but a cough stole his voice. Mrs. Cavanagh passed me a cup of water, and I couldn't stop the telltale shake of my hand as I lifted it across the bed. "Yes, it has. I have some water if you require it."

"Please." He rubbed his chin. "If the two of you would but help me up onto the pillows."

Mrs. Cavanagh's hands were like birds in the firelight, flying this way then that. She bustled to the far side of the bed, and I finally understood what she wanted me to do. Together we resituated him so he could manage the water.

He took a long drink before turning to Mrs. Cavanagh. "Leave us. I want to talk with Miss Halliwell alone."

Terror crossed Mrs. Cavanagh's face. I sought her wild gaze with my own, but she merely threw her hands up as if the request was a matter of course. She was forced to clear her throat, however, and add, "I'll be just down the hall dressing for supper if you need me, Miss Halliwell."

I gave her a reassuring smile. "Thank you."

Mr. Cavanagh waited for the sound of the door before extending his hand in my direction. "It is good to hear your voice. I remember how you and your brother used to run through these halls with my own children."

Carefully I took his wiry fingers into mine, all too conscious of the feel of his bones moving beneath his skin. Was he even eating anything?

"Yes. It was a happy time in my life."

"How is Arthur these days? Is he settled in America?"

I'd forgotten how close my brother and Mr. Cavanagh had become the summer before we left for Ceylon. They were always talking politics and chemistry. Arthur and he were very much alike back then. "I'm still waiting for a return letter from him, but the one I received in Ceylon before I left indicated he was doing very well indeed. My parents are quite proud of him."

"I'm glad to hear it. He was always a man to make something of himself. Far more so than some of my children, I'm afraid, which unfortunately brings me to why I asked you in here in the first place. I need to talk with you about Seline."

My muscles twitched, and for a moment I thought I saw spots before my eyes. "Oh?"

He patted my hand. "Do not take my questions amiss, although I do want the truth. I know the two of you were always close, and I desperately need insight from someone outside of this house. Mrs. Cavanagh and my boys tend to keep me at arm's length." He rubbed his forehead, his eyes fixed to the underside of the poster bed. "Did Seline talk to you before she left?"

I cleared my throat. "A little."

"Well, I paid Miles to leave that very morning, and I was confident we'd not see him in this county again, but now I'm to understand Seline left a note—that they've run off to Scotland. Lying here as I am, I cannot help but feel a fool. And I cannot believe there's not more to this business than what we already know." His voice softened. "I don't mean to make you uncomfortable, but what I must ask is, do you have any suspicions about whether Miles hurt her in any way, whether anything was forced on her?"

My heart nearly stopped.

And for a blessed second, I imagined my own father taking

me aside, asking me so tenderly about my incident in Ceylon, but the moment faded to darkness and to the bitter reality I knew to be true. My father would never ask in such a way. Not to mention our situations could hardly be compared. Seline had initiated what happened between herself and Miles Lacy, and mine was more than a simple kiss.

"I . . ." I paused a second to think. Seline would want her father to believe the situation was Miles's fault, but he had asked for the truth. "She knew she never should have made a habit of seeing him alone, not when there was obviously a mutual attraction, but I don't think she meant for anything to happen."

My voice took a strange dip as I went on. "She should have left the minute he came near her." My eyes slipped closed, the unspeakable details of my own night in the tea fields emerging from deep inside me, twisting and turning Seline's story into something more.

"I can only imagine that it happened quite fast. Her reflexes might not have behaved the way you'd think they would. She'd been so desperately alone for so long. Perhaps she wanted to believe someone cared for her . . . Then everything changed."

Mr. Cavanagh's hand curled tight around mine, his voice breaking the pensive silence of my thoughts like velvet ice. "I've already spoken with some of the grooms. There have been accusations about Miles in town. Seline said it was only a kiss, correct? You've no need to hide anything from her father, now. I only want the best for her."

His hand was so warm, his comfort so utterly real. I nearly mouthed the word *no*, but then I gave my head a little shake. We were speaking of Seline, not me. "Luckily, they were found straightaway before—"

"My dear Miss Halliwell. You're shaking. I never meant to

cause you any distress. I know how good a friend you've been to my daughter. I'm afraid this will be a delicate matter for some time to come, but you've helped me understand what happened a little better today. If we can only find Seline and bring her home, this will all be forgot. So if you know anything, anything more . . . Mrs. Cavanagh is convinced they'll return a married couple. I may very well be forced to send him money to keep him honest, but if Seline is able to come about in society, it will be money well spent."

I wondered how much Mrs. Cavanagh had told her husband about the disappearance. Did he know about my concerns?

"It may be a bit difficult for the new couple at first; however, if she or Miles reaches out to you, let them know I plan to stand their friend. They should go on as if there was never an incident in the first place. Attend parties, dance the night away. The scandal will fade away in time. It's simply a matter of moving on."

"I suppose so." I sat there in silence for several seconds. I'd always considered Mr. Cavanagh wise, and he was probably right about society. Seline would come about. But what about inside the person? What about me? I'd changed so much since my assault, but what if I could find a way to go on as if nothing had happened? No one knew, after all. Could I, too, find my way back to some sort of normalcy? Capture the essence of the person I had been before? The girl with the whole world in front of her and an unending zest for life.

My heart lurched, and I sat up straight. Wasn't that why I'd come to Loxby in the first place—to forget?

Strangely enough, Mrs. Cavanagh agreed to the dinner party with Hugh Daunt and Tony Shaw without even batting an eye. I don't know what I expected her to say or do, but it certainly didn't involve such a level of enthusiasm. She patted my cheek and smiled, adding rather sweetly that a night of conversation and cards might prove just the thing to turn her mind from her relentless fears about Seline.

It was Avery who seemed hesitant.

In fact, on the night of the occasion, I entered the drawing room to await the guests with the rest of the family, and he was still making a fuss about the whole idea. He'd managed to corner Piers by the fireplace, and by the looks of his stiff posture the conversation had not been pleasant.

"Dash it all. Our time would be better spent elsewhere." There was a sort of dig in his voice and he added a heavy sigh. "We haven't even heard from Uncle Charles yet. These fantastical notions of yours could all just turn out to be a hum."

Piers averted his attention from Avery as I approached, and he dipped his chin.

As if aware of an added presence in the room, Avery stepped back and spun to face me before running his fingers through his hair. "Oh, it's you. Good evening, Charity." He checked his sullen behavior, adding a bit too boisterously, "And what a gown! You do clean up rather nicely."

Oh dear. I took a quick glance back through the door and let out a slow breath. Thank goodness Mrs. Cavanagh had not descended the grand staircase as of yet.

"Care for a drink?" Avery had always possessed a heightened degree of boyish charm, but after what I'd witnessed between him and his brother, the show felt unnatural.

I offered him a smile. "Thank you, but no."

Piers didn't move, regarding me out of the corner of his eye. At least I thought he did, but he was always so good at deflection—

something about that restrained posture yet steely countenance. I pulled my arms in close. Avery and I were friends. Why should I care what Piers thought?

Piers had donned a silver waistcoat and black jacket for the impromptu dinner party. His black pumps gleamed in the firelight. We'd said nothing to each other throughout the day about Seline's disappearance, but we both knew this party could prove vital to uncovering where she had gone.

Avery checked his watch and held up a finger to Piers who had opened his mouth to speak. But Piers was already ahead of him. "I have one more thing to add, and then we shall put this conversation to rest. We shouldn't hear from Uncle Charles for days yet. If Tony or Hugh saw anything"—he shot a glance at me—"I should like to know straightaway."

Mrs. Cavanagh bustled into the room, effectively stifling any response from Avery. She crossed the rug amid a flurry of purple satin and gold trimming, her hand lightly caressing the base of her hair, which was swept up and pinned with a single ostrich feather. She paused for a dramatic pose by the sofa and angled her chin. "I hope this will do. You will not be embarrassed by your mama?"

"Well done." Avery went dutifully to her side and continued to lavish the praise Mrs. Cavanagh so evidently sought. I couldn't help but see the resemblance to Seline in her speech and mannerisms. Seline would have loved to be the toast of the evening on such a night.

Mrs. Cavanagh took Avery's outstretched arm. "What time are we to expect our guests?"

She had left the invitations as well as the preparations to me and Piers.

"Six o'clock, ma'am."

She wrinkled her nose and turned to Piers. "I suppose Mr. Daunt was more than pleased to accept our kind offer." She moved her hand to conceal her words but spoke loud enough so everyone in the room would be sure to hear. "For we all know his pockets are to let."

"Mama!"

I was caught off guard by Avery's outburst.

He ran a hand down his face, working to temper his tone. "It's no secret that the Daunts have had a rough few years. Hugh is doing all he can to keep Rushridge afloat." He cast a curious glance at me. "Besides, we all know Tony Shaw is the better catch for any eligible young lady."

I froze as a single pulse of dread tore through my chest. First Seline then Piers—did Avery also consider Tony a suitor for me? I turned away, wandering over to the large central window before feigning an interest in the front drive. Why must every conversation around a single young lady involve marriage?

Within seconds Piers was at my side. He rested his arm on the window frame. "Allow me to apologize."

"There is no need."

He let out a long breath. "Then permit me to say that I don't believe any of the Cavanaghs possess the least degree of tact." When I didn't answer, he stared down at me. "No flaming retort? Are you well this evening?"

I gave him my best casual shrug. "Perfectly well. Why do you ask?"

He inched his foot onto the windowsill. "I wouldn't dare wager a guess, but I will endeavor to point out that your face is a bit pale at present, and after you made clear your thoughts about marriage, I—"

"You meant to rescue me from the likes of Tony Shaw?" I gave a breathy laugh. "How valiant you are."

"That's not what I—"

"Trust me, Sir Galahad, I can handle an old friend who's never shown the slightest interest in me."

"Possibly." His finger grazed the edge of my sleeve. "Or not. I daresay Avery was in the right of it. You shall find Tony's continued indifference a bit more difficult to attain with your, uh, selection of gowns this evening." His eyes flicked up to meet mine. "You look exceptional."

Warmth filled my cheeks, and I spun to the window like a mouse, my heart wild. What did Piers mean by complimenting me in such a way? He'd already made his intentions clear. Did he hope to inspire me into a marriage with Tony?

I choked out a thank-you before adding a bit more confidently, "Rest assured, I didn't wear this gown for him."

Piers stared at me for a moment, then his eyes widened in that infuriating mix of surprise and confidence. I could have scratched him.

Phenomenal job, Charity. If a way existed to make the situation more complicated between Piers and me, I'd certainly found it.

I rushed to snuff out the resulting silence, pointing through the window. "There. I can almost see the silhouette of the abbey in the moonlight. At least I think those are the ruins on the hill over there." My shoulders felt heavy, my throat thick. "What do you suppose your brother and his friends were doing there the night Seline left?"

Piers turned his back to the window, his arms crossed. "Searching for ghosts perhaps."

"Don't be ridiculous."

"I wouldn't put anything past Avery and his friends."

A wry smile curved his lips, and I couldn't help but deduce that his mind was on something else. He nudged my shoulder. "There have been rumors for the last hundred years of a spectral monk who walks the ruins."

"And you mean to suggest that Avery was hoping to meet this monk?"

He let a small laugh slip. "He always has been fascinated with the beyond."

I dipped my chin. "Speaking of the *beyond*"—I motioned out the window—"our first guest has arrived."

Piers cocked an eyebrow. "Here we go."

At length Mr. Baker entered. "Mr. Hugh Daunt and Miss Daunt."

Piers leaned down near my ear, his voice a mockery. "He brought his sister."

"Don't look so smug. I invited her."

He raised his eyebrows. "I hope you don't regret it."

Priscilla Daunt had been twelve years old when I left for Ceylon. Though she'd been able to hold on to the wide-eyed innocence of youth, she'd also grown into a lady in my absence. Her blond locks were twisted into braids and piled neatly on her head, while the white roses in her hair matched perfectly the smooth satin of her gown. She recognized me at once and hurried through a curtsy to Mrs. Cavanagh before tugging her brother to meet us in the center of the room.

I felt Piers's hand at the small of my back. "Hugh, you remember Miss Halliwell?"

Hugh swept a questioning look from Piers back to me, and it wasn't the first time I wondered if he knew of Piers's and my secret relationship. Before I left for Ceylon, Hugh had mentioned rather coyly how much Piers was going to miss me.

Of course that turned out to be far from the truth.

Today Hugh flashed a keen smile. "Indeed I do." Then he bowed. "May I present my sister, Miss Daunt."

Priscilla had always had a lovely voice and pretty manners, but she tossed them aside as she grasped my hands. "No need for formalities here. I perfectly remember Miss Halliwell."

I squeezed her hands in return. "And I remember you."

Her voice came out in waves, like a song building to crescendo. "I was absolutely giddy when I heard of your arrival in East Whitloe. You and Seline must call on me as soon as the both of you are free. I am sorry to hear she is indisposed at present."

It seemed Avery had already initiated a viable rumor. I didn't bat an eye. "We would be pleased to do so as soon . . . as Seline has fully recovered."

Mr. Baker announced the arrival of Mr. Tony Shaw as well as his older cousin, Miss Susannah Shaw, whom I'd been forced to add to the party to keep up the numbers. All eyes turned once again to the door. The spare guest was ushered in before her cousin, and I found her a dainty little bird with black hair and wire-rimmed spectacles. She was slow to move and even slower to smile—the complete opposite of her jovial cousin.

Tall with a large frame, Tony Shaw couldn't help but chuckle as he drew up beside her and bowed to the room. The removal of his hat left a few scraggly pieces of hair at the back, and he smoothed them into place. Years ago he had been forced to crop his diminishing locks quite close and brush what was left forward. It didn't appear he would be able to do so for very much longer.

I gave him a wide smile. Though Tony tended to laugh a bit too loud for most drawing room conversations, he also possessed the immensely desirable mix of goodwill and humor. A favorite at parties, he and Avery had always got on quite well. I knew when he flashed that brilliant grin of his in response to mine no time was lost between us.

Dinner was announced within the half hour by Mr. Baker, and we all made our way into the formal dining room in something of a muddled crowd. I was pleased at the opportunity to seat myself between Avery and Tony, regardless of the insinuations about us. I liked Tony and I always would.

The dining room was comfortably warm as we awaited the first course. A fire snapped in the grate. The white walls danced with candle-strewn shadows, which were created beautifully by the grand central candelabra. Mrs. Cavanagh had selected a bold china pattern for the evening, dark blue with golden heart-shaped leaves and stems.

The servants emerged from the hall in matching gilded livery to serve the first course of bouillie soup, and I focused my attention on Tony.

"I am so pleased you were able to join us this evening. Are you having a fine time?"

He swallowed his first bite of soup. "More than fine. Deuced glad you decided to return. We've all missed you, especially Seline. I'd be lying if I said your name wasn't mentioned by her more than once or twice a month at least." He shot a glare across the table. "And your arrival finally brought Piers back from that curst hole he was living in near Liverpool."

"Oh, it wasn't me. Piers dashed home to take Avery to task after he was rusticated from university."

Tony narrowed his eyes. "Quite right. I had, uh, forgotten about that nonsense with Avery." He took a sip of his drink. "Tell me about you. What are your plans?"

"Rather awkward at present, I'm afraid."

He leaned in. "Does that mean they still involve Piers?"

"Goodness no!" What had he known growing up?

I heard a creak from his corset as he leaned back. "Then another gentleman—"

I set my spoon on the table with a clunk. "I see you are as bold as you ever were."

He laughed. "You know I'm only teasing. I am well aware your aspirations likely have nothing to do with men."

"You are quite right. I have a mind to take a position as a governess."

He nodded slowly as if pondering my suitability for such a position. "Considering your family and travels, I have to admit I was expecting something a bit more interesting, like an elephant herder or tiger trainer."

"You've been visiting the Royal Menagerie again, haven't you?"

"It has the most fascinating animals—tigers, zebras, kangaroos. Every time I'm at the Strand, I can't seem to stay away." He shook his head, then looked back at me. "A governess, eh?"

"I plan to start inquiring about a position as soon as I can."

He gave me a smile, but it felt forced. "You will make an excellent governess of course. I'm fairly certain you could do anything you set your mind to. But don't decide too quickly."

"I thank you for your confidence, but it has been a long few years, and I'm ready for simplicity."

He nodded. "I could use some of that simplicity as well. Got quite a bit of money riding on Lord Kendal's curricle race. Dashed nuisance if he doesn't win. I may have to sell off some of my land. Not as tight as Hugh, mind you, but I could stand for some luck."

"The curricle race?" I asked, fishing for more information about what Avery had already mentioned.

"Just put it in the book at White's last week. He plans to wait till after his engagement party of course, but he shall make the race from Whitecaster Hall right past Kinwich Abbey."

My nerves twitched at the mention of the ruins. "Speaking of Kinwich Abbey, I understand Seline came upon you and a few other gentlemen there the other night."

His eyes shifted and his chair squeaked. "Uncomfortable business there. Must not have heard about Kendal's engagement. Turned into quite a scene."

"Avery said Lord Kendal and she had an argument."

"And a bitter one at that."

Desperate for information, I realized I might have to take Tony into my confidence if I was to get any real information. I made certain everyone else at the table was absorbed in their own conversations and took a measured breath, hoping I wasn't making a terrible mistake. "I know I can trust you, Tony."

"Always."

I hesitated to go on, but Tony had always been a friend to me, and I had little chance of learning anything playing it safe all the time. I bit back my doubts and plowed on. "No one knows at present besides the family, but Seline disappeared that very night. A note was found later in her room indicating she'd eloped."

"Eloped!"

"Shhh! To Gretna Green. And you cannot tell anyone."

He leaned in. "With who?"

"Miles Lacy."

His eyes darted about the room as he processed my revelation, then whispered again, "Are you sure?"

"Do you have reason to doubt it?"

He frowned. "I do."

"Why?"

He adjusted his jacket. "This may come as a shock to you, but a year or so ago I found myself in something of a pickle, and I decided to offer for Miss Cavanagh. She nearly laughed in my face. I cannot imagine her running away with the likes of Miles Lacy, not when she could have had me."

CHAPTER 8

Mrs. Cavanagh escorted the ladies back to the drawing room following dinner, and I meant to take the first opportunity for a comfortable coze with Priscilla. Though she and Seline ran in very different circles, Priscilla had always been quite close to her brother. Something might be gleaned by the association.

It took me a moment to secure her attention, distracted as she was by Mrs. Cavanagh's infernal pacing. A pat of the sofa cushion and I urged her over beside me. She cast one last glance at Mrs. Cavanagh before taking a hesitant seat at my side, her nose wrinkled. "What do you suppose has upset her this evening? I did hope to make a good impression."

I recrossed my ankles beneath my gown for the fifth time. "Probably anxious about Seline's recovery."

"Oh yes." She thought for a moment. "But I understood Seline's illness was only slight in nature—nothing to worry over."

My shoulders sank. I hated to carry on in any kind of a falsehood, but it was vital to protect Seline's reputation. I gave a credible shrug. "Yes, but one never does know with a fever."

Priscilla nodded, and her attention strayed back to Mrs. Cavanagh, her lips pursed in anticipation.

I tried a smile. "Won't you tell me about your brother? Five years has been a long time to be away. I must confess, I hardly recognized him."

"Oh." A blush stole across her cheeks, and she lowered her head. "I can imagine it would be startling to see . . . if you didn't know. The last few years have been difficult for him."

I had posed the question merely to make conversation, but something about her reaction piqued my interest. I took a glance at the door. Perhaps there was more to Hugh Daunt than I was yet aware.

I waited for her to look up. "How so?"

She fumbled with her fingers in her lap. "I really can't say where it all began, but somewhere over the last year or so, we've all witnessed Hugh—change. First it was the terrible streak of lethargy, then the slow, insidious wasting away." She gripped my hand. "Charity, he's managed to withdraw nearly completely from the world. He used to be so full of life. You remember . . . and now . . . nothing. Avery and Tony are dears to try to think of ways to get him out of the house." She gave my fingers a squeeze. "I can't tell you how grateful I am he decided to come tonight. It's the first spark of interest I've seen in him all week."

She narrowed her eyes, and then a smile emerged. "You know what I think? This sudden elevation in mood must have everything to do with you returning to East Whitloe. Maybe it will be like old times again."

"I do hope so, but I cannot credit his decision to attend our dinner party with anything to do with me. We were never all that close."

"Perhaps not." She glanced away. "He did speak a great deal about Avery on the drive over."

A low rumble of voices resonated in the hall, and Miss Susannah Shaw flew to her feet, hightailing it to the pianoforte. A grand shuffling of papers, and the selected melody pounded into the room on the delicate strokes of a horse at full gallop.

Priscilla released a small laugh. ". . . come . . . now. What a . . ."

The music effectively drowned out Priscilla's words, and I was left to plaster a smile across my face. I leaned forward and attempted to focus on her lips, but it was no use. I'd missed too much to follow her now.

I mirrored her emotions as best I could—like I'd done a thousand times before. Throughout my illustrious ballroom days, I'd perfected the art of pretending I'd understood what my dancing partner had said. Having anyone repeat their words in a loud room rarely helped and merely frustrated the person speaking. After all, who wants to repeat the same thing over and over again?

The gentlemen entered the drawing room, marking the blessed end to Mrs. Cavanagh's frantic pacing. She collapsed into a chair, her hand resting at her throat.

Avery nodded at me as he made his way across the room to his mother's side, and for the first time I wondered if their relationship might not be entirely healthy. Of course Seline had run off and Avery was only trying to calm his mother, but Piers handled things so differently. Consciously aloof was the best way to describe him. Granted, Mrs. Cavanagh tended to keep him at arm's length.

Avery whispered in Mrs. Cavanagh's ear and then helped her to the card table in the corner of the room.

Priscilla brightened almost immediately. ". . . I should . . . a game of Whist. Will you join us?"

I took a quick glance at Hugh as I struggled to speak over the piano hammering in my ears. "No, thank you, but I'm certain

Mrs. Cavanagh shall be pleased by your company." The last thing I wished to do was try to make conversation over a card table situated so close to the pianoforte.

Besides, I knew full well it wasn't Mrs. Cavanagh who had captured the fascination gleaming in those baby-blue eyes. No, I understood the situation perfectly now. Priscilla Daunt had set her cap at Avery. It was a good match, disposition wise, but if the Daunts were in desperate need of money, as Mrs. Cavanagh had indicated, it might spell trouble for the marriage, as Avery would likely inherit very little.

I whirled back to the room in search of Hugh. He was the one person I hadn't had the chance to speak with as of yet, and considering how close he had been with Seline, he might have some insight about the night she disappeared.

I rose to take a calculated turn about the room when Priscilla motioned Hugh to join them at the card table. "We . . . need a fourth . . . Whist." He nodded as he passed by.

I let out a sigh and turned back to find Piers but a step away, resting against the wall beside the sofa. Startled by his sudden presence, I fell into my seat.

He covered a laugh with his hand. "I didn't mean to . . . you."

I lifted my eyebrows, and he nodded, moving in closer and raising his voice. "I didn't mean to frighten you."

"You didn't frighten me. I was simply surprised to find you, uh, standing there . . . so close. I-I mean, I didn't see you walk over."

"Too busy making mischief with Priscilla?"

"Don't be ridiculous."

His attention moved to the card table and Hugh, and his smile faded. "I do find the elder Daunt a bit more worn around the edges than I remember from when I last saw him."

"Which is one of the reasons I hoped to speak with him this evening."

"Good luck. He's quite proficient at evading conversation. I've managed only a few words with him so far, and now Avery has him tucked neatly into a card game. Neither of us may get much of a chance."

Having finished her first performance to mild applause, Miss Susannah Shaw eagerly started in on a second piece, perhaps even livelier than the first.

Piers touched my arm. "Would you . . . step . . . the terrace."

My eyes widened, and he bent to my ear. "I know very well you can't hear a word I'm saying with that rackety song in the background, and I have something important to tell you."

I nodded, slowly rising to my feet.

He offered me his arm, and I raised my hand to take it with little more than a passing thought. But as I settled my fingers on his jacket, a forgotten memory wafted into my mind on a breath of his musky cologne—the day he'd rescued me from my horse accident. I'd been so pleased to see him that day, so hopeful for the future, but he'd regarded me in the same confusing way, a curious mix of compassion and worry. How familiar the moment felt, but at the same time so tantalizingly unfamiliar. I glanced quickly away. There could be nothing between us, not now.

Ignorant of the thoughts swirling in my mind, Piers led me through the French doors at the back of the room and onto the waiting terrace. I'd expected some sort of comment from someone in the room, but we made our escape into the dampened air with nothing more than a few inquisitive looks.

The cloudy night had wrapped the countryside in a dreary blanket. What little wind there was snuck around Loxby's black corners like a clever fox, winding its way up my arms and across my shoulders. I gave a subtle shiver.

Piers turned to face me beside a large potted plant, the moonlight playing tricks with the expression on his face. "Are you cold?"

"A little, but at least I can hear you out here."

I caught a smile as he moved his head. "I enjoy a performance on the pianoforte as much as the next gentleman, but I'm not certain what you would call that monstrosity."

I popped his arm. "Quiet. She might hear you."

He lifted his eyebrows and laughed. "Not the way she's playing."

"What did you need to tell me?"

He regarded me for a moment. "All right. I'll behave." Then he gave me another smile. "Hugh happened to mention that Seline's horse showed up at Rushridge earlier today."

"Her horse?"

"Avery and I have assumed all along that she took it with her, at least until she and Miles were forced to change horses." He shifted his weight on the stone floor. "Avery thinks it's possible that Seline sent the mare off that night, but I have a hard time believing she would do such a thing." He shook his head. "And if I'm right and Seline was indeed on that horse, something could be terribly wrong."

The furtive breeze sent a leaf skittering across the terrace. I watched it disappear into the shadows as the tightening in my chest made it difficult to breathe. "What do you think could have happened?"

He scowled. "I fear Miles might have forced an engagement or perhaps something worse."

"I hadn't thought of that. Are you well acquainted with Miles Lacy? Would he do such a thing?" Was that why Mr. Cavanagh had asked if he hurt Seline?

Piers ran his hand through his hair. "I know his uncle quite well, and he's the epitome of respectability, but Miles came to Loxby only a year ago. I've not been home in that time. I'm afraid I've nothing to compare to."

"Perhaps Avery—"

"Not this time, Charity. This conversation needs to stay between the two of us." Piers paced the distance between the potted plant and the wall. "I'm not saying my brother was involved in any way, but the people who were there at the abbey that night all cry friends with him. I'm not certain he can be completely honest with us, not when he still believes Seline simply ran off. And one thought keeps circling my mind. Miles Lacy wasn't at the abbey. At least Avery didn't see him there—or admit he'd been there."

I thought for a moment, the quiet of the night humming in my ears. Could we trust Avery, or was he hiding something? "What do you think they were doing there so late at night?"

"That's what I'd like to know, and I haven't been able to get a straight answer out of Avery." Piers glared off into the darkness. Somewhere out there were the ruins of the abbey.

He lowered his voice. "I plan to ride to Kinwich tomorrow and begin my search for answers. It's the last location anyone saw Seline and the only place I have to begin the search for clues."

Piers and I returned to the drawing room, and the card game surreptitiously broke up on our arrival. This was the last opportunity I would have to speak with Hugh, so I skirted around the sofa to avoid Priscilla's gaze and headed to the sidebar where Hugh had stopped to pour himself a drink.

When he didn't initially turn, I cleared my throat. "Mr. Daunt?"

He spun to face me, a smile sneaking onto his face. "I don't think you've called me that in my entire life."

I laughed. "I think you may be right."

"We all missed you while you were away. No one more so than Seline."

Hugh had always been on the thin side, but up close, particularly when he smiled, I could see the shadows that highlighted his bones, the sallow color to his skin. Priscilla was right. He looked practically ill.

Perhaps he was. I tried to keep my voice light. "I'm quite glad to be back."

There was a strange, unsettled movement to his eyes as if he found it difficult to focus on my face. Then abruptly he froze. "Seline isn't ill, is she?"

My heart took a wild turn. "What do you mean?"

"You don't have to pretend with me. I heard her arguing with Kendal the other night. She was extremely distraught."

Uncertain how far to probe, I gave him space to talk. "Did you hear what the argument was over?"

He took a glance at his watch. "I thought she'd come to the abbey to address Kendal's sudden engagement, but something else must have driven her from the house so late. She said she was frightened."

"Frightened?" I stepped closer. "About what?"

"I don't know, but I'm certain of one thing. Kendal broke her heart. I could see it in her eyes." Hugh turned his attention to the painted ceiling as if he could see through the plaster to Seline's room. "Tell her when she's ready to entertain visitors, I want to come. We can meet in the garden as she likes to do. You'll tell her that, won't you?"

I blinked. "Of course."

Priscilla had said earlier in the evening that her brother rarely left the house. Interesting that he had continued to meet Seline in the place where the three of us had once enjoyed our pretend tea parties.

Perhaps Priscilla wasn't privy to Hugh's excursions after all.

"Hugh, I—"

"Charity, dear." Mrs. Cavanagh's booming voice stifled any further conversation. "Would you run and fetch my shawl? It's rather drafty in here after you and Piers had the ridiculous notion of opening the door in this weather."

My shoulders sank. My moment with Hugh was gone all too quickly, and I had so many questions. "Certainly, Mrs. Cavanagh. I'll hurry."

It wasn't until I reached the door that I felt Hugh's hand at my arm. He pressed in close to my ear, his words a fervent whisper. "Would you give this to her for me?"

Something smooth and cold slid into my hand, and I glanced down to see a folded note with Seline's name written on the outside.

CHAPTER 9

When I returned to the drawing room with Mrs. Cavanagh's shawl in hand, I realized all too quickly that I'd made the trip to her room in vain. Mrs. Cavanagh was in the process of declaring it time to retire for the night.

She gave a great show of it, but unfortunately her departure took with it all opportunity I might have had to engage further with any of the party guests, particularly Hugh.

Mrs. Cavanagh gave a fluttery whiff of her fan as she stole across the carpet, and Avery jumped up immediately to assist her. Of course the impending absence of Avery was all Priscilla needed to insist that she and Hugh should leave as well. It seemed she had nothing to gain by humoring the rest of us. My gaze fell to Tony, and as expected he and his cousin fell in step behind the Daunts.

Piers and I watched the guests amble from the drawing room to the awaiting servants in the front entryway, and Piers nudged my arm. "You must be tired. I'll see the guests to the front drive. No need to linger."

"No need to linger"? Did he want me out of the way?

My chest tightened, but I nodded nonetheless. After all, Piers's desire to escort his guests to their carriages alone was perfectly appropriate. He was the master of the house, and I only a guest. But something in the tone of his dismissal made me glare at his retreating form until he was lost to view.

Before I left for Ceylon, I'd never been made to feel like a guest at Loxby Manor, not by Seline or Avery. I circled around to the grand staircase as a rather disconcerting discovery struck me. The Cavanagh's were not exactly the family I remembered. Piers had arranged a duel for goodness' sake and then declined to show up. Moreover, he'd refused to explain himself to his friends or family. And after a bit of prying tonight, I'd learned that Seline had toyed with not only Hugh but Tony as well.

I leaned on the banister as I reached the top of the stairs, the letter Hugh had given me burning in my pocket. How much had changed at Loxby Manor. The people I thought I knew inside and out had proved to be mere shadows of their former selves. My mother told me before I left that I could never go back to the way things were, not really. But I hadn't wanted to believe her.

The air felt thick in my lungs.

Tony said he had actually proposed marriage—to Seline of all people. It was all so strange really. Hugh had always been the one enraptured with her, and she with Lord Kendal. And then Seline had had the audacity to turn around and insinuate that both gentlemen would be a good match for me! The entire notion was the outside of enough.

I turned down the dark corridor that housed my room before stopping at a small rococo table in the hall, the weight of discovery a fresh burden on my shoulders.

Interesting how our intimate group of friends had all managed to converge at Kinwich Abbey the night Seline disappeared. I reached for the door to my room in something of a fog, but everything changed when I heard a skittering at my back. How easily I could go from perfect ease to heart-pounding alarm.

I spun around and raised my candle into the all-encompassing gloom of the empty hall. At first I saw nothing, but achingly slowly, a round shadow emerged against the far wall.

My hand shook, and I nearly dropped the pewter candleholder as a scream lodged in my throat and burned like fire to emerge. Yet it was only an insidious shadow, growing and shrinking as I moved the light. I forced myself motionless. Now was not the time to revert to the frightened girl from Ceylon whom I loathed with a passion. There was no one at Loxby Manor who might attack me.

Then I heard it, and my chest heaved with relief.

A soft, glorious meow.

Carefully I lowered the solitary flame to illuminate the carpet at my feet. The little white cat I'd met on my first night at Loxby had found her way inside once again. Carefully I set the candle on the floor and rubbed the ache from my chest, the pretty little creature with ice-blue eyes watching my every move.

I extended my hand. "Here kitty."

The cat remained deathly still. She was as scared as I was.

I inched a bit closer, but even the slightest movement incited panic and she jerked away. I sat back on my feet unmoving, simply regarding her. I daresay the poor little thing had not been met with kindness in this house, certainly not by Seline or her mother, and I understood her fear all too well. I would have to let her be to come to me on her own terms.

I stood and made my way back to my bedchamber door, peeking behind me every few steps. She watched my movements with her paw raised to bolt until I mimicked the soft meow I'd heard her make before. She tilted her head to the side. I repeated the sound, and just like that, she took a hesitant step forward. One more time, and to my infinite surprise, she trotted right up to my feet.

It was almost as if we understood one another. At least I hoped so. Everyone needed to feel safe.

I was cautious to touch her for fear I'd scare her off again, so I nudged the door wide and made my way to the center of the room before kneeling on the rug. One more heartfelt meow and the fluffy white bundle leapt straight into my waiting arms. It seemed Seline's unwanted cat just might be my newest friend.

Her silky fur was as soft as I remembered and her movements as dainty. I carried her to the seat by the window and let her relax into my lap. "I don't believe you have a name, and that will never do if we're to be friends."

She stretched, then licked her paw. She had a sweetness to her face, an innocence to be protected.

I simply held her for a long moment, relishing the feel of her warm body. I hadn't realized how much I'd missed the affection of another being, even a feline one. Then I leaned down near her silky ear. "You know, when I had to move to Ceylon, I missed my home in Britain terribly. There was one awful week when I wasn't certain I could go on. I found myself at the house of a friend of my mother's, and the lady showed me the snowdrops she'd planted in her garden.

"It was a little thing, but somehow she knew I needed that reminder of home. I decided right then and there that somehow I would find a way back to Britain, which is why I came here. What do you think, Snowdrop? Do you like your name? I think it suits you quite nicely. You can help me remember why I'm here."

Snowdrop wriggled inward as I ran my fingers along her soft back, and the tension in my muscles eased.

We sat for some time just so, enjoying each other's company, the blessed silence of companionship filling the space between us. At length I rested my head against the side of the bow window only to sit forward once again.

I rubbed my eyes to be certain I'd seen what I thought I had.

A light . . . in the valley?

I took a sharp glance down at Snowdrop as if she might hold the answer I sought. "What on earth?"

Shining like a beacon beneath the crescent moon, amid the stony remains of Kinwich Abbey, was a light. Not just any light—the same one I'd seen the night Seline had disappeared.

My heart ticked to life, all kinds of suppositions racing through my mind. Who could be out there in the gloom . . . again? Avery? Tony? Hugh? Or someone else entirely? Like Seline?

I set Snowdrop on the floor, and she skittered beneath my bed like a wild animal. Her frantic flight left me biting cold. I inched my gaze to the door as a sinking feeling spread through my chest. My sixteen-year-old self never would have questioned a romp through the woods at night, particularly if it meant that I might glean some answers. So why did my legs resist now? I was back in Britain, after all, in the countryside where I'd always felt free.

I closed my eyes. Pretend . . . First, I had to believe I was still the person I had been before. Everything else would come later—the confidence, the joy.

By hook or by crook as they always said. I only needed time.

I wandered to the wardrobe and retrieved my pelisse, determined to keep my dark thoughts at bay. Perhaps I could make my way into the garden to see if I could catch a glimpse of who might be returning home. Surely I could do that alone.

I took a deep breath as I fastened the buttons on my coat, then forced my legs to carry me through my bedchamber door.

Why did the corridor seem darker than before, the shadows deeper? The solitary candle in my hand proved a poor companion as the layers of darkness shifted around me, yet I was determined to take a step forward, even if it was a small one.

At the landing I was forced to peer into the murky floor below, and my heart deserted me. On the crest of a cold wave, the hairs on my arms prickled to attention. All too easily I could imagine the twists and turns of Loxby concealing a presence, that someone or something lurked just out of sight . . . waiting for me to descend the stairs.

I shook my head, my hand finding the balustrade. I was being ridiculous as usual. There was nothing down below.

Carefully I descended the stairs on a tingling surge of terror that seemed to dissipate at first, then charged once again to the surface with the far-off click of a door latch.

My eyes snapped open wide, and I froze at the bottom step. "Is someone there?"

Only silence replied—the buzzing emptiness my mind filled readily enough with the suggestion of ghostlike whispers.

The circle of light I'd relied on up until now felt like a hindrance as the depths of the room beyond the reach of the candle's glow faded to black. Instinctively, I blew out the flame to keep from being seen, which plunged me into the sickly gray light of the moon.

Several agonizing seconds passed while I waited for my eyes to adjust. Then I crept across the entryway to the hall that led to the back of the house.

The cool air felt like ice in my throat, and I considered returning to my room more than once, but eventually I made it to the side door, the one that led to the rose garden, and pushed through it.

The night had come alive since Piers and I stood on the terrace. The surge of the wind, the hush of leaves, the intermittent rustling of small nocturnal animals. The scent of woodsmoke lingered from the day's fires. I wrapped my arms close about my middle and stepped into the clearing, hoping I might get a better view of the abbey.

Then I heard it—a faint sniffle.

I spun to find Mrs. Cavanagh seated on a curved bench beneath the large, central oak tree. My hand flew to my chest. "I-I didn't realize anyone was out here."

She had a handkerchief gripped tightly in her hand and dabbed it generously at her eyes. "I'm sorry if I woke you."

"You didn't . . . wake me."

She hadn't changed her gown from the dinner party, and I wondered how on earth she'd found her way to the garden after she journeyed to her room. I took a seat at her side. "You should be in bed. It has been a long day."

She shook her head, but it was more of a slow quiver. "I can't sleep, not anymore. 'Pon my word, I'm not certain I shall ever do so again."

"Should I fetch Mr. Baker to summon the doctor? Perhaps he can give you something that might help."

"Thank you, my dear, but he has already done so. The only thing that can take this ache from my heart will be for my daughter to return home."

The clang of an iron gate jerked our attention to the far side of the garden as a dark figure passed into the moonlight.

Avery.

I had been right. The garden was the perfect place to wait for whoever had journeyed to the abbey. Now more than ever I wanted answers, but we were not alone. I assisted Mrs. Cavanagh to her feet, and Avery sidestepped through a rather awkward pause as he took in the two of us waiting for him beneath the oak tree.

He spoke naturally enough. "Mother, Charity, what brings the two of you out here so late?"

"We could ask you the same question." I wished I'd hid the interrogation from my voice a bit better as Avery pulled slightly away.

He spoke to his mother. "You shouldn't be in this damp cold. Come, let me take the both of you inside."

As Mrs. Cavanagh moved, Avery cast a piercing look at me, quelling the questions forming in my mind, and I was relegated to walk behind them as they traversed the short garden path back to the door. It wasn't until Avery held the door wide for me to pass through that I saw what was tucked into the crook of his arm.

It was none other than a black cloak.

I woke early the following morning, determined to catch Piers before he left on horseback for Kinwich Abbey. I had been eager to search the ruins since the night Seline disappeared, but after seeing that light again last night, then Avery with the cloak in his arms in the garden, there was no way Piers was going on a hunt for answers without me.

I called for my maid and dressed quickly in my favorite dark green riding habit. A hasty bite of a muffin and I hightailed from the house, straight to the wide, double doors of Loxby stables where I couldn't help but stop short. I knew Mr. Cavanagh was well-known as a horse man in the district. I'd heard that even after his accident he still kept a fine selection of cattle, as Piers and Avery had both been brought up with the same horse-mad affliction. But nothing could have prepared me for this new stable complex.

Piers had expanded the large central room, which now held rows of cribs, each wooden post decorated with the Cavanagh crest. A groom whistled as he waltzed from the harness room, a bridle in his hands. "Good morning. Can I saddle a horse for you, miss?"

"Why yes, I'm to ride with Mr. Cavanagh this morning."

"Ah." He smiled. "I'm just getting Gypsy ready now."

My heart gave a stir. Gypsy? I'd not seen him in years. I took a few steps forward to get a better look at the stallion around the crib wall. He was as magnificent as he'd been five years prior. His dark brown eyes found mine, and I ran my hand down his nose. "Good to see you, too, boy."

I wondered if Piers's horse remembered me as well as I did him. Piers and Gypsy had always made a striking display when they crossed the fields. I used to watch them from my bedchamber window at Flitworth Manor every morning.

I took in a long, sweet breath of hay.

"So you plan to steal my horse now? I suppose he always did like you better than me."

Piers stood in the doorway, a riding crop tucked beneath his arm. He cast a shrewd glance at Gypsy. "Traitor."

"Don't be ridiculous. He's far too spirited for me, but I have come to join you on your quest this morning."

Piers stood still as he considered my announcement, his eyes wandering to the nearby groom. I was a bit surprised when he returned a rather pleasant, "I would like that."

"In all this grandeur have you a horse I may ride?"

He laughed. "She's still here, you know."

My mouth fell open and I whirled to face him.

"That's right. Jewel's here."

My hand sought my neck. "You mean you actually kept her all this time?"

He gave a slight shrug, then lifted his eyes to mine. "She was far too pretty to get rid of."

I looked around. "Where is she?"

He extended his finger. "Fourth crib on the right."

My legs were moving before he'd finished his sentence. Papa had paid Mr. Cavanagh to stable Jewel for me, but when we departed for Ceylon, he had left instructions to have Piers's father sell her off. I couldn't believe my eyes.

How I wished I'd brought a treat for her. The sweet gray mare I'd come to love seemed uninterested at first as I walked to the front of her crib. That is, until I spoke her name.

"Jewel."

Her eyes immediately perked up and she tugged against her lead, nudging her long nose up against me. My heart melted, and I ran my hand along her silky neck.

Piers hooked his arm around the edge of the post. "I thought you might come back someday and want her."

I couldn't even form a response.

He motioned behind him. "Let's allow the grooms to do their business. The horses will be ready soon enough." Then he offered his arm.

I smiled as I took it. "I don't know what to say. Thank you. I can't tell you how happy it makes me to see her."

He touched my hand. "You're welcome."

He led me to a shaded area beneath the stable archway and clock where he pulled away. "I am glad of the company this morning, but I have to ask, what brings you to the stables so early?"

I raised my eyebrows. "I saw a light at Kinwich Abbey again

last night. The very same one Seline and I viewed from my window the day she left the house. So I went to the garden, and who should arrive home but a few minutes later? Avery."

Piers flexed his fingers. "He didn't say anything to me."

"Which is why I'd like to take a look around the abbey. Just the two of us. Something is going on at that place. Something Avery's not telling us."

After a moment he nodded. "Agreed."

"And there's more." I reached into the pocket of my habit and pulled out the note Hugh had given me the previous night. "Hugh pushed this into my hand a few minutes before the party broke up. He asked me to give it to Seline. I didn't tell your mother because I wanted to speak with you first about what it said."

Piers took the letter into his hand and opened it in the bright morning light.

My darling,

Where were you yesterday? I waited all morning, and you know how I yearn for you. If you are in need of help, do not be afraid. It's past time the Society did something for me, regardless of what I have planned. Everything is set for next month. We cannot possibly fail.

Your faithful servant,

Hugh

I waited for Piers to read the whole of it. "What could it mean?"

He refolded the note. "Seline has always kept Hugh dangling on a string. I fear this is just more of her playacting."

"But he said 'the Society,' not just 'society.' And what could be set for next month?"

"There's no way to be certain."

I returned his steady glare. "Unless we confront Avery."

Piers stared down at the letter again as if he needed more explanation, but he wouldn't find any hidden in the text.

I laid my hand on his arm, and his gaze met mine. "I know neither of us wants to paint your brother in a poor light, but last night . . . Piers, he had a cloak. One that looked similar to the one Seline borrowed from me the night she vanished."

CHAPTER 10

The remains of Kinwich Abbey could be seen for miles around East Whitloe.

Built in the middle of an open meadow near the River Sternway in the thirteenth century, the small monastery included a gatehouse, an infirmary, and a bell tower. And as I'd learned from old paintings when I was a child, at one time, vast gardens and pools. For centuries the hallowed cluster of buildings was managed by a group of monks until it was dismantled officially by the Dissolution of the Monasteries around the year 1540.

Today little was left of the grand structures but a section of the gatehouse and one wall of the main building with two rows of crumbling cloisters, which at one time would have surrounded the central courtyard. Piers reined his horse to a halt a few feet from the gatehouse, and I directed Jewel beside him.

Creepers lined the ruins of the ancient walls as tall green grass carpeted every inch of the surrounding grounds. Pockets of dew clung to the dampened stones, glistening in the rays of the morning sun. In the open the gentle wind was almost constant, bathing the ground in a reverent hush. Leaves scattered across what was left of the gatehouse's stone flooring and danced in and out of the ancient corners as if an invisible hand enjoyed swirling them just so.

Caught up in the humble aura of the place, we both seemed hesitant to dismount, but Piers eventually swung from his horse and turned to assist me. His arms rose automatically to help me down. He was a gentleman, after all. But when his eyes met mine, there was an uncomfortable split second of indecision in his gaze.

He shook the moment off as quickly as it had come, slipping his hands around my waist, but the hesitation lingered in my heart. Though we had agreed to a working friendship—for Seline—I could no longer deny the unresolved emotions we still carried between us. Time had done nothing but intensify an attraction I couldn't begin to understand. What was it about Piers Cavanagh that arrested my good sense?

Piers motioned ahead. "After you."

The cloisters lay beyond the remains of the gatehouse, and I walked straight for the ruins, trying in vain not to read into the strain in his voice.

The sun gleamed through the open remains of a small circular window at the pitch of the main building, and I was forced to shield my eyes. "I don't suppose the ghosts come out in the daylight?"

Piers was but a step behind me. "I wouldn't know. My father did a pretty good job of scaring us all when we were children. I've only ever come here a handful of times."

I grimaced. "I remember. It was about a monk who was murdered, right?"

"I wish I could say my father's whimsical notions were completely false, but I've come to understand there was actually a tragedy at this place centuries ago. He must have based his ghost stories on the legend."

"Oh? I didn't know."

"Not a murder, but a man did lose his life in a terrible way." He pointed to the center of the courtyard. "In fact, the place where it supposedly happened is ahead. Follow me."

A chill skirted across my shoulders as we came upon the dregs of a fire, and I stopped. "Look here."

Piers touched his forehead as he stared one at a time at the five square stones encircling a pile of ashes. Clearly bewildered, he dropped his arms at his sides and paced across the yard. He stood at the base of the ancient abbey wall and yelled back, "It must have been a beast to move, but someone has done it."

I hurried over to where he was standing. "Moved what?"

"The notorious drifter." He pointed to a statue perched at the edge of the wall.

My mouth fell open as the inkling of a memory sparked in my mind. "The statue!"

"Then you do remember."

I ran a hand down the cold, chiseled stone. "A little. The ghost had something to do with the sculptor?"

"It is believed that one of Kinwich Abbey's resident monks set to work on this very statue. What inspired his sudden artistry is left to conjecture as he was never able to finish the face—a patron saint perhaps, or Richard the Second; various rumors have persisted over the years, some darker than others."

Perhaps it was the emotive stillness of the crumbling walls or the unsettled fingers of the wind, but when I peered up at the faceless form of centuries long past, an explosion of nerves cascaded down my legs, followed by an unnatural yet inescapable urge to step away.

Piers took my arm. "It's still looks as devilish as I remember it. Something about that empty space where a face should be—"

"Yes, I . . ." I stepped away from his touch, escaping to the center of the courtyard. "It must have inspired your father to make up that horrid story."

He followed me across the tangled grass. "As I said, the story was not entirely fabricated. Turns out the statue really did fall on the monk while he was working on it. He was killed, which is why it remains unfinished to this day. No one dared to touch it after that. In fact, years after the monk's death, the villagers came to the abbey to move the wretched piece at last, but somehow the statue fell again, mangling a man's arm in the process. Ultimately, the abbey was abandoned and the statue forsaken where it lay in the courtyard . . . until—"

"You mean, someone had the nerve to stand the awful thing back up and perch it in the groove of the wall of all places? How did they even get it over there?"

"I haven't the foggiest idea. It must have taken several people. And I cannot credit such a strange decision. It almost looks as if whoever moved it meant for the statue to preside over the courtyard. See how it glares at us."

I fought back a shiver. "All I know is I don't like it. They should have hauled it away from here and disposed of it."

Piers gave a little laugh. "Don't tell me you still believe the story of the ghostly monk? He's bound only to come out at night, you know."

"Don't be ridiculous. It's not that." I glanced once again at the hollow curve of lifeless stone, the shadowed emptiness where a face should reside but didn't. Beat by beat the sound of my heart thrashed into my ears. Driven by a cruel imagination, a cold pair of eyes and a long nose took shape on the stone facade. My legs felt weak as my mind filled in the details where the artist had left off—bit by bit my attacker from Ceylon emerged in the stone.

I stumbled backward, and Piers's arm appeared to support me.

His voice sounded tight as his eyes narrowed. "Perhaps we should move into the shade for a moment."

I nodded, and he helped me onto the remains of a stone floor in the shadow of the one remaining wall and knelt at my side. "Are you well, Charity? I keep getting the feeling something is wrong, and I don't mean Seline's disappearance."

I could read the question in his eyes, the candid tenderness of a life of shared experiences, the love we had never really been able to explore, but now was not the time to disclose what had happened. I could hear my mother's voice in the depths of my mind. *"Hush, Charity. You must never speak of this again. Your very respectability is at stake. Besides, such a thing makes people terribly uncomfortable."*

My throat felt thick. Indeed. Such a shocking revelation would do nothing but change things between Piers and me forever. I shook my head.

He settled into a seat at my side, his arm brushing against mine as he moved to adjust his jacket. The familiar urge of closeness tickled my skin, but the last thing I wanted from Piers was pity or even affection, for that matter. Hadn't I made myself clear from the start? I only wanted to be left alone.

I inched away from him and pressed my hand to my forehead. "I got a little overheated is all. I was thinking about Seline coming out here alone so late at night." It sounded plausible. It was why we were here, after all.

He glanced about. "The place is quite changed from the last time I was here. See those stones there." He pointed to the center of the courtyard. If I remember right, they've been moved as well."

"They look like they could be seats."

"And the fire—I daresay Avery has been using the abbey as a meeting place. See how the whole thing is arranged?"

"But why would he do so?"

"Privacy? Entertainment?" He shrugged. "Either way, I intend to find out." He pushed to his feet, then placed his hands on his hips, his eyes trained on the statue. "I shall ask him straightaway, and this time, there shall be no change of subject or conscious evasion. I have no time for anything but the truth."

I rose beside him. "Piers?"

He placed his arm against the wall, and I felt rather small beside him, tucked as we were in the corner of the old abbey. Piers had always possessed a sort of commanding presence wrought by his early maturity and a deference few could manage. It had been intoxicating in my youth, but I'd not seen the like since his return from Liverpool. I looked away of course. How could I bear to do otherwise? But his fingers brushed my arm, forcing me to meet his gaze.

"What is it?"

I swallowed hard. "Seline told me the night she left that she had a plan. She fled the safety of Loxby Manor knowing full well who was here at the abbey. What if everything went terribly, terribly wrong and it is one of our dear friends who holds the key to what really happened to her?"

I rushed to change into an evening gown of sea-green Indian muslin, a favorite of mine, then entered the drawing room quite early for supper. Piers had declared with a great deal of irritation that he intended to confront Avery as soon as his brother returned from his all-too-convenient afternoon trip to town, and I had every intention of being present when he did so.

I found the lonely drawing room an empty shell, and with

relief I took a moment to steady my breath. Twilight had crept over the house, plunging the ornate room into an ashen haze. Shadows blurred the furnishings' otherwise vibrant colors and chased me across the rug to the window where I stopped to rub a chill from my arms.

I heard a click and whirled around to see Mr. Baker enter the room. He gave me a nod, remaining silent as he set to work lighting the candles and stoking the fire, but I could feel the question in his pensive glance as if he'd spoken the words aloud. Why was I here already?

I was spared an uncomfortable response as Piers wandered into the room as well. "Good evening, Miss Halliwell." He allowed a small smile as he adjusted the sleeve of his dark blue tailcoat. "I see the both of us have arrived early for supper."

I shot a peek at Mr. Baker as he ducked from the room. "Your mother should be down shortly. I was dressed, so I thought I might do a little reading before the rest of the family joined me."

He dipped his chin. "Reading . . . in this light?"

"I suppose I might have overestimated the quality of Loxby's beeswax candles. I assure you, I read quite frequently at night in Ceylon."

"And what exactly did you read, Madam Bluestocking?"

I cast him a shrewd glare. "Fiction mostly, but we didn't have access to all that many books. I was forced to do with what I had. You would have been bored out of your mind—nothing on botany, I'm afraid."

"A travesty." He opened his hands. "And what book do you have to read today?"

I pursed my lips. "Oh, all right. I came to talk to Avery, same as you."

"My valet assures me he's returned and is changing his dress at present." He walked to the sideboard. "Care for a drink?"

There was an ease to his voice I hadn't heard since he'd returned to Loxby—it suited him. I relaxed my shoulders. Perhaps we could find our way to friendship after all.

"No, thank you," I said as I sat on the sofa, my hands falling restlessly into my lap. "For some reason I can't seem to get Kinwich Abbey out of my mind."

"Kinwich Abbey?" Both our eyes shot to the door as Avery sauntered into the room. "Now why would you be thinking about that place?"

Piers pounced at once. "Why don't you tell us, Avery?"

Avery shrugged as he poured himself a glass. "Devil if I know, other than it's where Seline disappeared from."

"Don't take me for a flat. I've been to the abbey. I want answers, and I want them now. What were you and your friends doing there so late at night?"

"Easy, Piers, you needn't yell." Avery flopped into a wingback chair. "We were just kicking up a lark, nothing to write home about. I had no idea Seline would come flouncing out there cutting up our peace." He cocked an eyebrow. "Trust me, no one was more shocked than Kendal."

Piers twirled his quizzing glass. "So the four of you were doing . . . What exactly?"

Avery tried to hide his sheepish smile, but he'd never been all that good at deception. "It's a sort of secret actually."

"Not a well-kept one if Seline knew what you were about." I drummed my fingers on the arm of the sofa. "With Seline missing, don't you think it past time we all know the truth?"

Avery turned his attention to Piers. "But I gave my word."

Piers edged forward, settling his elbows on his knees. "Is your word worth Seline's life?"

Avery paled as he digested Piers's statement, then sat up stiff. "Don't gammon me. Seline simply ran away with Miles. Her life isn't in any danger."

"Is it not?" Piers ran his hand across his forehead. "No one knows Seline better than the three of us sitting in this room. Tell me Avery, note or no note, do you honestly believe she would run off with the likes of Miles Lacy?"

He sat for a moment, his fingers tracing the line on his breeches before he glanced up. "I'm not sure."

Piers let out a sharp breath. "Why don't you begin by telling us what the four of you were about at the abbey."

"All right, but it cannot leave this room. And in a way, you already know something of it." Avery shifted in his chair, the playfulness on his face long gone. "It all started about four years ago. I won't go into the specifics, but we initiated our own secret society." He melted back into the chair. "And here I am telling you all about it. I could get in serious trouble for this."

Piers merely flicked his fingers. "Go on." Being the elder of the Cavanagh brothers, Piers had always maintained a father-like hold over Avery, and today proved no different.

Avery had no choice but to continue. "We got rather out of control one night at the abbey. Like I said, we were kicking up a lark . . . I was not myself. Well, Kendal got it in his mind to move that old faceless statue. We all knew the story about the ghostly monk, and we were dipping rather deep that night, so we thought it might be fun . . ." He stared up at us. "It wasn't. The thing was beastly heavy, and Tony managed to roll it over his foot somehow. That's how it all started, you see. He planned to ride to Maidstone that very evening, only he couldn't because of his injury."

Piers opened his hands. "And?"

"Tony had an opera dancer there he'd made promises to . . ." He looked at me. "Dash it all, you don't need all the blasted details. It was a sticky situation, one I'm not proud of, but Kendal, Hugh, and I decided to ride to Maidstone on his behalf and pay the chit off. When we returned, we lit a lamp on top of the statue to notify Tony we had completed the mission. That was the first official meeting of our society."

Piers folded his hands together. "And Seline knew of this . . . *society*."

Avery nodded. "Guess so. She must have figured out somehow that Kendal would be at the abbey that night." He stood. "But that was the end of it. She arrived, had an argument with Kendal, and left. The society had nothing to do with whatever happened after that. The more I think about it, the more I believe she's standing in a church or even over a curst anvil in Gretna Green taking her wedding vows this very minute." He shrugged and started for the door. "Mother needs my assistance before supper. I forgot I told her I'd stop by, and here I am prattling with the two of you."

"Then, by all means . . ." Piers waited for Avery to leave before turning to me. "Quite a reaction, wouldn't you say?"

"It was indeed." A prickle worked its way up my back, and I widened my eyes. We hadn't even had a chance to ask about the look-alike cloak.

CHAPTER 11

I couldn't sleep that night, consumed by what Avery had and hadn't revealed about the abbey and the nonsensical beginnings of his secret society. I didn't know Lord Kendal all that well, but I knew Hugh and Tony would think long and hard before agreeing to such a ploy.

Of course it was just the sort of thing Avery would do. He'd always had a flair for the dramatic. I scrunched the eiderdown beneath my chin, the chill of the room hovering about me.

The question was—had Avery disclosed everything about the night Seline disappeared? My shoulders wilted beneath the covers. After he'd dashed off in such a way, I highly doubted it.

The next few interminable hours involved a great deal of tossing and turning before I finally pushed into a sitting position on the side of the bed. Late or not, I had best find something to read or there would be no sleep for me.

I eased from the bed and onto the cold floorboards, gathering my robe and slippers on my way to the door. The onset of night had brought with it a deathly stillness that had swallowed up every inch of Loxby Manor—the black silence, the distinct nip of vulnerability. I pulled my robe tight around my neck.

In some ways it felt good to stretch and move. But as I cracked open the door to my bedchamber, the merest prickle of unease scaled my neck and fanned out at the base of my hair. It was a familiar sensation, one I particularly loathed, for I knew what followed. Like clockwork a series of images rushed into my mind—the green leaves of the tea plants, the sliver of moonlight, a dark figure walking toward me. This time, however, when my attacker's eyes came into focus, the indeterminate glare of the faceless statue from Kinwich Abbey joined the all-too-real green eyes of the groom in Ceylon.

My breathing quickened and my muscles clenched.

No. I crushed my fingers into a fist. *Please, God. No more.* I was back at Loxby Manor and Captain Halliwell for goodness' sake—not a sniveling, fearful slip of a person. I stared up at the crossbeams on the ceiling of the corridor. *Take it away!*

A soft purr sounded at my feet, and I jerked my attention down as Snowdrop rubbed against my legs. The tension in my shoulders eased a bit, and though a bit unsteady, I was able to kneel down beside her.

The poor dear had found her way back to my hallway, probably on her way to my room. I stroked her head, running my fingers one at a time around her ears. She'd arrived just when I needed her.

Careful not to frighten her, I gathered her into my arms and pressed my nose into her soft fur. How did she know I wanted her? I glared down the darkened hall. Tonight Snowdrop and I would hunt a book together, and then maybe someday I could find the strength within myself to do so on my own.

I fetched the hall tinderbox and set Snowdrop down to light a candle at the turn of the corridor. The cat seemed happy enough to join me on my quest, so I allowed her to walk beside me. It was not until I reached the end of the family wing that I heard the ghostly murmur of a wail.

I froze. It was a woman to be sure, and she was crying. For a breathless moment I thought it might be Seline, but as I crept forward, following the gasping tears, I was led straight to Mrs. Cavanagh's door.

She'd not closed it completely, and I could see her darting about her bedchamber through a candlelit sliver, her white handkerchief wild in her hands. Though I doubted any intrusion by me would be met with approval, I also realized rather sadly that I was the only other lady in the house, and Mrs. Cavanagh might very well need me.

I rapped my knuckles against the door.

She whirled about. "Who's there?"

"It's me, Miss Halliwell, ma'am."

There was a creak of shifting wood as Mrs. Cavanagh thrust something into a desk drawer and slammed it closed. "You may come in."

She was wiping her eyes as I pushed the door wide. "I am sorry to disturb you." I motioned into the hallway. "I was in search of a book, you see, and I heard you crying."

She waved some smelling salts beneath her nose before flopping into her desk chair. "I-I didn't realize anyone was still awake." She sniffed and used her hand as a makeshift fan. "You needn't have bothered to check on me. I spend most of my nights as you find me."

Her arm shook as she rested it on the desk, which drew my attention to a spot of red near the tip of one of her fingers.

"Oh dear. Have you injured yourself?"

She quickly covered the finger with her handkerchief. "Nothing to worry over. I'm afraid my nerves got the best of me this time. I daresay I bit it to the quick." She closed her eyes for a moment before fumbling for her hairbrush. Several seconds passed as she watched herself in the looking glass before she spoke. "I suppose everyone will think me a terrible mother when they learn of what has happened—allowing Seline to rush off like she did."

I walked over to her. "I imagine it will be something of a shock, but at the same time, we all realize there is nothing you could have done to change what happened that night."

"Wasn't there?" Tears spilled onto her cheeks as she pivoted to face me, her gaze searching mine. "What a dear you are to try to comfort me." She squeezed my hand. "Of course it will be some time before you could possibly understand the complexities of being a mother." Her eyes grew cold. "Motherhood is nothing but worry and doubt, waves of unrelenting pain. You can do every little thing within your power for your offspring and end up with ungrateful children." She whirled back to the glass. "At least I have Avery."

And Piers.

I stood stone-still for several seconds, a wariness filling my chest.

How could a mother favor one son so clearly over the other? I knew how much Piers loved her. The entire affair was a sad business.

I opened my mouth to form some sort of response when Mrs. Cavanagh broke the silence with a shriek. "What is that *thing* doing in here?"

Snowdrop scampered to the safety of my legs, and I scooped her up. "It's only Seline's cat. She's quite friendly. See?"

"Don't come a step closer. I told Baker if that horrid beast ever found its way into this house again, I'd . . ." Her attention shifted to my wide eyes, and then she threw her hands in the air. "Don't tell me you formed a tender for such a vile creature."

Mrs. Cavanagh pranced to the wall, and I had little time to react before she tugged the bell pull—hard. "My maid will see that *thing* is taken care of once and for all."

As if Snowdrop understood the severity of what was happening, she squirmed to get away, but I drew her close to my chest. "Please, don't hurt her. She's a darling."

Mrs. Cavanagh's eyes flashed in the firelight. "Ha!" Her shoulders snapped back, her voice razor sharp. "What do you take me for? Hurt her indeed." She trounced back to the dresser. "'Pon rep, what a presumptuous young lady you have grown into, Miss Halliwell."

"I do apologize. That is not what I meant at all." An empty feeling settled into the pit of my stomach, and I spoke with far less alacrity. "You needn't bother your maid. I will see the cat removed from the house."

She seemed to relax a little, but the civility I'd experienced upon arrival was spent.

"I suppose that will do." She glanced about the room as if the darkened corners might provide her the words she sought. "I shouldn't have snapped at you so. I'm afraid I'm not entirely myself at present." She pressed her hand to her chest. "After Seline's utter betrayal, my nerves have been pushed to the limits. There are times I fear for my very sanity."

The word *betrayal* sent the hairs on my arms prickling, and I shifted into her line of sight. "Mrs. Cavanagh, what if Seline didn't go with Miles Lacy after all? What if it was something more serious?"

She pursed her lips, the balance of my words weighed in turn according to the lines on her face. "Does it really matter at this point? She'll be ruined either way."

I shook my head, the apathy in her voice echoing in my ears. *"Does it really matter?"*

My father once told me that the light of a solitary fire at night could reveal a great deal. I never really knew what he meant, not until that moment. My senses felt heightened, my perception far more focused. I watched Mrs. Cavanagh as she dabbed her dry eyes with the handkerchief she had wrapped around her bloody finger.

Had I truly ever seen her before? The real her—the very definition of duplicity?

She said she valued experience yet did everything she could to hide her aging body. She demanded allegiance from her children but cast them off without a thought. The firelight danced across Mrs. Cavanagh's sallow cheekbones, highlighting the depth to her intricate gaze.

Was Mrs. Cavanagh mourning the absence of her daughter or merely the destruction of her reputation—the same unforgivable act of disloyalty Piers had inflicted on her so many years ago?

Mrs. Cavanagh ran her fingers through a ruffle on her gown as she produced one last sniffle.

There was no way to tell—not until Seline returned.

Snowdrop made the perfect companion that night in my room. In fact, I slept so well I was late making my way to the breakfast room the following morning. I nearly missed Piers completely.

Thankfully I came upon him at the foot of the grand staircase.

He was dressed for riding, his pantaloons tucked neatly beneath a rather fetching pair of Hessian boots. The blue tint of his jacket matched his eyes perfectly. I found it difficult not to stare as I descended the final steps into his waiting grin.

"Good morning." There was a slight lilt to his voice, and I instantly read into those two simple words. Had something changed between us since our visit to Kinwich Abbey yesterday?

I offered him a slight smile, not too bold. "Where are you off to this morning?"

"I sent a note to Hugh yesterday at his estate, informing him I would call today. I had hoped you might want to join me, but"—he tapped his watch—"I had nigh given up on you."

"Yes, well, I was up rather late." I wasn't certain I should mention the confusing meeting I'd had with his mother. After all, I had little flattering to report and her words would only hurt him. Besides, whether I wanted to admit it or not, as much as our whirlwind romance had ended in disaster, I still cared a great deal for him. Coward or not, I couldn't help but think of Piers as a friend.

He offered me his arm, and my fingers tingled. I took a measured breath. Who was I kidding? He was more than a friend—but certainly not a suitor. No one would be allowed that place in my life, not anymore. Such a precarious relationship, particularly with someone like Piers, would only bring heartache, and I'd had quite enough of that.

I touched his arm. "If your plan is to take the horses, I'll need to change into my riding habit."

I could hear the groan rising from his throat, but he chose to flash me a smile. "You know where I'll be. Don't take too long. We haven't much time."

My heart betrayed me, squeezing rather painfully in my chest. I'm not certain those were the exact words he used when we ducked into the alcove on my last day in East Whitloe, but the wonderful moment came rushing to my mind nonetheless. I touched my lips. I'd never forget that day for the rest of my life.

His voice broke the silence of my memories. "If you plan to woolgather, I have other things I can do this morning."

I grasped the banister, turning recklessly at the top of the stairs. "No, you don't." And hurried down the corridor.

The Daunts had not lived in East Whitloe for more than two generations and, as a family who came into money rather late, had been treated for years by many in the district as beneath their touch, which unfortunately had included my own family. In fact, despite all the years Hugh and I saw each other as children, I'd never stepped foot inside Rushridge.

The house itself was not all that large, composed of square brown bricks and multiple white chimneys, but the grounds were superb. I'd heard that his sickly mother, Mrs. Daunt, still employed a fine gardener who had transformed the acreage into something of a prize garden, but nothing could have prepared me for my first sight. The manicured bushes and hedgerows had been cut into geometrical shapes, the green lawns stretching like an endless ocean behind perfectly placed rows of flowers.

We were met at the door by Hugh and also Priscilla who, once she saw that Avery was not one of the party, affected a merely passable performance of hiding her disappointment.

I took her arm. "Avery was forced to journey into town for the day. He was sorry to miss our visit."

Since we had told Avery nothing of our plans to call at Rushridge, I was fairly certain he would indeed be irritated. I was only hoping my explanation might keep Priscilla from mentioning our visit, but by the look on her pouty face, I doubted her silence.

She gave a little laugh. "Don't be silly. Though I am always pleased to see either of the Cavanagh brothers"—a firm yet inviting glance at Piers—"I most especially wanted to see you today." She squeezed my arm, and I couldn't help but take my own quick look at Piers.

Priscilla showed us into the adjoining drawing room, with the gentlemen lagging behind. The room, which had been papered with a rather attractive pattern of purple flowers, was a squarish affair with high ceilings and thick rugs. I made my way to the long sofa at the back and found the seat quite comfortable.

Tea was called for at once, and Priscilla took a seat at my side. "I am quite glad of a moment to speak with you alone."

"Oh?"

"It's about Hugh, actually. He's acting most peculiarly, and I hoped to get your opinion on the subject." She nibbled at the edge of her lip. "For instance, at supper last night I posed the idea of purchasing a new gown for Lord Kendal's ball, and he got quite cross with me. He said he wasn't certain we would go at all. But I know very well he means to do so. Avery mentioned it the other night."

I hesitated to get involved. "Perhaps he hasn't the money to provide you with a new gown just now."

"I am not completely ignorant of the state of our affairs, and I'm more than happy to wear an old one." She clenched her hands in her lap. "It's *how* he said it, as if something has changed to prevent us from attending, something he didn't mean to share with me. Has Avery said anything to you?"

"Not at all."

Hugh and Piers entered, and Priscilla seemed distracted as she went on. "Hugh has always been susceptible to the sullens, particularly whenever Seline is involved. For years now if I mention her name he flies off the handle. I've just never understood his fascination with her."

All too quickly the men were within earshot, Hugh pausing beside the sofa, his eyes on me. "Piers tells me you admired our gardens on the way in. Would you like to take a turn with me? I would love to show them to you."

I straightened in my seat. "Oh, please do. From what I've seen thus far, they are quite lovely."

As the four of us made our way from the room, a thought took hold. Had Piers noticed Priscilla's strange behavior and arranged the walk to secure some time alone with her? No one could have missed the sharpness of her voice or the ridiculous way she kept moving her hands. Clearly something was distressing her.

Or was the walk Hugh's idea?

As we rounded the first hedgerow, the purpose became clear. Hugh seemed determined to draw me ahead of the others, so I allowed him to, but I wouldn't stray too far.

His voice came sharp and quick. "Did you give Seline the note?"

Something was buried in that sickly sweet tone of his that I couldn't quite identify, almost as if he anticipated . . . What exactly?

My steps turned sluggish. Was it possible that Hugh already knew Seline was not at the house? Had Tony betrayed my confidence? Perhaps I shouldn't have been so easy with him at the dinner party.

The cry of a nearby blackbird filled the delicate silence between us. I would have to be wary how I answered. "She was far too ill to read your letter as of yet. I am sure she will soon."

He eyed me for a long moment, my heartbeat thundering in my ears, and then a flicker of discipline made over his face. "I'm sorry to hear her illness has progressed. You just never know how serious an ailment can be, can you?" He stooped over and gathered a few daffodils into a bunch. "Tell you what, why don't you bring her these." He said it with such calm deference, I began to question my previous confusion.

I gladly took them from his hands. "I believe I've made friends with another one of your *gifts*—a little white cat."

A smile broke through the indifference on his face. "I know what you are thinking. Presenting Seline with a cat was hardly proper on my part, but she and I have always had a different sort of relationship, or shall I say, there is an understanding between us."

He didn't allow me a response, as he shouted behind us, "Piers, this is the spot I was telling you about."

We'd come upon a small brook and a perfectly symmetrical ornate bridge. "I plan to build the folly right here." He turned to me. "Seline is always saying how much she loves this place."

I couldn't help but remember what Mrs. Cavanagh had said—how the Daunts were in the basket. How could Hugh afford such a project?

Piers must have been thinking the same as he followed with, "And when do you hope to start construction?"

"Within the month if all goes as well as I hope."

A quick glance at me. "Ah."

"Seline loves this grove as well as the brook. We've spent many a happy time here."

Though we were all good friends as children, it seemed Hugh's plans for Seline ran far deeper than I'd originally understood—he was already making changes to his estate. There had always been something quite private and special between them, which time had managed to grow, not diminish—at least on his part.

Piers and I were treated to a full tour of the massive gardens, followed by tea and cake, but my mind remained captured by the curious thoughts I had about Hugh and Seline. That is, until we set out on horseback to return to Loxby Manor.

Trailing behind Gypsy, I watched Piers's lithe form as he directed his horse out Rushridge's main gate. Piers had always been a natural at riding, but . . .

I sat quite still, the subtle tug of Jewel swaying me back and forth in the sidesaddle. Piers had been my first and only love, and he would not be an easy one to forget, not completely. Seline must be the same for Hugh. Though she flitted around like a butterfly from one flower to the next, Hugh's affection remained. He'd not had time away to gain perspective like I had to see what lay right before his nose. He could dream of building her all the follies in the world, but she would never marry him without a great deal of money or a title.

I urged Jewel alongside Piers. "What do you make of Hugh's preposterous notion?"

"You mean the folly."

"It is folly as far as I'm concerned. If what we understand about his finances is true, he'll drive poor Priscilla into destitution."

"Well, if she doesn't snag Avery first."

"Don't be absurd. Your mother will never allow such a connection. Avery will be forced to look for someone far better situated than Priscilla."

He cast me a knowing glance. "You've only been here a few days, but I can see plain as day you already know your way around my family." He shifted his attention back to the road. "However, you are also assuming I will be the one to inherit, not him."

"Well, of course you will."

He took a deep breath. "The decision is my father's of course, but Mother has been doing her level best to persuade him otherwise. And can I blame her? After my shocking cowardice and fall from grace, I have no thoughts of marriage. My conscience wouldn't allow such an arrangement, not when the lady would be forced to share in my disgrace. Which will also mean no children. Upon my death Avery or his offspring will inherit anyway." He shrugged. "Might as well make the whole thing easier and cut me out."

"That is ridiculous."

"Is it?"

"You're gambling on an uncertain future. You might very well marry after all. You can only assume that every lady values her place in society above all else . . ." I reined Jewel to a halt, distracted suddenly by a glint of light on the ground. "What is that?"

Piers pulled Gypsy's reins as well.

I pointed to the side of the road where a small round object flashed back at us in the sun. A wrinkle formed on Piers's brow, and he slid from his horse. Kneeling, he picked up the item and turned it first one direction then the next. "It appears to be a brooch of some sort."

"Will you bring it to me?"

He held it up, and I gasped as I took the familiar jewelry into my hands. "It's mine."

He took an uncomfortable look behind him. "Did you drop it on the way in?"

Slowly I shook my head. "This brooch was on the black cloak I gave to Seline. The one she borrowed the night she disappeared. I'm certain of it."

He seemed lost for words, his wide eyes doing the talking between us before he, too, shook his head. "That means she was here on this very path at some point that night."

The muscles in my fingers twitched against the cold metal of the brooch. Seline must have come to Rushridge after her argument with Lord Kendal. She wouldn't have had time to do so before, and the brooch proved she left the abbey to come this way.

I looked back at Hugh's house, the once beautiful gardens transforming into twisting plants and gnarled shadows. Hugh Daunt had said nothing about Seline coming to Rushridge, and he'd acted so strange about the letter.

The hairs on my arms rose to attention, and I pressed my lips together. Something about Hugh didn't feel right, particularly after all his sister had revealed. If Hugh was indeed hiding something, anything could have happened to Seline that night.

CHAPTER 12

I'd not encountered Miles's uncle, Mr. Lacy, since my arrival at Loxby Manor. He'd been promoted to head groom while I was in Ceylon, and the family thought quite highly of him. At least that was my impression. Few other families would have allowed him to retain employment following the scandal with his nephew.

It never even crossed my mind to seek him out—not until Piers and I came upon him quite by accident the very day we found the brooch.

We'd handed off our horses to an awaiting groom and departed the stables for the house when we saw Mr. Lacy lurking in the shadow of the clock tower. A small man, subtly wrinkled by years of hard work, we found him in something of a minor battle with a slip of paper. Catching sight of us out of the corner of his eye, he smashed the paper closed and buried it in his coat pocket.

There was an abject look about his eyes, a defeated curve to his shoulders. He stared off into the distance until he was confident of our approach, his countenance gaining composure. His hands, however, continued to worry their way around the brim of his hat.

He stepped forward rather awkwardly to greet us. "Good morning, Mr. Cavanagh, miss." He produced a wan smile, but it was impossible to miss the uncomfortable severity of his halting gaze.

Piers introduced me at once and Mr. Lacy nodded, shifting from one foot to the other. His voice came out a touch gruff, but not unpleasantly so.

His focus was tight on Piers. "I was hoping to have a word with you, sir, about Miles. I've spoken to Mrs. Cavanagh about my concerns more than once, but after this morning I believe I should talk with you."

Piers spoke with authority. "If you prefer privacy, I'll need to escort Miss Halliwell back to the house first; nonetheless, let me assure you that Miss Halliwell is a loyal friend of the family. She is more than aware of what has transpired and is considered the soul of discretion. We have all found her a great comfort during this trying time, particularly my mother and father."

My cheeks grew hot. Comfort to the family? Good heavens!

Piers went on without sparing me a glance, and I wondered what on earth he meant by such a flowery compliment. He certainly hadn't said such things before.

"We have no secrets from Miss Halliwell. You should remember her from when she was a child." A smile crossed his face. "She used to run all over this estate."

Run all over the estate indeed. If I did so, Seline, Avery, and he were right there beside me.

Mr. Lacy cast me a quick look, a wary one, hidden nearly completely behind a pair of pinched eyelids. He patted his jacket pocket. "I found a letter this morning, and I can't make heads or tails of it."

Piers lowered his voice. "A letter? From Miles?"

Mr. Lacy angled his shoulder. "The boy must have left it for me before he departed the estate. It was under some books in his room, and I missed it until today."

A line wriggled across Piers's brow. "Did he mention Seline?"

"Not at all. That's the thing. His words were rubbish really, just some outlandish ideas about moving on and such, taking advantage of opportunities elsewhere. He seemed to imply he had found the answers to all his monetary troubles."

Piers rubbed the back of his neck. "Answers? Surely, he meant marriage with Seline, although I find that difficult to believe, as her dowry is not all that large. If I may, do you know how deep Miles is in the basket?"

Mr. Lacy raised his eyebrows. "I didn't know the whole of it till he was here at Loxby. Miles was never constant, you know, not in any area of his life, taking positions here in Britain and abroad, playing deep. He was nigh cleared out if I had my guess." He pressed his lips together. "When I suggested he come to Loxby, I had hopes he might settle down, but the entire notion was a terrible, terrible mistake. My brother fairly deceived me about his character. Trust me when I tell you he was not the man I thought him to be. If Miles did run off with Seline, I'll never forgive myself."

My mind focused on the word *if*. Did Mr. Lacy share the same suspicions as Piers and me?

Piers laid his hand on Mr. Lacy's shoulder. "The repercussions of your nephew's lack of judgment are his and his alone. You've been a loyal retainer for years. You could not have anticipated all that has happened."

I stayed silent throughout the emotional exchange, anxious not to intrude on the conversation, but the word choice Mr. Lacy had used lodged in my mind and only grew the more I thought about it. "If I may ask, earlier you used the word *if* when you spoke of Miles's elopement with Seline. Why was that?"

He considered me a moment before dipping his chin. "Like I told Mrs. Cavanagh from the start, I can't put my finger on it exactly, but

I had a conversation with him the night he left. It made me question things. For one, he appeared scattered. What I mean is he was acting rather odd, rushing around here and there, thrusting his clothes into a bag. He kept repeating over and over again that he hadn't any time, that he had to leave straightaway. The whole interaction has never sat well with me. And then this letter? It just doesn't add up."

Piers chimed in, "Perhaps he was only following my father's instructions. He did demand that Miles leave the estate. There were terms to his exit."

"As there should have been, but Mr. Cavanagh knew full well Miles planned to depart in the morning. He told him so in my presence. Mr. Cavanagh was more than gracious enough to grant us that. The whole blasted business was arranged for me. Mr. Cavanagh felt compelled to do right by me, and Miles threw all of it away. Believe me, that boy was happy enough at the time to agree to Mr. Cavanagh's commands. Something else must have transpired to cause such urgency that night."

"Perhaps Seline proposed an elopement and they set off at once," I said.

A look of doubt blew once again across Mr. Lacy's weathered face. "I tell you right here and now my nephew was afraid, Miss Halliwell. I don't care what this note looks like. He was afraid. Something must have got beneath that tough skin of his, and he saw no recourse but to leave Loxby Manor as soon as possible. It is the only conclusion I can come to." He plunged his hand into his pocket and retrieved the note, shaking it in his hand. "He must have left this letter to appease me."

Piers crossed his arms, tapping his finger against his jacket sleeve. "Did you recognize the handwriting?"

"It's his all right. No doubt there." He spread the letter into the light.

Piers shrugged. "I cannot say I have any recollection of Miles's handwriting, so I will take your word that this is his."

I moved in close to Piers, scanning quickly what I could of the script.

> Uncle,
>
> I write this in haste as I depart Loxby Manor for the last time. I've been granted a lucky opportunity for protection, and I would be a fool not to take it. My monetary troubles will be over soon, and I hope you can rejoice in my newfound fortune. Such is the way in life. One man's trouble is another man's gain, or something like that. I shall always remember you stuck your neck out to help me. Consider my leaving straightaway as a favor for you.
>
> Miles

Mr. Lacy ran his hand through his hair. "What I don't understand is if that nephew of mine meant to flee with Miss Cavanagh to the Scottish border"—his eyes flashed as he looked up—"why wouldn't he simply say so? Moreover, where the devil are they now?"

That night I returned to my bedchamber to find something of a surprise. A square, white card lay propped on my escritoire. The unexpected flash of white startled me at first. That is, until I moved a bit closer.

Overcome, my hand flew to my mouth, for I knew just what it was.

Piers had loved to study plants since we were children. He kept a journal where he recorded his various experiments in the garden. He gathered seeds from all over the world, and once the plants grew to adulthood, he'd sketched every inch of the beautiful creations. I used to sit and watch him for hours as he detailed every last curve of the flower, sculpting the delicate shade of the petals. Once I even grew an orange tree in our hothouse from a seed he gave me.

It wasn't until our secret courtship that he began drawing the flowers only for me. He would pen out each plant's Latin name on the back and leave the sketches in various places where I would be sure to find them. I kept each one in a book in my room where I then spent hours admiring them.

Strange that I'd not thought of those drawings in years. I took the card into my shaky hands.

A chrysanthemum. The flower of friendship.

I melted onto the bed, pressing the paper to my chest for a long moment before holding it out once again to read the Latin name on the back, but the words didn't seem correct. What Piers had written was a phrase, not the flower's name.

I'd studied Latin years ago when Piers had been working with a tutor. Slowly, I mouthed out the words he'd written, journeying back into my memories.

Cras enim a die.

"Tomorrow is a new day," I said aloud, proud I'd remembered the vocabulary before the deeper meaning sank in. It was one of the sentences we'd studied together. I ran my finger along the chrysanthemum's petals, then closed my eyes. He'd remembered too.

I stood to place the drawing in my bedside table drawer when a flash of light out the window caught my eye. My heart constricted as I rushed to the glass. The glow seemed to move across the edge of one of the remaining walls of Kinwich Abbey, like a ghost, bobbing and weaving in the night, illuminating a dark hooded figure.

The spectral monk?

A transient chill slithered up my arms, prickling my hairs to rise. And then nothing.

The light vanished.

It was two days later when Mrs. Cavanagh received the much-anticipated correspondence from Piers's uncle Charles, which she promptly shared with the group of us gathered in the drawing room.

> My dear sister,
>
> I have searched every thoroughfare from East Whitloe to Gretna Green and have come up empty-handed. If the runaways journeyed to Scotland, they most certainly did not come to Gretna Green. I shall make haste back to Northampton where a local innkeeper swears he saw a gentleman that matched Miles Lacy's description who was accompanied by a person he claimed was his sister. Seline perhaps? The gentleman gave his name to the inn as Fitzgerald. Do not lose hope. I shall endeavor to come up with the pair, although at this point we must assume they are already married or shall be so very soon.
>
> Your loving brother,
> Charles

Avery flopped against the back of the sofa. "See, Mama, it is not as bleak as we once thought. Uncle Charles will come up with her."

Though Avery made a show of addressing his mother, I couldn't help but feel he spoke more for Piers's and my benefit.

Mrs. Cavanagh's face brightened before it dissolved into a heavy sigh. "But to be married to that fiend." A sly glance up. "What a travesty."

Piers crossed the room and took a moment to read the letter himself. He cast a look at me over the paper before folding it. "This does give one hope, but I cannot be easy until we've set eyes on Seline. This gentleman Uncle Charles is chasing to Northampton could be anyone. It would be prudent for me to return to the villages a day's ride north of here and see if anyone has used the name Fitzgerald."

Mrs. Cavanagh waved her hands in the air as if fighting a swarm of flies. "Heavens no, Piers. Are you daft?"

He formed a steeple with his fingers and rested his chin on top. "A matter of opinion, I suppose."

Mrs. Cavanagh flicked open a fan. "You'll simply get all those tongues wagging again, and then where will we be? Your sudden and, pardon me, notorious presence in the district is cause enough, but if you go riding from one end of Kent to the next asking all sorts of questions about Seline, she'll be ruined straightaway too."

The weight of disgrace hung heavy around Piers's neck as he lowered his head. "I would never wish to cause anyone in this family any further harm, but I fear—"

"If only you had as much consideration when you chose to avoid that duel."

Avery pushed to his feet. "That is enough, Mama. You needn't drag up the past once again. I've grown bored of such a topic. Piers said he had a reason. He's had reasons for everything he's ever done, and I for one don't intend to guilt him into sharing this particular one with me."

Mrs. Cavanagh's hand flew to her mouth to cover an audible gasp.

Avery measured his tone. "I shall be happy to spend a few discreet days on the road." Then he turned to Piers. "Besides, it would be better for you to stay at Loxby in case we receive word of Seline's whereabouts. You're a much better rider than I, and speed may be a factor if we're to track her down."

Piers nodded, but it was half-hearted at best, his focus settling on the rug.

Mrs. Cavanagh seemed to recover from her shock rather quickly, waving Avery to come closer. "Send word as often as you can, my dear, even if there is nothing to report."

The room felt colder somehow as I watched Avery saunter to the door, Piers curiously still at my side. Perhaps Charles Cavanagh was right, and Seline was simply on the road with Miles Lacy. It would be a great relief to know she was safe.

No. I stiffened. A nice thought indeed—Seline and Miles deeply in love, possibly already married—but as quickly as the idea had come, it turned to ice in my chest. My gaze fell to the folded piece of paper lying in the center of the small table.

Interesting that Seline had left a note, just like Miles Lacy, and— The image of my brooch lying in the dirt flashed into my mind, followed by Seline's haunting whispers. She meant to return to my room that night. I was certain of it. After all, she'd promised to return my brooch. Something or someone had prevented it. And if I was right and Seline's letter was indeed a forgery, might the note Mr. Lacy had conveniently found days after his nephew's disappearance be as well?

I pulled the cross on my necklace back and forth. Someone could be working quite hard to make us all believe she had simply run away. I pictured her riding through the night on her way home from Kinwich Abbey as a terrible thought struck—Seline Cavanagh might never come home.

CHAPTER 13

The first moment I could steal to myself I returned to Seline's room, wondering all the while why I'd not thought to do so already. If Seline really had come back to the house to leave a note the night she disappeared, she would have invariably taken some of her things with her. Even if she didn't elope with Miles Lacy and was planning to go elsewhere, she would have needed something.

Seline's bedchamber lurked as unnaturally still as it had the fateful night of her disappearance, yet somehow in the midst of lonely shadows and the palpable thrum of silence, her essence remained. A half-burned candle on the bedside table, a book left open on the escritoire, a hairbrush at an angle on her dressing table.

The door felt suddenly heavy. I inched it shut behind me and made my way across the thick rug. Strange how I could hear the *whoosh* of my slippered steps and the beat of my heart. Carefully, as if the fabric might come apart in my hands, I opened the heavy chintz curtains at the back window, allowing the bright light of afternoon to flood in around me.

Seline's jasmine scent seemed to hang in waves about the room, and I was forced to rub a chill from my arms. It was almost as if she stood beside me, watching me. Goodness. I took a deep breath. I only meant to look about her room, nothing more. I was hardly an intruder to her private world.

Uncertain exactly what I hoped to discover, I headed to her dressing table and looked over her toilet. I'd paid little attention the night I found her missing. Granted, I had known Seline quite well at one time. We would spend hours together in each other's rooms, talking, dressing for supper. Surely she hadn't changed her habits all that much.

I cracked open the first drawer, shuffling through brushes and various containers of powder and rouge. The second drawer housed a rather fine collection of fans, and the third hairpins and papers. On the table's surface lived the familiar bottles of perfumes she'd always loved as well as a wooden jewelry box.

Her jewelry box. A twitch wriggled up my neck.

Gently, I lifted the lid and scoured over the few pieces inside. Nothing remarkable, which in a way was remarkable. Seline had exceptional taste, and I remembered her begging her father for jewelry when we were younger. My fingers settled on a groove, the very place a necklace might have been kept, as well as spots for presumably missing rings. Perhaps Seline had come home and fetched her favorite pieces of jewelry—or she could have been wearing them that night. I bit my lip. Unfortunately there was no way to know.

I heard a loud pounding beyond the wall and my hand jerked back. The jewelry box slammed closed, sending a puff of dust into the room. As if struck by lightning I fell back, unable to move or breathe. Was someone in the hallway? On their way to Seline's bedchamber? My chest felt numb and I wondered if my heart was beating at all.

Footsteps, and they were approaching fast. I held so still I thought my feet might take root to the floor, but Seline's bedchamber door remained shut. The footsteps drifted on, and like a slow-moving waterfall, the tension in my muscles gradually ebbed away. But I could no longer search in relative calm. Whoever was out there might still interrupt at any moment, and then what? I had no reason for invading Seline's room. Either way, I had to hurry.

I flew to the wardrobe and ran my hands through her beautiful gowns. If she had taken her jewelry, she might very well have taken a gown. I pushed past one to the next. Were any missing? How on earth could I even tell? I'd not been privy to her wardrobe over the last five years. And she would have had little room in her valise. It was entirely possible she would have selected only one gown to take with her. I threw my hands up, abandoning the wardrobe search, and turned instead to her bedside table. Nothing. Everything. How could I know what was here and what was missing? I'd been a fool to think I might find a clue within her room.

I flopped onto the bed, taking one final meticulous look over every inch of the apartment in a veiled attempt to discover something before I abandoned the idea entirely.

It was in that very moment that I noticed the dresser that held her water urn and wash basin and the small item lying next to it—Trotter's Oriental Dentifrice, or Asiatic Tooth Powder.

My mouth dropped open, and I stood before racing across the room and seizing the small, round container. Sure enough, Seline had left her tooth powder. I spun back to the dressing table. And there was her favorite lotion, Olympian Dew. No way would Seline embark on an elopement without her beloved toilet.

I shook my head as the last of my trickling doubts disappeared into a pool of certainty. I'd come to Seline's bedchamber to find something missing, something to prove she had returned to the house and left on an adventure. But it wasn't what Seline had taken with her that provided the frightful truth looming ever-present in my mind; it was what she had not.

I set the tooth powder on my dear friend's dresser, my fingers quivering as I drew them to my side. There was no doubt in my mind; Seline had not returned to the house. The letter we'd found the night she disappeared had to be a forgery, which could only mean one thing. Seline could be in terrible danger.

I'd no intention of sharing my newfound assumptions with Mrs. Cavanagh, but when I arrived in the drawing room later that day, I found her standing at the bow window, her hand perched on her hip, a look of contemplation on her face.

Though I knew Piers and Avery hoped to spare their mother any undue anxiety, I began to wonder if such a tactic was indeed the best course, particularly when urgency was most definitely upon us.

Mrs. Cavanagh knew her daughter better than anyone. She might prove useful in our investigation. I stared down at the red-and-yellow Aubusson rug and clasped my hands at my waist. It wasn't my position to disclose the whole of what Piers and I had learned, not when he'd specifically asked me not to, but perhaps I could pose something of a question for Mrs. Cavanagh to ponder, something that might help me understand what happened the night Seline never came home.

I cleared my throat, gaining Mrs. Cavanagh's attention. "Ah, Miss Halliwell, you startled me." She motioned for me to join her on the sofa. "I was lost in thought."

"It must be difficult . . . as you are forced to wait for news."

She seemed to move as if in slow motion, every inch of her body exhausted from worry. "Sometimes I believe I might never recover from Seline's departure, and then other times I imagine her waltzing right through the front door and declaring she never left. My dear Miss Halliwell, it is a strange world that I am forced to live in now—a terrible dreamland I fear I may never awaken from."

There was a moment of silence as she arranged the folds of her skirt. "Seline was always a headstrong child, and some people you simply cannot save. I suppose she has no one to blame but herself. Yet at the strangest times of the day, I feel"—she shrugged—"I guess you could call it an inkling of remorse for my part in failing her as a mother."

I cannot say what came over me in that instant. I'd not felt a connection with Mrs. Cavanagh since I'd arrived, but somewhere within the creases of her rambling hid an intimation of emotional truth, which Mrs. Cavanagh rarely exposed. Though she had been hurt by Piers and pushed him away and now by Seline, I knew that deep down she loved all of her children. What mother wouldn't?

I took a seat on the sofa. "I just came from Seline's room."

Her eyes widened, and then the muscles in her arms stiffened. "Her bedchamber?"

"Yes. I went there hoping I might make some sense of why she left that day."

Mrs. Cavanagh cocked an eyebrow as she sucked in a deep breath, but her voice came out steady. "And what did you find, my dear?"

"Nothing of any consequence—not exactly, that is."

She regarded me as if I were one of her embroidery palettes and she was determining where to place the next stitch. "I've been over that room more than once. If Seline had left anything that might help us locate her, I certainly would have found it."

"But you see, she did leave something."

Her eyes widened further. "What do you mean? Tell me at once."

The palpable strain in her voice caused me to pause, yet I couldn't help but continue down the path I had already begun. "Her tooth powder and lotion, actually."

Confusion swept across Mrs. Cavanagh's face.

"The items may mean nothing, but don't you think Seline would have taken them with her?"

Mrs. Cavanagh's pinched eyes flitted back and forth before fixing on a spot on the rug. She let out a tight sigh. "I daresay she simply planned to buy all she needed for her journey once they left. I shall be sure to send Avery into town as soon as he is back to inquire after such a purchase." Then a smile emerged. "Yes, this might just give us a direction of travel."

She took my hands into her claw-like grasp—a mix of desperation and demand—and I was shocked by how cold her fingers were. I nodded readily enough and produced a faint smile. Of course her conclusion did make some sense. Miles had funds to support their flight. His uncle had said as much earlier in the day. But Mrs. Cavanagh was not quite ready to explore the darker thoughts that plagued my mind, that took me to a place far different from what she imagined.

I pressed my lips together. Perhaps Piers was right and I should handle her with a bit more caution. After all, her emotions were so very thin and, in many ways, bound up tighter than a spring.

I rose to take my leave, feigning interest in an afternoon stroll, but she stopped me at the door, a curious bend to her pale brow. "If you find out anything further regarding Seline's flight from the house, you will share it with me, won't you?"

Had she read my thoughts?

A slight hesitation and she regulated her voice to mimic the way a mother would speak to a small child. "I know I can trust you to keep me informed."

I leaned against the doorframe. "I only want to be a help to you in this house. I feel so out of place at such a time yet equally glad I can be of service to you and your family."

She lifted her chin, a smile spreading. "I did have my qualms about you coming here at first, but I am so glad now that you did."

Later that same day as I was crossing the landing, intent on the hall to my room, I happened to catch sigh of Snowdrop's willowy white form disappearing into a room down the family wing. I was convinced it was Mrs. Cavanagh's room, and I rushed to intercept. A few paces forward and I realized it was actually Mr. Cavanagh's bedchamber she had taken a fancy to.

I paused a moment, certain I should leave Snowdrop to whatever fate befell her. After all, I'd promised to avoid Mr. Cavanagh whenever possible, but Mrs. Cavanagh's swift justice came to mind. On second look, the poor dear was but a few steps inside the dark room, cleaning her paws on the rug as if she hadn't a care in the world. She gave me an innocent look, her eyes flashing in the light from the hall.

Goodness, how could I possibly abandon my friend?

The nurse's chair was empty and Mr. Cavanagh lay stone-still within his canopy bed. In all likelihood he was asleep. No one would even know I had been inside. I tiptoed through the door in a crouch, reaching silently for the fluffy ball of fur—

"Who's there?"

My arm froze in midair. Dread trickled through my chest as I inched my focus to the rustling sound emanating from Mr. Cavanagh's bed. Apparently he hadn't been asleep at all.

His face lay in shadows, but I could tell he'd been freshly shaved. It made him appear somewhat younger, more approachable. I knew I could have snatched up Snowdrop and tiptoed from the room without a word, but one glance at his muddled face and my heart wouldn't let me. Here lay the head of the Cavanagh family, packed away in this terrible room and forgotten day after day. I could no more leave Mr. Cavanagh to his fate than I could Snowdrop.

I stood. "Good afternoon, Mr. Cavanagh. It's Miss Halliwell." I thought it best not to mention Snowdrop, who darted into the shadows the instant I set her on the ground. I squinted in the dim light, trying in vain to keep track of her. But it was no use. "Do you mind if I open the drapes? It's so very dark in here."

He chuckled. "Is it? I wouldn't know." He motioned into the air. "Do as you please. It makes no difference to me."

As I moved to the window and thrust open the velvet curtains, my gaze fell to the wilting flowers on the dresser. Forgotten indeed. "Please excuse me, I shall be right back."

I hurried into the corridor outside his room and gathered Hugh's bouquet of flowers from the table at the landing.

Upon returning I moved the Sevres vase to Mr. Cavanagh's bedside and took a seat. "There. Can you smell them?"

His lips scrunched up. "Smell what? Please don't tell me you've brought supper."

I wafted the flowers beneath his nose. "Not food. Take a deep breath."

"Ah." His face relaxed. "You brought me daffodils. They're my favorite."

I raised my eyebrows. Like father, like daughter I supposed. "Well, your bedchamber looks a bit more cheery at any rate. And now that I have some light, I can see plain as day that I need to speak with the maid who is supposed to be tending your room. There is a great bit of dust in here."

A wrinkle crossed his brow. "Is there? I just assumed Mrs. Cavanagh was seeing to all that."

I considered his words. "Well, she does have her hands full at present. Seline's disappearance has turned the entire household upside down."

"And Piers has returned. I'm afraid his sudden arrival has only reminded her of what happened five years ago. You see, my accident in the stables occurred shortly after Piers's disgrace. Of course that blasted horse had nothing to do with his forced retreat from society, yet sometimes I wonder if she believes the incidents were somehow related. One scandal, then another."

Here it was, the chance I'd been waiting for. If anyone knew why Piers had permitted the world to think him a coward, his father might. I was glad Mr. Cavanagh couldn't see me biting my fingernails as I formulated the order of my words. I had to be careful if I meant to learn the truth.

I ran my fingers along the coverlet. "Perhaps Mrs. Cavanagh's emotions have become confused in her head. It was quite gallant of Piers to arrange the duel to avenge Seline's honor, but then to disappear . . . I wonder why he's never said what happened that day."

A long sigh. "Sometimes you must allow a man a secret. Trust me, the entire ordeal was quite trying for Piers, particularly because"—his arm twitched—"his heart was involved."

I sat up straight. "His heart?"

"Piers was caught in a bad way. And though he's never told me the whole, I know my son."

My eyes went wild about the room. "Had it something to do with Miss Gervey?"

"No, it . . ." Mr. Cavanagh remained quiet for a moment, then licked his lips. "Speaking of Miss Gervey, have you heard the news?"

"Of Lord Kendal's pending marriage? Certainly."

He searched blindly for my hand on the bed. "Poor Piers. Mrs. Cavanagh held out hope for him and Miss Gervey till the bitter end, but he'd best forget her now."

Mr. Cavanagh's fingers were soft and warm, and I allowed him to hold mine as Piers's clear blue eyes came to mind, his darling smile. "I don't know how one can do that—forget someone, I mean."

"It is not an easy process, but when the lady has made promises to another gentleman, he must do so and straightaway."

Thankfully Piers had made promises to no one, only himself. I'd been spared that at least. I leaned forward, emboldened by Mr. Cavanagh's openness. "I do think Piers has a handle on things. He told me he never means to marry."

"True. He's spoken of remaining a bachelor to me quite frequently as well. He has no intention of sharing his disgrace with anyone, but love can be a tricky thing, my dear. Sometimes it clouds our vision, when other times it allows us to see."

He rubbed his face, a companionable silence filling the room. Though I urged my mind away from Piers, I found my thoughts narrowing in nonetheless on Mr. Cavanagh's surprising words about the duel. *"His heart was involved."* A sinking feeling filled my chest. If it wasn't Honora Gervey to whom Mr. Cavanagh had been referring, whom exactly did he mean?

My eyes widened, and I drew my shoulders back. Wait.

If I understood correctly, the incident occurred around the same time I left for Ceylon . . . The same time. Every muscle in my chest tightened and twisted as the sharp pieces of our past clicked together. It had been staring me in the face since I'd arrived.

My accident on the road!

If Piers had planned the duel with Lord Kendal for the morning I unexpectedly arrived home, he would have had to miss it because he was helping me. Oh dear. I nearly stood before thinking better of such a hasty move, pressing my free hand to my head instead.

I was right. I had to be. Piers never would have left me on the side of the road that day, and he would have been forced to keep quiet about his whereabouts to protect my reputation. I had been out all night, after all. What a fool I had been. Everyone would have thought . . . My stomach turned as I remembered the look on his face. I'd known something was wrong.

Mr. Cavanagh adjusted his position on the bed, startling me back to the present, a smile taking over his pensive face. He could have no idea of the emotions churning within me.

"You know, after you left the other day, I spent a great deal of time thinking about your brother. He was a good friend to me before your family departed so suddenly for Ceylon."

My voice felt a bit shaky in my throat, but I pushed through. "Arthur would have liked to have seen you again, but I don't know that he ever means to leave America. He loves it there."

"I was thinking I might dictate a letter to him. Baker handles all those sorts of things for me now. If I did so, would you be willing to enclose it within one of your own?"

"Certainly. I would be happy to."

"Good. Then I shall summon Baker at once."

He reached for the bell rope, and I took the opportunity to retreat. "I will leave you to it. Good day, Mr. Cavanagh."

He raised his chin. "You will come again another time? Perhaps bring a book to read?"

I was glad he couldn't see the flush on my warm cheeks. "I would be honored to."

I made my way to the door before taking a long glance back into the room. With everything so unsettled in the house, in a way I was glad Mr. Cavanagh had asked me to return. Of course Mrs. Cavanagh would not be pleased. I suppose she only wanted to protect her husband, and I did understand caution to a point. He was pale and feeble. But at the same time, if the appearance of his room was any indication of his neglect, it was high time someone took an interest in him.

I sealed the door shut with care, pausing in the hall. It felt good to have a father figure in my life once again, and Mr. Cavanagh had given me much to ponder about Piers.

Piers. My heart contracted.

Mr. Cavanagh was right. Love was tricky and confusing and complicated. Piers Cavanagh was not the man I'd thought him to be for five long years. So what was I to do now?

CHAPTER 14

It was a full week before Avery returned home. I saw little of Piers during that time and never unaccompanied as he was caught up in estate business with his father. Thus I was forced to contemplate alone my role in Piers's scandal, the presence of Seline's tooth powder, and the continued lack of communication from her uncle.

Well, not alone exactly. After I disclosed my thoughts about Seline's tooth powder to Mrs. Cavanagh, I saw more and more of her about the house. Perhaps I'd caused her more worry than I originally thought. Every afternoon, like clockwork, she'd slink into the drawing room as if it took great effort for her even to consider company, and then she'd happily proceed to instruct me on the finer intricacies of my needlepoint.

I suppose with Piers busy and Avery away, I was the only person in the house she could turn to for comfort, and comfort she needed. Her behavior remained odd at best. Some days she would sit and stare out the window for hours, jumping at the littlest sound. Other days she would speak constantly, as if conversation was the only balm to a wounded spirit.

Though our exchanges were tentative at first, within a few days something changed between us. She had just finished praising the initials I'd embroidered on the corner of a handkerchief when she stopped midsentence and her eyes clouded over.

"Oh, my dearest girl." Her face was white and her hand shook as she covered her mouth.

I hesitated a moment before touching her chilled fingers. "Are you well, Mrs. Cavanagh?"

It took her a great deal of effort to respond, but at length she began in a whisper. "That handkerchief you are working on for your father. Well, it brought back a rather difficult memory of my own. I-I had one like it at one time. It was ruined the day Mr. Cavanagh was injured."

I looked down at the curly *H* I'd just completed. "Oh?"

I hadn't the least idea what to say to such a declaration. Mrs. Cavanagh had been terribly tight-lipped up until that point, and I didn't want to pry, not about something so personal.

But she was eager to talk. I could feel it charging the air between us as she laid down her needle.

I knew it was prudent to embark on such a conversation with caution, yet Mrs. Cavanagh had swung open the door and clearly left it gaping for me to step through. I took refuge in a sip of tea, asking almost as an afterthought, "Is it difficult to think about?"

Her eyes narrowed, and she shifted her weight on the sofa. "In most ways, yes. In others . . . no."

My eyes widened. "I—"

"It was the day I finally knew myself." She motioned into the air. "What I was able to overcome."

"Was Avery home at the time?"

"Yes . . . he was." Her face fell strangely stationary. "It took us years to find our footing with Piers gone, and now . . . I fear all my efforts have been wiped away by Seline's thoughtless decision. I did everything for my children's futures. Everything."

Slowly I turned to my needlepoint, my hands a little less steady than they had been before. Mrs. Cavanagh had been dealt one difficult card after the other.

A shuffle sounded at the door, and Avery waltzed into the drawing room.

Mrs. Cavanagh flew to her feet. "What news have you brought us?"

The road had left a sprinkling of dust down Avery's jacket and breeches, but even more noticeable was the weariness of his bearing. He collapsed in the closest chair, his hand finding his forehead.

"A complete waste of time. There has been no word of a Fitzgerald or anyone matching Seline's description in any direction. The whole curst escapade has proved to be nothing but a blasted inconvenience. I could box Seline's ears for forcing me to ride all over the district. Mark my words, she can marry her stable hand with my good blessing. I'm finished chasing a veritable ghost."

Mrs. Cavanagh threw her hands up and shrieked. "Don't say such a terrible thing."

Avery quailed beneath the weight of his words. "I didn't mean ghost exactly—"

"Not that." Mrs. Cavanagh fanned her face with her hand. "The part about her marrying a stable hand. I'd rather just about anything happen than that."

Mr. Baker entered the room to announce the arrival of Tony Shaw and Hugh Daunt.

My gaze shot to Avery just in time to catch him mutter under his breath, "Figures."

The gentlemen bowed and we all took our seats once again, but Avery seemed decidedly uncomfortable, leaning forward, raking his hand through his hair. In fact, everyone in the room had caught a whiff of Avery's irritation, and no one seemed to want to be the first to initiate the conversation.

Avery finally glanced at the ceiling before drumming his fingers on his knee. "Just rode in from Canterbury boys. Haven't even had a chance to shed these dusty clothes."

Tony produced a smile. "Don't you always look like that?"

Avery laughed and the room seemed to relax, at least some of it did. The sudden arrival of Avery's friends had forced a lid on Mrs. Cavanagh's pot of boiling questions, and she wasn't happy about it.

She finally swayed to her feet. "I believe I shall retire to my room to rest before supper."

The gentlemen waited for her departure, and then all eyes turned to me. Goodness, was I supposed to leave as well? I adjusted the folds of my skirt, then folded my hands on my lap. Even if Piers had taken a break from the investigation, I had no intention of doing so.

Tony ran a hand down his face, then turned to Avery. "We were just up on the rise and we saw you ride in. I thought a little air would do Hugh some good. Then we got to talking. How about you ease our friend's mind and tell us you are still planning to attend the ball at Lord Kendal's in a few weeks."

My attention shot to Avery. "A ball?"

A spot of red entered his cheeks and he sat up. "Kendal's planning a dance the night before the curricle race. Something of an engagement party."

Hugh came to life. "Then the race is still on."

"Why wouldn't it be?"

Hugh shrugged. "With his sudden engagement, I did worry. I've got quite a bit of money riding on the outcome."

Tony chuckled. "We all do."

Each of the boys joined in the laugh, but I couldn't miss the hesitation in their voices and the sideways looks they passed around the room. Something was not as it seemed. If only Piers were here to witness it as well.

I cleared my throat. "Are you all attending?"

They stared at me for a long second, and I added quickly, "The ball."

"Oh yes, of course." Tony stood, startling me by his hasty movement. "We were really on our way home. No wish to tarry. I don't think Hugh should be out of his house for much longer. I'm pleased to learn Kendal has not lost all his senses over a bit of love. Good day, Miss Halliwell. Avery, I know you'll keep us informed."

Informed of what?

I opened my mouth to form a question, but Avery mumbled something about clothes as he made his way to the door. Hugh, it seemed, meant to beat him to it, calling out his farewells as he rushed into the entryway.

Then silence. The life of the drawing room disappeared into the incessant tick of the grandfather clock. I stared across the empty room at the flames in the fireplace. Those three gentlemen were hiding something, and if I had to guess, it had something to do with the night Seline disappeared.

Later that same day, hours after I'd retired to my room, I heard a scratch at my bedchamber door. I stared for a moment at the closed door before moving. My first thought was of my maid, but the notion trickled from my mind, skittering its way down my back like an insect. She would have no reason to return to my room.

I clutched my robe from my bed and threw it around my shoulders. "Who is it?"

The person answered with another knock, but this time it had a pattern to it, as if that alone should reassure me whoever stood on the other side meant no harm.

"Just a moment."

I grasped the poker from the fireplace and inched my way to the door before turning the lock and stepping into the shadows. "It's open."

The door swung inward slowly as my heart thundered. A figure appeared in silhouette, and I raised the poker above my head.

"Don't you dare hit me with that thing."

My arms relaxed, and I dropped the iron rod to my side. It was Piers.

I took a few steps forward and then stopped, the realization of my lack of dress filling my cheeks with heat. I pulled my robe tight about my neck. "What are you doing here?"

"Charity." My name came out a little more than a whisper, but then a laugh entered his voice. "Who were you expecting?"

I placed the poker back into its holder near the fender. "No one. Which is why I couldn't be too careful."

"Oh?"

I turned back to face him as a peculiar feeling swarmed my chest. He just stood there, watching me, his arms crossed, his shoulder pressed to the wall as if the past few years hadn't even happened. He seemed different. Did he somehow know what I'd discovered from his father?

I swallowed hard. Or was it me who was different?

A familiar stir of anticipation, one I hadn't felt in some time, settled in my core. I forced it to bend to my will. We were older now, both changed by our experiences. Both wiser, hopefully.

Not once during the few blessed weeks of our secret relationship had I ever been alone with him in my room. Outside, yes. Hidden in the hall alcove, once. But this intimate setting, the most private of places, felt like something else entirely.

I rubbed my arms, but I couldn't completely wipe away the urge to step nearer, to test the boundaries of my delicate emotions, to find out what I feared most of all—was intimacy possible for me after so much pain?

Piers had always been perceptive, but never more so than in that moment. His brows drew in and he seemed almost careful when he asked, "What is it, Charity?"

The sound of his voice broke the tension that had sprung up like a plague, forcing me back to the present, to reality. "Nothing. You just surprised me is all. Why are you here?"

He crossed the room, his gaze never leaving my face. "I need to show you something."

A beat of terror coursed through my body. "What is it?"

He stalked to the window and thrust open the drapes. He pointed into the inky blackness. "There on the hill. A light."

I rushed to his side. Sure enough, across the meadow a light twinkled on the horizon, darkening what was left of the rugged stones of the Kinwich Abbey cloisters. "And Avery just returned today."

Piers dipped his chin. "Care to join me for a midnight stroll?"

The familiar flash of fear drew heat to my cheeks once again and then a startling cold.

Piers took my hand. "I'll be with you of course." He motioned to the window with his head. "It's only Avery and his silly friends out there."

Then his face changed. "Forgive me if I was improper in coming to your room. I thought you might like to join me. I can certainly venture to the abbey by myself." His voice dissolved into a mumble. "Asking you to come had nothing to do with any fear on my part. I— Never mind." He pulled away.

"Wait!" I followed him to the door. "I'm coming with you. I wanted to go more than anything the night Seline disappeared, but I couldn't bring myself to do so alone."

Piers eyed me for a moment as if he didn't believe me, then nodded. Goodness, he probably thought I changed my mind to appease him, that I actually thought him the coward he'd been labeled. After all, the Charity he remembered wouldn't have batted an eye at such an idea.

I reached for the door, and he chuckled. "I am glad you've decided to join me, but I don't think it would be all that wise to go dressed like that."

I grimaced, then lifted my chin. "Give me five minutes."

The ridiculous charm he liked to strike to life like a candle in the most awkward of moments bubbled to the surface. He'd never been all that good at social games, but sometimes he possessed this look . . .

He raised an eyebrow. "You know, someone might see me in the hallway. Perhaps I should simply turn my back."

I pressed my lips together. "Dare I risk it?"

He splayed his hand across his chest, feigning indignation. "I thought you knew me better than that. Last I checked I'm not a rake"—then more seriously—"nor would I ever betray your trust."

The long months in Ceylon came to mind after I'd received his letter, but I shook off the memories. Everything I thought I knew about our prior relationship had to be called into question, re-examined from a new angle. The drawing he left me came to mind. It was time to start anew, and we were only friends now.

"If you will stand over there, I'll hurry."

I waited until he'd taken his stance in the corner, his back to me, before slinging my robe from my shoulders. A twinge of embarrassment snuck down my spine and washed over my bare arms, but I realized in that strange moment that I did trust Piers, more than anyone else.

I threw a simple frock over my chemise before sliding my arms through my long pelisse. Though the day had been a warm one, I knew the night would not be so kind. I dropped into a chair at my dressing table. "All right, you may turn around."

My voice must have sounded a bit serious, for when he whirled to face me he wore the oddest expression, as if he'd not seen me for some time.

He pushed off the corner of the wall and was behind me in one fell swoop. My fingers went to work on my hair, but the strands felt slippery under his watchful eyes. Suddenly rather clumsy, I dropped one strand then another as I attempted a quick chignon.

"Can I be of assistance?"

I met his gaze in the looking glass and my heart all but stopped. Hadn't I dreamed of such a moment? Piers and me, alone in our bedchamber preparing for the evening. The whims of a different time and place.

He didn't seem to notice my discomfiture as his fingers brushed my neck to hold the bottom part of the coiffure. My hands clenched briefly, then released. After all, it was the first intimate touch I'd received from a gentleman since the assault, and the shock of it left me frozen to my chair, but not in the way I'd imagined it would.

No, this was quite different.

He gave a breathy laugh that tickled my shoulder. "I can't say I know what I'm doing, but I suppose I won't make it any worse."

As Piers leaned over to secure a hairpin, I caught a tantalizing whiff of his familiar cologne and it transported me back in time. Carefully I focused on the warmth of his skin, the delightful trickle of nerves that radiated down my back. It was strange really, how a simple touch could be so utterly wonderful yet alarming at the same time, like riding on the back of a runaway horse—the initial rush of exhilaration, followed quickly by the all-too-real and desperately terrifying loss of control.

I grasped another hairpin and forced my chignon firmly into place before dropping my arms to my sides. "There." As I sat, inwardly quivering, I employed a great deal of control to add over my shoulder, "And thank you."

It was impossible to know what he was thinking, but as he stepped away, I caught a fleeting expression on his face. He, too, had sensed the invisible emotions passing between us. Turning to the window, he raked his fingers through his hair, but he couldn't completely hide the waver in his voice. "We'd better hurry."

CHAPTER 15

The dark of night had brought with it a galling wind that surged against Loxby's ancient stones and cast a spell of considerable unease on the horses.

Piers kept Gypsy close as we started up the narrow path toward the crest of the hill. We could no more bring a lantern than announce our arrival to the people at the abbey, so the hazy white light of the moon flickering through the clouds stood as our only guide.

Piers had been quiet most of the ride, but as I followed him into a grove of trees, he motioned me closer, his voice a whisper. "This is a good spot to dismount and tie up the horses. We'll have to be careful as we make our way on foot across the open valley." He dismounted and secured Gypsy before coming to assist me.

I slipped into his waiting arms. I'm not certain his hands lingered at my waist any longer than was proper, but heavens, it felt that way. At length, I shied away, pretending the need to adjust my pelisse but, more importantly, the gallop of my heart.

He took my hand, tugging me close. "I'd like to make our way around the back of the abbey. There's a cut in the land there where we won't be seen. That is, until we climb the small cliff. Do you think you can you manage such a thing?"

I nodded, unable to answer aloud, certain my voice would betray the wave of nerves feathering up my arm from the warmth of his hand.

We dodged the sharp fingers of low-hanging tree branches and the sticky nails of dense shrubs as we exited the small grove where we'd tied off the horses. More than once I had to free my pelisse.

We crouched as we skittered across the meadow, through the tall grass, and wound our way closer to the River Sternway. There was a small outcropping of dark rock that terminated into a plateau.

As soon as we were safely out of sight and with the river burbling behind us, Piers pulled me close once again. "I'll give you a boost onto that ledge and then swing myself up." He cupped his hands and I placed my half boot into his fingers. With little effort I was thrust upward toward the edge of the rock where it was up to me to pull myself the rest of the way. I used my forearms to give myself just a few more inches before finally catching my knee on the ledge. It certainly wasn't ladylike, but with one hard push I was able to roll into the cleft of the rock and now lay panting in a pocket of damp soil and dead leaves.

I closed my eyes, refusing to consider what insects might call the unfortunate spot home.

Piers's fingers appeared at the cliff's edge, and I sat up to watch his approach. He launched himself off a nearby tree, using it as leverage to scale the short face of the rock as if he'd done so a thousand times.

Still on his feet, he crouched to make his way to my side and pointed to the ledge above us before slowly raising his head where he could see. He dropped his arm back from the rock's upper edge and curled his fingers, urging me to follow his ascent. I scrambled up beside him.

I'm not certain what I expected to see over the top ledge, but it wasn't three bowed heads swathed in black cloaks and huddled around a small fire. There was no conversation on the breeze, only a low hum, as if one of the men were chanting. I glanced at Piers. Were they?

He had a sour look about his face, his brows low, his nose wrinkled.

I opened my mouth to whisper a question but stopped when I caught a flurry of movement out of the corner of my eye. The strange cloaked group stood, and the men followed each other in a circular pattern around the fire, mumbling the same words over and over again. It only took me a moment to be certain they were speaking Latin.

Piers's arm tensed at my side as he lifted his hand to wipe his face. There was a solemn intensity in his gaze, and I bit the inside of my cheek.

What on earth was Avery a part of?

The billowing wind ruffled the long black cloaks for several minutes, causing the firelight to dance in and out of darkness. Finally the members of the society took their seats on the remains of broken stones.

It was Hugh who spoke first, his tone anxious. "I am sorry to have to summon you both here on such short notice, but with so much at stake, particularly for me, I have to have my questions answered."

Tony's voice rent the night air like a low ship's horn. "Don't go up into the boughs, Hugh. We've all placed our bets same as you."

"But neither of you will be ruined should our scheme fall apart."

I could see Avery's shoulders move as he spoke. "I planned to come to your house straightaway. You needn't have summoned us. With guests at Loxby, you put us all at great risk."

Hugh popped to his feet. "It's been over a week. What did you expect me to do, sit around and wait?"

Avery's arm shot out. "Sit down. Stop making a cake of yourself, and I'll tell you all."

There was a second of strained silence, but Hugh did as he was told, retaking his seat at an angle, his fist pressed to his chin. "Well, go on then."

Avery's covered head faced Hugh then Tony. "Lord Kendal says everything is in place. His engagement changes nothing."

"But he's already sent out invitations for the ball. You mean to tell me he doesn't care a fig that all those people will be scrambling about his house? What if our benefactor learns of what we have planned?"

Avery shrugged. "Kendal assures me that won't be the case. We all took a solemn vow, Hugh, and I for one don't plan to put any of our lives at risk. Kendal says the two events are to remain completely separate. His allegiance to our plan, or more importantly his friends, has not changed. And I believe him."

Hugh's voice almost squeaked. "You would."

"What is that supposed to mean? Of course I do, as should you. The bond between the four of us goes way beyond this society. And we know who his secret bearer is."

Tony leaned forward, his cloak billowing forward until he shoved it out of his face. "We need to get back on task. Now, I've agreed to the modifications to the chap's curricle, but I don't want to see him dead."

"Nor do I." Avery's shoulders crunched forward. "Truth be told, I'm not easy about any of this business, particularly with Kendal involved. He's got a hot head and an even nastier temper."

Hugh's hands shot up. "Listen to the two of you. What do you want, a compassionate stroll down the lane? This is my estate and future we're speaking of as well as Priscilla's. I for one am glad we have someone like Kendal bound to our society. Some things just need to be taken care of, one way or another."

Avery sighed.

Hugh thrust out a finger, "Admit it, Avery. You never did like the man. It's not Kendal's fault that your brother hadn't the nerve to face him on an open field."

Avery shoved to his feet. "If I hadn't taken an oath, I'd call you out right here for that."

Tony pushed them apart. "Calm down. What are we, children?" He turned first to Avery. "Piers can defend his own honor. He'd be embarrassed to see the way you're acting. And, Hugh, no more secret meetings. Everything is arranged. There's no turning back now. The society will meet again after the ball, not before."

I felt Piers's strong hand in the darkness seconds before he pulled me close. "We need to hide . . . to the horses . . . quickly now."

He slithered down the incline, then raised his arms, his voice little more than a breath on the wind, "Careful."

I shimmied to the corner of the rock and swung my legs into the black abyss behind me, crawling on my stomach until I tipped over the edge. Dangling there, my hands slipping on the wet dirt and cold rock face, there was a second where I felt myself falling before Piers's hands were at my waist guiding me to the ground.

I could hear the scuffling of feet above, and Piers and I both looked up the moment the light moved. They were dispersing, and Tony and Hugh would inevitably take the river path home, but if we tried to cross the meadow, we'd be seen by Avery. With his right hand at my back, Piers motioned me into the dense brush that lay between the rock and the river, and I pushed my way into the brambles. His whispered voice directed me to a small opening on the ground.

There was little room to move, let alone stretch out my feet, so I pulled my knees to my chest and pressed back as far as I could against the cold, hard rock face. Piers was right behind me, forced to slide in close at my side. It took only a moment for us to realize we might not both fit. He tried his long legs first one direction then the other before letting out a frustrated sigh.

"Perhaps if we stack them just so." I pointed to the ground. "Here, extend them under mine."

The moonlight revealed how wide his eyes grew at my suggestion, but I don't think he knew I'd seen the gesture as his voice remained a calm whisper. "If you think it best. This is hardly proper, but it's imperative the group doesn't know we were here."

I shrugged. "Nothing about this night has been proper."

We scrunched in closer and closer, determined to remain hidden, and though I'd started out on the frigid ground, somehow I ended up in Piers's lap, his warm arms wrapped around me, a bittersweet breath from the past. I'd made the suggestion without really thinking how utterly close it would bring us and what that might inadvertently ignite.

I'd feared intimacy since the attack, afraid of the pounding race of my heart and the resulting panic as my throat swelled shut. Granted, I'd suffered such an episode only once since the assault, at a dance in Ceylon a few months later, and the fear of its return was stifling at times.

But this was Piers with me now. Nothing was ever the same with him.

I felt his laugh without hearing it. "I can't say I ever thought I'd be in this position again."

"Again?"

"Shhh!"

I'd spoken too loudly, but really, what was he referring to?

He guided my ear close to his mouth. "Remember when you hurt your foot that day on the road?"

My heart stopped. "Well, of course I do. How could I forget?"

His body seemed to relax. "You had me a bit worried there. Sometimes I get the strangest feeling you don't remember anything about us." An awkward pause. "You were in my arms at the gate-house, I mean. You were cold. Remember?"

"I suppose I was."

"Things were so different then." His voice sounded almost mel-ancholy. "We were different."

I fought against the ache filling my chest. I owed him a great deal for all he'd done for me, but I knew myself too well to allow the conversation to proceed any further. Piers would never under-stand what transpired a few months after I left for Ceylon.

I felt his muscles stiffen. He yearned to know my secret, that hidden piece of me I didn't share with anyone.

It was in the resulting silence that we both realized the sounds at the abbey had died away, and we were entirely alone. I crawled from our hiding space and shook off the dust from my pelisse. Piers emerged a few steps behind me, and we made our way across the meadow to the horses.

I slowed my approach, allowing him to draw up beside me. "What do you think about what our friends said regarding Lord Kendal's curricle race?"

His voice came out grim. "About rigging it? I'm shocked."

"I cannot believe Avery would do something so foolish. Not after your family has been through so much."

Piers let out a long breath. "Neither can I."

"And the risk to the other driver—Tony seemed to think that possible."

Piers took a moment to answer, his focus on the far-off trees swaying in the moonlight. "It is concerning indeed, but I was actually thinking about something quite different."

We'd reached the horses and I turned to await his help to mount, but he didn't extend his hands, not yet at least. "What if Seline was somehow involved in this scheme? She saw the light on the hill that night and knew exactly who would be here. If Avery can be trusted with his explanation, she came to speak with Lord Kendal."

My mind replayed every detail of the night in my room. "She did say she had a plan. What if she knew something about Kendal's curricle race?"

He lifted his eyebrows. "Or she overheard it that night."

A painful gasp escaped my mouth. "Of course that gives us . . ." I could hardly finish the sentence, my mind awash with the implications such an idea posed. "A plausible reason for one of our dear friends to wish to silence her."

CHAPTER 16

I passed the remainder of the night in a state of fitful agony, the sleep I did manage ruled by dark thoughts. Each member of Avery's secret society shared a special relationship with Seline. Though I could no more imagine any one of the four gentlemen harming her, they did have a reason to be concerned about her knowing their secret.

Hugh was clearly taken by her, but he also had the most to lose should the curricle race not take place. His family was in the basket and he was depending on the money to turn everything around. Both his mother and his sister were counting on him. And then there was my brooch. Piers and I found it on the main road to his estate. Seline must have made her way to Rushridge at some point.

Lord Kendal's reputation was as sharp as his temper. Everyone knew he won any contest he entered—at any cost. He'd actually put a bullet in his own cousin during a duel, even when his cousin swore he'd delope. Lord Kendal would have no scruples where the race was concerned, and he would do anything to ensure his deception remained a secret.

Tony had told me he had money riding on the race as well, and his father was a stickler for rules. He could not chance the possibility of getting disinherited. He would be left destitute.

Then there was Avery. Confident, affable Avery. What possible motive could he have to silence his sister? Unless he feared the ramifications of another scandal in the family. He wasn't the heir; however, he would lose something else he so desperately clung to—his mother's affections. She could never forgive him if he betrayed her too.

I was still hashing through the possibilities when I crossed the landing the following morning. I knew Piers would be gone on his morning ride, and part of me was glad he'd be absent. More had passed between us the previous night than simply the investigation. He still cared for me, one way or another.

I had always been like a member of the Cavanagh family. And of late I'd hoped Piers could find a way to look upon me like a sister. But after a night spent crouching in his arms, I knew it could never be, not for either of us. My skin would always tingle. My fingers would ache to touch him. And the dreaded question of what would happen next might forever hang in the air between us. I stopped at the head of the grand staircase, my gaze drifting to the alcove, then to the carpeted steps at my feet.

As soon as we discovered what happened to Seline, it was time to begin my search for a governess position. Loxby Manor could never be a place of refuge for me. I'd been fooling myself since the moment I came back. Even after he left the estate, Piers Cavanagh would haunt the halls of the house as well as my heart.

The breakfast room was quiet, and at first I thought I was alone, but as I took in the whole of the room I found Mrs. Cavanagh brooding over a plate of ham.

I tried a smile. "Good morning."

She returned a nod, but I could tell it would be one of her sullen days when conversation would be difficult to manage, and I wasn't all that certain I would be up to the task after the night I'd had.

I secured a plate of food, some bread and cheese and a cup of coffee, then took a seat at her side. Mrs. Cavanagh had a pewter visage—ashen face, cloudy eyes, the long stare of days of worry and pain.

I took a sip of coffee, my attention drifting to her meager plate of food, which looked untouched. "Have you been able to eat anything today?"

She shook her head. "It all tastes bitter in my stomach these days."

"Even a few bites would help. You must keep up your strength."

Her focus slid across the table, but she didn't make a move for her food. "I've been pondering what you said the other day, about the tooth powder. I think you may be onto something. I don't believe Seline would have left without it."

So that was the reason for the black mood. Mrs. Cavanagh was finally coming to understand the mystery surrounding Seline's disappearance.

She rested her forehead on the palm of her hand. "If Seline did not go to Gretna Green, then where is she?" She took a quick peek at me from beneath her fingers, and I could almost feel the imperceptible pull, her thirst for my answer.

"What do you know about Seline's relationship with Hugh?"

She perked up at once. "I won't deny they've a history. Hugh's been in love with her since he could put two words together."

"And they've remained close?"

"Seline revels in his attentions. She loves flattery and Hugh is one of the best, but she has no real intentions where he is concerned."

I took a bite of bread. "Do you think he fully understood the status of their relationship? He showed me the other day where he'd like to build a folly on his estate. He mentioned how much Seline would like it."

Mrs. Cavanagh coughed out a laugh. "What a fool that boy has always been. Everyone knows Seline would never stoop to marry someone like him."

A twinge brought the hairs on my neck to attention. "But everyone was so willing to believe she had run off with Miles Lacy."

Mrs. Cavanagh shifted in her seat, her fingers scurrying to the handle on her cup. "We didn't know what to think. Mark my word, I never believed she'd kiss him in the stables either. In daylight, no doubt! Where anyone might see. And here I thought she was clever all this time."

"What about Tony Shaw? He did propose at one time."

"That was merely to appease his grandmama. He'd been caught in a rather delicate indiscretion, and she demanded a proposal. I daresay he picked the only girl who would satisfy his relations and whom he was equally certain would refuse him."

Mrs. Cavanagh tapped her fingers on the white tablecloth. "What are you getting at with these questions?" Her voice sounded almost eager. "Do you believe Tony or Hugh could have something to do with her disappearance?" She added with a sly whisper, "A secret marriage perhaps?"

I supposed a marriage to either gentleman would be preferable to Miles Lacy, but I didn't share her rosy conclusions. "All I know is four gentlemen were the last to see Seline before she vanished, and it's high time we figured out what happened that night."

Her eyes took in every detail of my face in her controlled, detached way. Then they opened wide. "I've never been more glad of your visit to Loxby Manor. You're right of course. One of those boys must be hiding something, and Avery is far too close to them to decipher the truth." She took my hand in hers. "I'm counting on you to expose their lies—to find Seline." She gripped harder, driven by an overwhelming wave of emotions, no doubt. "Wait . . . You said four gentlemen. Was Lord Kendal also there that night?"

I was forced to seek out Piers that same day. We needed to make plans for what was next to be done. Lord Kendal had to be investigated of course, but how? Piers would never be received at Whitecaster Hall, and I could hardly go there myself.

Mr. Baker pointed me to the library where I found Piers deep in the process of searching out a book. He didn't hear me enter the room at first, and as I stood there in the doorway, I found myself hesitant to alert him to my presence.

Loxby Manor boasted a considerable library, and as I breathed in the musty scent of paper, I took a quick glance about the room. Although the books stood in dire need of a good dusting, they were handsomely displayed along three tall bookcases. A small, white, scrolled fireplace centered the room and peeked at me behind two crimson winged chairs.

Piers had removed his jacket and climbed the central bookshelf ladder to peruse the uppermost shelf. A scholar at heart, he'd spent little time refining his physique, but there was a lithe gracefulness to his movements, a familiarity that sparked the same fascination I'd had before. I could barely take my eyes off him.

He extended his arm, leaning as far as he could to reach a book. All at once, the ladder tipped to the side.

I raced across the room, but he'd pushed the old wood as far as it would permit. Just as the tips of his fingers crested the edge of a book, the ladder took one last moan and creaked beneath his feet, separating at the rungs. He clawed at the bookcase as he attempted to slow his descent, but the frantic movement only loosened the top shelf. I arrived a split second after he hit the hard floor. Then the first book struck my shoulder, and I threw my arms over my head, the resulting deluge lasting but a few seconds.

Silence followed the stridency of literature, and slowly I lifted my arms. Books lay sprawled around us, some open, some torn, the ladder split like a banana peel in a heap on the floor. I sneezed, puffs of dust glistening into the air.

My shoulder felt numb, limp even, as if my arm simply hung from the joint. Instinctively, I cradled my elbow.

Piers was quick to my side, his hands urgent but restrained. "Are you hurt?"

I shook my head, but I knew something was wrong.

Relieved, he rested his back against the bookshelf, an amused expression sneaking onto his face. "Regardless, I daresay help will be here soon. They could probably hear your pert little scream from the stables."

I slid a few more books from my legs. "Oh, did I scream? I didn't know it."

"No?" He chuckled. "What brought you in here?"

"I thought I was saving your skin."

"Ah, but I'm afraid you took the brunt of it. Here, let me help you to your feet."

I tried to extend my hand, but I couldn't.

He stepped back, his smile fading. "You're not all right."

"I may have injured my shoulder when the books hit it and I fell, but you needn't concern yourself. I doubt it's broken. Perhaps if I were to lie down in my room."

"You shall do no such thing." His arm slipped around my waist. "Come with me to the sofa at once."

I allowed him to carefully seat me. "Did you fall directly onto your shoulder?"

"I'm not certain. All I remember is extending my hand to prevent the fall." I attempted to lift my arm once again. "I can't even move it."

He felt around the shoulder joint and then winced. "There's a rather large groove here as well as a bump on the back side. I'm afraid your shoulder may have slipped out of place."

"Out of place?" My heart stopped. As a child I'd seen such a thing happen to a groom after being bucked from a horse.

Piers's hands were gentle. "I do have some experience with this sort of thing." His gaze fell to mine. "Will you trust me to help you?"

"Always." I swallowed hard.

One simple word, but how it hung on the air like a swirling mist, clouding my vision. I did as Piers instructed and lay down, but my mind could do little more than churn through the complexities of such a word.

I did trust him. The bonds we'd forged in our youth hadn't broken, not by time or distance, my experiences or his shame. So much had changed for me while I was in Ceylon, but somehow Piers hadn't.

He knelt beside me and took my hand, lifting my forearm at a ninety-degree angle. "You might want to brace your feet, but try to relax your shoulder."

I pressed my feet against the armrest and closed my eyes as a sharp slice of pain ripped through my shoulder, then relief.

"Charity?"

Piers sounded as if far away, but then I felt his fingers swipe a loose strand of hair from my forehead and I opened my eyes.

"It's done. Do you think you can sit up?"

I nodded, and he used my good shoulder to assist me into a sitting position. The room swirled for a moment, then settled into place. Carefully I moved my injured arm and was relieved the pain had significantly abated.

Piers moved away a few inches from me on the sofa. "I don't think you should move it too much as of yet. I'll call Baker for the materials for a sling."

I waited as he tugged the bell pull.

"What were you looking for?" I motioned with my chin. "Up there?"

His focus retreated to the uppermost shelf. "I got to thinking after witnessing Avery and his friends at the abbey. A while back, my father told me he'd been part of a secret society called the Ancient Noble Order of the Gormogons. He was only a member for a short time, since it was my understanding they were disbanded along with all the secret societies except for the Freemasons by an act passed in 1799. The group was formed by a collection of Jacobites but later went on to focus more on charitable dealings. At least that's what Father said.

He rubbed his forehead. "I'm not certain he meant to disclose anything about the society to me at all. I simply stumbled onto a medal in his room that he'd buried in a drawer and forgot about. It was a round silver medallion, which had the sun and a dragon on one side and a large gentleman sitting on a throne on the other. My father, mistaken by the source of my questions, thought I'd come across a book he'd hidden in the library and decided to tell Avery and me something of the society, if we kept it secret of course. I thought little of the group and never even pursued the book he mentioned. I had my own troubles at the time."

I sat up. "Is that what you were about up there?"

"I thought maybe I had found it when the shelf fell."

I pointed with my good hand. "Then by all means, go see at once."

He smiled. "I believe I will."

He crossed the room and knelt at the pile of books lying in a heap on the floor. Carefully he sifted through each one, opening and closing them until he came to a thin leather volume with rumpled pages. I could see the print was handwritten from across the room. He glanced up over the book's edge. "Lucky break."

He pushed to his feet and made his way back to the sofa, sitting close so we could both see the pages.

Neither of us heard Baker until he cleared his throat. "May I help you, sir?"

Like a guilty child, Piers scooted away. "Ah, Baker, as you can see, Miss Halliwell has injured her arm. We'll need some cloth and bandages to fashion a sling."

His eyes slid to the broken shelf. "I understand." Then he turned and left the room.

We watched his retreating figure until he disappeared from sight, the tickling fingers of embarrassment fighting for control of the situation. I felt a hint of a laugh on Piers's breath, but we were far too interested in the book he'd found to give it rein. We crouched in again, his arm sliding neatly across the back of the sofa behind me. My finger brushed his as I moved to turn the page, and he looked up ever so briefly at my face.

A heaviness hit my chest and I forced a breath. I knew in my heart he'd made no move to get close to me, not after what happened at the abbey, but here he was so real and my every waking thought of him so confusing. He only wanted friendship from me, so why did my mind keep slipping back to another place and time?

I imagined inching forward and kissing him. Goodness, my muscles still remembered the movement and ached to do just that, but could I actually bring myself to do so after everything that had happened—to willingly surrender myself to another man? And what would it feel like? What would I feel like? Would he kiss me back?

The moment passed as quickly as it had come, Piers clearly not as affected as I was. He pointed to a picture on the second page, his voice steady. "Look, this is similar to the medal I found in my father's drawer, but smaller, and this one has a ribbon of Persian ivy. See the large leaves."

I squinted at the sketched picture. "Only you would know that. It also has the sun you were describing earlier, but this one is a collar jewel."

Piers snapped me a sideways glance before turning the page. Scrolled across the top in large letters were the words *Members* and *Loyalty Pledge*. We read in silence for several minutes, each handwritten line more interesting than the last.

The book seemed to be an outline for membership as well as the means by which each person took what they called a loyalty pledge. Apparently in order to join the Gormogons the pending member would have to relinquish condemning information regarding himself or one of his family members, which would then be kept by the society as absolute collateral for loyalty to the organization.

Piers flipped through the remaining pages, but one section was torn out. He slid the book onto a nearby table. "My father said he was not in the organization long."

"What collateral do you think he gave them?"

He shrugged. "It could have been anything. The Cavanaghs have not been the wisest group of people."

I wanted to laugh at the truth of his statement, but pain was evident in his eyes.

Though the world had branded Piers disgraceful, I had never thought of him that way, even before I knew the truth. As a young man he was bright, methodical, conscientious. Nothing like his siblings.

"Do you think Avery is following in your father's footsteps? He did call it a secret society."

"But they disbanded years ago. This group or whatever he likes to call it seems more to me like playacting."

"Yet they've arranged for some kind of mischief at the curricle race. Sabotage is nothing to take lightly."

"No, it isn't." Piers angled against the back of the sofa, his arm behind his head. "And Avery is too far involved to stop it now. I'm afraid we've little choice but to go to Whitecaster Hall and do a little hunting ourselves."

My eyes widened. "You mean to the ball? Will we even be invited?"

"Mother will certainly have an invitation. Kendal's fiancée, Honora, is a distant cousin of ours. Mother will need an escort."

"Yes, Honora . . ." My voice felt weak. "I know I already asked, but what exactly happened between you and her?"

He took so long to answer I began to wonder if he'd heard the question at all. But then his eyes met mine and he spoke rather softly. "You know full well it was wrong from the start. I knew it. She knew it. But our parents were so pleased by the association."

"Was she one of the reasons you wrote me that letter?"

The color seemed to drain from his face.

I added quickly, "I'm not accusing you of anything. I just wondered."

He spoke with determined calm, but I felt the charge of the silence that crept into our conversation, starting and stopping his words. "I told you before you left that I had to settle things between Honora and me. But life has a way of changing things when you least expect it. In that same time I was branded a coward, shunned by society, disdained by my mother. I could no more pursue you than any young lady. Honora publicly rejected me, which only added to my shame. It probably sounds strange for me to say so, but I'm glad she has found happiness with Lord Kendal."

My chest tightened. "But what about you?"

He forced something just short of a smile. "I strive each day to take care of my father as well as his responsibilities, keep Avery on the right path, and provide for Seline. Trust me, I'm a busy man."

I searched his eyes. But not a happy one.

Baker walked into the room then with an arm full of supplies.

Piers rose and accepted the bandages. "Thank you." He set them on the sofa at my side and knelt casually before me, almost as if we'd not had such an intimate conversation. "You'll only need to wear this for a short time, but I'm afraid you'll feel the effects in your shoulder for a while."

He draped the fabric under my bent arm and around my back, then tied the ends on top of the opposite shoulder. "Now how does that feel?" He rested his hand on my good arm.

And for some odd reason I fought back a surge of tears. My arm felt better, really. So what was driving my rampant emotions? I watched as Piers folded the extra bandages and slid them back into the medical box, his fingers always so precise.

And then it hit me.

Piers had always been the one person in East Whitloe I could count on, the one person who understood me. For years I'd grieved the loss of our relationship, but had I ever really considered the loss of our friendship? I simply missed him.

And here we were sharing in the same comfort and affection we had so many times before, but with one terribly painful caveat—there would never be anything more between us. His shame was a public one; mine private. We were standing on two very different mountain peaks yet staring at the valley below with no possible way to meet in the middle. Piers Cavanagh was a gentleman. Avery would carry on the family name and his children would eventually inherit Loxby Manor. And I knew in my heart that marriage was not the right choice for me, not after all I'd been through.

I needed to start looking for a governess position and sooner than I'd originally thought.

CHAPTER 17

The invitation for Lord Kendal's ball finally came the following week. It had been long in its arrival, and I was beginning to wonder if we were to be invited at all. Piers caught my eye across the drawing room as he folded the letter closed.

"It seems we've been invited."

Mrs. Cavanagh sat up at once. "Well, I should say so." Then she slumped back down. "Of course, how could we possibly travel to Whitecaster Hall with Seline still unaccounted for?"

Avery was quick to pipe up. "I'd be happy to grace the ballroom as the representative for our family, to give the happy couple our good wishes of course."

Piers shot me a look, then steadied his gaze on Avery. "Though I do thank you for such a generous offer, I daresay it prudent for us all to attend."

Avery gave him just what Piers was watching for—a rather sharp glare followed all too quickly by a pout. "You do realize that Honora will be there."

Mrs. Cavanagh's growl echoed her son's. "Yes, Piers, I do not think—"

"I daresay it's past time I was able to speak with Honora Gervey."

Mrs. Cavanagh flicked open her fan and quivered it before her face. "'Pon my word, you don't mean to make a scene, do you? Because I absolutely refuse to—"

"No, Mother." Piers picked at a piece of lint on his breeches. "I merely mean to wish her good fortune in her marriage."

"Well," she huffed. "If that is the case . . ."

Avery, however, grumbled on, "What about Kendal?"

"I suppose I shall endeavor to avoid him."

Avery's eyes narrowed. "As I imagined. But if I may, why the sudden interest, brother?"

Piers crossed one boot over his opposing knee, an air of distraction about him, but I knew better. He cleared his throat. "Kendal was the last person to speak with Seline before she left. Aren't you the least bit curious what was said?"

Avery shifted in his seat. "I guess so."

Piers lifted his eyebrows. "You *guess* so?"

"Oh, all right. It makes perfect sense to question the gentleman. I just wished I'd thought of the idea first."

Mrs. Cavanagh seemed to brighten. "We should all go. After all, it would be remarkable for me not to do so, considering I never miss a social occasion. It would certainly be remarked otherwise, and we mean to maintain Seline's innocence as long as possible."

My lips parted. "But what about her supposed illness?"

"I've never hovered over a single one of my children. It would be odd for me to start doing so now. We shall simply remark in passing that I employed a very fine nurse, for you must accompany me as well, Charity dear. I could not bear the ordeal without a companion by my side." She had a suppliant expression, well-practiced, which she employed to full affect. I found myself equally agreeing in my heart all the while shrugging off a chill.

Why the sudden invitation? Would something be required of me at the ball?

My going was settled before I'd had a chance to answer. Avery declared it a remarkable idea, and with Piers agreeing so readily, I daresay it was what he'd wanted from the start. In fact, with such enthusiasm, I began to warm to the idea. After all, it would give us a chance to snoop around Whitecaster Hall.

It wasn't until later that evening that I had the chance to speak with Piers alone about the idea. He timed his move perfectly. As I finished the last few notes of a song on the pianoforte, he feigned interest in the darkness beyond the bow window—the perfect spot for a tête-à-tête.

His finger caught my arm as I brushed past him on my way to the sofa. The room's well-placed pillar provided the intimacy he sought. "Can you understand me here?"

I nodded, a wave of nostalgia washing over me. Piers had always managed to find various ways for the two of us to be alone. Even in a room full of people, he was attuned to my needs.

He dipped his chin. "What do you think about my plans for the ball?"

"I believe you were right to encourage us to go. The opportunity might indeed prove useful."

He edged in a bit closer, closing the gap between the column and the wall. "While we're there"—his voice sounded strained—"do you think you could tempt Lord Kendal into asking you for a dance?"

I blinked, an uncomfortable laugh aching to slip out of my mouth. "And how exactly do you expect me to do that? Lord Kendal and I barely know one another, and he's never shown any interest before. You know I'll never be considered a toast."

Piers gave me a curious look. "Why do you do that?"

"Do what?"

"Joke as if you've nothing to recommend yourself."

Then I did laugh. "Because I don't."

His face grew serious and it took him a moment to respond. "I would consider Lord Kendal a fool if he gave up a chance to dance with you."

My cheeks filled with warmth, and I turned away. "What if he does ask me? What then?"

"Use the moment to question what exactly he and Seline talked about. You're her friend, and she would certainly take you into her confidence. It would be only natural that you harbor concern for her. Tell him she's fallen into a decline."

My shoulders felt heavy, my left one still harboring the faintest ache from the fall in the library the previous week. "You are forgetting one rather important detail."

"What's that?"

"I won't be able to hear anything he says in the middle of the dance floor." My hand sought the comfort of my throat. "You know with any noise, I can't—"

I felt his light touch at the small of my back, and my focus snapped toward the room. Avery and his mother were deep in conversation near the fire. Neither was the least interested in what Piers and I were doing hiding beside the pianoforte. His touch felt personal, closed away as we were from the rest of the company.

Piers seemed confused by my expression, then jerked his hand off my back. "I do apologize. I, uh, momentarily forgot my place. It won't happen again." He propped himself against the column. "What if you were to go about your dance with Kendal in a different way? You could plan the dance, but at the last minute declare you'd rather take a turn with him in the garden."

"Wouldn't that be a bit bold of me?"

"Seline certainly would, and if I take Honora there myself, Kendal will be chomping at the bit to follow."

The garden.

I pressed my hands together to hide an inward shiver. Piers didn't know that I'd rarely visited any gardens at balls. Could I actually go there—with Lord Kendal?

Piers watched me with that probing look of his, and I was caught in his gaze. Then his shoulders relaxed. "You needn't worry. I'll be in there watching you the whole time. What happened with Seline and Kendal was no more than a silly lark. Touch her ankles indeed. I never should have called him out for it."

"It's not that."

Slowly, a knit formed across his brow. "Then what?"

For a breathless moment I thought I might actually tell him, but the bell of self-preservation rang loudly in my mind.

I gave him a passable shrug. "I'm simply worried I might not be able to uncover the information we seek. After all, I'm hardly a Bow Street runner."

He mirrored my tentative grin. "All we can do is try."

I nodded, and just like that I'd agreed to an intimate conversation with a gentleman I barely knew in a garden, of all places. I thought I might be sick.

The next few times I visited Mr. Cavanagh in his room was of my own choosing. The very idea of him lying there day after day with little more than a tight-lipped nurse would be more than many could bear. And I'd never expected it, but I'd come to enjoy his conversation.

He was a great deal like Piers, actually. An easy listener with calm mannerisms, a wise counsel with none of the confusing feelings of attraction.

Mr. Cavanagh's deep scowl transformed into a smile as I swept the gown of my skirt beneath my legs and took a seat at his side. "How are you today, Mr. Cavanagh?"

He reached out his hand for mine. "A great deal better now, and I'm happy to report I have been a bit stronger this week. I've spent more of my time in my chair as you suggested, and it seems to have done me a world of good. I'm not certain why I'd not done so before. Everyone keeps telling me how weak I am, but you are in the right of it. How am I to get better if I don't ever push myself?"

"That's wonderful."

His lips twitched. "Are you to attend this ball I keep hearing about?"

The question was a surprise but an equally prudent reminder that Mrs. Cavanagh liked to talk. "I shall accompany Mrs. Cavanagh of course. Although, on the whole I'd rather not go."

"Not go?"

I realized my mistake at once. What reason could I possibly have for wanting to avoid a ball? "I suppose I loathe the idea of everyone staring at us, sneering at the Cavanagh family. Since Seline's scandal, I mean. They've probably all heard what happened between Miles and her in the stables."

He scrunched up his nose. "I'm told by Baker that we've done a fair job of managing the whole thing, and your being there will help put to rest any further rumors. Most in attendance will be blissfully ignorant of what transpired that day."

"I suppose you are right." I wished I'd controlled the hesitation in my voice a bit better.

Consternation crossed his face. "You can consider yourself one of the Cavanaghs while you are under my roof. Hold your head high."

A Cavanagh. If only I really were one.

He went on, "And Piers will be there. He of all people has a far bigger burden to bear. He shall be forced to face Honora Gervey after all this time."

My gaze snapped to the bed. "I suppose Mrs. Cavanagh informed you he planned to join our party."

"No, but I'm certain she will. Piers told me himself this morning."

My mouth fell open, but I can't say why. Certainly Piers would meet with his father. He was managing the estate, after all, but the very idea of them discussing matters of the heart . . . It felt so, so strange. I'd had little relationship with my own father, and here was Mr. Cavanagh well versed on each of his three children's personal affairs.

Mr. Cavanagh held up his finger. "You must keep your promise now. Not a word to anyone about Seline. This family might come about after all. Do you know that Piers mentioned taking up residence once again at Loxby Manor?"

"No. Did he say why?"

"He's still terribly resolute about remaining a bachelor, but he no longer wishes for life to simply pass him by. I lay that spark of interest firmly at your door, my dear. In one way or another, you've made him remember what he owes the family. I don't know if you were aware, but Piers was very much in love with you at one time.

I daresay you know as well as anybody that such feelings are not easily cast aside."

A letter from my mother arrived the following morning. My initial delight at seeing her familiar handwriting faded rather quickly into fear of what the letter might contain. I'd written her about the scandal, and I knew all too well her solution to my awkward placement would involve my removal to America. Though I knew it prudent to make plans to leave, I wasn't ready to depart Loxby Manor, not when Piers and I were so close to figuring out the mystery surrounding Seline.

I took the letter to my bedchamber and settled comfortably onto the window seat. Carefully I broke the wax seal and unfolded the paper. To my great surprise, a second letter fell from the inner pocket of the first, onto the floor. What on earth? I hesitated before recovering the small interior note, lost as to who might have included one with my mother's.

I turned the paper over. Arthur?

I tore into the second seal. Arthur had indeed dashed off a note to me. I recognized his stilted handwriting at once. Though he'd written to me before, it had only been the one time to tell me he'd settled in America. I glanced at the window. What would prompt him to do so now?

> Charity,
>
> Mama is wholly unaware of my including this note within her letter, and I would prefer she and the Cavanaghs remain in the dark. It was a decided risk, but I thought it might go unremarked hidden as it was.

I write to beg you to be careful. There is much you don't know about the people who reside at Loxby Manor. I had no idea you were to spend the year there, or I never would have let you go. As soon as you can arrange passage to America, do so and straightaway, but tell no one of your plans. I dare not say any more in writing. Trust no one.

Your loving brother,

Arthur

CHAPTER 18

Arthur had been right. There was a great deal more going on at Loxby Manor than people were aware of. What he knew, I couldn't guess, but now was not the time to book passage to America. I had to get answers first—for Seline. And Piers would protect me.

The Cavanaghs had received a letter as well from Piers's uncle Charles, which only intensified my need to speak with Kendal alone. It seemed Uncle Charles had found nothing. Seline had truly vanished.

My only chance for answers was to attend Lord Kendal's ball.

I donned my best evening gown that night, a round robe of gold crepe laid over a white satin slip with bows decorating each shoulder. I gave my maid free rein with my hair, which she divided down the middle, then swept up in a beautiful coiffure atop my head, leaving a few loose curls on either side of my forehead.

I thought the resulting creation rather attractive. I'd not worn my hair in such a way before, but it did little to squelch my concerns. Not only was I expected to lure Lord Kendal into the garden for a walk, which could only be considered presumptuous of me, but there was Arthur's warning in the letter. And Mr. Cavanagh's words about Piers were never far from my mind.

Had he truly loved me before I left for Ceylon? He'd never said so, not exactly. I knew he cared for me a great deal, and I him. He'd risked everything for me. But after I received his letter so long ago, my memories had shifted. It was so easy to convince myself I'd been nothing more than an enjoyable distraction. Avery and Seline had certainly echoed my thoughts by the tone of their letters.

Piers, however, was not a man to be distracted by anyone. I knew that now. Really, I knew it then. Just one more reason I adored him. I stared at my reflection in the looking glass. Somewhere along the way the girl of five years ago had turned into a woman—a damaged one. I touched my pale cheek, startled by the warmth beneath my fingertips.

I swiped a bit of powder across my nose. If I was to understand the Piers of today, I had to understand everything that happened to him the years I was away. So much of the scandal that rocked the Cavanagh family rested firmly at my feet, but so much more had gone on while I was away. What better person to expose what happened than Lord Kendal?

Mrs. Cavanagh had instructed me to join the family in the receiving hall at six o'clock, which is where I found Piers waiting alone, deep in thought, his arm perched on the fireplace mantel. As I took in the stoic figure he presented, I nearly stumbled, grasping the banister to avoid complete embarrassment. He turned at the sound, his brow tugging inward, the pocket watch in his fingers slipping to the far end of the fob.

He straightened and his black tailcoat fell neatly into place. "And here I thought I was the only one in this household who possessed the ability to arrive on time."

He crossed the room and offered me his arm. "I'm certain you've noticed how Avery and my mother enjoy being fashionably late."

The air felt dangerously thin between us as his eyes met my own. "You look lovely. Do you feel ready?"

A rush of nerves filled my chest, and I came rather close to blurting out, "For what?" before it donned on me what he was referring to. He meant the investigation of Lord Kendal of course. Nothing about *us.* Goodness, I'd put far too much thought into what Mr. Cavanagh had said.

I moved into the roving heat of the flames, my heart flighty at best. "I shall do my utmost to uncover something we can use."

Piers's hand was at his chin, his gaze pinned to the roaring fireplace. "There is something I need to tell you. I spoke with my father this afternoon and—"

Footsteps pounded from a far-off corridor, and I could have screamed as Avery pranced into the front room. He headed straight for the window, his gait rushed, his face bereft of the good humor he so often employed to his benefit. He stared out before turning to face the room. "I won't be returning in the carriage tonight. I'm to stay at Whitecaster with Kendal. I'm to assist with the curricle race."

Piers didn't miss a beat. "Then Kendal still plans to race first thing in the morning."

"It's all arranged. Really no reason to change it now."

Piers cast me a sideways glance. "I've heard the book at White's has gained quite a few more bets for this particular race, which involve a great deal of money."

He scowled. "Really? More?" Then he sauntered over to the hall chair and flopped down. "All I know is Kendal will beat Blakemoor handily, and it shall be a good thing for my pocketbook."

"You're certain of this? Interesting that everyone else in London thinks otherwise."

Avery shifted his weight in the chair. "Well, not exactly. What do you take me for, a soothsayer? Blakemoor is cow handed. We've all been saying it for years. And Kendal's got some prime horseflesh."

"What horses?" I asked.

"Got 'em from Tattersall's a few weeks back. A couple of high steppers, and in the hands of Kendal, they'll be nigh unbeatable. And Blakemoor's cow handed, I tell you. He'll lose the race sure enough."

Baker entered the receiving room, and I assumed he'd come to speak with Piers as he made his way across the rug, but he headed straight to me and held out a folded piece of paper. "I'm sorry to disturb you, Miss Halliwell, but I was asked to give this to you."

After my letter from Arthur, the note felt cold as I took it into my fingers. Captured by the questioning looks of Piers and Avery, I kept the note firmly in my hand and stood. "If you will excuse me."

They nodded and I escaped to the back hall with a candle where I carefully opened the note. I didn't recognize the handwriting. It appeared rushed, the ink smudged, and it took more than one read through to fully understand the message in its entirety.

Miss Halliwell,

I've had another letter from my nephew, and I must speak to you at once. Please meet me beneath the archway to the stables before you depart Loxby Manor. It is a grave matter that warrants your utmost attention.

Mr. Lacy

Head Groom

I took a quick look behind me, the darkness suddenly alive with sounds. What on earth could Mr. Lacy need to tell me tonight? And should I involve Piers with Avery so close?

No, I knew I couldn't risk it.

Instead, I was forced to circle around the upper floor and utilize the side entrance beyond the great hall. Even then, I was careful not to make a sound as I swung open the heavy door and slipped into the night.

The moon was in and out of the clouds, but I hadn't far to walk before I saw Mr. Lacy lurking in the shadows of the stables' arched entryway. He scraped his hand through his hair in short, jerky movements as he watched me approach.

"Thank you for coming, Miss Halliwell. I wasn't certain I should involve you at all, but you were the only person who came to mind. I'm lost as to who to trust. You are the only one I'm certain is outside of all this. He shook his hand before plunging it into a coat pocket. "I've had another letter from Miles."

"Oh?" A wave of unease splashed across my chest. "What did he say?"

Mr. Lacy tugged at his shirt collar. "Miles's in a muddle, I tell you. Never had any sense, that boy. Which is why I couldn't possibly speak with Mr. Cavanagh—my very livelihood hangs in the balance." Another tug on his shirt before he pushed his hand to the back of his neck. "It seems Miles didn't leave the area as he agreed to."

I leaned forward, the hairs on my arms prickling in the cool breeze. "He didn't? Why ever not?"

His gaze turned somber before it plunged to the ground. "He's at Whitecaster Hall."

"Lord Kendal's estate?"

"Apparently Kendal paid Miles to assist with the upcoming curricle race."

I pressed my hand to my forehead. "I cannot believe it." Then I eyed the head groom, a curious thought taking shape in my mind. Why was Mr. Lacy telling me all this?

His fingers shook against the loose paper in his hands. "I'm afraid for my nephew. He sounds desperate this time. I hoped you might be able to speak with him when you go to Whitecaster today, remind him what he promised me from the start. I don't know what I'll do if any of the Cavanaghs hear of this. Servants talk, and I'm afraid the gossip will alight tonight at the ball. Mr. Cavanagh cannot know. My very future is at stake."

Ice twisted in my chest as I glared back at the house. Piers would be coming this way at any moment. Why had I dropped him that note? Poor Mr. Lacy only wanted to keep his position, to set things right.

Mr. Lacy's shoulders curved forward under the weight of his anxiety. "Mrs. Cavanagh has been to the stables daily, asking for word about Miles. She'll not allow me to stay on if she learns my nephew has not held up his end of the bargain. I curse the day I ever stuck my neck out for that maddening boy."

I touched his arm. "I'll do my best to speak with Miles, and I understand your concern."

"Thank you. I hoped you might." He sounded so hopeful, but his momentary relief faded all too quickly as he balled his fingers into a fist at his side. "I fear certain something terrible is planned for that race. The amount of money he's been paid, well, it's far too much for a simple groom's work."

The sabotage!

I took a step back. Could the Gormogons have employed Miles Lacy to carry out their plan?

"Did your nephew say anything else, anything specific I might go on?"

He rubbed his chin. "I'm afraid not. He simply wrote for me

to trust him, that his staying in the area would eventually pay off. He seemed to imply he meant to compensate me for my troubles."

A surge of wind shook the trees and howled its way beneath the stone arch. Mr. Lacy stared into the darkness around us as the shadows seemed to edge in place. My focus fell to the piece of paper in his hand. If Miles Lacy was at Whitecaster Hall, then Seline most certainly did not run away with him.

"Mr. Lacy?"

"Yes." His voice sounded gruff, his eyes like an owl's in the dim light.

"Do you still think Miles had nothing to do with Seline's disappearance?"

He shook his head, but I wasn't to hear what he said as I heard a door in the distance. I jerked a glance behind me. "Thank you for trusting me with this information, but I must go at once. We'll speak again soon, and I promise you I'll try to find Miles as soon as I can once I've arrived at Whitecaster Hall."

I whirled away and walked off at a brisk pace, caught up in not only my fear of accidental discovery but the first definitive proof of what I'd anticipated all along. Seline did not write that note the maid found in her room. Miles Lacy might very well hold the key to determining what really happened to her. I had to talk to him. Of course there was one rather big question: should I do so without telling Piers?

CHAPTER 19

I'd heard Whitecaster Hall was magnificent, newly built and elaborately sculpted—a rectangular palace with symmetrical outcroppings and pillars like the pantheon in Rome. However, as we were late leaving Loxby, there was no light with which to view Whitecaster Hall in all its splendor.

That is, until we breached the front door. Nothing could have prepared me for what I found inside.

We were met by a brilliance of light like nothing I'd ever seen. It spilled down from every angle, arresting each guest as they traversed the entryway door—hundreds upon hundreds of beeswax candles. The whispered awe of the ladies around me ran rampant as they moved to count every last candle. A woman wearing a particularly large ostrich feather in her hat turned to her companion and declared the spectacle a fine tribute to honor Lord Kendal's affianced bride.

I found the sentiment a bit difficult to grasp. Who would spend such a ridiculous amount of money on a hallway?

Piers was no doubt thinking the same as his left eyebrow inched upward. He caught my incredulous stare and covered a laugh.

"Careful." I took in our surroundings. "We don't want to offend our host after we've just arrived."

Straightening, Piers offered me his arm. "I swear nothing shall surprise me after what I've seen tonight." A few steps forward and we'd created enough space between us and his mother and Avery for some semblance of privacy. He touched my gloved hand. "Are you ready?"

How to answer such a question? Ready for my tête-à-tête with Lord Kendal? Hardly. And worse, I now had the added stress of seeking out Miles Lacy.

I looked up. "And what about you? I'm greatly concerned Lord Kendal may not be as receptive to your presence in his home as you seem to think he will be."

Piers shrugged. "It's possible he'll continue to cut me, but he'd never make a scene. Not when Honora is the guest of honor."

"Have you seen her recently?"

He shot me a curious glance. "Certainly not. We did not part on the best of terms. Granted, she was always . . . How to describe it . . . Tactful with me." He glared off into the shadows for a moment, then turned back to me. "Rest assured, she was no more in love with me than I was with—"

He wasn't to finish his sentence, as Lord Kendal and Honora Gervey appeared directly ahead, greeting the guests as they passed into the ballroom. I could feel the muscles tighten in Piers's arm.

I took a deep breath. This would not be easy for either of us, but we had each other.

Honora was the first to spot us through the crowds. With her raven-black hair and snow-white cheeks, no one could have missed the flush that crept across her face. She touched Kendal's arm to gain his attention and whispered into his ear. His eyes snapped forward, and he stared at us a long second before the insidious workings of a smile crossed his face.

A few charged steps and we were before them.

Kendal spoke first, but he made certain we understood he was directing the conversation to me and me alone. "Miss Halliwell, if I'm not mistaken, it's been some time."

I lowered my chin. "I've just returned from Ceylon where I spent the last five years."

"Five years!" His eyes brightened. "How can it possibly have been so long?" He slid a glare at Piers, then came back to me. "It was good of you to accompany Mrs. Cavanagh tonight as Seline could not. I do hope you enjoy the evening."

Avery was behind us now, and Lord Kendal purposefully dismissed us. It was Honora's sheepish gaze that graced our exit, but she didn't say a word.

Piers motioned me through the ballroom door, and we made our way into the throngs of people. He kept a look of indifference across his face, but he couldn't deceive me, not completely. Some part of him had hoped to be acknowledged by Kendal. It would have gone a long way toward salvaging his reputation, but Kendal would not be so kind.

I considered each hard face around us. Years had passed since the fateful moment Piers had been labeled a coward, and yet polite society in East Whitloe would never forget. I could only imagine what he'd suffered through while I was away—all for me.

He tried a smile. "Would you do me the honor of the first dance? After that, I daresay I shall retire to the card room as I shan't burden any other partners."

I lifted my chin. "I shall be pleased with a dance of course, but there will be no card room for you after that. You must wait with me until I can approach Lord Kendal for our walk in the garden. I've no intention of dancing with anyone else this evening either."

Piers rubbed a chalk drawing on the floor with the toe of his pump before moving close to my ear where I would be sure to hear him. "I don't need your pity if that's what this is. I'm not a lost puppy, you know."

"Don't be absurd." I pinched his arm. "Trust me, I've had quite enough smiling and nodding over the years. If anyone wants to secure my affections, they can very well do so off the dance floor and out of this maddening noise."

A smile creased his lips, and he leaned in once again. "Are you trying to make me believe you don't like dancing?"

"I simply like hearing what people are saying, and the older I get, the less and less patience I have for pretending."

He paused this time before returning close to me. "You know, I didn't think it possible, but I believe I like you even better since you've returned from Ceylon. That adventurous spirit of yours has turned into a shrewd one, and God help the man who tries to harness it."

As Piers pulled back, I could hardly look at him, let alone breathe. What did he mean by such a statement? Perhaps Mr. Cavanagh was right about my effect on Piers. He had found a way to shake off his isolation, and it had loosened his tongue.

He offered me his arm as the noise of the room barreled into our conversation. "Shall . . . take a turn . . . the room?" He leaned in close once again. "I'd like to give everyone their chance to cut me at the outset. That way I can focus on the task at hand. We're here for Seline. All the rest of this is simply a distraction."

I'd never experienced the full censure of polite society, not until then—the searing glares followed by the turn of the shoulder, then the comments, spoken just loud enough for others to hear. We'd only crossed the length of one wall before Piers was forced to halt our progression, bending his head to ask me if I thought it wise to continue as his partner. He did not want to completely ruin my reputation in a matter of minutes. But he didn't understand the emotions broiling in my chest. Quite frankly, I didn't understand my desire to spite them all, to find some way to defend him.

After my attack I'd closeted myself away in my family's home in Ceylon. I thought that somehow my friends and acquaintances would take one look at me and know instantly what had happened, yet here I was holding the arm of a man who bore his own public humiliation with dignity and grace. It may have taken him a few years to do so, but the courage he displayed was freeing—not only for him but for me.

I urged Piers onward across the room. The dancing would begin soon, and quite suddenly I was looking forward to sharing the moment with him—for it wasn't only his moment of triumph; it would be mine as well.

The musicians in the balcony cradled their instruments, poised to begin the first dance. Piers found my hand as the performers struck up a short march signaling the dancers to take the floor. Honora Gervey called out a waltz, and the lull of the crowds wafted into the background, my heartbeat pounding its way to my ears.

Though the waltz had been introduced at Almack's last year, I had yet to perform the steps in company. I shot a glance at Piers and he gave me one of his rather entrancing smiles, that perfect mix of humor and anticipation. Thank goodness I'd agreed to join him.

The collective gaze of the people in the room prickled down my back as I placed my left hand on his upper arm, my right touching his gloved fingertips, but Piers swiftly grasped my entire hand. The subtle change brought a rush of warmth to my cheeks and my eyes to his face. I'd heard the various debates about the waltz—the degree of personal familiarity that rendered it liable to abuse—but I hadn't understood the arguments. Not really. Not until that moment. Not until I met his eyes.

Various couples took their places around us and the music began. The steps were slow at first and my feet felt almost sluggish, but Piers kept me moving and smiling. He maintained his promise and said nothing as we twirled around the dance floor; however, something more important passed between us—the first spark of uncomplicated happiness.

Awash with nerves, I felt tears forming in my eyes as the small discovery blossomed in my heart. This was what I had been yearning for; not Piers exactly, not simple attraction to a man, but a connection, something real, something secure. I swayed to the music as the tempo increased. For the first time in five years, I felt alive.

The music ended all too quickly and the lines returned to Piers's face. He pulled me into the shadow of one of the columns. "Now is the perfect moment to approach Honora. Do you think you can get Lord Kendal to ask you to dance?"

I sank against the wall. "I don't know. He seemed amiable enough when we arrived, but I can't help but worry."

"I'm going to make my way over to Honora during the next dance, hoping I might delay her afterward. She wouldn't dare take a turn with me on the dance floor, but she owes me a conversation at the very least."

"And that is when I should seek out Lord Kendal?"

He nodded, but his eyes seemed to say just the opposite.

"You don't think I'm in any danger, do you?"

He rested his hand on my shoulder as if he were privy to my secret. "I won't let you out of my sight. Not for one solitary moment."

He meant to encourage me, but the gravity of his words only caused my fear to escalate. Could I do this? Could I wander the gardens with a gentleman I barely knew? The calm I'd felt only moments before on the dance floor disappeared into thin air, my muscles tightening in turn.

What was I thinking coming here, acting as if it was so long ago? Everything about my relationship with Piers was complicated, and he had problems of his own. True intimacy would always be a great unknown for me. I was a fool to think otherwise.

He'd told me he had no intention of taking a wife, but convincing his heart might be an entirely different matter. Piers and I had been drawn to each other since we were children. Nothing would change that but time and space, and the only way I could bring myself to leave Loxby Manor was to uncover what happened to Seline.

I took a measured breath. "I'll get Lord Kendal to speak with me, one way or another."

We shared one last long look before setting off on our separate missions.

Seline had been in love with Lord Kendal for as long as I could remember. He was suave, handsome, and titled, and he'd never spent one minute thinking of me. So why on earth would he ask me to dance? He'd never done so before.

Chairs squeaked in the corners of the room. The musicians rearranged their instruments in the balcony. Boots scuffled across the floor as the roar of conversation pressed against my ears. Where was Lord Kendal? I scanned the throngs of people milling in every direction before a stream of cloudy moonlight caught my eye, pouring in through the floor-length back windows, illuminating our illustrious host. I flicked open my brisé fan. It was now or never.

Carefully I pretended to search for someone in the crowds as I made my way closer and closer to the earl, stopping but a step away. I took a few calculated glances across the dance floor before settling my hand on the edge of the white wainscoting circling the room.

Lord Kendal watched me for a moment before rather slyly edging closer. His expression remained one of haughty indifference. "Lost your escort?"

I batted my eyes as I'd seen Seline do hundreds of times before. "Not at all. I was merely looking for Avery Cavanagh. We arranged a dance, and I'm afraid he may have forgotten."

There was a bend to Lord Kendal's dark brow, followed by a heart-wrenching second of indecision, but I simply waited for him to appraise me, hoping my ploy would not go awry.

Finally he gave a sigh of amusement, his attention narrowing in on my face. "Well that will never do now, will it?"

I had to stay close to him if I was going to hear his words accurately. "It is neither here nor there. I suppose I shall simply have to sit this one out, unless you can suggest an alternative." I moved as near as I could while staying within the bounds of propriety.

Of course the sudden familiarity I'd been forced to create inadvertently played to his never-ending vanity. A wry smile slid like satin across his face, and I was reminded of how easily Seline's charms could get under one's skin.

He offered me his arm as if he was doing me a great favor. "Would you do me the honor instead?"

A strange mix of emotions hit me as I accepted his offer. I suppose a part of me was giddy—the young dreamer from long ago who was rarely given any attention, particularly by a noted Corinthian. Over the years I'd grown and changed. I was no longer a slave to societal expectations, not really. I'd seen the dark side of a person, and I would carry the scars for the rest of my life. Fear, anger, disillusionment—all fought for the balance of my attention.

And then I looked up. Lord Kendal was just a man, and Piers would be watching us—he'd promised me he would. My body stiffened, but I affected an innocent smile. "Would you prefer to take a turn in the gardens instead? I believe I need a breath of fresh air."

Piers had timed his own walk perfectly. As Kendal took a sideways glance at the terrace doors, he was struck dumb by the sight of Honora embarking on her own garden stroll—with Piers, no less. Kendal's eyes narrowed and the grooves in his chin dimpled as his jaw clenched. Yet he was far too practiced at deception. His evident shock subsided as quickly as it had come, and he casually touched my hand. "I daresay I could stand for a stroll myself."

He redirected our path toward the French doors with a sharp turn, and a lady and gentleman were forced to jerk out of our way. Kendal thrust the left side of the door wide, and we erupted into Whitecaster's renowned garden, swept silent by the quiet hand of night.

On the terrace stood a couple in deep conversation, and to their right, a pair of friendly bachelors, but there was no sign of Piers and Honora. I took a long breath of dampened air, the stilted breeze abuzz in my ears. The rolling gray mist had thickened over the course of the evening.

We descended a row of wide stone steps, which narrowed around a circular pond and disappeared between dense hedgerows. I'd heard Lord Kendal's garden hailed on more than one occasion to be something quite special, but I couldn't remember exactly why.

I narrowed my eyes, straining to see down the curvy paths that split in all directions. No budding flowers or manmade ponds, simply greenery as far as the torchlights could illuminate—so much like the tea plantation in Ceylon. A prickly chill filled my chest and my legs began to feel heavy. Where precisely did Kendal mean to take me?

The bushes grew taller the farther we walked, plunging the path into feathered darkness. I thought I heard Kendal swear under his breath, and strangely enough, his doing so comforted me. Kendal slowed his steps as he came to the same conclusion I had. Piers and Honora had found a way to be alone.

CHAPTER 20

What a strange garden.

Each turn in the thick hedgerows brought another path exactly as the last.

Then I remembered. All the greenery, the winding paths were a maze. Whitecaster Hall was known for its small, intricate maze at the back of the property. I'd heard Seline describe it years ago.

One last corner and we came across a moonlit statue of Venus. Lord Kendal seemed hesitant to walk any farther from the house. "I thought perhaps Piers Cavanagh had come this way, but he's nowhere to be found."

I rubbed the chill from my arms. So there was to be no pretense between us. I glanced once more behind me. "I'm not certain which way they went, but rest assured, I know Mr. Cavanagh to be an honorable man. I doubt he came this far." Granted, we had.

"Honorable." Lord Kendal laughed. "I beg to differ on that point." Then his face grew quite still as he drew a circle with his finger in the air. "Was this some sort of arrangement between the two of you? You distract me while Cavanagh takes a turn with my fiancée?"

"Certainly not."

"Then what are we doing out here, Miss Halliwell? Because I don't believe for a second you needed a whiff of fresh air." He spoke calmly enough, but his eyes were like daggers in the darkness. "Did Seline send you?"

I hesitated to answer as a stray gust of wind sent the leaves on the bushes quivering. A whisper of caution? Perhaps. I'd rehearsed what I might say over and over again in my room, but nothing could have prepared me for the expression on Lord Kendal's face or the way it would make me feel.

I stumbled over my next words. "I-I did wish to speak with you about . . . well, Seline, but not in the way you suppose."

He picked a dried leaf from the sleeve of his jacket. "I have nothing further to say about Seline." He made no move to leave.

"I—" This would not be easy. Lord Kendal and I were practically strangers, yet at the same time we shared a connection through Seline. Standing there alone, buried in the heart of the maze, caught in Kendal's dangerous glare, I knew I could not fob him off with a manufactured lie. I let out a long breath. The truth was always best. "Seline never came home after your society meeting at Kinwich Abbey."

The moonlight betrayed the scowl that took shape on his face. "What do you mean she never came home?"

"Just what I said. A rumor has been circulated that she is ill, but the truth is she's been missing since that night."

His mouth slipped open, his eyes growing wild as he searched the bushes for answers.

I stepped forward. "There was a letter found in her room stating she had run off with Miles Lacy, that they were bound for Gretna Green."

His head tipped back slightly, followed by a pointed huff. "But that is—"

"Impossible."

"Well, yes. Miles Lacy is here this very night in my stables, and trust me, I'd know if Seline was with him."

"It is my understanding that you were the last person to speak with her the night she disappeared. And it was an argument."

He dipped his chin. "When do we *not* have an argument?"

"If I may ask, what was she angry about? I'm attempting to piece together everything that happened that night, and your point of view is vital if I'm to figure out where she has gone."

He crossed his arms. "So you think I might have something to do with her disappearance?"

"That is not what I said, but surely you see that I must question everyone, particularly the person she specifically went to see that night."

He raked his hand through his hair. "The little minx thought she had me at last. Her excitement was palpable." He cast me a sideways glance. "She liked to hold little secrets over us—all of us. Hugh, Tony, Avery. No one was left out of her little web. Of course Hugh always thought he was different—that she was being honest with him. He'd scored some sort of promise out of her. I, thankfully, had not been blessed with such a burden." His gaze flicked to mine and held. "Believe me when I tell you, she did not know about Honora that night."

I played with a stray leaf on a nearby bush as I pondered his story. "You said she thought she *had* you. What do you mean?"

He shrugged, but the lines on his face only deepened. "She had a plan to trap me into marriage. She seemed to think she'd found out something about my upcoming curricle race, something she could use against me."

The exchange I'd overheard at the abbey echoed in my mind. "I believe the word you are looking for is *sabotage*."

His eyes rounded. "Curious little thing you are. Now who told you such a farradiddle?"

"I overheard a conversation that seemed to suggest—"

"Oh, you did, did you?" A smile crossed his face, but it wasn't a comfortable one. "And you really think, as a member of the Four Horse Club and a notable whip myself, I need stoop so low?"

Arrogance, it seemed, was like a second cousin for Kendal, and it flashed its way to the surface on a bolt of lightning.

I'd hit a nerve. He began to pace. "You can take your curst insinuations and leave my house this instant—with your escort." He stopped suddenly to grasp my arm. "After all, he's the master of avoiding anything unpleasant."

Caught up in Lord Kendal's wave of anger, I let him drag me like a dog to the corner of the hedgerow where, like lightning, a fist sprang from the shadows, striking him square in the face. I had to jump away to avoid his limp body as it flopped onto the gravel like a sack of flour.

Honora screamed.

Piers shook out his hand, a curve gracing his lips. "I think Kendal is right. It might be about time for us to leave, Miss Halliwell." He turned to Honora, his eyes more determined than I'd ever seen them. "Miss Gervey, you may accompany us back to the house, or we'll be happy to send someone back to help you." He flicked his fingers in the air. "And your illustrious fiancé."

Piers offered his arm, but Honora refused, trouncing off in the direction of the house, an expression of pained irritation across her face.

Fighting my own level of shock, I tried to keep my voice low, but it was nigh impossible. "What were you thinking?"

"I didn't like how he was manhandling you."

I gasped. "Then you *were* watching us the whole time."

"As I told you I would." Concern swept over his features, and he pulled me close.

I should have thrust myself away the second he did so, but I didn't move, not at first. It was almost as if my muscles were momentarily paralyzed, but not unpleasantly so. His arms were safe, familiar even, and my heart galloped.

I heard him expel a breath of relief. "Charity."

Then we were moving, shuffling, inching away from each other.

He ran a hand through his hair. "Did he hurt you in any way?"

I touched my previously injured shoulder. "No, I don't think so. But what about him?"

"He'll be fine, besides the devilish headache he's bound to have when he awakes." Piers knelt at Kendal's side, jabbing his finger into the earl's waistcoat pocket.

Shaking off my rampant emotions, I knelt as well. "What are you doing?"

"Help will be here soon enough. Thought I might do a little snooping." He ran his hand down his face before resting his fingers on Kendal's lapel. There, twinkling in the moonlight, was a small silver collar jewel. "What's this?"

We leaned in together, the etched dragon taking shape in the dim light.

Piers met my eyes. "The Gormogons. Look, it even has the same Persian ivy border as the one in the journal. Quick, check his other pockets."

I dipped my hands into Kendal's jacket, and I was rewarded with a folded slip of paper. I held it out, spreading it open at once.

Kendal,

Lest you forget, I have access to your loyalty pledge. Don't fail us or the cause. We need each other in times of success but, more importantly, in times of trial. We're trusting you to carry on as planned.

Piers refolded the note. "It seems we were right. Only, this is a bit worse than I anticipated. 'The cause'? I begin to fear this secret society is larger than just the four friends Avery indicated."

A shiver scaled my neck. "What if the group never dissolved like your father thought it did? Could it not have carried on in secret?"

"Possibly, but when pressed, my father admitted that the group did little of anything, originating merely to oppose the Freemasons. There would be no reason for it to continue."

"Unless they found a purpose, something to unite them?"

"Avery has always been an idealist. If he thought he might make changes in Britain for the good of society, he would definitely want to be a part of it."

The sound of footsteps lit the air and we glared at one another. Like lightning, Piers shoved the missive back into Kendal's pocket.

Two servants burst through the opening in the hedgerow just as Piers gently patted Kendal's face. "Wake up, my good man."

Kendal moaned, then opened his eyelids. He was confused at first, his gaze darting about the garden, and then his eyes narrowed.

Piers stepped back to allow Kendal's servants to assist him to his feet, then whispered to me, "See, he's well enough."

His confidence was intoxicating, yet what had he set in motion with his rash behavior? "Oh, Piers, he'll call you out again, and then what?"

"I'll be sure to meet him at dawn this time."

Kendal stepped forward, the fire in his stare for Piers alone. Silence roamed the bushes like a tiger, coming to rest at Kendal's feet. "You'll meet me for this, Cavanagh." He wiped a spot of blood from the edge of his lip. "Considering our past, perhaps we should forgo the seconds and finish our duel right here, right now. Swords or pistols, if you please?"

Piers didn't flinch. "A pleasant thought indeed, but I've no intention of doing this in such a havey-cavey way. My seconds shall call upon you tomorrow. And I assure you, this disagreement between us shall be put to rest . . . once and for all."

"Trying to regain some semblance of honor?" Lord Kendal spat on the ground. "Believe me, there will be no chance for an apology, not with a blow to the head. You'll meet me on that field, or you can slink back to that cottage in Liverpool even more of a coward than you already are. And if you fail to show up this time, you bet I'll announce it in church."

"I should expect nothing less . . ." Something drew Piers's attention beyond the gardens.

It was Avery, racing across the side yard. He stopped but a few feet in front of us, winded and his face red. "Something has happened at the stables." He eyed Kendal for a moment, then went on. "It's the new groom . . . He's been murdered."

"How? Why?" The words were out before I'd even had a moment to think.

We departed the maze as a group, but once free, Kendal took off at a run.

Piers touched my shoulder, his voice firm. "I think it best for you to go to my mother in the card room. Avery and I will investigate what has happened."

I nodded, but at the same moment I saw Mrs. Cavanagh bustling across the yard on her way to the stables."

Avery threw up his hands. "What the deuce does she think she is doing? Mama!" he cried as he raced off to intercept her.

Piers and I hurried to the group huddled behind the stables, the hum of fear circling the crowd like the eerie sound of animals brought to life at night. The air had grown cooler over the course of the evening, but it was a stale chill, damp in places, stuffy in others, almost as if Whitecaster Hall had been sealed up within a cave.

We arrived in time to see Mrs. Cavanagh push her way into the woods, her voice far shriller than the others. "I was told he was a servant at Loxby Manor. Let me through."

My gaze snapped to Piers and I mouthed, "*A servant?*"

Forgetting his earlier reticence to keep me from whatever horror lurked behind the stables, I was tugged along behind him into the forest.

There were several Whitecaster servants milling about a small opening within the trees where I could see the ominous reminder of what they'd found—a motionless pair of feet lying at an angle in the shadows among the leaves.

I was surprised to hear Tony's voice at my side and grim at that. His focus remained on Avery, his eyes like slits in the torchlight. "I found him like that just moments ago."

Avery plunged his hand through his hair. "And you didn't hear or see anything? I thought you planned to overnight in the stables."

A layer of unease tinted each of Tony's words as if he were trying much too hard to say everything and nothing at the same time. *"I was in the harness room with Hugh, and then I left to deliver"*—he mouthed words only to Avery; speaking aloud again—"to Kendal at the ball. I returned to find him missing. We searched the stables for some time before one of the grooms turned up and said our boy saw something out the window, and we charged out the back door."

Piers piped up. "And where exactly is Hugh now?"

Tony shrugged. "His horse is gone. He must have left earlier. Of course he never planned to stay the night."

Mrs. Cavanagh crept up near the body before Avery took notice and tugged her back, returning her hurriedly to my side. He motioned to me with his chin to take her away. "We'll leave as soon as I can get out of here. I doubt there will be a curricle race now."

I clasped her cold fingers, her face a ghostly white.

"Oh, my dear Charity. The rumors were true. He never left . . . But murdered? I cannot believe it. I cannot . . . I feel faint."

I refrained from pointing out that it was she who had forced her way forward.

She was a ball of quivers and gasping breaths.

I grasped her arm. "We should make our way back to the house."

Piers, having got his first view of the body, nodded to me, his eyes wide.

Her voice was barely audible. "I think that wise, my dear."

We pushed through the swarm of people, but as soon as we were out of earshot, Mrs. Cavanagh came to life, tugging us to a bench beneath a willow tree. Darkness lurked in patches beneath the branches as the moonlight fought to break through.

The evening chill sought to remind me of the advanced hour, yet I was determined to hear what Mrs. Cavanagh was so anxious to say. I rubbed my arms and leaned in close. A shiver skated across my shoulders as I tried in vain to make out the complexities of her face, but they were lost in the shadows. Her fingers felt almost claw-like as she pulled me close.

"It was Miles Lacy!"

Her words were like cold water splashed in my face, and it took me a moment to form a response. "Are you certain?"

Her voice dipped. "I'd know that man anywhere."

"Did you see . . . I mean . . . Did anyone say how he died?"

"Clubbed over the head, if I were to make a guess. There was a great deal of blood on his forehead and a rather large wound."

My hand retreated to my neck. "However will we tell Mr. Lacy?"

Her voice came out of the gloom far more flippant than I was expecting. "He was never all that fond of the boy."

"No, but to lose anyone in such a way . . ."

"That is neither here nor there. I brought you to this spot to discuss something far more important. With Miles Lacy dead, where is my darling Seline?"

I had already surmised that Seline was not with Miles Lacy, but Mrs. Cavanagh had not. I understood now why Piers wanted me to get his mother away from the stables. I ran my hand around her back and urged her to stand, speaking quietly in her ear. "All we know at present is that the letter Seline was supposed to have left us was indeed a fabrication, or she was lying. Everything else is speculation at this point. We'll wait for Avery and Piers before making any rash judgments. Do not give up hope yet."

I glared back at the stables, opening my mouth to speak, then closing it just as quickly.

After all, who on earth wanted Miles Lacy dead?

CHAPTER 21

I assisted Mrs. Cavanagh back into Whitecaster Hall where we were confronted by the sights and sounds of a ball filled with people completely ignorant of what had transpired. Dancers swirled about the floor as a low hum buzzed from the card room. Servants bustled by as they prepared the supper table.

The house felt a blur, almost as if I were witnessing the spectacle from outside my body. A man had died only a few yards away, and here we stood, caught up in the throes of a different world. Mrs. Cavanagh begged leave to sit on a chair where we shared the next few minutes with little to no conversation.

That is, until something snapped in her demeanor, and she dipped forward. "I daresay it may be some time before Avery and Piers will be able to escort us home, and I swear I cannot just sit here and fret. It will do my heart no good." She worried her hands in her lap. "Perhaps a card game might distract me for the time being."

A card game? Now? Mrs. Cavanagh had always been a curious creature to me, but never more so than in that moment. I drummed my fingers on the wooden armrest. Or maybe she was right. She would be nothing but a rattled mess if I were to leave her to her own devices. At least in the card room she'd have the comfort of friends.

And a place to gossip, no doubt. A scandal that had nothing to do with her family—her lips were itching to spread the news.

I gave her a wan smile. "If you think a game of Whist will calm your nerves. I, however, am completely unable to concentrate on anything, let alone a game of skill."

Her eyes narrowed. "Well, I can hardly leave you here alone. It just wouldn't be proper."

I chose not to point out how often she did so, nodding instead as I rose to accompany her into the card room, but Piers appeared through the door.

Catching sight of us, he hurried over. "Avery's determined to assist Lord Kendal at the stables. He'll find his own way home. I think it best for us to leave at once."

"Whatever you suggest." Mrs. Cavanagh's voice had taken on a leaden tone.

Piers extended his arm, and we made our way to the front hall to await our carriage. Mrs. Cavanagh was pleased to find a friend there waiting as well. Her predilection for gossip allowed Piers and me a precious moment to ourselves.

The multitude of candles still blazed, revealing the disquiet on his face. He crossed his arms as he tilted against a nearby pillar, his eyes on the bright lights. "What an infernal waste of money this all has been."

I breathed out a laugh. "I quite agree."

Small talk felt foreign on such a night, and I could see it sour in Piers's eyes. He pressed the palm of his hand against the column. "Tony said something out there that I cannot get out of my mind."

I moved in close. "What was that?"

"You were there. The bit about him taking something to Kendal in the ballroom."

"You think it was the note you found in Kendal's pocket."

His eyes flashed. "Exactly." He played with his quizzing glass. "You know, I was standing quite close to Avery when Tony was speaking to him, and I could have sworn I felt a muscle stiffen in his arm, almost as if he flinched."

I stepped forward. "What if you are right and there's more to Seline's disappearance than what we think we know? Miles Lacy was not murdered by accident. Miles and Seline have been connected since the scandal, and Miles didn't leave the county when he swore he would. Something must have kept him here."

Caught up in the moment, I laid my hand on Piers's arm, which drew his sharp gaze. I pulled away, the silence of the hall buzzing in my ears.

He let out a sigh, but I couldn't read the intricacies buried within that halting breath. His hand brushed my arm. "Habits can be difficult to break."

"Yes, yes they can."

"Listen, I spoke to the groom who witnessed Miles leave the stables. The groom said Miles acted quite strange, as if something had shocked him. When the groom went to the window himself, he thought he saw a figure in the trees, but he couldn't make out who it was."

Mrs. Cavanagh drew up at Piers's side. "Our carriage is here and I have no intention of staying one moment longer in this house. I daresay it isn't safe at all." Piers gave me a knowing glance, then offered her his arm.

But I didn't move, not yet, churning over what Piers had discovered. So the groom had seen someone in the woods. Hugh perhaps? Or Tony? It could have even been Avery.

I said little as we traversed the front door and moved into the swirling night, my hopes for the evening vanishing into thin air. All our efforts to uncover the details regarding Seline's disappearance, and we were no closer to figuring out what had happened. Miles was dead, and now Piers had the duel to contend with. Our plans had been designed in vain.

I climbed into the carriage as the thoughts I'd been wrestling with arrested my steps.

The air around me shifted, scaling my arms and sliding across my shoulders, and for a moment I thought my legs would give out beneath me.

Was I right in my earlier assumptions? Had Seline disappeared without a clue because, like Miles Lacy, she was no longer alive?

Piers sent a note by my maid the following morning. I was to meet him in the entrance hall at three in the afternoon. He'd arranged for a carriage to take us to Tony Shaw's estate.

I spent the morning held up in the drawing room by Mrs. Cavanagh, whose spirits were surprisingly light after all we'd endured the previous day.

She caught me watching her from my seat on the scrolled end sofa. "What is nagging you, my dear?" She set her needlepoint on her lap, her shrewd eyes quick to follow me.

I slipped my book closed on my lap, keeping my finger between the pages. "I must have been woolgathering. Please forgive me."

"Humph." She pressed her lips together. "I suppose you think my elevated mood out of place on such a day."

"Not at all."

"Don't lie." She lifted her eyebrows. "It can become a nasty little habit."

I paused. "I was wondering if you might have received word about Seline? You seem different today."

"No." A deep breath. "When I returned to my room last night, I set aside some time for thinking. I do that on occasion, you understand, because I find the practice remarkable in improving the mind. You really should try it. Not too often, mind you, or it can irritate the nerves."

She straightened her skirt. "In fact, I take Mr. Cavanagh's pocket watch and when ten minutes have passed, I've either solved whatever crisis drove me to my thinking time in the first place"—she waved her hand in the air—"like what I should wear when I call on my neighbors, or the problem can simply wait till I think on it the next time." She looked up as if she'd solved some great dilemma. "Thus, I don't have to worry with whatever plagues me outside of my thinking time."

She flicked open her fan, souring at my obvious bewilderment. "I daresay such a practice would be beneficial for you as well. It improves conversation, at the very least. No gentleman wants a lady who is dull."

"And I daresay no lady wants a dull husband either."

She snapped her fan closed. "Don't be impertinent. Gentlemen can be whatever they wish as long as they provide you with a certain level of comfort. Take your cousin Samuel for instance."

Oh dear. My mother had to have written her. I shifted on the sofa. "And this thinking time has given you a new perspective on our troubles?"

"Well, yes." She frowned, but she couldn't quite keep her lips pressed tight, almost as if a secret satisfaction ached to slip out.

Not only was Mrs. Cavanagh prone to rambles and fits of nerves, but she was also a bit mysterious in how she managed her day-to-day life. She would retire to her room for a good portion of the day bemoaning her troubles, then emerge from her self-inflicted cocoon only to lecture me on how I might snag a husband.

She leaned forward to secure her teacup, then took a long, careful sip. Her eyes met mine over the cup's rim. "I had a thought . . ."

"Oh?"

"If Miles Lacy is no longer with us, that means Seline has not married the fool."

All I could do was nod. Nothing Mrs. Cavanagh said at this point could possibly surprise me. I glanced down at the book in my lap. She was difficult to watch really—her ability to wade through a shallow pool of thought, coming up only to ensure that those around her met her expectations. I ran my finger along the cover, a cold sensation filling my chest.

Was I so very different from Mrs. Cavanagh?

I'd kept my assault a secret to retain my reputation, even though I knew full well I no longer held any intention of marrying. The idea was a sobering one, perhaps not exactly fair, but something to ponder nonetheless. I had a long way to go if I was ever really going to understand myself. Perhaps Mr. Cavanagh was right and I should simply move on, pretend, or otherwise. Inwardly I sighed. If only it were that easy.

I tapped my finger on the book. "Have you heard anything from your brother-in-law in regard to his search?"

"Charles's letters have been few and far between, but he did write and there is no further news. Seline has simply vanished." Her voice turned a touch dismal, and I was forced once again to reexamine my perception of Mrs. Cavanagh. She did love Seline in her own way, as she no doubt loved all her children. And she seemed to worry a great deal about Seline's return. So why did I feel uneasy in her company, almost as if she were keeping some sort of secret?

I watched her pick at her needlepoint as if the two of us were simply enjoying a fine afternoon, but on occasion there was an urgency to her movements. She jerked the needle up and down, her breathing short and fast as her eyes slid readily to the door, the very feel of the room ever changing.

Suddenly Baker entered the drawing room and the silence snapped. Mrs. Cavanagh jumped to her feet, her hand flying to her chest.

He didn't respond to her hasty movement, but I could see plain as day it had affected him. He cleared his throat. "Mr. Cavanagh requests your presence in his room, ma'am."

It took a moment for her to answer. "You may inform him I will be there shortly." Her voice was strong, but when she whirled around to stow away her sewing bag, I caught a glimpse of her face. It was only a second, and I could have easily been reading into what I saw, but her eyes looked pinched, her mouth quivering in a scowl.

I stood as well. "Is there anything I can do to help?"

Her eyes met mine, and I was startled to see them shiny with tears. "How kind of you, but as you well know, I am merely passing the days as best I can until I hear word of Seline. Mr. Cavanagh needs me just now, and I should not keep him waiting."

CHAPTER 22

Piers entered the receiving room at precisely three o'clock. I stood in the warmth of the front windows when I heard my name, turning to see a rather well-dressed gentlemen in dark blue waiting for me in the doorway. I couldn't help but notice again how refined Piers had become in my years away.

"Good afternoon."

Society had never considered him to be naturally handsome, his features a tad unremarkable, his mannerisms a bit clumsy at times; however, when he smiled, I mean really smiled, he possessed the momentary ability to capture one's attention. I'd tried to put my finger on his allure years ago with little luck. There was just something about his face when it changed. I found myself smiling back.

He accepted his hat and gloves from a waiting servant, and I made my way to join him at the open front door. Beyond the portico stood the waiting curricle, and I cast a questioning look back. "I didn't know you intended to drive."

We exited the house and he crossed in front of me, maneuvering into place to assist me into the vehicle. "It is a lovely day, and I'd much rather drive than ride. What do you think? You'll not catch a chill on the return trip?"

"I have my pelisse. I think a curricle ride sounds delightful."

I accepted his outstretched hand and mounted the steps up and over the large wheel of the vehicle, where I settled into a long black leather seat. Piers rounded the equipage and swung into his place at my side.

He squared his polished boots on the floor and secured the ribbons, offering me a quick glance before flicking the reins. The vehicle swayed into motion with a lurch, and I gripped the side of the carriage.

Piers's curricle proved well-sprung, and as we rounded the front drive and began our way down the long road that led out of Loxby, he seemed to relax at my side. The sun was balmy on my skin, and it took me all of three seconds before I found myself drifting back into the past—to the last time Piers and I went driving. I'd been so excited to have a few precious moments alone with him, the chance to sit close, the delicious possibility of more.

I stared down at my lap. How much had changed since then. Today there was a good six inches between us—six inches of impenetrable hurt and shame, an invisible wall we would be fools to cross again. So why did every inch of my being want to do just that?

Piers caught me staring at the bench. "I must confess, I selected this carriage with the intent purpose of speaking with you alone."

"Oh?" The spring wind was a fragrant one and bluebells littered the roadside. I breathed them in, hoping to control my heart rate. "I'm glad you did."

He smiled, prodding the butterflies in my stomach to life.

Again I took a deep breath. "I have some things to tell you too, but you first."

He stared down the road for a long second, a curious wrinkle to his brow. "I wouldn't normally discuss such a topic with a lady, but you were present at the, uh, challenge."

"You mean of the duel with Lord Kendal." I folded my hands in my lap, focusing my gaze on my fingers.

"Yes." He slowed the horses so he could steal a glance at my face. "I'm sure the murder has kept him busy thus far. He would not be so foolish to meet me with the authorities crawling all over Whitecaster Hall."

"Then you still intend to—"

"See it through?" He sighed. "Certainly I do."

"That's not what I was going to say. I was simply wondering what the arrangements were going to be . . . What you had chosen to use."

He kept his focus on the road. "It shall be pistols, as I've heard Lord Kendal is deadly with a blade. Though I've trained with a sword, I would be hard-pressed to call my skills refined."

"You always had your nose in a book, no time for anything else. You were busy preparing to apply for a fellowship in botany."

A momentary pause. "You remember that?"

"Why wouldn't I?"

The curricle swayed as we rounded the corner, but Piers fell silent.

My mouth slipped open. "You never did apply, did you?"

He made no movement, but I knew my words had affected him. "Life took me on a very different journey."

"It has a way of doing that."

He ran the ribbons through his gloved fingers. "What I wanted to tell you is that I've gone ahead and sent my seconds to meet with Lord Kendal's. I hope to have this business over and done with as soon as we're able to."

"Who did you arrange to second you?"

"Avery of course, and Tony Shaw. It's the best I could do on short notice." He chuckled. "It's not all that important really. I'm planning to delope."

"And Lord Kendal, will he shoot into the air as well?"

"I doubt it." Sarcasm tinted his voice.

"Then you simply plan to stand there and take the bullet?"

He shrugged. "What other choice do I have?" His fingers clenched the ribbons, then relaxed. "I just wanted you to know . . . in case something happened. I'll need you to look after my father and mother. Avery will have a difficult time of it."

"Don't say that, Piers. I know you'll come back." The muscles in my back stiffened as I imagined Mrs. Cavanagh learning of Piers's injury or worse. Regardless of how she acted, it would devastate her. And me. I watched the trees as they passed by to keep my worries at bay.

"Speaking of your mother, I had a rather peculiar conversation with her today. She seemed relieved by Miles Lacy's death."

The carriage rattled onto the bridge over the River Sternway, the horses' hooves echoing off the ancient stones. The oak trees were larger here, stretching their gnarled branches over the bridge's exit, their roots dipping deep into the hillside to produce the massive plants.

The carriage was still shifting in the shadows when Piers turned to me. "My mother is a complicated creature. I will not claim to understand her, but I know she cares for Seline. Her thoughts become scattered when she's nervous."

"Or perhaps afraid?"

"Well, yes."

The grove of trees broke at the base of a slight incline, and green grass lay as carpet over the slopes.

I leaned forward to see as far as I could across the horizon. "I'm anxious to see Grovesly again. We must be getting close."

"The outer gates are just over that hill."

There within the slight valley I caught a glimpse of Tony's ancestral home. The redbricked structure graced the manicured lawns like a perfectly planted flower, its vast white chimneys pointing to the heavens like petals and the entire affair mirrored on the surface of a motionless lake.

I smiled. "It's just as beautiful as I remembered."

Traversing the long drive took several minutes. Finally we coasted to a halt before the grand front entrance where a cluster of blue-liveried servants were prompt to meet us.

We alighted from the curricle and were shown through a small receiving area. Down a long hall and around the corner, we were deposited in a salon of pale green walls and gilded moldings to await our host.

I wandered to the fireplace at the center of the long wall, running my fingers over the familiar intricate surround, which displayed two female figurines, arms stretched upward to support the mantel.

It wasn't long before Tony barreled into the room on the whiff of a laugh. He stopped just inside the door, turning to speak at the last second to someone behind him. "Tea and cake, if you please."

He crossed the room, stopping but a few feet in front of us, the genial smile he wore so well fixed on his face. He looked far more at home at his own estate.

"It's an honor to have you both to Grovesly." He spoke easily enough, but I noticed a slight hesitation in his voice, or was it merely a weary remnant of the previous few days? It was he who had stumbled upon the body of Miles Lacy, after all.

"Your home is just as lovely as I remember it." I moved to take a seat on a nearby sofa, which encouraged the gentlemen to be seated as well.

Piers, it seemed, had no time for small talk. "I'm going to be straight with you, Tony. We've come for answers. Miles Lacy is dead, and though we've kept it somewhat a secret that Seline's been missing since the night she had an argument with Lord Kendal at Kinwich Abbey, we can do so no longer."

Tony dipped his chin prettily enough and covered his mouth with his hand, but there was no denying the fact that he already knew of Seline's disappearance.

Piers recounted what we knew so far as Tony sat stoically rubbing his chin. "I'll do all I can to help of course, but I have little information to share with you about that night. I was the first one to leave, after all."

"Then we should start with Miles Lacy. He was mentioned in Seline's note, which we now believe was forged. They were supposed to have eloped, but clearly they did not."

His face blanched, and he shrugged defensively. "I never met the fellow in my life before I found his dead body lying behind Kendal's stables."

"What exactly happened the day of the murder?"

Tony's knuckles whitened on the armrest. "I promised Kendal I'd overnight in the stables. Lot of money was riding on that blasted curricle race. I'd never seen anything like it." He scrunched his lips up. "I'm sure everyone is in a pucker since it had to be postponed due to the murder. I don't even know if Kendal ever means to have the race now. If he doesn't . . . Have you been by London to see the book at White's?"

"No, but Avery made some offhand comment about there being quite a few bets."

"And then there were so many people at Whitecaster for the engagement ball. I got a little nervous myself. Thought it might be best to watch over Kendal's horses. When I was asked to give him a small token of luck from Hugh, I only left for a moment."

"So Hugh was there at the stables?"

"Just for a short time to make sure everything was ready. I sent him home at once. He didn't look well."

Piers nodded. "Then what happened?"

"I found Kendal in the ballroom and gave him the letter. Then I returned to the stables." Tony's eyes glazed over. "When I entered, it was eerily quiet. I found out later the grooms had gathered upstairs to enjoy some ale. I intended to walk straight to Kendal's private stall, but a groom drew my attention out the window. That's where I found Miles, flat on his back in a grove of trees, his skull broken, blood everywhere . . ." Tony glanced at me. "Forgive me, Charity, I don't mean to be gauche."

Piers didn't flinch. "Then he was hit over the head. But why on earth was he at Whitecaster Hall in the first place?"

I startled both gentlemen as I spoke. "I may be able to shed some light on Miles's presence there. You see, Mr. Lacy received a letter from Miles a few days ago." I had their attention now. "He told his uncle that he'd taken a job—a lucrative one—at Whitecaster Hall."

I wasn't prepared for the wide eyes Piers turned on me, nor the unease on Tony's face. I wish I'd had a moment to tell Piers about my secret meeting with Mr. Lacy.

Piers was clearly off stride. "When did you speak with Mr. Lacy?"

I turned first to Tony then back to Piers. "I'm so sorry. I should have found a way to tell you before now, but Mr. Lacy sent me a note before we left Loxby the night of the dance. I ended up meeting him at the stables, where he asked me to speak with his nephew at Whitecaster, to try to talk some sense into him. He wanted Miles to leave the country as they'd arranged with Mr. Cavanagh. He thought Miles might be in something deep."

Tony rested his elbows on his knees. "I hesitate to speak, but so much has happened . . ." He ran his hand down his face. "Apparently Miles is the one Kendal contracted to rig the curricle race."

Piers remained oddly silent for a long moment. "You were all in on the sabotage?"

"Listen, Piers, don't blame Avery. It was Hugh's dratted idea, and he would broker no opposition."

"What happened after we left the stables that night?"

Tony shook his head. "Kendal was shocked, barking out all kinds of orders. It was mayhem, I tell you, servants running in every direction. I was eventually sent to fetch the magistrate."

Piers drummed his fingers on his leg. "Tell me about the Gormogons."

Tony nearly fell out of his chair.

Piers didn't flinch. "I followed the three of you to the ruins of the abbey. You were talking about the curricle race. What does one have to do with the other?"

Tony squirmed in his chair. "I don't know what you're talking about."

"Don't play coy with me. We've been friends our whole lives. If you think I can't tell when you're sporting a lie, you will be gravely disappointed. Besides, Avery has already revealed a great deal."

"Avery, huh? Hugh will have his head."

Piers sat forward. "Then it was Hugh who revived the Gormogons?"

"Couldn't say. I'm not a charter member."

A slight smile creased Piers's lips. Unwittingly Tony had just confirmed what we'd wondered since finding the medallion—the group was indeed connected in some way to the one Mr. Cavanagh had been a part of.

An innocent diversion of a group of friends? Possibly. That's certainly what Avery wanted us to believe, but a man was now dead and my friend missing. Everything took on a more sinister tone.

Piers angled his chin. "Then tell me this, Tony. When Kendal was flat on his back in the garden, I ran across a particular note—the one you delivered, no doubt." Piers couldn't stop a slight smile. "Within the text were the words *loyalty pledge*. I saw something similar in a book my father keeps hidden in our library. Perhaps you can save me the trouble of ferreting it back out. What does the term mean within the Gormogons?"

"You opened Kendal's letter?"

Piers lifted his eyebrows. "The one Hugh brought you, correct?"

Tony slapped his leg. "Dash it all, Cavanagh! You were always too clever for your own good. Listen, you two, you can stop your games. I'll tell you what I know, but it isn't much.

"I joined the group on a whim. Actually, Hugh got me involved. I had a little trouble with a lady friend of mine, you see." He adjusted his collar. "I agreed to pledge myself to the betterment of the society and my troubles went away. Simple as that."

"How did you pledge yourself?"

"Each Gormogon member holds a damaging secret provided to them by a new member. Except for me, because I was the last one to join our small party. Avery holds my pledge and Kendal has Hugh's. I know that. The secret has to be of great importance, evidence that would cost the person his livelihood, standing in society, or worse. Avery is my 'secret bearer.' If I betray the group in any way, he can choose to expose my secret." Tony ran his hand along his forehead. "Which is entirely possible since I've told you both all of this."

Piers shook his head. "With my father a former member and my brother involved, you can hardly be found liable."

I leaned in. "What if a person wants to join, and they don't have a secret?"

Tony dipped his chin. "Everyone has a secret."

My chest felt heavy, and I looked away, a mix of shock and embarrassment pumping through my veins. Tony was right in a way. Even I had a secret.

I only hoped one of the gentlemen didn't see through the unease crawling across my face. To my great relief, neither said a word. That is, not until Piers and I were alone in the curricle on the road back to Loxby.

He slowed the horses to a walk, then halted them altogether beneath the sweeping branches of a nearby elm. He said nothing at first.

The sun had only intensified over the hour we'd been at Grovesly, and I retrieved my fan from my reticule. "Why have we stopped?"

"You looked a little green back there."

I gave a rather unconvincing laugh. "I don't know what you mean."

A knit formed on his brow. "You're a puzzle to me in so many ways, Charity. You always have been. When you were young, I thought you quiet and shy, then came to learn you were full of imagination and curiosity. You were the only one who would listen to my lectures about the plants in the garden. You came nearly every afternoon to visit Seline, yet more often than not I found you wandering my garden alone. Were you always waiting for *me*?"

My face felt impossibly hot. "You know I was. You were a breath of fresh air for a young lady exhausted by the tedious instructions of watercolor. I will never be an artist."

"And then we met that day on the eastern slope. You remember, you told me you'd escaped your governess. I can still see every detail of what you wore, how your arms swung at your sides. You'd found an orange, if I remember right, and you vowed to grow a tree from one of the seeds. You were relishing every minute of freedom. I was intrigued. I was lost." He looked up. "I'd never felt anything like it before."

"That was the day you gave me one of your flower drawings for the first time."

"We had precious little time to make sense of what happened between us. And then you were gone, and my entire world turned upside down."

I glanced up. "And then you wrote that letter."

"Yes, I did." He swallowed hard. "After everything that happened with Lord Kendal, I believed at the time it was best if I removed myself from your life. Your brother certainly thought so. But I want you to know, now I understand what a terrible mistake that was. I fear your adjustment to Ceylon could not have gone smoothly. Seline read me your first few letters. Though I struggled to do so, I could not hear you in them. They felt like nothing but empty words."

He ran his hand down his face. "Earlier today I saw you flinch when Tony mentioned secrets, and I shan't pry; however, I want you to know that I will always stand your friend." He shook his head. "I guess what I mean to say, rather badly mind you, is that I have no intention of abandoning you again. We practically grew up together. I'll always care for you."

I raised my eyebrows. "Like a sister?"

He chuckled beneath his breath. "All right, not precisely like a sister."

Everything I thought I knew, all my plans, all my intentions fell about me like frozen rain, little ice pellets that scattered on the flagstones in all directions. I wasn't ready to tell anyone my story, but Piers wasn't just anyone, was he?

As if he followed my thoughts, he slid his hand closer to mine on the bench, carefully extending his pinky finger beneath mine. I couldn't speak or move.

A subtle gesture, but the ramifications were endless.

My heart quivered as a delicate gust of wind sent my bonnet ribbons fluttering across my gown.

Piers knew me better than anyone, but I couldn't focus, not with his hand so utterly warm against mine. My head swelled with dizziness, my mouth went dry. He wanted me to take his hand. But I couldn't do it. I just couldn't do it.

What if I panicked? What if I pushed him away when I needed him the most? I lowered my head as the true depths of my fears and isolation took shape in my mind. It wasn't Piers I was afraid of—it was me.

CHAPTER 23

Piers said little on the remaining carriage ride back to Loxby, though he acted normal enough. Perhaps I'd read too far into his innocent gesture in the first place. Intimacy had always come naturally with us. It was a kind move he'd intended for a friend . . . Nothing more—an olive branch, so to speak.

At least that's what I told myself as I was forced to take his hand while he helped me out of the curricle, and then again when he delayed me on the front drive. "Will you be willing to accompany me back to Rushridge? After what Tony said about Hugh coming to Whitecaster, we have no choice but to approach Hugh again."

"When do you plan to go?"

"Tomorrow if at all possible."

I looked away, my gaze following the sweep of the horizon, the subtle shades of an evening preparing to rest. "I'm afraid I've sorely neglected your mother and father. What they must think of me, I cannot guess."

He paused. "I'll be happy to wait for you if you so desire, but if you'd rather I go alone, I can certainly do that as well." He gave me something of a smile, but it wasn't an easy one. The tenuous nature of our friendship hung so delicately in the balance.

I did my best to appear unfazed. "Wait for me."

It was an innocent enough response, but the way Piers's face changed made me acutely aware of the bond we'd forged in the past and how those precious moments would affect us forever.

He gave me a little nod, doing his best to lighten the mood. "Two days, then. In the meantime, I certainly have estate business I've been avoiding. I'll send Hugh a letter to expect us."

"Thank you."

Piers moved to walk away, but I grabbed his arm. "Seline will appreciate all you're doing to help her."

He paused to roll a stray piece of gravel back into place with the toe of his boot, and then his face fell. "Assuming she's still alive to thank me."

Piers's ominous words followed me throughout the evening and into the next day, like a vicious specter hovering constantly over my head, threatening to descend at any moment and expose that which I feared the most. A tremor flashed across my skin as I glanced at the small casement clock in my bedchamber, the roots of fear plunging ever deeper into my heart. With every passing day, the likelihood of finding Seline alive slipped farther and farther away.

Glad no one was present to read my thoughts, I rested my hand on Mr. Cavanagh's door latch. The very decision to stay at Loxby had been difficult enough, but now things had taken a dark turn and I had been left to drown in a muddy lake.

Mr. Cavanagh's visits proved to be the only respite I got from the overwhelming anticipation of the household.

Every last person was awaiting something. Mrs. Cavanagh, a

letter from Charles; Piers, his duel with Lord Kendal; Avery, the curricle race; and all of us most of all waiting desperately for a word about Seline. I couldn't help but wonder how long it would be before someone reached their breaking point.

Carefully pushing into the room, I was a little surprised to find Mrs. Cavanagh at his bedside. She seemed a bit shaken by my sudden arrival, for she dropped her sewing onto the floor and fumbled rather dramatically to retrieve it.

Though my eyes went straight to the bed, I was equally startled to find Mr. Cavanagh seated in a large wingback chair near the fireplace, his cane gripped in one hand, the other busy patting the armrest of the chair. "What do you think, Miss Halliwell? I've managed two hours today."

I darted Mrs. Cavanagh a worried look, then turned back to Mr. Cavanagh. "That's wonderful."

A smile spread across his face and I knew I'd made the right decision to come.

"Won't you join me by the fire for a coze?"

I forced my legs to carry me across the rug to his side, knelt to kiss his hand, and took a seat in a nearby chair. Though I could feel Mrs. Cavanagh's eyes on me, I kept my voice light. "How did you know it was me at the door?"

He folded his hands in his lap. "You have a nervous little twitter to your steps, my dear. I hadn't noticed it before, but I certainly do now." He rubbed his whiskered chin. "What has kept you away the last few days? I've waited for you to come every afternoon."

"I'm afraid that's my fault." Piers's deep voice startled me, and I turned to see him waltz into the room.

Mr. Cavanagh had always had a hearty laugh, and it slowed my pounding heart. He grasped the hand Piers laid on his shoulder.

"Here I lie day after day with not a single visitor, and then everyone arrives at once. Good afternoon, son."

Piers seemed a bit lost for words, his eyes tracking mine as he neared the fireplace. "I didn't mean to intrude. I merely came to discuss repairs, but I can see now that you are more pleasantly engaged."

"Don't run away, boy. I'm glad you've come."

There was a shuffle at the back of the room as Mrs. Cavanagh flew to her feet, and her voice came out a bit jarring as she huffed, "You may take my chair, Piers. I have a basket of letters to attend to."

I waited to see if Mr. Cavanagh meant to delay her, but he seemed only too pleased to have us to himself. A flounce of muslin, an irritated sigh, and the couple's connecting room door slammed shut.

Mr. Cavanagh crossed his legs, an expression of derision darkening his features. "Mrs. Cavanagh thinks I know nothing, living as I do in this room day after day." He hesitated a moment, then ticked his finger back and forth between Piers and me as if he could see us sitting there. "Now tell me, when's the wedding?"

A rock hit my stomach, and Piers coughed. "What wedding?"

"Why, Miss Gervey and Lord Kendal's of course. Who else could I mean?"

Piers's eyebrows slanted upward as he looked away, a whisper on his breath. "Who else indeed?" Then, for his father's benefit, he said, "We've not had our invitation as of yet, but the banns have been read." Piers's voice sounded hollow as he grappled to fill the silence. "It shouldn't be long now."

"Ah." His father made a show of nodding. "I hope your mother hasn't quibbled with you about Miss Gervey, for I thought her a silly little chit who was always beneath your notice."

A strange smile crossed Piers's face. "We never were suited

for one another, were we? Mother should have seen that from the start."

Having stumbled all too awkwardly into a private conversation, I began to wonder if the two of them had forgotten I was there, which is precisely when Piers gestured to me with his chin. "There was something else I came to speak with you about today, Father, and I hope you won't take my mentioning it amiss. You see, Miss Halliwell and I stumbled upon an old book of yours in the library."

Mr. Cavanagh shifted in his seat. "Oh?"

"It contained information about the Gormogon's society you were once a part of. Do you remember telling me about your secret group?"

Something flashed in those lifeless eyes. "My dear boy, I'd forgotten all about that book, but yes, I remember discussing it with you and Avery long ago. What brings that to your mind now?"

"Several things actually. First, answer me this: the society was disbanded in 1799, is that correct?"

He was slow to nod. "As I understand it, yes."

I inched forward in my seat. "A secret society? Will you tell me about it?"

Mr. Cavanagh stifled a small chuckle. "Not a topic for a young lady, I'm afraid."

I feigned irritation. "Well, since it was disbanded long ago, can you at least tell us what the society was for? If it's not too impolitic, that is."

A smile joined the wrinkles on Mr. Cavanagh's chin. "The Ancient Noble Order of the Gormogons was never impolitic, my dear." He rested his head on his hand. "The society was brought over to Britain from China, but it was really a Jesuit scheme to establish a Jacobite club. The members of my particular sect, however, weren't Jacobites at all." A raspy laugh. "No, we simply enjoyed ridiculing the Freemasons . . . and the government at times." Then his face grew serious. "Regardless of our affiliations, joining was a serious matter, and every member gladly did so to seek justice for the people of Britain. Such a commitment was not taken lightly."

Piers stood, his brow tight, before pacing to the window. "Have you heard from any of the former members of late?"

"Not at all. I suppose they've all moved on with their lives. The society was for young, healthy men, not gentlemen in their dotage. I daresay my friends and I would make a poor set of revolutionaries now." Mr. Cavanagh turned his attention back to me. "Did you bring a book to read to me today?"

Caught off guard by the sudden change of subject, it took me a moment to answer. "I did actually. I found a copy of *The Monk* by Matthew Lewis."

Piers cleared his throat, darting me a look. "Apropos, I daresay." Piers had not finished his questioning, but we both knew Mr. Cavanagh had ended any further conversation on the subject.

I attempted a slight shift. "I must confess, I've never read *The Monk*, but the other day Piers reminded me about the stories you used to tell us as children—to keep us away from the remains of Kinwich Abbey. I found the book in your library earlier today. An inspiration perhaps?"

Mr. Cavanagh dipped his chin. "I'd forgotten all about that silly novel. It's been some time since I read *The Monk*, but if my memory serves, I must warn you that it has a decided horror aspect to it."

Piers smiled as he paced back to the fireplace. "Dare you proceed, Miss Halliwell? Doing so might keep you up at night—with that view of the abbey from your window."

"I've never been one of the simpering females I detest." I settled the book on my lap and opened the cover. I tempered my voice. "What do you think, Mr. Cavanagh? Shall we proceed?"

"I believe so, but pull the bell, my dear, if you would. I'd prefer to move back to my bed. I've had enough sitting up for one day."

Piers took a step toward the door. "If the two of you will excuse me, I must beg my leave. Father, I shall visit you again before nightfall to discuss the business I came about. Though I'd enjoy doing so, I haven't the time to sit and listen to *The Monk*."

Though I thought him curiously anxious to leave, Piers bent down to my ear on his way to the door, his voice a fervent whisper. "Rose garden. One hour. Understand?"

I looked up helplessly, and he raised his eyebrows.

Caught in his pointed gaze, I couldn't help but nod. If Piers requested to see me, I would always go.

I found him an hour later as planned in the far section of the garden where we used to meet in our youth. He stood with his back to me, his arms resting on the trellised wall. Piers had always been a thinker, a student of the world before him, and I found his mind a restful one. When we were younger, I could watch him for hours as he drew every last detail of whatever small plant he was curious about at the time.

Today his focus was on the fields as the sun melted into a far hill, crafting rose-colored hues that swept across the clouds and the countryside below. Small insects glistened in the waning light, dipping in and out of the tall grass; the ruins of Kinwich Abbey stood artfully within the valley's thin mist.

Slowly I drew up beside him. "Beautiful."

He turned at once, surprise clearly written on his face. "I didn't hear you enter."

I motioned beyond the wall. "I found the sunset so reverent; I didn't want to disturb it."

"Gardens have always been a special place of mine . . . of ours, I mean." He glanced around. "I'm pleased to see the undergardener has done a fine job of keeping it up. The plants are healthy, the flowers as sweet as I remember."

"Have you a garden at your home in Liverpool?"

He relaxed into a sigh. "Indeed I do. I've spent years cultivating it as well as an orangery." His eyes found mine. "You'd love it. I know so much more about the plants since my studies. My current wilderness has a symmetry and beauty to it . . . I . . ." He tucked his hands in his pockets. "Standing here though, I think I realized something—something I've been searching for. My garden in Liverpool doesn't feel like home, not like this place."

My eyes misted, and I was forced to look away. I, too, was searching for a way back. "I understand what you mean. I may never see my childhood home again. Flitworth Manor is leased, but it almost doesn't matter. It was here at Loxby where the vast majority of my memories were formed—at least the ones I cherish today."

"For years I thought it best to stay away—from everyone in my life. But standing here, breathing in the world I left, I'm not so certain anymore."

Piers had always had depth to his thoughtful demeanor, unassuming mannerisms, careful words, but my mouth went dry as I raced to understand what he was discovering about himself and what he meant to do with it. "Then you plan to stay at Loxby indefinitely?"

He shrugged. "For the time being. I see now I've neglected not only my family but the estate as well . . . Among other things."

He took a step closer, feigning interest in a rosebush at my side.

The familiar rush of nerves splashed across my shoulders and trickled down my arms. We'd been so close before—sharing every part of our lives. Should I not tell him what animal lived in the shadows of my mind, what would always exist between us?

I glanced up to find him watching me. "Oh, Piers. How does one find their way back when they've lost so much of themselves along the way? It's like the whole world is blurry and no matter how hard I squint, I can't seem to see clearly."

He extended his arm slowly, carefully wrapping his fingers around mine. "I'm not certain anyone can go back, not really. It's more about finding a way to go on, to move forward, to trust that God will take something bad that has happened and work it for good." He stared down at our hands. "It doesn't mean the path will be easy. I just know now that I don't want to take it alone."

For a moment everything fell motionless, the warmth of the sun, the look in Piers's eyes, the living garden around us. Then a bird took flight from a nearby tree, rustling the branches, effectively snapping the spell.

The moment was lost.

I recovered my hand and moved to take a seat on the bench where I sat still for several seconds. When he said he didn't want to take the path alone, did he mean his family . . . or me?

Piers hesitated at the rosebush, a far-off look about his eyes. Then he walked over to join me on the bench. "Did you leave my father well earlier today? He seemed much improved this afternoon." Piers had regulated the sound of his voice, his lightened tone feeling almost foreign amid the murky waters of my turbulent emotions.

"I did, though he seemed a bit tired from my visit."

"I must admit, though I was hesitant at first for you to visit him, I do think your doing so has done him a deal of good. The doctors worry about him greatly. Avery has been forced to handle him with kid gloves, and now me. Particularly of late. Some days he can scarcely move from his bed." He took a deep breath. "I don't look forward to the day we must tell him about Miles's death . . . and what it must mean about Seline. I'm afraid the truth of what happened might very well push him over the edge. My father has fallen into bouts of reclusiveness, even before his accident. My mother always describes him as passionate. Passionately happy, passionately sad, fiercely loyal."

"He's lucky to have a son who cares so deeply for him."

Piers wiped a hand down his breeches. "My father and I have never been all that close. Years passed where we rarely exchanged more than two words with one another." He looked around. "Strange how things turn out so differently than planned. In a way, when I left for Liverpool I knew everyone would change while I was gone, but I never expected to return to this—Avery grown up, Seline disappeared, my father withering away. And you . . ." He shook his head. "Needless to say, I don't intend to let time pass me by again. Life is far too precious and short."

My ears buzzed. "What do you mean . . . *me*?"

He picked at the chipped paint on the bench. "Over the years I always imagined you married with children. I suppose I found it easier that way."

"Easier than . . . ?"

A second of stormy silence crept by as he stared at the far garden wall. "The terrible regret I experienced after losing you."

For years I'd thought of no one but myself—the painful dissolution of my dreams, the way I'd been forced to change, the scars that would never really heal. But in that vulnerable moment, it was as if I saw Piers for the first time or, more importantly, the hard iron bars of his cage. Such a solitary existence had demanded a toll.

"Piers . . ." Fear crept into my voice, but as I lifted my eyes to the one person who had always understood me, I was compelled to speak. "Something happened to me in Ceylon."

Slowly, he turned to face me, his gaze sharp as a knife. "What do you mean?"

I felt my hands trembling in my lap and stood to shake them out. "There was a man . . . a groom of one of the British government officials . . . He followed me into the tea fields . . . It was dark . . . We were alone." Tears stole my voice as my throat grew so thick I could scarcely swallow.

Piers flew to his feet and grasped my shoulders, gently but willfully forcing me to face him. "What happened?" His voice was a whispered mix of pity and dread.

"Oh, Piers, he didn't take everything, but at the same time he did. Please don't make me say it aloud."

His arms went lifeless at his sides as he fought to make sense of what I'd revealed. "I knew something was wrong. I've felt it since I arrived. Darling, I—"

We both froze, as he'd not used the term of endearment since before I left for Ceylon. An accident of course. But what had brought it to his mind now?

I stared into those familiar blue eyes, glossy with unshed tears, and my heart contracted. Piers Cavanagh, the man I'd loved, then loathed, but never stopped thinking about, felt sorry for me. He'd never look at me the same way again, not as an ardent suitor or as a close friend. I was a victim now, damaged goods—another person in his life whom he must handle with kid gloves.

It was all I could do to continue. "I-I never meant to tell you, certainly not in this way. I don't even know what you thought or felt about me two minutes ago. I only know where I left my heart. Rest assured, it is not your public scandal ensuring nothing will ever happen between us; it is my private one."

My emotions hit a boiling point, and I whirled away, my shoulders careening into the plants as I escaped to the house. I'd learned long ago it was best to cry in private. But as I fled the garden, I found myself compelled to take one last look back.

I had known from the start there would be no chance of romance between the two of us; however, no one could have prepared me for how I would feel when I saw the expression on Piers's face—the moment he realized the same thing.

CHAPTER 24

I lay down to sleep that night trapped within a body that didn't feel like my own. It had all the right moving parts of course, but as I slid the silky covers along my skin, I barely felt them.

Piers knew everything now.

I stared at the shadowed beams in the ceiling as a crack of thunder rattled the windowpane. The whir of heavy rain followed all too quickly, filling my bedchamber with an uncomfortable hum as the angry gusts beat against the walls.

I wasn't afraid, not exactly, but each rolling pound of thunder sent my muscles twitching, the very fabric of the storm a breathing reminder of my unsettled mind. I buried my head in my pillow. Why had I ever thought to come to Loxby Manor? I'd spoken with such authority to my mother, declaring my return to East Whitloe would be a haven. At the time I believed Loxby the only place I could find what I'd lost in the tea fields of Ceylon—the promise of hope.

But my journey back to Britain had not gone as planned.

Searching for Seline had driven Piers and me round and round in circles, and it would be nothing but painful to have to face him now. I'd delayed my search for a governess position for too long. It was time to start looking at options. Perhaps Mrs. Cavanagh might know of a family. In the morning I would finally broach the subject with her.

However, when I descended the stairs the following day and entered the drawing room expecting to find her present, I was met instead by an argument between Avery and Piers. I checked at the doorway, immediately thinking better of entering, but Avery had already seen me.

"Charity." He motioned me into the room. "You are just the person to talk some sense into my brother."

I'm certain my face must have blanched, for a tingle spread across my cheeks. I had to fight hard to avoid Piers's steady gaze.

Avery didn't bat an eye. "Piers had the gall to suggest I forgo joining the two of you on your visit to Rushridge. Believe you me, I know what lurks beyond such a suggestion. He only means to keep me away from Priscilla, and I won't stand for it." He crossed his arms. "And after I kept your prior relationship a secret. It's the outside of enough."

Shock unhinged my tongue. "You mean you knew . . . about us?"

"Well, of course I did. And I wasn't the only one. Seline and I had the two of you pegged months before I happened upon you in that alcove."

My head felt light, my eyes a blur. Avery had seen the kiss. I reached for the back of a chair to steady myself.

Piers's voice came out cool and calculated. "That's enough, Avery. You needn't be crass."

Avery huffed as he turned back to me, belatedly reading the expression on my face. "I beg your pardon, Charity, but you understand, don't you? I've known Priscilla for years. She has a way of getting under my skin, and I can't seem to shake her. In fact, I don't mean to. I don't care what Mother says. I think we suit quite well."

I gave him a weak smile. "If only the world were as simple as that—a place where you could follow your heart free of all the complications that come with it." I was careful not to look at Piers. I could only guess what was churning in his mind.

Avery seemed a bit put off, stomping to the door to open it. "Well, at any rate, I'm coming with you today whether you two like it or not. We can ponder the intricacies of the heart as well as all the other secrets of the universe another time."

We opted for horseback on our journey to Rushridge, and I must say, I did tolerably well avoiding any intimate moments with Piers both in the stables as well as the open fields. Every fiber of my being wanted to know what he thought of my confession, but I'd grown tired of the burden of hidden pain.

With what little interaction we did share, I found Piers decidedly more subdued, but with Avery present the stifling embarrassment or the pitiful looks I'd fully expected never really materialized. We were all just childhood friends set out on one of our adventures.

The previous night's torrential storms had vanished with the dawn, leaving a bright sun amid a blue, cloudless sky. I took a deep breath, my gaze wandering the dithered valley to the crisscrossing hedgerows and beyond. For the first time in as long as I could remember, an inkling of peace had found its way into my heart. Perhaps telling someone had its merits after all.

If only Seline were with us.

Her absence was the one blight on the perfectly beautiful morning. Piers must have been watching me, because his voice felt like the delicate strokes of a painter, an omniscient one. "Seline would have loved to be here with us."

"How did you know I was thinking of her?"

"I suppose because I am always doing so myself."

Avery had drifted a little ahead, and I moved to urge Jewel forward when Piers's arm shot out, his fingers curling around my reins. "Charity, we didn't get a chance to finish our discussion yesterday. I'd hoped to have a moment of privacy with you . . ."

"I said all I mean to."

"Well, I didn't."

I closed my eyes. "Not here, Piers. Please."

There was an edge to his voice I couldn't place, but his eyes were soft. "Another time, then?"

I was spared an answer by Avery's startled shout. Piers and I jerked our attention toward a small grove of trees several yards off the roadway. Avery had dismounted his horse and was on his hands and knees. "Piers, come at once! Oh God, no!"

Piers spurred Gypsy forward, and I followed as quickly as I could. He was off the horse's back in seconds, rushing to Avery's side. He, too, dropped to the ground before clawing at the dirt, his hands feverish at Avery's side.

He must have heard my approach as his head shot up. "Don't come any closer!"

"What is it?"

Avery nodded and Piers pushed to his feet before stalking to the side of my horse. His hands were at my waist, and I slipped onto the ground.

His face was bereft of life, his eyes stone-cold. His voice came out more like that of a ghost than a man. "I've feared for some time this day was coming, but I never could really make myself believe it possible . . ."

Coils of ice wrapped my heart as I took a closer look at Avery's desperate hands and the tears pouring down his face. "No!"

"It's Seline." Piers shook his head achingly slow. "Someone buried her battered body in a shallow grave. The heavy rains last night must have washed away some of the earth, exposing a piece of her gown."

Disbelief still prowled my mind. "Are you certain?"

He closed his eyes for a long moment. "Quite certain, I'm afraid."

Carefully I reached for his gloved hands, which were wet and muddy from the ground. "How?"

His voice was choked by emotion and he hesitated to answer, letting out a ragged breath. "It looks as if she was hit over the head." He squeezed my fingers, pain so evident in his eyes. "Are you well enough to ride for Rushridge? It's just over that rise. I dare not leave Avery in such a state. Priscilla will be there."

All I wanted to do was help him somehow. "My legs are a bit weak, but I can manage."

Almost mindlessly he cupped his hands, and I placed my boot into his waiting fingers. I was thrust back onto Jewel and sent cantering down the road before I had much of a chance to process the last few unthinkable minutes. But as I steered my horse through Rushridge's elaborate gate, it hit me all at once.

Seline was gone. Dead. Here I'd been worried about my own problems when my dearest friend had been . . . What?

Murdered? My chest tightened. Someone had placed her body so carelessly in that grave—on Hugh Daunt's property, no less. Suppositions flashed through my mind until I could bear to think of them no longer. All I knew was Hugh must know something, and I was riding alone to his very doorstep.

Priscilla was fetched from her room straightaway and made quick work of sending a servant to inform the authorities about Seline's death. After several seconds of disordered pacing, she took a seat beside me on the sofa, oddly undecided about whether we should tell Hugh.

I was still nursing quite a range of shock when I rounded on her. "Don't be ridiculous. Hugh must be appraised of the situation and at once."

She grimaced, the delicate lines on her face pulling tight. "I suppose you're in the right of it, but I shudder to think what such appalling news will do to him."

"Do to him?" Hugh edged into the room, having caught the last breath of our tense conversation.

Priscilla flew to her feet, mumbling as she raced across the room, roused into fawning all over him.

Some part of what we were discussing must have shown on our faces, for Hugh would have none of Priscilla, plunging his hand through his hair. "Quit your prattling and tell me what the devil is going on."

Priscilla cast me a desperate look, and I moved to intercept. "Please, come into the room and sit down, Hugh. There is something you must know, and it will be difficult to hear."

I watched him closely, anxious to soften the blow in some way, but as I picked my way through the words to use, I had a strange thought. Would Hugh be as distraught by the news of Seline's death as we all thought he would? Though Priscilla had assured me he was teetering on the brink of madness, I wasn't entirely sure I agreed with her.

He took a seat, then motioned with his hand. "Well, get on with it."

"It's about Seline." I slowed my speech to give him time to process all I was about to reveal. "We haven't told anyone, but she's been missing since the night she had the argument with Lord Kendal at Kinwich Abbey. A note was found that same night detailing how she'd run off to Gretna Green, which we all believed at first. We had hoped to keep her reputation intact . . . Last night's storm washed away some of the earth as well as a great many of our questions. We discovered her . . . moments ago in a shallow grave." I lifted my eyebrows. "On your estate."

He seemed utterly lost as his gaze searched the floor, a myriad of emotions flashing in and out of his harried eyes. Finally his hand crept to his mouth. "You mean to tell me . . . Seline is dead?"

"And has been these past few weeks."

I'd had time to consider the possibility of something terrible happening since the night Seline disappeared, but Hugh had been wholly unprepared for the news. He slumped into his chair, covering his face with his hands. "How could this have happened?"

"I hoped you could shed some light on the situation. Seline must have come to Rushridge after your society meeting at the abbey. Did you speak with her? Did you see her?"

"I-I didn't get the chance." Slowly, methodically, he looked up to meet my eyes. We stared at each other for what felt like a full minute. At length he spoke, his voice altogether different. "Are you accusing me of something?"

Priscilla rushed to his side and knelt on the carpet. "Don't be ridiculous. We're both just terribly concerned about what happened. And about you. Perhaps you should—"

Hugh jumped up and Priscilla was thrust backward.

"Where will I find this grave?"

"Off the main estate road. Piers and Avery are there now. The authorities will be on your property shortly." My words felt strange as they left my mouth. It was as if I'd wandered into a dreamland where all my childhood acquaintances had elevated themselves to villains of their own stories. Well, sort of. Hugh was brass and cold, morose at times, but after witnessing his reaction moments ago, I didn't think him involved in Seline's death.

He paced from the room without looking back, and as with Priscilla, a fresh wave of anxiety washed over me. How would he handle seeing her body? Thank goodness Piers would be there.

Priscilla saw her brother to the door, then made her way back to the sofa and slid down beside me. "I didn't know Seline all that well. A part of me hated her for what she did to Hugh, but I never would have wished her harm."

Priscilla's voice grated against my ears, the numb shock of Seline's death melting whatever resilience I'd been able to manage thus far. However, something she said caught my attention. "What exactly did Seline *do* to Hugh?"

She let out a long sigh. "Hugh spoke of some kind of agreement between them. He actually thought she meant to marry him someday. I overheard him and Tony talking about it last night. They were angry and didn't know I'd come down to the kitchens for some food. I couldn't help but listen."

Interesting. "What did they say?"

She toyed with the edge of her lip. "I probably shouldn't repeat it. Hugh would have my head for doing so, but I don't want you to think he played any part in Seline's death." She folded her hands in her lap. "Seline's absence will be a terrible wound for him. I only hope he may find a way to come about."

She took a glance at the door, and I nodded for her to go on. Now was not the time for secrets.

"Tony was saying something about how Hugh had tried to leave. I can only assume he meant Seline, because he went right into discussing a curricle race. Apparently Hugh bet a great deal of money on the outcome. Hugh said that once he had given Seline his name, he could find a way out."

I sat back. "A way out?"

"That's what he said. I assume he means the crushing debt we've been living with for the last few years."

"But Seline doesn't have a large dowry."

"No, and I also don't believe for one second that she ever really considered marrying Hugh. She did revel in his attentions, but I daresay she's the biggest flirt I've ever known." Priscilla's hand flew to her mouth. "Oh dear, I shouldn't have said that. I never meant to disparage the dead." She closed her eyes. "I still can't believe she's really gone. She had that boisterous personality that no one could ever believe extinguished." Her icy fingers curled around mine. "How did she die?"

It took me a moment to produce the words burning on my tongue. "She suffered a blow to the head. We can only assume that is what killed her."

"A blow to the head?" Her whispered words echoed my own astonishment. Then a wrinkle formed on Priscilla's brow. "I must say, that does make me think of something." Her eyes flit about the room. "You know, the night Hugh went to the abbey I went looking for him. I even walked to the stables to see if his horse was indeed gone."

"And was it?"

"Well, yes, he'd taken it with him. But on my way back to the house, I heard a scuffle then the pounding of horses' hooves. I thought it was Hugh returning home, but he didn't appear like I thought he would. I started toward the main road to intercept him, but it was the strangest thing. I saw a shadow heading the opposite direction."

"A person? What did they look like?"

"I'm fairly certain it was a man. Well, I'm partially certain. The figure was a long way away and moving fast. Then Hugh arrived. We walked back to the house together, and I thought no more about it." She leaned forward, her eyes growing wide as saucers. "You don't think we were a few yards away from a murderer, do you?"

CHAPTER 25

The next few weeks shot by in a blur, the effects I still have not completely recovered from. Tony brought word that Piers's duel would continue to be delayed and the curricle race likely to be canceled entirely. The authorities were in and out of Loxby Manor at all hours, asking questions and taking information.

Mrs. Cavanagh went straight into seclusion, emerging only for the events surrounding the funeral and the arrival of her brother-in-law, Charles, leaving Piers and Avery the difficult task of telling their father what had transpired.

At the close of the week, I was informed by a servant that the doctor was summoned due to Mr. Cavanagh's deteriorating health, but thankfully the concern passed within the next few days. Even so, Piers and Avery decided it was best to remain at their father's bedside for the immediate future. Rightfully so, I was not asked to visit or share in his care, but I had grown fond of Mr. Cavanagh, and the sudden removal of him from my life only furthered my isolation.

Thus, I was left to process the reality of Seline's tragic death in my own time and my own way. The days leading up to the funeral and shortly after were the worst. I found it hard even to think or move. After all, I was the one person who could have stopped her from leaving the house that night—at times I found the crushing guilt almost too difficult to bear.

Snowdrop rarely left my side as I spent the long hours in my bedchamber or alone in the library, my favorite refuge in those difficult days. It wasn't long before I realized books offered me a blessed escape that calmed my mind and refocused my purpose in remaining at Loxby Manor.

Though I'd hoped with all my heart to find Seline alive, soon enough questions about the strange circumstances of her demise began to trickle back into my mind. If I couldn't save her, perhaps I could do some good in bringing her killer to justice.

It was a passing thought that took root, deeper and deeper, in the weeks that followed, which only hardened my resolve to uncover the truth. Piers and I had made quite a bit of progress in our prior investigation, yet something remained elusive, a piece of information we had yet to learn, and I was determined to figure out what it was.

My gaze flicked to the bookshelf, to the very top where Piers and I had found the leather journal detailing the intricacies of the Gormogon secret society. Though at first Avery had scoffed at the idea that his group of friends could somehow be involved in Seline's disappearance, now everything had changed. Nothing could be glossed over or dismissed. Seline, my dearest friend, was dead and not in any normal way. She had been struck over the head, as Miles Lacy had, and buried where her murderer meant for her to be forgotten.

I tapped my fingers against the soft fabric of the sofa. All the clues thus far pointed back one way or another to that secretive group of Avery's. If I had to guess, the key to what happened to Seline lay somewhere in the complexities of the Noble Order.

I sat motionless for a moment, breathing in the fresh scent of a rolling fire, the flames swaying before my eyes. Piers had said the order was abolished with all other secret societies by a law in 1799, but what if factions of the group had prevailed? Or someone had revived it at a later date? But for what purpose?

Avery, Tony, and Hugh seemed to think their little group a pledge to friendship, but there was something more, something devious to the ritualistic practices of the meeting I'd observed—and the even more surprising movement of the faceless statue.

I imagined the men huddled in their cloaks before the fire. I could see them all sitting there as if the meeting had happened yesterday. Avery, Hugh, Tony, and Lord Kendal.

Wait . . . My eyes widened. There had been five stone seats encircling the fire at Kinwich Abbey, yet there were only four members that we knew of. I stiffened, my nerves prickling across my skin like a horde of spiders. What if there was a fifth member?

I flew to my feet and made my way over to the bookcase. The servants had repaired the shelf and ladder and replaced the books in their proper places, but a few steps forward and I could already see that something was different.

The leather-bound journal was gone.

I searched for Piers all afternoon, as he could have easily been the one to take the book about the Gormogons, but it was he who found me on the east rise as I strolled the grounds.

He had to make a bit of a dash to catch me and drew up beside me panting. Then he laughed. "I'm not certain I've run so far in years."

I mirrored his amusement. "Then I'm glad I provided you with some exercise."

We stopped in the shade of an oak tree, Loxby Manor tucked behind the far hill. It was the time of year where the sun was hot but the shade a blessed cool.

"How is your father today?"

I was happy to see that the dark circles that had lived beneath Piers's eyes for the past few weeks had faded a bit. His face was far less pale. He affected a smile. "I believe he is a little better today. He allowed me to help him to his chair. I think Avery and I can turn over most of the nursing duties to the staff at this point."

"And your mother?"

He looked down. "She continues to keep to her room, but I asked if she'd allow you to visit, and I do think she would appreciate a change in her daily routine."

"Then I shall go to her at once."

His arm shot out. "Please, will you stay for a moment with me? I have something I wish to talk to you about."

It took me a moment to answer, but I could think of no excuse. "All right."

He paced the shadowed ground. "I had a dream last night. It was about Seline, only I never really saw her face. I saw a cloaked figure on horseback, and it brought something to mind."

The breeze was a refreshing one, a cool splash of spring, and I turned my head to enjoy it. "Yes?"

"You see, I woke in a panic, the images my mind had created still lifelike before me. That's when I made the connection." He stopped, his eyes finding mine. "When we recovered Seline's body, she wasn't wearing a cloak."

My heart seized in my chest. "She wasn't?"

"No." He shook his head. "Nor was one recovered anywhere nearby."

I felt almost dizzy as I reached for a nearby branch. "The murderer must have removed it."

He shrugged. "Or she took it off somewhere else, but why would she? And if that is true, why haven't we found it?"

I started pacing. "We found my brooch on the road to Rushridge. Perhaps the cloak fell off sometime after that."

"That is just what I think. Particularly if there was a struggle, the brooch could have easily come off then."

I imagined what the gruesome scene might look like and my stomach turned, but not before an idea popped into my mind, which I rolled around in my thoughts before lifting my eyebrows. "You said you assumed the figure in your dream was Seline, but she was wearing a cloak and you couldn't see her face. What if the murderer experienced just the opposite? What if he mistook Seline for someone else, and she was dead before he realized his mistake?

Piers flopped against a tree trunk as he ran his hand down his face. "You mean the killer thought he'd come upon Hugh on his way home?"

"Exactly."

We both stood in silence, my suggestion far too plausible to dismiss. What had Priscilla overheard the day Seline's body was found? Something about Hugh wanting out. Was it possible that he was trying to leave the Gormogons?

Piers crossed his arms. "I need to speak with Avery again. I don't think we've even scratched the surface of this secret society. I continually get the feeling everyone is hiding something."

I told him my suspicions of a fifth member and he hung his head, the lines that had set up residence on his forehead deepening with each revelation.

I touched his arm. "And the journal in the library has disappeared."

His eyes rounded.

"It's time to reopen the door to the investigation. Are you ready?"

"I will admit, the past few weeks have been like nothing I've ever experienced before." He peeked down at my hand resting on his arm. "I don't know what I would have done if you weren't at Loxby."

Startled, I pulled away. "I did little to warrant any gratitude."

"Just your being here, your wise council, your calm spirit. Believe me when I say it's made all the difference. I may never be fully ready to learn who took the life of my sister, but at the same time, I cannot rest until I do. I know you feel the same way."

The gentle tug of his fingers urging me closer was nearly imperceptible, but with little more than a passing thought, willingly I stepped forward into his waiting arms. The embrace was soft and gentle at first, like two friends, but as his hands made their way up my back, he drew me closer . . . closer . . . until my body pressed tight against his, his warmth seeping through my muscles like the relief of hot water on a bitter winter day. We held each other in comfortable silence for I don't know how long, his head resting on mine, his arms terribly tight, as though if either one of us were to let go, the other might simply slip away.

I didn't dare move as my heart beat wildly and my thoughts dissolved into the shimmering residue of fireworks that fall from a dark sky. He felt so good, so safe. The one man I could trust.

The one man I could trust. I repeated the idea over and over again in my mind, my muscles relaxing in turn as tears filled my eyes. Was this what I had been searching for all along? Had I simply confused the absence of pain with the absence of affection? With some half-baked idea of self-preservation?

Eventually Piers's hold slackened, and he took a step back, his gaze darting around the small grove as if lost.

It seemed the embrace had snuck up on both of us.

He gave me a tentative smile. "It's time I walk you back to the house."

I nodded, as was the proper answer to give, moving at once to accept his outstretched arm. But as I slid my hand onto the crook of his jacket, a new, far more daring thought surged to the forefront of my mind, one I would be pondering for the days to come—for the first time since the assault, with Piers and Piers alone, I would have been willing to stay right there in his arms, to finally breach the wall of uncertainty I'd built to protect myself, to finally find out what would happen next, what hidden demons waited in the darkness beyond the wall.

Avery spent the weeks following the funeral at Rushridge with Hugh and Priscilla. Though Mrs. Cavanagh disparaged his choice to abandon Loxby, I knew he left because he had to find a way to survive the overwhelming guilt, the never-ending sadness, the hole Seline's departure had left in all our lives.

None of us would ever be the same, not on earth at least.

I doubted Avery would return home for some time. Thus I had quite a shock when I found him standing in the first-floor sitting room staring out the large central window the very day I'd embraced Piers on our walk.

He glanced over his shoulder. "Good morning, Charity." Gone was the carefree smile he'd always shared. Dark circles surrounded his eyes, matching the black band on his arm. "I came to speak with Piers. Baker is fetching him for me."

I crossed the room in silence, hesitant at first to come close, as I felt a bit of an intruder, but then I caught sight of the prospect beyond the glass. Small openings in the thick clouds had allowed the sun's textured rays to filter through, painting ribbons of warmth and light that stretched from the heavens to the earth. I, too, was transfixed.

Avery didn't look at me as he spoke. "Sometimes I imagine her gazing down on us, wondering why the devil we don't just get on with our lives. Seline never did have any patience for introspection. She was far too impulsive for that—and I loved her for it."

"We all did." I moved into his view. "Avery, I want to ask you something."

I thought I saw his arm clench. "Yes?"

"It's about the secret society. You told us some time ago that Tony, Hugh, Kendal, and you initiated the group. However, lately I get the feeling someone else might have been involved."

He pivoted to face me, his eyes colder than I'd seen them before. "Let Seline rest in peace, Charity. You'll only make things worse by meddling in something you know nothing about."

I felt something inside me crumble. What was hiding in that mind of his? That he mourned the passing of his sister was certain, but how many secrets had he been forced to swallow?

Piers crossed the threshold into the room just as Avery made a move for the door.

"It's good to have you home."

Avery cast me a quick look, his face indeterminate at best, then took a tattered breath. "I've brought news from Lord Kendal . . . and it's not pleasant."

The color drained from Piers's face. "What is it?"

"The date for his marriage is set, and he means to have the duel before then. He sent his seconds to Rushridge with a written letter."

I jerked forward. "But that is absurd—now of all times? Seline's only been gone a few weeks."

"It'll be a month tomorrow since we found her, and"—Avery raised his eyebrows—"Kendal's been waiting on this duel for far too long as it is."

I whirled on Piers in desperation. "Surely you don't mean to meet him now, after everything that has happened."

Piers didn't spare me a glance. "You may arrange the meeting for dawn the day after tomorrow on the green beyond the upper branches of the River Sternway. It is sufficiently remote and secluded there. Tell Kendal I am more than ready to put this unfortunate business behind me as well."

I heard Avery swallow. "That's miles on the far side of Whitecaster Hall. You'll have to overnight in Eastward."

"Indeed, as I intend to keep the duel as far away from Loxby Manor as I can get. We've had far too much death around here already."

Avery shoulders slumped. "Swords or pistols?"

Piers's eyes narrowed to slits. "Pistols of course."

CHAPTER 26

Waiting was never easy, and I swear that's all I had done since I'd arrived at Loxby Manor—first for Seline, then for answers about her disappearance. Well, now I was waiting for the blasted duel to arrive that would take Piers away from me.

Sleep proved elusive, and I woke with the servants the day Piers had arranged for his afternoon departure. As the duel would take place near Whitecaster Hall, he'd planned to overnight at the Dovetail Inn in Eastward.

After an early morning spent drinking chocolate and a bit of distracted reading, I decided to pass the hours with Mrs. Cavanagh in her bedchamber. Though I couldn't tell her about the upcoming duel and would be forced to pretend nothing had changed in the house, it was also time I broke her self-inflicted isolation. Piers continued to worry about his mother, and considering she had not emerged from her room in several days, I worried too.

I entered the dark space with a candle, having received no answer to my knock. I found her sitting in a chair by her desk, her attention glued to an open drawer, but I doubted she saw anything beyond her troubled mind.

"Mrs. Cavanagh?"

Slowly she turned to face me, her eyes so still she reminded me of a doll. Though I'm certain her maid had arranged her hair beneath her cap first thing in the morning, her gnarled fingers had been hard at work, pulling and twisting. She bit at her lip, the muscles in her thin cheeks straining beneath the effort.

Finally she opened her mouth. "What is it?"

"Avery and Piers will be gone for a few days. I thought—"

"You needn't concern yourself with me." She scowled. "I require little these days."

"I hoped you might allow me to read to you. I've missed our conversations."

A breathy laugh stole across the room, but she didn't object. I moved a chair beside her and took a seat where I was able to get a closer look. Clearly the last few weeks had been unbearable.

She ran her fingers back and forth across the handkerchief in her lap before her gaze snapped to mine. "Things are not always what they seem, are they?"

I hesitated to answer, lost as to what prompted her words. "No, they aren't."

"The world is a vicious place, my dear—liars, thieves, murderers—you could be sitting right next to one and not even know it."

Uncomfortable, I shifted in my seat. "What do you mean?"

Her head seemed to hang on her neck, bobbing as if caught up in a breeze. "I suggest you leave this house as soon as possible. You never, never should have come back here." She turned to close the drawer as a shiver shuddered down her back.

"You're cold."

She pushed my hand away. "Leave me be."

I stood almost mindlessly and headed to the wardrobe. "Have you a shawl in here?"

She took a half-hearted glance over her shoulder. "I believe I left it in the connecting room."

I made a move for the interior door, and she screamed, "No!" My feet went numb as my hand flew to my chest.

"Just hand me the blanket there on the bed and leave my presence. I shall send in due course for my maid." She pressed the handkerchief to her forehead.

"Piers is—"

Her eyes flashed and my breath caught.

"You and Piers." She erupted into a coughing fit, but when I came close to assist, the venom in her eyes chased me away. "It was always you with him, or he never would have permitted the scandal that tore this family apart."

I did my best to ignore her insinuations, but I knew the truth.

Her eyes widened with triumph. "That's right. I see you've worked out all the details at last. He made me swear not to tell you at the time, but I had no idea what would happen then." Her tongue skirted across her dry lips. "He was out all night, you see, worrying about the upcoming duel. He'd acted rashly in calling out Lord Kendal, but he knew his duty. He would not disappoint his family."

"And then?" The tone of my voice fell flat. I knew very well where the story was going, but I needed to hear it once and for all.

"And then he found you, alone, lying in that ditch with an injured leg. He could no more leave you than he could cut off his right arm. At first he thought he might come about somehow, explain things to Lord Kendal, but he couldn't. He'd made Kendal look a fool, and that would never be tolerated. You were a reckless, headstrong girl to set out so late in the day from the coaching house on horseback."

Mrs. Cavanagh ran her finger along the embroidered letter on her handkerchief. "Piers told me he meant to bring you to Loxby Manor at first, but during the long, arduous trek, he realized all too clearly that none of the servants would believe for one moment that the two of you had not been out all night together. So he took you to the empty gatehouse where you waited until the sun rose into the sky and your very respectability was less in question. Then you told everyone you had just arrived, the day they had all been expecting you.

"Things happened rather quickly after you left for Ceylon. Lord Kendal demanded an explanation, but Piers had none to give. He could not tell him or anyone else the two of you had spent the early morning hours together alone—not if he meant to spare your reputation."

My eyes clouded with tears as a swirl of emotions rattled my chest. I had been right. He'd risked it all for me.

Mrs. Cavanagh flicked her hand in the air. "Go on now. You've done enough here already."

My heart pounded like a blacksmith's hammer, slow and painful thumps. Eventually I uttered a whispered, "As you wish," and fled the room.

I escaped straight to the garden where I was afforded an hour alone, but even then tears stung my eyes and my heart lay open before me like the final pages of a book.

I never dreamed Piers would find me in such a state.

He was slow to advance, wandering a bit before taking a seat on the curved white bench at my side, his gaze questioning me. "I've been searching for you for some time. Has something happened?"

I gathered myself as best I could. After all, I didn't want to burden him before the duel. Anything might affect his performance, and I was determined not to be the cause of something dreadful—*again.*

I attempted to rid myself of the shroud of turbulent emotions with a light shake of my head. "I went to see your mother, although I don't think she was too pleased to see me. She said some things that needed pondering is all." I glanced up. "Like my leaving Loxby as soon as possible."

He breathed in a sharp breath. "She said that?"

"Demanded, more like."

He perched his elbows on his knees and lowered his head into his hands. "I fear her mind is not what it should be since Seline's death. She's barely eating or sleeping these days. All this while I've been worried about my father's frail health when I should have been equally concerned about my mother's. Avery has always been better with her. His being at Rushridge is no doubt taking a toll." Piers looked down at his hands before splaying them wide. "She and Avery share something I will never understand. It doesn't help that I've been gone these last five years."

"Piers, I . . ." Trapped by the knowledge of how my own actions had played an integral part in Piers's removal from Loxby, I wasn't certain how to proceed. "You and I have shared nearly everything over the years . . . even when we were children."

He smiled. "Do you ever wish you could go back to those days, where the world was small and our dreams unequally big?"

I fell motionless as the garden buzzed to life around me. The sweet scent of flowers on the breeze, the warm sun on my back, Piers sketching before me. The vision almost felt real. Slowly, I lifted my eyes. "With all my heart."

He stared off into the rosebushes, silence settling on the bench between us. I daresay we both mourned the loss of what might have been, packaging up those dreams into crates that will never be opened again.

But it was what he said next that caught me by surprise.

"Strange how indulging in the idyllic world of yesterday can make living in the present so terribly unfulfilling, particularly when something happened that changed the course of life." He folded his hands in his lap, his voice dipping lower. "Over the last few weeks, I've come to realize something, Charity. That rosy picture of the past is just an illusion." He sighed. "And a dark one to lose oneself in. Over time those happy memories grow sweeter, the edges soften, the images blur. They become the fragrant scent of remembrance that remains forever out of reach.

"I don't believe God made us to be looking back all the time, calculating every mistake we've made, measuring our worth by actions we can no longer change, particularly when such a practice comes at the expense of our future."

I leaned back against the cold iron of the bench, the emotions I had fought so hard to keep at bay bubbling to the surface, playing with the twists and turns of my beliefs. Was I, too, guilty of painting an unrealistic picture of the past, holding it up as the ideal?

I had come to Loxby to escape my present pain, to lose myself in a happier time and place. But Piers was right; my doing so had turned out to be nothing but an illusion. In the end I had not been able to run away from *me*.

I felt his touch on my hand, and I looked down as he slid his fingers through mine. "I never meant to lecture. In fact, I came here to say something quite different." He took a deep breath. "I don't know what will happen on that field tomorrow morning."

"Please don't say that."

"Say what? The truth? We both know all too well that life is short, and I've done a fine job of wasting what I've been given thus far."

He shifted his position on the bench, the honesty in his eyes betraying the thoughts he wanted so desperately to string together. "Charity . . . I need to tell you something."

I had a moment of cringing anxiety deep within my core, but as we sat there staring at each other, the feeling ebbed away.

Then his words spilled out. "I've spent the last five years trying to forget you. I told myself it was noble I stayed away, that I was sparing you the awkward moment of refusing me, but I was a coward to do so. This thing between us has never been simple, and I know now it will never go away, not for me at least."

A gust of wind came so unexpectedly over the garden wall, rushing through the plants, that I pulled away from him, my father's words echoing in my mind. *"A sign of things to come."*

He held out his hand. "Please don't go, not yet. Regardless of what you think of me when I am finished, I know in my heart I cannot leave for the duel without saying everything on my mind."

I nodded, and he closed his eyes for a long second.

Silently I watched him fight the intense vulnerability I knew so well, and my heart shifted. It wasn't only that I had finally grasped the depths of his compassion; it was the stark realization that I had been given a rare gift—a man who understood the intertwining layers of guilt and shame and hope and pain. He was my equal in every way.

He glanced up. "The incredible truth is, I thought I loved you back then. I know now I had no concept of what that meant, what life would bring to the both of us. You've shared with me your unspeakable nightmare. We've mourned my sister together. We share a history no one on this earth can understand but us. This is love, Charity, not what society dictates or some fluttery feeling in my chest, which I assure you is growing inside me with every word I speak."

He took my hands again. "Love is you and me deciding to stand at each other's side to face whatever comes." He trailed his thumb along the lines of my hand. "It's thinking about you every second, aching to see you when we are not together, knowing each other's faults and choosing patience time and again. It's forgetting the past, all the terrible details that weigh us down. It's forgiving ourselves and each other over and over again."

My heart felt unfamiliar, a remnant of another time and place, my muscles tightening and twisting throughout my body, but I knew without a doubt I had no intention of moving one inch away. I loved Piers Cavanagh with all my heart, and he was right. I wanted everything he'd said. Fear of the past or even the future could not steal the hope I felt stirring in my chest, not anymore.

He ran his finger around my hairline and rested his hand at the back of my neck. His touch was familiar yet terrifying and captivating all at once. The very intimacy I'd run from for five long years turned out to be so utterly different from what I'd expected. A tint of embarrassment warmed my cheeks, and my hands quivered beneath his touch.

He dipped his head. "I promise you I'll not take one step for granted. I can wait forever if that's what it takes." He gave me a rueful smile. "After all, there's nobody waiting to marry me."

I lifted my chin. "That's where you are wrong . . . I am."

A smile transformed his face, his eyes brilliant in the afternoon sun, the tendrils of his hair fluttering in the hands of a spirited breeze.

"Charity."

I wasn't certain if he'd spoken my name aloud, for it felt more like a soft whisper on my skin.

My heart pitched forward, and I can't say I know exactly what happened, but I know it must have been me who moved first. Piers never would have done so.

All at once my lips were pressed to his. And slowly, cautiously, deliciously, his arms wrapped tight around my shoulders, inching me closer and closer still. My head swam as my hands felt their way up his back. I'd dreamed of such a day for so long, but I could not have anticipated the overwhelming freedom that one simple kiss wrought about in my soul. As I melted into his arms, I was lost in the stirring moment of hope. I knew without a doubt I'd taken the first step in overcoming that which I never thought I could.

The wind curled once more around the small garden, and I yearned for Piers never to let go, but we could not stay there forever. Gently he pulled back, holding me at arm's length.

"I am sorry, but I have to go."

Fear numbed my arms, but my fingers curled tighter on his arm. "Do you indeed plan to delope?"

He gave me no sign of emotion. "Of course I do. I'll send word as soon as the duel is complete. Avery is bringing Dr. Knight. I'll overnight again in Eastward, but only if I need to."

I gripped his arm. "What about Lord Kendal?"

"Don't fool yourself, Charity. Lord Kendal has been waiting for this duel for five years, and he always shoots to kill."

CHAPTER 27

Piers and Avery left an hour later to little fanfare. Mrs. Cavanagh chose not to emerge from her room to say goodbye, and Piers was forced to visit her in her chamber. I only prayed she said nothing of our prior conversation.

Thus, the secluded evening ushered in the first supper since I'd arrived at Loxby Manor where I dined completely alone. Baker seemed to sense the tension in the house and did his best to ease the strange, palpable quiet of the dining room, but he could not do so completely, not when I sat alone at the large symmetrical table.

With dinner disposed of, I decided to forgo any time in the drawing room and made my way upstairs to my bedchamber where I flopped on the bed. A part of me wanted to revel in Piers's and my newfound connection, but the duel tainted everything. I could not allow myself to dream, not yet.

The hours grew stagnant, the room suffocating, and I rose to see if I could find Snowdrop. She'd been missing from my room the last few days, but I'd seen her near the stables when I watched Piers leave. Though I enjoyed her presence many of the nights I spent alone, on this one I *needed* her.

I began my search on the ground floor, scouring the house,

the front portico, and the back terrace. I dared not go too far in the blustering night, but I had to try, meowing as I liked to do to get her to follow me. But there was no sign of the little white cat.

It wasn't until I scaled the central staircase that I heard a faint meow on the still air. So she had found her way into the house once again. I started for my room, but I realized all too quickly that the sound had not come from my hallway at all, but rather from the family wing.

I crept from one room to the next, straining to hear another call. It was near Seline's room where I was finally rewarded by Snowdrop's sweet meow. But all too quickly my heart turned cold. The sound was coming from Mrs. Cavanagh's room.

I inched forward, hoping I had misheard the cat, certain I would never enter Mrs. Cavanagh's domain again. My heart could not take another lashing from Piers's mother, not after what she had said to me earlier.

But as I reached Mrs. Cavanagh's closed door, I realized the cat's plea was coming from somewhat behind me.

In Mr. Cavanagh's room . . . Not again.

Surely not. I made my way closer to his door and a similar deflection of echoes resulted. I stood there a moment in confusion until the answer came to my mind.

The connecting room between Mr. and Mrs. Cavanagh's bedchambers.

Somehow Snowdrop had found her way in there. I might have a chance to recover her after all, and if Snowdrop had got herself trapped, Mrs. Cavanagh would not react kindly. It was a wonder she hadn't heard the cat already, but if she was asleep, it was possible.

I stood there for several seconds debating my next move. Both bedchambers connected into the shared room, which was likely to be an intimate space. I could be discovered at any moment. But with any luck, Mr. and Mrs. Cavanagh would already be sound asleep, and I could tiptoe my way in and out without anyone the wiser.

I held my breath and cracked open the slender door. The dressing room lay dark within, and slowly, carefully I tiptoed into the drab, motionless interior. The back drapes were drawn tight, leaving me little to no light to work with, and I was forced to stand still in the entryway, my back pressed to the door until my eyes adjusted to the gloom.

The door to Mr. Cavanagh's room stood ajar, and through the opening, I could see his curved silhouette highlighted by the moonlight on the bed. His nasal breathing surged in and out of the transient silence.

A chill roamed the small chamber, which appeared to be more of a dressing room for Mrs. Cavanagh alone than a shared space. A portable hip bath stood to my right and a dressing table filled with feminine luxuries to my left, flanked on the far end by a large painted screen.

"Snowdrop," I whispered, moving at once to locate the cat.

The room was eerily quiet, the shadows far more menacing. I knelt and tried again. "Snowdrop."

Then I heard it, a small pitiful meow, coming from the far side of the screen. Carefully I inched around the partition, the feathered moonlight playing tricks with my vision. First I thought I saw her in the corner, then beneath a small cushion bench, but it was behind the slim wardrobe that she'd managed to wedge herself.

I attempted to coax her out of the slit between the furniture and the wall, but she would have none of that. I gave her a faint meow and was pleased to see her start my direction only to stop, her hind legs caught up in some clothes that had slipped behind the wardrobe. All I needed to do was grasp her middle and pull her toward me, the piece of clothing still hooked by her back claw.

I cradled her to my chest. "You silly little kitty. I wonder how long you've been sleeping back there. You're lucky Mrs. Cavanagh hasn't found you before."

As I reached to disengage the piece of clothing, something shifted in the dim light. Slowly, carefully I lifted the heavy fabric into the threads of moonlight and gasped.

My cloak. The one Seline had borrowed that fateful night. Snowdrop had been using it as a bed.

I felt dizzy and fell onto the bench, my hand pressed to my forehead. How in the world had the cloak made its way into Mrs. Cavanagh's dressing room? Thoughts stormed through my mind, each far more unsettling than the last. Was Mrs. Cavanagh somehow involved in her own daughter's murder?

I thought back through each painful detail of the night Seline went missing. I'd heard someone in the hallway, someone I'd never identified. Could it have been Mrs. Cavanagh on her way back to her room? She had been awake that night, and I had been surprised to find her dressed when I entered her room.

But what possible motive could she have had for killing her own daughter? Surely Seline's scandal could not be the inciting incident that brought about something so horrific. My heart lurched. Mrs. Cavanagh had been at Whitecaster Hall when Miles was found dead, and her behavior was certainly odd at the time.

I heard the floorboards creak in the adjoining room, and my heart snapped to life. Mrs. Cavanagh was not asleep as I had supposed, and here I sat in her very dressing room. My cloak felt like lead in my hands as I thrust it back behind the wardrobe. If

Mrs. Cavanagh had killed before, she wouldn't hesitate to do so again. If only Piers and Avery hadn't left when they did.

I strong-armed Snowdrop against my chest and turned to leave. My feet slid across the floor as I made my way to the door, but I never looked back toward Mr. Cavanagh's open doorway.

"What do you think you are doing?"

Breathless, I turned into the hollow gaze of Mr. Cavanagh's night nurse, standing in the shadows of the doorway.

It took me a full second to regain my heartbeat as well as my addled thoughts. "I came to retrieve the cat. The poor dear had gone and got herself trapped in here. I'm on my way out with her now."

"Shhh." The nurse pointed behind her. "You'll wake him." The quiver in her voice was unmistakable.

I nodded, anxious to make my escape, when I heard a grunt from inside the room. "Is that you, Miss Halliwell?"

I closed my eyes for a brief second, wishing I could sink into the floor. Slowly I set Snowdrop on the ground. "Yes, Mr. Cavanagh. I didn't mean to wake you." I angled around the nurse just enough to see the darkened figure move on the bed. His hand was at his hair, smoothing and combing.

I took a step back. "Please excuse me for disturbing your sleep. I'll be on my way at once."

"Don't disappear, not yet at least. I have something to say to you." His head pivoted in the darkness, his voice directed at his nurse. "You may leave us until I call for you."

I watched the nurse scuttle away from the door. Then I caught a flutter in the moonlight, like Mr. Cavanagh had flicked his hands in the air.

"Come closer." His voice was demanding but not unkind.

Confusion weighed my steps as I approached the bed. Though

Mr. Cavanagh and I had grown close over the past few weeks, I swallowed hard.

I moved in the darkness until my thighs pressed against the soft edge of the bed, my hand retreating to the post. "It was abominable for me to wake you this way."

He cleared his throat. "If it eases your conscience, I do understand why. We all know Mrs. Cavanagh cannot abide cats."

I could hear Mrs. Cavanagh in the next room and the hairs on my arm pinged to attention.

Mr. Cavanagh cleared his throat. "Tell me, did you write to your brother in America?"

For a moment I scrambled for words. "Yes, of course."

"And included my letter? When was it sent?"

My eyes still trained on the connecting room, I nodded. "Yes. Weeks ago."

"Good, I—"

The sound of the door cut off Mr. Cavanagh's sentence and we both turned to see Mrs. Cavanagh holding a candle that illuminated her startled face. "Why, Miss Halliwell . . ."

I shook my head as I clutched my chest. "Please, excuse my intrusion. I heard your cat and it brought me into the connecting room. I didn't mean to wake either of you. I shall be on my way at once."

Her gaze crept from me to Mr. Cavanagh then back to me, like an animal waiting to pounce on its prey. "I don't see any cat."

I glanced at the floor around my feet. "Oh dear. She must have run off."

Mrs. Cavanagh tilted her head. "Just so." She watched me a moment, the candlelight flickering in her narrow eyes. "Unable to sleep?"

I wished I could see Mr. Cavanagh's face in the shadows of the bed, but he'd slipped into the clutches of darkness.

"Yes, I . . ."

Her tone turned accusatory. "I think it best you return to you room."

My skin tingled. "I understand."

A tight smile creased her lips.

For a breathless moment I considered laying my suspicions before Mr. Cavanagh, but I had no proof of Mrs. Cavanagh's involvement, and my presumptions stemmed from nothing more than an article of clothing and a feeling that was growing by the second.

I locked my door that night, plagued by fear and questions surrounding Mrs. Cavanagh. Could she be the fifth member of the secret society? Was she playing a deep game? Those thoughts, coupled with anxiety for Piers, kept me from sleeping.

Morning, however, brought its own problems. Baker burst into the drawing room, a salver in his hand. "This just came for you, Miss."

I slipped the letter from the silver platter with a great deal of trepidation. I didn't recognize the handwriting, and for whatever reason, that frightened me. "Thank you, Baker."

I waited for him to leave before breaking the wax seal.

Miss Halliwell,

Rest assured, Piers Cavanagh is alive and well, but he did take a ball to the right shoulder, inhibiting him from writing this very letter. The doctor says it was a clean wound and he should recover nicely, but he shall be laid up here in Eastward for a bit. Hugh Daunt has offered his services should you need anything in the days to come as he is returning to Rushridge and will deliver this letter to Loxby on his way home.

Your servant,

Tony Shaw

I folded the letter closed, my heart constricting. If Piers was too injured to ride home, it was more than a simple wound. Tony had no doubt written me the letter to belay my fears, but nothing could stop them now, not until I laid eyes on Piers once again. All this time I'd been pushing him away, and now I couldn't imagine life without him in it.

CHAPTER 28

I didn't see one member of the Cavanagh family the rest of the day. That is, until I stumbled upon Mrs. Cavanagh on my way to bed.

She'd stopped at the foot of the stairs. "Care to join me in the kitchen for a bite to eat?"

I touched my forehead, dread climbing my arms. "I find I'm a bit tired this evening."

She didn't move. "I have something I wish to say to you." Then she glanced behind her, her fingers wrapping tightly about the banister. "But not here."

One by one my muscles tensed as my thoughts dropped into a muddle of fear and expectation. How could I refuse my host? But should I take one solitary step with a possible murderer? Of course the servants were only one scream away. What could Mrs. Cavanagh really do? And I'd wonder all night what she wanted to say to me if I didn't find out.

Slowly I nodded before following her into the servants' wing, my steps tentative at best.

The kitchens were dark beyond the glow of the solitary candle in Mrs. Cavanagh's unsteady hand. She went to work at once scrounging up some pastries from the larder and settled in across from me at a long wooden table.

Once seated she waited for me to take a bite before hunching over her own plate, her fingers fidgety with her pastry. "I'd like you to speak to Avery and straightaway."

"Avery?" I'm not certain what I expected her to say, ensconced as we were beneath the veil of secrecy and darkness, but it definitely didn't involve him.

Her movements were edgy in the candlelight, and she was quick to glare over her shoulder. "He hasn't been speaking to me of late, and I had a terrible shock today. I dare not say anymore, but I have to know what he offered the society."

I, too, took a sideways look at the door. "What do you mean?"

Her hand quivered as she ran her fingers across her forehead. "Everything has changed now. His pledge was not in the book like those of the other members from before."

Ice enfolded my heart. "You're talking of the Gormogons." So it was Mrs. Cavanagh who had the book.

Her gaze shot to mine. "I have to know before I do anything, before it's too late." Her chest caved in with each breath. "Don't look at me like that. I told you to leave this house. Why didn't you do so when you had the chance?" She shook her head. "He'll kill again . . . and again. Whatever it takes to achieve the power he so desperately wants. And you've learned far too much already, my dear."

"He, who?" *Avery*?

A sound echoed from somewhere beyond the walls, and she flew to her feet. "We haven't time. Promise me you will go to Avery as soon as he arrives back at Rushridge and demand the truth." She looked around frantically. "The walls have ears, my dear, and the darkness hides many things. I would advise you to head to the village, but it is getting late . . . very late indeed." Her voice shook. "I fear something terrible might happen before morning. It would be too easy, far too easy. Please be careful. Go to your room at once and lock your door. I don't know what I would tell your mother should something happen."

Piers had said his mother's mind might be slipping, but this flurry of ideas was full-on madness. How could I believe anything she said? Particularly when all the signs pointed to some level of her involvement in Seline's death. I'd found the cloak in her dressing room of all places. And this new business about Avery—what a dilemma. He would not take kindly to my interference, nor feel at ease to tell me anything about what he offered the society.

"I shall return to my room as well." Her voice sounded sickly sweet as she grasped the candleholder. "These things are out of our control, after all. What right do we have to tempt fate?"

I watched as Mrs. Cavanagh slunk out the kitchen door, my nerves coiled like springs throughout my body.

I sat stock-still in the dreariness of the kitchens, afraid to think, afraid to move. Whoever had killed Seline and Miles was intimately involved with the Cavanagh family. That was certain. Finding the cloak in Mrs. Cavanagh's room had proved that.

And if Mrs. Cavanagh was to be believed, here I was, alone in the depths of the grand Loxby Manor with Piers miles away—a perfect target, but for whom? And why?

Mrs. Cavanagh had focused in on Avery's offering to the society. If I remembered correctly, Tony had detailed the process when we visited him. The book Piers and I had found in the library had done so as well. At least now I knew where the book had gone. I glanced at the door. I had no intention of stepping one foot inside

Mrs. Cavanagh's room to retrieve it. I thought back hard, reliving as best I could Tony's conversation.

A loyalty pledge—that's what he'd called it. Any new member to the Gormogons was forced to relinquish condemning information to join, which would be kept by the society as collateral. My eyes widened. Why would Mrs. Cavanagh want to know what Avery had turned over to the group?

Was that the piece of information we'd been missing?

The letter we discovered in Lord Kendal's pocket mentioned something similar in regard to him. Whoever wrote the note held Kendal's pledge. I tapped my fingers on the table. Who held Avery's pledge?

The conversation at Tony's estate returned to my mind. Tony had said Avery held his pledge and Kendal had Hugh's, thus Hugh might very well have Avery's information.

My eyes widened as the depths of Loxby Manor grew cold around me. What if Mrs. Cavanagh was right and I was indeed in danger? Except for a few servants, I was wholly unprotected. How easy it would be for someone to slip into the house.

Tingles crawled across my skin as the dark corners of the kitchen grew darker still. My gaze darted from one gloomy corner to the next, my imagination filling in the gaps where my eyes could not, and all the while the unnatural feeling that I was not alone scaled its way up my neck.

I stood.

Rushridge was not so very far and Priscilla would be there to assist me, to keep me safe until Piers and Avery returned from the duel.

But I dare not tell anyone at Loxby of my plans. I would have to creep my way to the stables alone.

Alone.

The word hung like a vicious wraith in the darkness, leering at me from the shadows. The road to Rushridge would not be an easy one, but Loxby Manor was no refuge. I tightened my fists and raised my chin. I could do this. I needed to do this.

My steps were small and my heart sought to betray me, but I made my way to the side door and swung it open nonetheless, breathing in the journey I had before me.

The night was warm but eerily still, every sound begging to be heard and contemplated. I stood on the doorstep for several seconds, scanning the surrounding wilderness. Life had indeed made me cautious, but I wouldn't let it strangle me, not anymore.

I pulled the door closed behind me and scurried down the path to the stables where I found Jewel waiting for me in her crib, her stoic strength a balm to my pounding reservations. I rushed through the harness room, readied Jewel in relative silence, and led her carefully from her stall.

A mounting block lay near the door and I utilized it to swing into the sidesaddle. I kept her to a walk until we'd departed the paddocks and crossed the open yard. Loxby Manor and all its questions and fear melted into the darkness behind me.

Centered firmly on the road to Rushridge, I spurred Jewel forward. Her powerful muscles contracted beneath my legs, the sudden and desperate surge of exhilaration rushing over me like the wind. For a breathless second I was free, flying through the trees.

Jewel's stride widened as we hit level ground, her gallop strengthening with each powerful step. The sliver of moon proved a poor guide on the open road, and I was forced to trust her instincts.

The minutes passed and the familiar open landscape drifted away. Jewel didn't slow till the gates of Rushridge materialized in the gloom ahead, the black iron bars glinting in the moonlight. I couldn't help but stare down at the side of the road where Seline's body had lain in the shallow grave for weeks. There was little trace of the precious life that had been there, a bit of disturbed earth, nothing more, but I would never forget what had happened there.

Having passed through the gates, I rounded the front drive and scrambled from Jewel's back at the last second, only to nearly lose my footing as I hit the ground. I looked up at the house, relieved to see a light on in one of the ground-floor rooms. I prayed Hugh and Priscilla were still awake as I looped Jewel's reins over an iron post.

I mounted the stone steps and descended on the front door of Rushridge, pounding out a knock against the heavy wood.

Silence.

With a tight fist, I tried again, my hand aching with each thrust.

Finally the door cracked open an inch to reveal the beady eyes of the Daunt's elderly butler.

I stepped into the beam of candlelight extending beyond the door. "I must see Hugh Daunt at once."

The butler angled his chin, but he must have recognized me from my earlier visit, for he swung the door wide and bade me to enter.

I raced into the open hall, only to catch sight of Priscilla in the drawing room doorway. I breathed out a sigh of relief. "Priscilla."

Her eyes widened. "Charity, you look a fright. Whatever are you doing here at such an hour?"

It took me a moment to catch my breath. My gown was rumpled from the ride and I tugged it into place. "I must speak with your brother. Is he able to see me?"

She stole a peek over her shoulder, then took a breath, lengthy and determined. "He's in the drawing room, but he's had a difficult time this afternoon."

I crossed the carpet to grasp her hand. "I wish I could come another time, but this is urgent."

Her face fell. "You may find him a bit strained at present." At length she motioned me to precede her into the drawing room.

Entering as bade, I found Hugh beneath a blanket in a chair near the fire, his gaze fixed on the window. Though I'd raced from Loxby as if chased by an animal, all of a sudden everything slowed, my thoughts, my steps. It was as if I approached a stranger, one I should be afraid of. He wore a grimace, but it wasn't the disconsolate mood that transformed my own. It was his eyes. I could not see Hugh in them. No wonder Priscilla had been worried.

I took a seat at his side. "Oh, Hugh."

He barely gave me a glance, his words flippant. "You mustn't worry. Piers is a Cavanagh. He'll pull though."

His monotone voice sent a fresh wave of ice into my chest. "Though I'm glad to hear that Piers will recover, I've come about something else entirely. I need to talk to you about the Gormogons."

His eyes flashed and he coughed as he shifted to face me. Priscilla raced over with a glass of water, casting me a sharp glare. I waited a moment for Hugh to regain his bearings, but I wouldn't be silenced, not now. "Am I right in guessing that you hold Avery Cavanagh's loyalty pledge?"

His eyes closed. "Those blasted pledges." His fingers curled into a fist on the armrest. "What does it matter now? I wanted nothing more than to escape the group, to expose the man responsible, but I'll never be able to get out now. Believe me, I never joined to become a traitor to my country. What a fool I've been—we've all been." His voice grew cold. "We've been played like a curst stack of cards."

"Treason?" I touched my throat, shocked at these revelations. "And you made plans to get out of the secret society?"

His fingers came to life on the armrest, pushing and pulling the fabric. "For months now. I'd rather die than directly finance revolutionaries in France."

My head swam. Wouldn't Avery feel the same way? "Did any of the members know of your intentions?"

"Avery did, but I swore him to secrecy." Hugh lowered his head into his hands. "I was waiting for the payout from the curricle race to finally make my exit. I had it all arranged. My loyalty pledge involved the state of my affairs. If I could have overcome that hurdle, I might have come about."

I sat very still. The motive for murder I'd been looking for was now abundantly clear. When the person killed Seline by mistake, his intention must have been to silence Hugh.

"Can you tell me again everything that happened that night at Kinwich Abbey?"

His shoulders slumped. "Why does it matter now? She's gone forever."

"Piers and I believe the murderer had a different target in mind. Please, I need to hear what happened that night from your perspective."

He ran his hand through his hair. "I was the last to arrive. Kendal was already getting nervous. He wanted to know how far we were willing to go to ensure the race went in his favor. Avery was trying to calm him down. He told Avery he'd hired someone he trusted not only to tamper with the other driver's curricle but to ensure his victory as well."

My eyes widened.

"We were never more shocked when that very person turned up dead."

"You mean it was Miles that Lord Kendal hired?"

"So we all learned upon his death."

My mind raced to make sense of the connection. After all, who would want to kill the very person hired to sabotage the race? And how did any of this relate to Hugh or Seline? "Go on. What else happened the night Seline disappeared?"

"We were all arguing about the importance of the race when Seline wandered into the circle and took a seat on the empty stone chair. For a moment I almost thought she was someone else." He looked up at me. "But then she removed her hood. Avery sprang to his feet, ordering her back to the house, but she demanded to speak with Kendal first. We all knew of Kendal's engagement. He'd told us at the start of the night. I thought that was why Seline had come. We all did. She pulled Kendal aside and they had one of their impassioned turn ups. The whole deuced affair was uncomfortable. I don't even know what was said at the time, only Kendal stomped off angry."

"You didn't know at the time?"

"The meeting broke up; only we didn't go home, not for a while. I met with Seline first. She was terribly upset. She thought she could blackmail Kendal into marrying her. Apparently this wasn't the first time she'd eavesdropped on one of our meetings. She knew about the sabotage and was planning to use it against Kendal. But his engagement was already announced in the papers. He couldn't draw back. Her hands were permanently tied, and she knew it.

"I thought that would end things between them, that she'd finally fulfill the promise she made to me years ago. I started to tell her that, but we were interrupted by Tony. He needed to talk to me about the race. He had questions about whether we could trust this anonymous person Kendal had hired. We all had far too much riding on the outcome, you see.

"Seline was so distraught, she wouldn't go home. I told her to ride ahead to Rushridge and wait for me there. As soon as I was done with Tony, we could talk. She agreed—and I never saw her again."

"What about Avery? Did you see him go straight home?"

"I cannot precisely recall. I did see him talk to Seline for a moment before she left. I assumed to encourage her to go home."

I glanced up at Priscilla as I considered Avery's role in all this. He had plans to marry a lady his parents didn't approve of, one with no money or connections. He had been open about the society in the beginning, but was he only telling us what he believed we already knew? Piers had been told about the Gormogons in Avery's presence, and Seline was well aware of the nightly pursuits of the neighbors. I folded my hands in my lap, praying for wisdom. "I ask again, what was Avery's loyalty pledge?"

Hugh ran his hand down his face. "I don't remember precisely, something about his mother."

"His mother?"

He flicked his fingers in the air. "He saw something a long time ago. It didn't really make any sense to me."

"Can I see it?"

"All the loyalty pledges are hidden at Kinwich Abbey . . . in the faceless statue."

"Is that why you moved it?"

"The statue was to remind us of our commitment and what we would personally sacrifice for a better world."

I narrowed my eyes. "This better world you speak of, what on earth did you hope to accomplish with this group?"

"I'm sure you've seen the soldiers who've returned from war, desolate, starving. The Corn Laws will only further the devastation. When Kendal spoke of change in this country, I never knew the group had ultimate ties to France. We weren't informed about that part, not until it was too late." He glanced up. "And you should know they've got their sights on you as well."

"Me?" I gasped.

"Well, not you exactly—your brother and his influence in Boston."

"Arthur? Don't be ridiculous. He's a chemist. He has no time for political intrigue."

Hugh looked away. "Don't underestimate them, Charity."

I bit my lip. "Will you come with me to Kinwich Abbey?"

"Tonight?"

"It has to be tonight. I don't know who to trust, and I fear something terrible is going to happen. I need to see those loyalty pledges as soon as possible."

CHAPTER 29

Mist had already begun forming in swirling clumps along the road, clinging to the base of the trees and gathering in the dips of the earth. The remains of Kinwich Abbey stood in a meadow, flanked on one side by the River Sternway, the perfect breeding ground for the ghostly dampened air.

Having dismounted our horses, Hugh and I trudged our way through the tall grass, the disturbed water droplets clinging to our clothes with each step as the fog grew ever thicker. Hugh pointed ahead, saying something about the abbey, but the haze made over his words, muffling them, changing them, as if the hallowed ground demanded silence.

The ancient stones looked like black daggers plunging out of the earth, wrapped neatly in a gray veil. Hugh stalked straight for the larger structure and I did my best to keep up. I couldn't help but feel as if I was walking blind.

The center of the crumbling cloisters was strangely free of the thick mist as the five rock seats remained perfectly placed in the semicircle I remembered. I called out to Hugh and he turned.

"Five stone chairs?"

He seemed a bit confused as he motioned to the ground. "Five members . . . Five seats."

"Then tell me, who is the fifth member?"

He stopped midstride, inching around to face me. "You don't know, do you?" There was a breath of wind that swirled between us, then he gave a lifeless shrug. "Surely you realize we've had several members beyond our little group of four. For example, there's a benefactor who funds a great deal of the society. I've never even met the gentleman." A visible shiver stole across his shoulders, and he motioned behind him. "The statue is just ahead. Let us be done with our nightly pursuit. I don't like leaving Priscilla and my mother unprotected at the house."

I edged in near as we made our way to the remains of the abbey wall, the black depths of night inching closer, fed by the endless crumbs of my imagination. Then out of the gloom, the faceless statue took shape before us. The gruesome details of the monk's tale came to mind as the vision I'd seen from my window gave its indeterminate glare an all-too-eerie life.

Hugh offered me a harried look before sidling forward. One by one he used the broken stones and mossy outcroppings on the wall as a ladder of sorts to access the backside of the statue. He spoke over his shoulder as he went to work tugging on the stones. "There's a secret compartment somewhere in here."

There was a moment of charged silence before I heard the scrape of stone, and he slid a fold of the statue's cloak to the side. Almost in response, the night came alive, the leaves quivering in the darkness as the wind prowled its way into the remains of the abbey. I took a wild glance over my shoulder, my heart thundering, but the shadows remained motionless, the clumps of mist blurring the lines between the blackened stones and the ground.

Hugh, too, seemed affected, his gaze scurrying about the remains of the abbey. He hesitated as he recovered a brown envelope and returned to my side.

"Here it is." It was strange how his voice sounded out of place among the fervent hush of nature. "I have to be honest, I was a little worried these wouldn't be here, but we've all been faithful up until now."

I thought of the torn pages from the Gormogon book at Loxby's library. "Wouldn't destroying this information set you all free?"

The feathered moonlight crept in and out of the clouds, revealing the scowl on Hugh's face. "Unfortunately each of us told one other person—our secret bearer—and all was reported to the benefactor."

"Oh." My attention fell back to the envelope. "Then go on and open it. We have to know what we are dealing with."

He slanted me a look, his brown eyes like black marbles in the darkness. "Quite so."

His fingers shook as he broke the wax seal and drew out a stack of papers from the inside. "The first one is Tony's."

"I fear we must read them all."

Hugh gave a painful nod, his eyes never leaving the paper. "It says here Tony fathered a child out of wedlock. The society paid the mother to disappear."

My heart ached. Could I really bear to hear the mistakes of my childhood friends?

Hugh went on, "Lord Kendal is next." His eyes widened as he read. "It seems it was he who forced the duel with Piers so long ago. Kendal knew just what would set Piers off and he planned the encounter for just such an end. After Piers failed to arrive, he went so far as to pay some men to spread the rumors about Piers's cowardice." He lowered the stack of papers. "Kendal gave Piers no choice but to leave town."

It felt like an iron ball dropped into my chest, and I nearly ripped the pledges from Hugh's hand. "But why would he do that?"

Hugh shook his head, a wraithlike swishing side to side. "Charity . . . I didn't know. It simply says here he was compelled to do so."

Hugh shuffled on to the next. "This one's mine." He smashed his eyelids closed for a long second. "It's no secret my family has had a gambling problem. My father managed to lead us up the River Tick five short years before his death." He thrust out the paper. "Do you wish to read the details? I'll not stop you from doing so, but I cannot."

"No, keep going."

"Here is Avery's."

I held my breath as Hugh scanned the contents. "I still don't understand the whole thing. It says Avery witnessed his mother go into the stables with his father on October 21, 1811. He heard a scream, and he entered to see his mother holding a large silver candlestick. Mr. Cavanagh had collapsed on the ground."

What?

If I'd had a dry place to sit, I would have. Seline had told me her father was blinded by a horse, not by Mrs. Cavanagh. All my prior fears raged to the surface. Is this why she approached me, demanding to learn what Avery had revealed to the society? To protect herself? Was she intending to kill her husband? My mind raced for answers. Every one of the victims had been hit over the head—just like Mr. Cavanagh—but something didn't add up. Avery was terribly close with his mother. If she was the cause of his father's dreadful accident, why would he be trying to protect her?

Hugh touched my arm. "What is it?"

"I just don't understand how all this relates to Seline's murder, or Miles Lacy's for that matter."

"Well, if you're right, Seline wasn't the target, and it was really an attempted murder on me. I was the one trying to leave the group, after all." He started to refold the pledges when something caught my eye. "Wait, there's more. You didn't read those last few pages."

His mouth scrunched up at the corner. "It's simply the record of donations to the secret society." His arm fell lifeless at his side. "The proof I need to leave the society. Names, dates. It's all here." He shook the paper. "All the money listed is bound for a resistance group in France, one that has ambitions to release Napoleon from St. Helena."

I gasped. "Napoleon? But the Bourbons—"

"Have been overturning most of the changes made by the French Revolution. As I came to find out but a few months ago, the Gormogons' support is extending those changes, even here in Britain, not reversing them."

"But that's treason."

"Exactly."

"But Avery—"

"Was drawn in like the rest of us. Each one of us was presented a society that was formed to better all our lives, a sort of gentlemen's club. We thought we were helping each other, not some grand foolish cause, one that included the utter betrayal of our country and everything we hold dear."

"I'd like to see the papers." I held out my hand.

He eyed my open palm for a moment. "I plan to take this to Whitehall straightaway." He met my gaze, but his hand inched toward his pocket. "I don't think anything will be gained by you seeing this."

"Oh, you don't, do you? Whether you like it or not, I'm a part of this. Don't you dare hide anything from me now. Hand it over."

Indecision deepened every line on his gaunt face. "There's

something else here besides the ledger I spoke of. It's another loyalty pledge."

"Oh?" I lifted my eyebrows. "From who?"

"The fifth member of our little group."

I extended my hand farther. "No more secrets, Hugh. They all stop here."

The paper felt cold, the air thin as Hugh slid the last remaining notes into my waiting fingers. It took a mere second before my focus narrowed on the name at the top.

Arthur Halliwell.

My stomach turned. How can this be?

Hugh pawed at the ground with the toe of his boot. "Your brother was one of the charter members, Charity. Your parents were wise to flee the country and take you all to Ceylon. It gave Arthur the escape I can only dream of."

My thoughts rambled every direction. "So my parents knew . . . about all of this?"

"No." He held up his hand. "They only knew Arthur got himself in deep with French traitors. You see, they came across a secret letter from a contact of ours in France. Arthur fessed up and the decision was made to flee. Avery told me about everything when I made the decision to leave myself. As far as I know, your parents never knew about the Gormogons. Of course it was several years before I learned the truth in its entirety as well. The society has always been quite good at protecting itself. Your parents wouldn't have believed we were all involved at any rate."

"I always wondered why we left for Ceylon so quickly, why my parents wouldn't even discuss staying. It makes perfect sense now that Arthur chose to study and practice in America."

I examined my brother's loyalty pledge one last time. "It says my grandfather was once a member of the society too." My brooch—the one my grandmother had passed along to me—had originally belonged to him. Whether she knew what it represented or not, I could never guess.

I took a deep breath and absently flipped to the next page in my hands. Hugh was right about the rest of it. The remaining pages were a ledger of donations, but as I read each line and moved to the next, a new, terrible inkling of fear sent the hairs on my arms jerking to attention. I'd seen the handwriting before. Not all of it, just the large first letter of each line. It was an elegant hand, made more so by the loops and curls.

The same curls that had been in the letter Seline had supposedly written to her mother the night she eloped with Miles Lacy—the night she had really been murdered.

"Who wrote all this?"

"The ledger?"

I nodded.

"The benefactor handles all the money, all the threats. He's the backbone of this society. I would assume it was written by his hand."

Was this the clue I'd been searching for all along? "And you don't know who this benefactor is?"

"His identity remains privileged information. Some of the earlier members know—Avery, Kendal. I'm fairly certain about them. Kendal's usually the one to speak on his behalf."

The moment of Seline's death came flooding into my mind as the words on the paper blurred before me. Hugh was certainly the intended target. He wanted out, had vital information about the organization, and meant to expose them. But how could this benefactor make such a horrendous mistake? The two riders would have had cloaks on, but Seline did not look all that much like Hugh.

All at once, an image flashed into my mind. The ground seemed to shift beneath my feet. I covered my mouth with my trembling hand, at first unable to give voice to the one thought that made everything fall into place. What if the murderer confused Seline for Hugh because his eyesight was impaired?

I reached out to steady myself on the uneven stone wall, the truth materializing in my mind.

Mr. Cavanagh had been a member of the society at one time. He'd asked me to enclose a letter to my brother, for goodness' sake. He had access to Mrs. Cavanagh's dressing room where he could have stashed the cloak . . . And those footsteps I'd heard the first night . . .

Tap, whoosh. Tap, whoosh.

They tiptoed back into my mind, and my eyes flashed wide open. Mr. Cavanagh utilized a cane to move about his room. I'd seen it the day I found him in his chair. If I was right, one way or another, *he* had been pulling the strings of everyone all along. I pressed my hand to my forehead. Moreover, he had inadvertently killed his own daughter.

I shook my head in disbelief. Mr. Cavanagh was barely ambulatory, yes, but on a horse, there was no reason he couldn't be deadly. He must have forged the note to cover his tracks. It was right around Seline's disappearance when he had taken a bad turn—due to guilt?

He would have carried on the charade with me to further distance himself from the brutal act. But he could not have managed to bury Seline's body alone. He was far too weak for that. I let out a long breath. Mrs. Cavanagh must have figured it out too. She'd changed over the last few days, her actions fearful at best. Then today she was out of her mind. She told me to lock my door. There was only one other person in the house besides the servants.

But what about Miles Lacy? He was in Mr. Cavanagh's employ.

Perhaps he had been utilized in another way. Miles changed his plans and departed the estate prematurely. Mr. Lacy said his nephew was scared. Miles suggested in the letter he was paid for his efforts. We'd all assumed his money came from the curricle race, but it could have come just as easily from Mr. Cavanagh.

Hugh stuffed the papers back in the envelope. "I think it best if we—"

A gunshot rent through the night air, echoing off the ancient wall. Hugh grasped my arm. "We've got to get out of here."

We bolted for the cover of a nearby wall, inching toward our horses, but we were met by the barrel of a pistol glinting in the moonlight. Mr. Cavanagh used the half wall as support as he inched forward. "Not another step."

Hugh and I froze at first, and then he shoved me behind him. "It's me you want. Leave Miss Halliwell out of this."

Mr. Cavanagh smiled. "You're not in any position to make demands, Hugh. I promise you, I won't miss a second time, not at this range. And don't worry about Miss Halliwell; this particular shot is for you. I need Miss Halliwell to entice her brother to fulfill his pledge. There are many people in America who support the French cause."

Hugh squeezed my hand and for a breathless second I knew what he meant to do, yet I was powerless to stop him. He whispered over his shoulder as he lunged forward. "Run."

But I didn't. My feet were frozen to the ground, my muscles stiff. My mind screamed, *Get away, hide!* But I simply stood there, my whole body shaking like that night in the tea field.

The shot was deafening. The smoke burned my eyes. Hugh stumbled back a pace. At first I hoped he'd merely reacted to the sudden sound as I had, but a large crimson stain fought its way through his shirt and waistcoat, spreading across his left chest. He touched the dark circular spot a moment, dumbstruck as he groped at me, then fell backward to the ground.

I raced to support his head, but it was no use. Mr. Cavanagh had hit his mark. Hugh Daunt was already dead.

I pushed to my feet, starting first one direction then the next, eventually stumbling back against the fractured wall. My gaze tightened on Mr. Cavanagh, who was groping his pockets for what I could only assume was another pistol. I fled around the wall's edge and into the inner L of the abbey ruins.

"Let me assure you, Miss Halliwell, I have another pistol, and you've backed yourself into a corner. I've only to wait you out." Mr. Cavanagh stepped into a beam of moonlight, utilizing the empty window ledge to support himself. "But I will say, bravo, Miss Halliwell. You've been a rather pleasant distraction these last few weeks. I had a feeling you might eventually figure out everything, which is why I already sent that note to your brother informing him of my concerns for your safety. I had hoped to negotiate with you. I even tried to nudge you into the arms of my wayward son, hoping I could use that as leverage with Arthur, but I see now none of that will be possible. Hugh will do nicely as your murderer. After all, when everyone finds out it was he who killed Seline, they shall be ripe to believe this as well."

I edged closer to the wall, keeping to the shadows so he wouldn't get a clear shot. "It was you who placed the brooch on the road to Rushridge, wasn't it? You wanted us to think it was Hugh who had killed Seline."

"It certainly would have been easier to get him out of the way, but this will do just as well. Arthur has always hated the nobility, and if I nudge him into thinking the authorities are corrupt in the handling of both Seline's and your murder? Believe me, your brother will be much easier to manage with the right reason to join our little revolution. His sympathies have never lain with the Crown."

"He would not be so utterly foolish. He's grown up from the lad you remember." Caught between the stone remains and the river, I knew I was trapped. If only I could keep him talking, I might think of something. "And Avery—I suppose you've been manipulating him as well." Carefully I crept closer and closer to the ledge that held the faceless statue.

"Love is always the perfect manipulator. Throw in a bit of misplaced affection for his mother, and I knew I didn't need to worry about him. He did not want to see his mother taken to Newgate prison for attempting to kill her own husband."

"You forced him to write that testimonial—the loyalty pledge. You told him you'd never fund a marriage between him and Priscilla otherwise, didn't you?"

He smiled. "What a clever chit you are. Of course I did."

I could feel the hard edge of the statue with my left hand, and Mr. Cavanagh was inching forward. He would be assured of a shot in a matter of seconds. I felt desperately for the crevice between the statue and the wall.

Piers and I were masters at finding secret places. I doubted anyone besides Avery knew of our alcove at Loxby Manor. Was there enough space for me to slip in here? It would be terribly tight, but possible, I thought. I would have to make my move at just the right moment. Mr. Cavanagh only had one shot, after all.

His steps seemed to hesitate as he talked, thus I kept him doing so. "What about Miles? Why kill him?"

"Who do you think helped me bury Seline? Miles found me minutes after I made the terrible mistake. I paid him, or shall I say blackmailed him, to assist me in burying her. I could not have done so alone. He would have made an easy murderer, but I had already decided Hugh would fill that role. After all, it was his fault she's dead."

"But why kill Miles later?"

"He was supposed to leave the country. Kendal must have enticed the fool to stay for that ridiculous race those boys were plotting. I never would have allowed the thing to go off, not if it helped Hugh in any way. Besides, I don't make empty threats, my dear. Baker has been my informant in the house. Servants talk. It was quite easy to learn of Miles's decision to remain at Whitecaster Hall. When everyone left me alone at Loxby the night of the ball, it was rather easy to make my way to Whitecaster on horseback and lure Miles from the stables. He was never all that bright."

I gritted my teeth. We'd given Mr. Cavanagh the perfect opportunity to sneak out unobserved.

Another inch closer and my arm slipped into the depths of the opening between the statue and the wall. "When did Mrs. Cavanagh realize you weren't completely blind?"

"Oh, I've always been rather ingenious. It's been a well-kept secret by Baker and myself for many years, although I daresay my wife began to suspect my duplicity of late. At the beginning I saw only shadows for some time, and I knew I would never be myself again. I decided to utilize Avery and his intrepid friends to bring about my wishes, keeping the truth about my condition to myself. It wasn't hard. Those boys were ripe for a gentlemen's club. It has only been in the past year that I began pushing myself, using the night to gain strength. Now . . ."

He stopped and lifted his arm to aim the pistol, steadying his hand with his other. My moment had come.

In a flash I bent and jerked my body into the black shadow

of the faceless statue, but I heard no shot. I'd moved prematurely. Mr. Cavanagh's eyesight, however, was not good enough to track where my movements had led me. To him, it must have looked like I simply disappeared.

Gasping for breath behind the cold stone, I watched as he glanced about, dipping his head both one way and then the next, but he never directed the pistol away from the small alcove. "I know you are there somewhere hiding, probably congratulating yourself on your ingenuity. But remember, all I must do is listen."

I cringed, tugging my arms into my chest. Unexpectedly, the statue moved. It was only a wobble, but my heart leapt into my throat. The large, menacing structure was somehow off balance. Perhaps that is why it had fallen on its creator in the first place. I wriggled my hands farther up my body and placed them flat on the statue's smooth, damp back. Again, the mountainous stone tipped forward before rocking back into place.

It would take a great deal of effort, and I would have to time my attack perfectly, but I now had a chance. I closed my eyes for a brief second and opened my mouth. "You'll be hanged for treason." I peeked around the edge of the stone.

The moonlight lit a smile on Mr. Cavanagh's face. "How so?" He stalked forward, his gaze tight on the statue.

"Because Piers won't rest until he knows all."

Mr. Cavanagh placed his boot on the narrow ledge, and my muscles contracted, thrusting my body forward with every bit of strength I had left. At first I thought the surge would not be enough to unseat the structure, but I was able to wedge my foot against the wall, which gave me the leverage I needed to send it crashing forward straight toward Mr. Cavanagh.

He screamed, attempting to dodge the heavy stone, but he was too slow, his movements far too clumsy. The years he'd spent lying in his room had taken a toll. The rock caught the back of his legs, pummeling him down to the grassy field below.

The inescapable sounds of the collision reverberated over the ancient walls until the last stone lay motionless and a deathly calm descended over the once hallowed ground. I dared not move for a full three seconds, my heartbeat galloping, my breaths coming shallow and quick.

Mr. Cavanagh lay utterly still, the statue lengthwise across his middle, and I knew he would not walk away a second time.

Pounding hooves drummed their way across the meadow until I could see a small band of riders approaching fast. I slunk against the abbey wall, my hand pressed to my chest, until I made out one face in the shifting moonlight.

It was Piers.

Then I saw Avery and Tony . . . and Lord Kendal?

Piers began his dismount strides before his horse drew to a halt. His eyes were only for me, and I raced to meet his plunging embrace. His hand was at my neck and then my head and shoulders. "You're not hurt, are you?"

I shook my head, and he pulled me tight once more.

He gasped for breath, his voice a ragged whisper. "Thank God. I never should have left you alone."

My pulse ran wild as I looked up into his eyes. "How did you know to come back? And your arm!" I took a step back to assess him. "You rode all this way?"

"Thankfully the wound has remained free of infection." He took a quick glance at his left shoulder. "It still plagues me, but nothing could keep me away from you, not after my mother sent that terrifying note."

"She what?"

"She sent Mr. Lacy earlier today with a letter saying she feared you might end up dead if I didn't return at once."

My lips parted. "Well, she was right!" Suddenly my arms felt heavy at my side. "Oh, Piers. It was your father all along. He had so many twisted plans. He's a traitor and a murderer."

Piers lowered his gaze. "I know it all. Kendal has been apprising me of his dealings while we rode to stop him. But it seems you already had him in hand. How did you get out here? We were riding for Loxby but heard gunshots."

"It's such a long story." I touched my forehead. "Hugh is dead, Piers. Your father shot him."

Piers went white in the moonlight as Avery walked up and gripped my arm. "I don't know what we would have done if we'd not found you standing here."

I gave him a small smile. "Priscilla is waiting at Rushridge, and is probably in a fearful state. She must be told of what happened to Hugh."

Avery nodded, but it was a difficult one. I didn't envy what lay ahead for him.

Piers helped me to a seat on a nearby stone. "All is settled between Kendal and me. He had every intention of shooting slightly wide, but he had to make it look real. My father would have heard otherwise. He's been controlling him for years. Kendal intended a flesh wound at the most or to miss completely, but his nerves got the best of him."

"A flesh wound?"

"He told me it was my father who kept up the Gormogons in secret after the law was passed. They had far-reaching plans for France and Britain. I suppose they thought it noble at one time, but somewhere along the line everything changed. He used Avery and his friends to do his bidding when his own years and infirmity kept him in his room."

Piers ran his hand down his face. "He forced Kendal to enrage me into the duel five years ago. My father needed me out of the way. He knew I would never align with his principles about France. He figured I wouldn't survive the duel, but when I didn't show up at all, he cornered Kendal into denouncing me."

I shifted closer. "Oh, Piers. Hugh and I read the loyalty pledges before he was killed. Your father paid several others to cut you in London. You had no chance to come about. He wanted to send you scurrying off to the countryside to hide."

Piers let out a tight breath. "It was his idea that I move outside of Liverpool." He put his arm around my shoulders. "Seline was indeed an accident, but I don't think he lost much sleep over her death. He had disconnected himself from his family years before, if he even ever knew how to love. He was a bitter man whom I will never understand."

He stood and extended his hand. "Let me take you back to Loxby. It's time we speak openly with my mother."

Mrs. Cavanagh sat perched on the settee in the drawing room when Piers and I entered the house. A grave look had settled into the lines on her face, her shoulders hunched over like a crow. So subtle was the spark of interest that glinted in her lonely eyes as we walked into the room, I'm not certain I'd seen it at all.

"Where's Avery?" Her words were more of a grumble than a question.

Piers stepped forward. "He's ridden to Rushridge to see to Priscilla. Hugh Daunt was killed tonight."

Her eyes widened, but Piers gave her no chance to respond.

"As well as Father."

Her hand shot to her mouth, then quivered against her lips, her voice tumbling out in an incredulous mix of whispers. "He's gone. Dead?"

"He was crushed beneath a statue at the abbey."

Her eyelids narrowed as she shifted her gaze to me. "Then it is done at last."

I took a seat at her side. "We're safe."

There were several seconds of tears, but I did not think them wrought by grief; relief more like.

Piers joined us on the sofa and took a deep breath. "I've been appraised of what happened five years ago between you and Father, and I must admit, I'm left reeling from the revelations this day has brought. I need you to tell me once and for all what happened in the stables that day."

Her hands went to work on her handkerchief. "It was an impulsive decision, one I've regretted since the moment I struck him." More tears.

I'd seen a great deal of drama from Mrs. Cavanagh since I'd arrived, but for the first time her sentiments felt real, as if we'd found our way to the last act of the play.

Her eyes slipped closed, her hand finding Piers's on the cushion. "You see, you had left for Liverpool only a month prior and I was still caught up in the aftermath of the scandal. Quite by accident, I stumbled upon a private conversation in your father's office. At first I paid no mind, but then I heard your name.

"Mr. Cavanagh was gruff and short. He said you were growing

to be quite a problem. He was upset with how open you'd been about denouncing French ideals, and he was worried you had found out too much information about his little group. The other man in the office, who I didn't know at the time, asked if Mr. Cavanagh would be willing to do whatever it took to silence you, and he agreed, just like that—like it was nothing to him. Like you were nothing. He said the cause was more important than blood."

I couldn't help but gasp.

Mrs. Cavanagh didn't skip a beat. "I was shocked to the core, angry beyond belief. Who was this man I had married? A monster? I suppose I wasn't thinking straight from that moment on. I hid in my room for some time before I saw him out my window heading to the stables. That's where I found him and revealed what I'd overheard. He merely laughed. Laughed!

"I don't even remember bringing the candlestick in with me, but there it was, in my hands. Avery saw the whole thing from the stable door, as did Mr. Lacy. We were all caught up in a nightmare, and they've both been forced to protect me ever since."

She went on. "Avery and I decided at once it was best for you to stay in Liverpool where you were safe, and I knew I couldn't face you again, not after what I had done. I thought if I kept you at arm's length I could bear the shame and keep you safe at the same time. I even thought to keep you out of the will so Mr. Cavanagh wouldn't turn his sights back on you.

"I hid the broken end of the candlestick in my handkerchief and kept it in my desk drawer as a reminder. I would take it out from time to time and look at it to keep me from writing to you. When Mr. Cavanagh awoke the next day, we told him that a horse had kicked him and caused his memory confusion. He never knew it was me, at least not at first.

"But then Seline disappeared and everything went sideways. Knowing the monster that lived in our house, I couldn't help but consider your father. But how could it be true? How could he do such a thing, blind and feeble as he was? So much of me wanted to believe Seline had really run off with that stable boy. I never even considered the idea that Mr. Cavanagh wasn't blind. He had us all fooled . . . and for so long. Baker must have been his confidant for years. I know that now.

"I found Mr. Cavanagh's room empty for the first time but a few days ago. I was terrified at what such a thing could possibly mean. I began watching him, studying his movements. Then I caught him yesterday in my dressing room without assistance, rummaging around behind my screen. He had full control of his faculties, and I knew for certain his eyesight was not as poor as he'd led us to believe. Everything was moving too fast, and you and Avery had already left. I didn't know what to do."

The weight of her words drew her shoulders back against the sofa.

Piers cast me a quick glance before turning back to his mother. "It is good to know it all finally, and I realize exposing your role in all this must have been extremely difficult. But shame is an insidious illness that only seeks to weaken and destroy you. I know that better than most.

"Baker shall have to be turned over to the authorities." He dipped his head. "I have no intention of leaving Loxby Manor, nor any of this family ever again. We have a great deal to sort out and much to understand and forgive, but we shall mourn our losses and find a way to move on together."

CHAPTER 30

The following weeks passed by surrounded by a large black cloud. I rarely saw Piers, as the official investigation into the murders had begun. We all knew there would be no way to sidestep the inevitable scandal Mr. Cavanagh had brought upon the entire family.

Though we were still in Mrs. Cavanagh's ordained mourning period of six months, no one came to visit Loxby Hall beyond her expected four-week seclusion as a widow. It would be some time before the Cavanagh name wouldn't be tainted by tragedy. However, I don't think Mrs. Cavanagh gave our social isolation a second thought.

The death of her daughter had changed everything.

I spent most of those long mornings with her in the drawing room and the afternoons walking the grounds alone. That is, until I changed course one warm spring day and made my way on foot to Flitworth Manor, my childhood home. At first I only wanted to see it again, spurred on by thoughts of Arthur, but as I neared the wide, menacing structure, something else sprang to mind.

I'd never met the tenants, nor had the least idea how to approach them, but after all I'd endured, I, too, had changed. I no longer lived my life in fear. So I approached the entrance, and when I was introduced to the lady of the house, I raised my chin and asked with conviction to be shown to the greenhouse.

I set the small potted plant I'd fetched from Flitworth Manor beside me on the bench, my eyes trained to Loxby's garden gate, my heart reckless as I waited. Though I'd left Piers a note to join me, I had no idea how long he would be or what he would think of what I had to say.

The sun had dipped below the far wall, the gray warmth of twilight softening the plants and cooling the earth. A pop of the latch and the gate swung open.

Piers paused a step into the garden, my note still in his hands, an inquisitive calm relaxing his face. "You summoned me?" A smile emerged as he made his way to the bench.

"Yes. I've been a bit busy today."

"Have you?" He motioned at the small plant. "What's all this?"

I slid the plant onto my lap. "I fetched this for you from Flitworth Manor. Do you recognize it?"

He stared for a moment. "Should I?"

"Not exactly." I ran my finger along a green leaf. "When we were children you gave me an orange once, and after I'd eaten it, I told you I meant to grow a tree. You laughed at me at the time, but you also didn't know that Flitworth Manor had a hothouse, and I was a favorite of the undergardener, Mr. Wynn, who is actually still in residence."

"Is he?"

"Well, I had a mind to see my past today, and while I was there, I asked to visit the greenhouse where I happened upon Mr. Wynn. This little plant here was grown from a seed of my original orange tree."

"Was it really?"

"It was. I had hoped to retrieve a single orange, but Mr. Wynn suggested I take the whole thing."

Piers smiled and took the plant into his hands. "It looks to be quite healthy. But we'll have to reopen the greenhouse if it's to make it through the winter."

"I brought it here for you. It's a gift."

His brows drew in. "For me?"

"I hoped it might be a reminder."

He angled his chin.

"You sacrificed everything five years ago to protect my reputation, but I don't want that one mistake to ruin the rest of your life. You see, this little plant here is ready for a new start at Loxby Manor, the same as you.

"Oh, Piers, just because society rejected you, doesn't mean *you* need to reject you. You're the same brilliant man you were before I left for Ceylon. You possess the same hopes and dreams, the same wonderful passions that make you who you are. I don't know if a fellowship is possible now or what it would entail or when the investigation will come to a close here, but at the same time, I know you deserve to see what's beyond that door you closed so long ago."

He dropped his head into his hands, and we sat for a long moment in restive silence before he turned to look at me. "My darling, what would I have done if you hadn't decided to come back here?"

I smiled up at him and for a breathless moment I thought he might kiss me, but he settled back against the bench and ran his arm behind my back.

"I suppose I could send a letter to Lord Hereford and inquire. He never really understood why I stepped away. I've been a fool not to do so already."

"That sounds like a very good start."

He sat up quickly. "But for now, we need to find a place for this little plant. Care to accompany me to the greenhouse? I have a mind to get that room in order, and I shall certainly need your opinions."

It was later that same day when I saw a small square card lying on my pillow, and my heart contracted. It was another of Piers's drawings, and a beautiful one at that—a single solitary rose, the symbol of passion and love. I flipped the card over as I moved it quickly into the candlelight.

Focus iam in mundo est.

My fingers tingled as I remembered each Latin word, writing them down until I had the sentence in its entirety.

The world is now in focus.

I collapsed into a seat on the bed, my hand pressed to my mouth. He'd remembered every word I'd said to him in the garden before he left for the duel. I read on; the postscript was written in English.

> You're right as you always are, my darling. I promise not to give up on myself any longer if you won't give up on us. I have a

plan to wait for you every day before dinner. Come when you're ready. And don't worry; I can wait forever if it comes to that. You know where I'll be. Take your time. Don't rush. When I see you, I'll know what it means.

All my love,
Piers

What a sweet, wonderful fool. I didn't need days, hours, or even minutes to contemplate our future.

I flew down the hall, stopping only briefly at the landing to comb through each thought and feeling pounding in my chest. Piers had tugged me into the shadows of the alcove so long ago. If only we had known then how the intimacy would change us—the feeling of being held and wanted, the surge of emotions that swelled into that perfect kiss. It had been surreal.

But today, when I pressed forward against the balustrade and saw him waiting for me in the alcove, smiling up at me in that enchanting way of his, choosing me again after all we'd been through, I knew my memories of that day so long ago would pale in comparison to this moment.

I descended the stairs, my hand clasped to the railing as if I might float away, my feet jittery on the steps. I suppose a part of me still remained cautious, a niggling twitch of doubt I would fight all my life, but as I reached the ground floor and inched my way to the edge of the curved wainscoting, my heart felt light, my steps assured.

Piers's arm stretched out of the shadows, and I slid my fingers into his hand, knowing full well my life would never be the same. Gently, he tugged me into the crevice behind the well-placed column that had been our secret and our joy, the one place where we hid ourselves from the world but laid our hearts open wide.

His smile slowly built until he ran his hands up my arms. "You came . . . already." A muscle twitched in his cheek. "I had a speech prepared, but dash it all, it can wait."

He drew me against his chest, moving his hands beneath my chin, his fingers extending into the delicate tendrils of my hair.

"Oh, Piers."

I remember a clock ticking from somewhere beyond the hall, the familiar scent of his cologne as I took in a breath, the prickling feel of my skin beneath his touch, the inescapable pull of desire.

I lifted my chin and his lips met mine, the kiss deepening into a culmination of five years of waiting, hoping, and dreaming—the precious beginning of our new life together.

Eventually he drew back, his eyes glassy from the surge of emotion. "You know, I almost cannot remember a time before I loved you. The years you were in Ceylon changed me in ways I didn't expect, but your absence proved terribly important. It gave me perspective. I know now that our love is a powerful bond, but it's also a gift, one I will never take for granted." He grasped my hands, stretching the silence between us as far as he could, a torrid of emotions claiming every groove on his face. "Marry me as soon as I'm out of mourning?"

Every last muscle coiled in my chest. "I hope you haven't spent one second worrying I would keep you waiting. Of course I will marry you, and the sooner the better. I love you beyond words and beyond fear. Whatever life brings our way, I shall be right by your side."

Piers pulled me into another embrace, and as I closed my eyes I drank in the warmth of his arms and the strength of his promise.

What he had written on my drawing was true for me too. My world had shifted into focus. Somehow, through the depths of loss and the darkest pits of betrayal, we'd scaled our own wounded ladders to find them curiously intertwined at the top. We were survivors, he and I, and how good it felt to climb on together.

EPILOGUE

Six months passed before the first snow brought not only the announcement of Priscilla's engagement to Avery but my wedding as well. I daresay we were all ready for a celebration, and it proved to be a happy one.

Though scandal still hangs over all our heads, each of us has found a way to move on, to find joy in what really matters. Piers gave Avery his cottage outside of Liverpool, the perfect place for Priscilla to start anew, a haven from the painful memories of her brother and the tragedy that happened so near. Mrs. Daunt decided to stay at Rushridge.

Tony still visits quite frequently, particularly when his pockets are to let, and I always look forward to those days of love and laughter. Some friends are friends forever.

Piers and I spend a great deal of time hosting and visiting Lord and Lady Kendal as well. I never could have dreamed a bond would develop among us, but after Mr. Cavanagh's death, nothing was ever the same, not for anyone. After all, there are only a few people who know what really happened that terrible summer.

Piers turned over the Gormogon's ledger to the authorities at Whitehall, and every facet of the group has been snuffed out, hopefully never to be heard from again. Baker was taken to prison to await transportation, and Arthur remains safely in America, continuing his work as a chemist. I do hope my parents will visit East Whitloe soon. I have so much to show them.

There are days now when I don't think of Seline, but they are few and far between. Her joyous laughter and zest for life still cling to the halls of Loxby Manor as well as our hearts, and I am glad to say she will never really leave us.

Mrs. Cavanagh still instructs me on the fine art of needlepoint, but there are no more suggestions for how I might interest a man. No, these days she says she can see Piers's love for me written across his face, and I feel the same about my husband. Piers and I both know what it felt like to be apart, and we don't want to waste one single second of our life together.

This past week Piers received a letter granting him a chance to study with Lord Hereford and the Royal Society with hopes of applying at some point for a fellowship. We shall soon be happily forced to divide our time between London and Loxby Manor. But we won't stay away for long periods of time, not now. Piers is determined to have his child grow up in the country, to get the chance to race over the hills like we did as children, to feel the love of family, to find his or her passion and never ever let it go.

ACKNOWLEDGMENTS

Travis, my husband and best friend, after nineteen years of marriage, I still fall more in love with you each day. My writing would not be the same without your constant support, encouragement, and inspiration. Thank you for our silly late night chats, my forced brain-storming sessions in the car, and for loving my mysteries as much as I do.

Megan Besing, where do I even begin? Your thoughts and critiques made this story what it is. Nor could I possibly survive as a writer without your encouragement and friendship. #iheartyou #wemesh

Mom, you passed on to me a love of fiction and the determination to see a project through to the end. Thank you for sharing my passion for traditional gothic romances and everything Regency. At all the stages of our lives our already deep friendship has only grown. I thank God for you every day.

Audrey and Luke, Bess and Angi, thank you for sharing my joy.

The entire Wilson clan, thank you for loving and supporting me.

Tony Smith, I had such a blast bringing you to life in this story. Though I did take a few liberties with the character of Tony Shaw,

Charity's regard for him mirrors my own. Thank you for your friendship and encouragement in my writing. And, you never know when Tony may pop up again.

My awesome agent, Nicole Resciniti, your support and wisdom elevates my writing at every step.

Becky Monds and Jodi Hughes, my fantastic editors, you took this story and molded it into one I'm so proud of. I'm blessed beyond belief to have you both working alongside of me. And to the entire team at Thomas Nelson, Paul Fisher, Kerri Potts, Laura Wheeler, Margaret Kercher, you guys have given me such phenomenal support. I am thankful every day I get to work with such a brilliant group of people.

And to my Lord and Savior Jesus Christ. To you alone be the glory.

DISCUSSION QUESTIONS

1. Charity decides to return to Britain to a time in her childhood where she remembers feeling safe and happy. Have you ever longed for moments from the past? Do you think she found what she was looking for?
2. After Piers missed the duel with Lord Kendal, he believed that removing himself from Loxby Manor would help everyone in his family, but what did his abandonment inadvertently cause?
3. Charity takes an emotional journey over the course of the novel where she finally learns to accept herself and her past. Is there something in your own life you have yet to make peace with?
4. In what other ways did Charity grow over the book?
5. What specific characteristics does Charity possess that will continue to help her heal after all she's been through?
6. Did you suspect Mr. Cavanagh's involvement in the secret society or the murders?
7. Do you think Mrs. Cavanagh had just cause for how she reacted to her husband's infamy?

8. Secret societies have played a significant role in both British and American history. Would you ever consider joining a secret group if you were convinced they worked for the greater good of society? Would you be willing to give anything up to join?
9. Do you think the constraints of the Regency period had any bearing on how Charity reacted to the assault?
10. Who was your favorite character and why?

ABOUT THE AUTHOR

Abigail Wilson combines her passion for Regency England with intrigue and adventure to pen historical mysteries with a heart. A registered nurse, chai tea addict, and mother of two crazy kids, Abigail fills her spare time hiking the national parks, attending her daughter's diving meets, and curling up with a great book. Abigail was a 2020 HOLT Medallion Merit Finalist, a 2017 Fab Five contest winner, and a Daphne du Maurier Award for Excellence Finalist. She is a cum laude graduate of the University of Texas at Austin and currently lives in Dripping Springs, Texas, with her husband and children.

Connect with Abigail at acwilsonbooks.com
Instagram: @acwilsonbooks
Facebook: @ACWilsonbooks
Twitter: @acwilsonbooks